A Thriller

Mike Baron

WordFire Press
Colorado Springs, Colorado

WHACK JOB
Copyright © 2012 Mike Baron

ISBN: 978-1-61475-086-4

Cover painting by Jeff Herndon

Cover design by Bob Garcia

Book Design by RuneWright, LLC
www.RuneWright.com

Published by
WordFire Press, an imprint of
WordFire, Inc.
PO Box 1840
Monument CO 80132

WordFire Press Trade Paperback Edition 2013
Printed in the USA
www.wordfire.com

:Dedication

To everyone who ever helped me write.

And my lovely wife Ann.

Acknowledgements

Many people helped me with this book. Thirty years ago, Franklynn Peterson and Judi K-Turkel tried to teach me how to write. Blake Kellogg encouraged me. As always, Mean Pete Brandvold (www.peterbrandvold.com) was there to guide me through thickets of prose with a machete and a flame thrower. Diggs Brown and Bob Garcia (http://gpsdesign.net/) offered invaluable advice and logistics support. Miguel Cima read the manuscript and made many helpful suggestions. Ellen Jo Baron provided logistics support.

CHAPTER ONE
LIBYA

The mission was FUBAR from jump street. Two SEALS, two Rangers and three spooks so that Ghaddafi's assassination would reflect well on at least three branches of service. Otto White looked around the cramped interior of the SH 60 Seahawk. It was crammed with men and equipment. Sound and vibration served as a constant reminder that they were carried aloft by a crazy machine that grappled with the laws of physics. The constant vibration felt like a passing freight train.

They'd been working on the intel for months. Ghaddafi was hiding out in one of his sixteen presidential palaces, the one at the Sarir Oasis one hundred miles from the Egyptian border. The seven heavily outfitted men hunkered in the belly of the stealth-equipped chopper, its McDonnell Douglas turbine muffled so that from a hundred meters it sounded no louder than a stiff wind.

Inside the helo was as loud as a boiler factory. There was nothing to see through the heavily tinted windows save the endless Sahara. The pilots saw a vast green ocean with frozen waves through their infrared. They flew beneath an overcast sky into the teeth of a 30 kph wind kicking up sand, the helo bucking and groaning like a ghost of the deep. Ghaddafi's Russian-trained pilots weren't good enough to fly in this weather.

The Inuit spook Ray Benson sat butt cheek to butt cheek on Otto's left, an Old Testament under his arm. He squeezed Otto's knee, turned his freaky blue eyes on him and carefully enunciated, "With a donkey's jawbone I have made donkeys of them. With a donkey's jawbone I have killed a thousand men." He grinned like a motherfucker.

Otto thought he was crazy. Everyone called the Inuit spook Quinn.

The satellite photo showed Ghaddafi's "palace," a concrete monstrosity covering 8,500 square meters; ten-foot walls enclosing what had once been the only available water for fifty klicks. The photo indicated the sad collection of stone and concrete buildings that comprised the village, the makeshift landing strip on which sat an Ilyushin Il-96, a gift from Vladimir Putin.

SEAL Master Sergeant O'Hern bopped Otto on the knee. They were over the drop-off. Otto gave a final screw to each earplug with his index fingers. He touched the crucifix tattoo above his heart and said a silent prayer. Quinn did likewise.

Otto was the bomb guy. It was his job to clear their infiltration by dismantling any booby-traps that lay in their way and use explosives to effect an entry, if necessary. Once inside, Otto would plant the homing device the Navy would use to launch its tomahawk. Master Sergeant O'Hern was the Ranger in charge. The other Ranger was Sgt. Tyrell Hathaway who clenched a Costa Rican cigar in his mouth. The SEALS were Lieutenants Osima and Al Dweeb and the other ops were a young spook named Hornbuckle and chisel-faced spook Ray Benson. Otto had met all six for the first time 48 hours ago. Three white guys, a black guy, an Eskimo, a Japanese-American and an Arab-American. All they needed was a lesbian dwarf.

Hornbuckle was after intel. Benson was a cypher.

At O'Hern's signal, they formed up. Al Dweeb pulled the door open and deployed the ropes. As the helo hovered ten meters above the sand tossing dunes into the air, the seven operators fast roped down to the desert floor. As soon as the last man touched down the helo rose, the co-pilot hauling in the lines.

The entire insertion took less than thirty seconds. The sound of the helo disappeared quickly in the blowing wind.

The land was not as flat as it appeared from the air but consisted of a series of gentle undulations stretching into the distance, cutting off the horizon, and providing cover for their infiltration. O'Hern shinnied to the top of a shallow dune and turned on the SOFLAM AN/PEQ 1 laser range-finding device. Putting on goggles to keep the sand out of his eyes, Otto shinnied up next to him. Ghaddafi's palace gleamed dully through the blowing sand three klicks to the southwest.

They could have used a drone but the CIC insisted on eyeball recognition. No more aspirin factories. Hornbuckle was after intel. The men followed O'Hern in silence over the dune and up the next. It was 0330 Zulu time. The shallow dunes stopped a half klick from the palace. They would have to cross that space with no ground cover save a handful of malnourished fig trees. The wind picked up, whipping pinpricks into every square centimeter of exposed flesh. Only Otto's chin remained uncovered.

They grouped along the last sand ridge, each man deploying his night vision scope. Ghaddafi's so-called palace looked like a concrete warehouse from the outside. The walls canted in toward the top at a ten-degree angle. The only concession to architecture was a lone minaret poking up from inside the near wall. A massive double steel door, closed, offered the only break in the featureless slab. Along the top Otto picked out one sentry hunkered down against the wind trying to light a cigarette in his cupped hands. After a few failures, he disappeared below the rim seeking a pocket of still air.

O'Hern signaled and they broke into two groups, O'Hern, Hathaway, Osima and Benson, and Al Dweeb, Hornbuckle and Otto. Otto's group circled the palace counter-clockwise, bringing them through a series of ruins, mostly abandoned cinder block shops and homes but also the remains of a Coptic Church. Those who chose to remain in the forlorn village had been forced to relocate 500 meters from the palace. Ghaddafi had had a single water outlet installed in the village center connected by pipe to the palace. He could turn it off at any time.

Otto took point fifty meters from the nearest ruin, his camo causing him to blend in. A minute glow lit the ruler-straight eastern horizon, but was cut short by the low-hanging blanket of sand. He crawled on his belly, cradling his carbine in his elbows. The nearest ruin was a gutted shell with scorch marks. It could have been ten years old or two hundred. Peering through a gap in the wall with his night vision Otto saw shifting green sands.

He made a circular motion and within seconds Al Dweeb and Hornbuckle had joined him. Spread out, they circled the palace, climbing over blasted sills or shifting rubble, the wind a constant presence whipping up little sand devils in the corners and peppering the skin.

The sentry on the south wall was more diligent, but he didn't look down. Otto, Al Dweeb and Hornbuckle converged at the south gate. While Hornbuckle and Al Dweeb hugged the wall, Otto got down on his knees and inspected the steel door, slightly inset due to the sloping walls. He pulled out a tiny battery-powered sniffer and waved it around the rim. He used a pen light to examine the gap between the door and the frame.

Satisfied, Otto removed a can of WD-40 from his pack and squirted the door's hinges. With a gloved hand, he pushed it open. It was unlocked, as their mole had promised. There was a minute squeak instantly lost in the wind. They slunk inside. Otto closed the door. Tinny Egyptian pop played from a tabletop radio next to a soldier in military drabs dozing in a tilt-back chair, feet up on a gunmetal desk.

The three ops entered a large dim cavern, the motor pool. The Agency had paid a million dollars for the intel and the open door. No one knew who the mole was. The room smelled of petrol, cleaning solvents and some exotic spice. Save for the dozing soldier, they had the room to themselves. The room contained a Mercedes limousine, an ancient Cherokee, a Russian Tiger with a roof-mounted .50, and an old olive drab bus. Intel estimated two dozen soldiers in the palace, plus Ghaddafi, plus "wife," and maybe one of his sons, all of whom the ops had learned to identify on sight.

Hornbuckle signaled them to cross the floor and form up by the door leading into the interior. As Al Dweeb was halfway across the floor, a dull thump resounded causing the earth to shift and dust to rain down.

A Team had detonated their distraction.

With a shout, the sleeping soldier came awake, slammed his feet to the ground and ratcheted his AK-47.

CHAPTER TWO

TOMAHAWK

O tto gripped his Sig and set. Without sighting, he envisioned a triangle between gun, eyes and target and squeezed the trigger. His first four shots ripped through the sentry's tunic and sent him sprawling. Hornbuckle was already through the door, gas mask on as he rolled a smoke bomb down the corridor. Their intel put Ghaddafi on the top floor in his "presidential suite."

Otto pulled on his mask and followed Hornbuckle through a steel door into a cinder block corridor with vinyl floor and acoustic ceiling. Hornbuckle stood sentry as Otto planted the homing device at the juncture of floor and concrete pillar. On their signal, *USN Corregidor* would launch a Tomahawk missile from the Mediterranean. The *Corregidor* remained submerged waiting for their sixty-second window of opportunity.

Hornbuckle and Otto ran past an open door glimpsing hallucinatory marble floors and a big indoor swimming pool glowing cerulean from underwater lights. A wave of obscene moisture struck them as they passed. They heard muffled shots and men shouting in Arabic. Hornbuckle paused at the next door to roll a smoke grenade into the big room. He and Otto followed splitting left and right. Through smoke Otto saw a Libyan soldier, pistol drawn, leaping down the broad marble steps three at a time. Hornbuckle drilled him with a head shot. The stairs ascended around the polished bronze doors of an elevator. The elevator doors were open revealing a space that would not have been out of place in a Las Vegas hotel. Gilt-tinted mirrors above a brass rail. Parquet floor. Hornbuckle tossed an illumination grenade through the open doors and bolted. The grenade exploded with a dull *whump*, belching smoke and fire into the room.

Hornbuckle and Otto took the steps two at a time, Otto's carbine banging against his side. The O'Hern-led ruse had succeeded in drawing the defenders to the north side of the building but Ghaddafi was never without his personal guard. They'd heard rumors that the Strong Man of Libya had hired lethal blond Belarus beauties whom he dressed in black leather outfits of his own design.

A hand grenade bounced merrily down the marble stairs and stopped at Otto's feet. Without thinking, he scooped it up and hurled it as far as he could across the marble lobby, falling to the steps beneath the fluted balustrade. The grenade detonated with an ear-puncturing report, metal shards pinging off the walls onto the floor for several seconds. Otto's earplugs protected him. He was up and following Hornbuckle as the staircase corkscrewed clockwise around the elevator shaft. Smoke rose with them, not all of it from the grenades.

They reached the fourth floor without resistance. Either they'd caught the guard napping or their intel was wrong and this was a skeleton crew. The intel could not be wrong. COC never would have signed off on the mission if he hadn't known for a fact Ghaddafi was in the building. A broad marble corridor led the way to the Presidential suite, double red leather doors with gold buttons set in a bronze frame.

A soldier in desert khakis lay on the floor outside the door, crimson pool the size of a garbage can lid beneath his head. His black beret had been knocked off and he clutched a Makarov MP-71 in one hand. He'd blown off the top of his head through the roof of his mouth.

Hornbuckle paused five meters from the door, hand up to pause. It was not supposed to be this easy. Hornbuckle motioned

Otto to the other side of the door. Otto examined the door and frame, got down on his hands and knees and peered under. The door was cracked open a quarter inch. From beneath the door, he saw Persian rugs extending to a massive marble desk, a pair of black boots planted on the floor behind the desk. Otto could not see any higher. The feet repositioned themselves.

Otto signaled Hornbuckle that someone was in the room. His heart raced in anticipation.

Don't anticipate, he told himself. *Be the mission.*

Hornbuckle stood on the other side of the door with his pistol in both hands. He stepped back and kicked the door, spiraling out of the way as soon as he made impact. The door swung back and smacked into its stopper. Hornbuckle rushed the room at an angle cutting away from the door. As soon as it was clear, Otto did the same going to the other side. They took position behind furniture and drew down on the figure behind the desk.

Not Ghaddafi.

The dark, thin, elegantly groomed young man smiled at them. It was Ghaddafi's son Malik. Every member of the team knew the entire Ghaddafi family on sight. The room was decorated like the office of a successful, but eccentric CEO. A copy of the Venus de Milo rested on a plinth. A gilt-framed poster of Anna Nicole Smith hung over a credenza topped with action figures including Conan the Barbarian. There were signed photographs of Michael Jackson and Snoop Dogg on the wall.

A big-screen TV, several generations old with a massive picture tube sat on a media stand. The east-facing windows showed the rising sun peeking over the horizon. A curving concave metal sheet mounted in native rock displayed an elegant *Qalicheh*. The room smelled of hashish and patchouli. There was a large brass hookah mounted on a delicately carved cedar table inlaid with mother of pearl. An open laptop faced Malik on the desk.

"Good morning, gentlemen," Malik said. Like all the dictator's children, Malik spoke perfect English.

"Where's the colonel," Hornbuckle snapped.

Malik spread his hands. "As you can see he's not here. If you plan to shoot me, don't delay. I embrace martyrdom as my destiny."

A muffled explosion shook the floor. Shouts and gunfire grew louder. Hornbuckle stepped up to the desk, gun trained on Malik, and seized the laptop.

"Watch him. I'll be right back."

"Where you going?" Otto said.

"I need to check something with O'Hern."

Hornbuckle left shutting the door behind him. The guard's body was still there.

Otto had a moment of misgiving. Why hadn't Hornbuckle used the radios? Did he fear they would be overheard? It was against protocol to leave a high-level figure like Malik with only one guard.

Otto walked counter-clockwise around the desk so that Malik came into full view.

"What do they pay you?" Malik said in a conversational voice.

"More than enough," Otto said.

"I will pay for my freedom. If you'll permit me to open this desk drawer." Malik's hand extended to the center drawer of the massive desk.

Otto motioned furiously with his gun for Malik to move back. "Don't touch it! Stay in the chair. Push yourself into the corner."

With Otto tracking his every move, the dictator's son had no choice but to obey. He scooted backwards on the chair's wheeled legs. Otto backed up to the desk drawer keeping a bead on Malik. He dare not turn away. Damn Hornbuckle for leaving!

Without looking, there was no way to tell if the drawer was booby-trapped.

Outside the wind howled and the sun turned bright orange, top lopped flat by the low-hanging clouds. He whipped his eyes back to Malik. The dictator's son sat in the corner grinning like a fool. His eyes glowed orange—or maybe it was a trick of the light.

Otto took a step toward Malik.

Streams of vapor poured from Malik's nostrils. He stood, smoke issuing from a corner of his mouth.

"Sit down!" Otto said.

Malik burst into flame.

Otto was momentarily frozen, awash in heat and the stink of burning flesh.

A flaming man?

Malik blossomed into a ball of white-hot phosphorus. A skillet of heat pressed down on every square centimeter of Otto's exposed skin. Wallpaper curled from the corners and ignited. The chair on which Malik sat exploded. Otto backtracked and tried the door. Jammed shut. He put his shoulder to it and shoved with all his might. Did not budge.

He had to get out of there. The heat was setting his clothes on fire.

He raced to the window and that's when he saw the Tomahawk.

CHAPTER THREE

AARDVARK

He was on an airliner headed down. There was a lot of screaming, but no sound. A sick, subdued terror seized his heart. He wrestled with his seat belt as the choppy sea rose to smash them.

He was afloat on some piece of jetsam. How long he drifted, he did not know.

Otto woke scorched, ears ringing. For long seconds he lay still waiting for the nausea to subside, fearful of what had happened to his body. Tentatively he lifted a finger. Five fingers. An arm. The other arm. A leg. The other leg. He was bruised all over, but there didn't seem to be anything broken. A ceiling lay mere centimeters from his face. He touched it—fabric. He placed both hands against it and pushed. The barrier was too heavy for him to lift but it shifted.

Otto turned his head and saw a strip of sand. He was lying on the desert beneath some kind of shield. Slowly, painfully, he crabbed sideways extricating himself from the sand. The steel-mounted *Qalicheh* lay next to him, convex surface up. He had been blown out of the palace on a flying carpet. Otto sat up, bracing himself with both hands. Twenty meters away Ghaddafi's palace, reduced to a pile of rubble, smoldered, sending a column of dark gray smoke whipping into the desert breeze.

The fierce winds of last night had abated, replaced by a steady 20 kph breeze that peppered Otto's face with pins. Otto sat behind the carpet that had saved his life. He'd flown out of the palace's fourth floor, forty meters into the sand on the eastern side, away from the village. He heard gunfire from inside the blazing ruin as vehicles vanished down the dirt road belching black smoke.

The Ilyushin roared to life and began to taxi.

Otto checked himself. Gun gone. Radio gone. He still had the tiny GPS transmitter, but he was too close to the Libyan Army to risk it. Amazingly, he still had a quart of water strapped to his belt. He had to get away. The palace was the center of too much attention.

Had Ghaddafi even been there?

Why had Hornbuckle left the room?

What was on the laptop?

Who fucked with the timing on the transmitter?

He slithered like a lizard away from the burning palace, heading east toward the truncated sun.

In the days that followed Otto had plenty of time to review the events in his mind and try to figure out what happened.

He lived in the desert like some feral beast, laying low during the day, hunting and moving east at night. He would require a minimum two gallons a day for survival, up to five gallons if he exerted himself. On the second day, he found a furze of green at the outside curvature of a wadi, dug down until he felt moisture and built a still out of a sheet of plastic and a straw they all carried for that purpose. At the end of the day he had accumulated maybe half a cup. He ate one of his two precious energy bars.

He lay up during daytime in a shallow grave he'd carved from the carapace of sand. The ground surface was thirty degrees hotter than that a foot below. He considered pissing in the hole like the Kalahari bushmen, but didn't have enough piss to make a difference.

By night the desert looked like the set of a vast black-and-white movie. Moon and star glow reflected off the quartzite rock and pale sands. Otto nearly stepped on a fat-tailed scorpion. He saw it at the last minute, foot paused in mid-air then slowly withdrawn. It was the Mother of All Scorpions. Five inches. Its chitinous, segmented body was the essence of evil, its sight repulsive and frightening.

Why had God made such creatures?

Who was he to question God?

There was no pursuit. Ghaddafi had his hands full with civil war. On the third day, Otto saw contrails to the north. He'd lost his GPS transmitter. Later that day he saw a caravan heading east several miles away on a ridge. Caravans were to be avoided at all costs.

He ate the last of his energy bars. His stomach screamed.

On the fourth day, he ate ants.

On the fifth day, he came upon a Canadian archaeological dig. Four white tents, some ruins, and two vehicles. He watched for several hours from a ridgetop with his mini binocs. There appeared to be two men and two women, plus a half dozen locals to help with the dig. Maple leaf patches adorned their backpacks, tent, and vehicles, a Nissan Pathfinder and an old Chevy pick-up.

Otto didn't have much of a choice. He had to take a chance. He hailed them from fifty meters. The men and one of the women were visible. They looked at him startled. He had appeared out of nowhere.

"Hallloooo! Sorry to bother you!"

As the two men and the woman turned to face him, unconsciously standing together, the other woman, middle-aged with a cap of silver hair, joined them. One of the men was tall and thin. The other was stocky, middle-aged, wearing those wrap-around shades that fit around glasses. The other woman was young and athletic, her long brown hair done up in a bun.

"Where did you come from?" she said.

"Otto White. I'm with Central Intelligence."

The tall man said, "You're a spy? An American spy?"

"We refer to ourselves as ops or agents. Listen, I hate to bother you, but I'm all that's left of a seven-man team. Do you have any water?"

As the stocky man handed Otto his canteen, the older woman said, "You have ants on your chin."

CHAPTER FOUR
SAM FLAMES OUT

Saturday.

Radio blasting Sis Boom Ba's "Boom-Ba Style," Sam Darling steered the Mercedes 350 SL with one hand and squeezed Sally's right breast with the other. Rural Virginia flashed by in emerald hues, the air redolent with honeysuckle. Sally laughed and twisted away.

"Eyes on the road, Senator."

Darling flashed his famous smile and shot a glance at his buxom thirty-six year old mistress, a lobbyist for Pendragon Oil. "How can I do that, darlin', with you by my side?" His hand fell to her knee. His touch was warm.

Sally's knee prickled with goose bumps. At sixty-five, the Senator looked like a man twenty years younger thanks to diligent workouts in the Congressional gym and a rugged outdoor lifestyle he'd brought with him from his native Colorado. Sally also felt the illicit thrill, familiar to half the players in Washington, of a clandestine affair carried out beneath the noses of the electorate, Senate leader and whip and the President, a model of moral rectitude who was rumored to be carrying on an affair with a foreign diplomat.

I owe this to myself, Sally thought, thinking of all the scheduling, work and deception that had gone into this weekend. With the enormous weight of Pendragon, its shareholders and board members on her shoulders, Sally knew she had to produce or be gone. As Chairman of the Senate Committee on Energy Independence, Darling was even busier. That they had managed to carry on their subterfuge for two whole years without *National Enquirer* or some freelance paparazzi finding out was a miracle in itself.

Never mind that Pendragon was behind Senate Bill # 465,002, lowering environmental restrictions on shale fracking in Western Colorado. So what if she was screwing the chairman? That's how the game was played. Besides—Darling was tall, charming and attractive and had promised to take her to Barbados for a long weekend in December. He was separated, but not divorced, from his wife of twenty-one years, Crystal. Although Darling had never said as much, Sally was certain he could be maneuvered into divorcing Crystal and marrying her. If she played her cards right.

They always think that, she mused sardonically.

She'd packed a few things to ensure a memorable weekend.

Darling had led a life of probity, at least until colliding with Sally. Or so he claimed. Journalists had been tracking his spoor for decades in hopes of digging up dirt that would derail the powerful Republican. They couldn't attack over his separation—half of Congress was in the same boat. So they scrutinized his every move, even going so far as to following his daughter Stella, a criminal defense attorney.

The two-lane blacktop wound through the piney hills northeast of Lynchburg, passing the occasional picture-book farm, sleek horses grazing behind white picket fences, until it came to a turn-off marked by an engraved wooden sign that would not have looked out of place outside an exclusive Georgetown boutique. Vernon's was a high-end low profile resort catering to D.C. power players. Owner Vernon Price was a former CIA officer and field agent, and had masterfully parlayed his credentials into a thriving business.

The smooth black macadam led between rows of blue spruce around a gentle curve to the administration building, a perfectly restored 19th century gingerbread farmhouse with a wrap-around veranda, green shutters and trim, and an old-fashioned bench swing suspended from two tractor chains affixed to a beam. One other car, an SUV with Maryland plates, two kayaks strapped to the roof and bikes on the bumper, was parked on the gravel.

Darling pulled up next to it and shut off the engine. He turned to Sally with a devilish grin, his eyes oddly yellow. Perhaps it was the late afternoon sun.

"I'll be right back, darlin'. Don't go anywhere."

Sally flipped down the passenger mirror and retouched her bow-shaped lips and lustrous fake eyelashes. Not bad for an old broad. Sally ran. Every morning, six miles along Rock Creek Park with a Beretta .25 in a fanny pack. Her belly was flat as Kansas. You could bounce quarters off her ass. Dabbing Donna Karan Delicious behind her ears, she placed the little glass container back in her purse as Darling emerged from the office holding a key on a big brass tag.

When he slid into the driver's seat, Sally noticed the sweat popping on his brow. "Are you all right Sam? You look a little feverish."

"It's called Potomac Fever, my love, and it's why we have to get away from time to time."

Starting the engine he slipped the automatic into reverse and stomped on the gas causing the little Mercedes to scoot back, spraying gravel like a singed Yorkie. He jammed the auto into drive and floored it, causing the car to fishtail wildly like a tire ad.

"Sam, is this necessary?"

"Sorry, Sal. I'm hot to trot." His hand fell to her thigh and squeezed. His touch was hot. They zipped down the gravel road past several neat bungalows to the last in line, green on white like the main house. Darling parked the car at a carefree angle, popped the trunk, popped out, grabbed the two overnighters and went up three steps to the front door. A hand-carved sign over the door said "Day Lilly Lodge." Setting down the bags, he unlocked the door.

He turned to Sally. "How fast can you change into something obscene, little lady?"

"Pretty damn fast," Sally said. Darling smacked her butt as she passed him, went through the cozy living room/kitchen decorated with Currier & Ives prints, through the bedroom with its walnut four-poster and crinoline skirt to the bathroom where she stripped, putting on a slinky silk peignoir from Mitzi's in Georgetown. She examined herself in the mirror, posing like a model, which she had briefly been following college. Small high tits. Thank God she didn't have humongous bazoombas like the typical Washington mistress. No boob job for her. Mama Crandall didn't raise no dummies.

Judging herself resplendent, she swung open the door and struck a pose. "Ta-DA!" Her smile froze.

"Sam?" she said.

The Senator stood on the opposite side of the bed wearing nothing but gray Calvin Klein briefs grinning vapidly. Vapor wafted from his mouth. His eyes were yellow.

"Sam, are you all right?" she said with quiet urgency.

Smoke spilled from his mouth, nostrils and ears. He incandesced into a pillar of blazing light and exploded releasing an expanding ball of white-hot gas and the smell of burning flesh striking Sally like a blacksmith's hammer and throwing her back into the bathroom.

CHAPTER FIVE
WTF?

Vernon Price smiled at the young couple from Maryland. He was a lean, gray man who radiated competence. "Okay. We're twelve miles from Tweedy State Park where there's a little lake. Or you can put into the James right here on the property. You can put in anywhere. We're seeing a lot of kayakers around here lately."

The young man handed Price his credit card. "Do you get HBO?"

"HBO, Showtime, every major league game, you name it, plus an extensive collection of movies on demand."

Sudden movement drew Price's attention to the window. Darling's delicious dumpling ran barefoot and half-naked toward the office. A prickle of alarm marched down Price's spine. Something in her desperate pumping told him she wasn't exercising. He flashed an apologetic grin at the young couple.

"Folks, if you'll excuse me one minute—it's just one thing after another around here."

The young man shrugged quizzically. "Sure."

Price bolted from behind the counter and exited the front door, taking the three front steps in one leap. He had to intercept her before she reached the office. Whatever had happened was not for tourists.

Price jogged toward her, hands up, palms out, stopping her twenty meters from the main house under a dogwood tree. "Whoa, Sally, whoa! What's going on?"

She collapsed into his arms wild-eyed, unable to speak, a peculiar smoky odor clinging to her skin. She gestured back down the road. Price looked up to see Day Lilly burst into flames. Poof, like a stunt out of *Fast and Furious*.

Gripping Sally by the shoulders, he marched her quickly to the nearest bungalow, Snapdragon, opened the unlocked door and led her inside. "Are you all right? Are you injured?" he said examining her carefully. She didn't appear to be hurt, just stunned and in shock. Price sat her down on the bed.

He pulled out his secure phone, the one the agency had given him, and hit the speed dial. Seconds later a man picked up.

"Contingency and planning, Baumgartner speaking."

"This is Vernon Price at Vern's resort, retired Service Contractor serial number 879002LP. Do you know where this is?"

"Yessir. What seems to be the problem?"

"I have a cottage that's burning out of control. Senator Sam Darling is trapped in the cottage."

"Sir, I'm dispatching a rescue team with medical personnel and fire fighters, but it will be … approximately seventy-five minutes before they arrive. Can you hold out?"

Price looked out the window at the bungalow, now completely engulfed in flames. Fortunately it was a hundred feet from the nearest structure and the humid summer meant little chance of the fire spreading. As Price watched, the young couple with the kayaks drove quickly away.

Nothing he could do about that.

It was all Price could do to stay put and not run for the fire extinguisher and the garden hose, but he knew from painful experience they would be of little help against such a conflagration. Priorities. First order of business: control the narrative.

Price went into the bathroom and filled a glass with water. He came out and handed the glass to Sally who had curled up on the bed and was weeping. She sat up and drank thirstily. Price knelt before her.

"Sally, I know this is difficult but we have to get our stories straight before the police arrive. What happened?"

Sally looked up, mascara running from her eyes like mudslides. "He seemed a little jumpy when we drove out and in the cabin he seemed feverish—he was sweating and smoke was pouring from his mouth and ears."

"What?"

"I know it sounds crazy! I swear to God he started smoking like a chimney! Then he blew up."

Price knew who Sam was. And he knew who Sally was. With the fracking bill before the Senate next week it seemed unlikely the senator's death was a coincidence.

The high wail of a first responder penetrated the bungalow. The Appomattox County Rural Fire Department was the first to arrive.

"Sally, can you stay in here until we get this straightened out? If they find out who was in the cabin there's going to be a big media brouhaha."

Sally swallowed and nodded. She knew how to play the game.

With a sigh Price went out to meet the fire department.

CHAPTER SIX
A NATIONAL CRISIS

Sunday.

The White House Situation Room was on the ground floor of the West Wing. Two Secret Service Agents stood at the entrance. A Secret Service agent guarded the White House elevator hidden in a pantry off the renovated kitchen, which led to the Secure Room, two floors below street level, lined with lead and designed to withstand a fifty-megaton hit.

Adjacent to the Situation Room was the computer room, housing a Cray XT5 with over 224,000 processing cores. A wall of monitors cast the only light in the climate-controlled op center, manned twenty-four seven by a staff of five including two West Point graduates, a Yalie, and two scruffy hackers who'd been recruited by the CIA. The President's, indeed, most of Congress' e-mail accounts were subject to unrelenting cyber-warfare.

There were hundreds of malware cells around the world whose sole goal was to disrupt the communications of the United States government. Iran alone sponsored thirty. China had an unknown number. The Russkies were said to have sixteen. Even allies such as Israel, Brazil, and Saudi Arabia tried to look up Uncle Sam's pants.

Hence the NSA's Advanced Networks Operations (ANO) team, a group of mostly young computing experts assembled in 2006 to hunt for suspicious activity on the government's secure networks. Their office was a nondescript windowless room in Ops1, a boxy, low-rise building on the 660-acre campus of the NSA.

Each of the twenty-one computers in the White House computer room was shielded by a metal box and had no connection to the internet or to each other. The shielding was to prevent their disruption by an electro-magnetic pulse. The system ran on a small nuclear reactor unconnected to any outside power grid that had been installed in spring, '02, at then-Presidential advisor Dick Cheney's direction. There were no wireless mice and no wireless keyboards because those signals could be intercepted and the data captured.

Those entering the room had to surrender their cell phones, laptops, even their remote control car door locks, because those devices were all capable of sending and receiving signals. Data was gathered at numerous CIA/HSA agencies around the country and thoroughly laundered through redundant systems before it was allowed to enter the secure room.

Inside the Situation Room, the President sat grimly at the head of a carrier-shaped mahogany table with a Sony iBook softly glowing at his elbow. Each of the seven others seated at the table had a similar laptop tuned to the news feed about the shocking death of Senator Darling in an automobile accident. He was alleged to have been driving alone when he went off the road, rolled down a bank and the car burst into flames. It was possible he was distracted by talking on his phone. The world waited for the autopsy report even as the Appomattox County coroner hinted that there might not be enough left to autopsy.

In reality the senator's remains had been transported to Bethesda Naval Hospital.

On the President's left sat National Security Advisor Margaret Yee, FBI Director Howard Lubitch, and CIA Director Luther Brubaker. On his right sat Homeland Security Director General Rolf Panny, Dr. Hayley Gross, a communicable-disease expert from CDC with a Level five clearance, and General Arthur MacCauley, head of the Joint Chiefs. At the far end of the table sat WH Chief of Staff Murray Compton.

The room was dimly lit by sconces set low to the lush cocoa pile rug, which along with the insulation removed all sharp objects from the ear. For a moment the only sound was General Panny clearing his throat and the gentle susurrus of the air conditioning. A funk of anxiety permeated the air.

"Ladies and gentlemen," the President said, "As you know, Senator Darling did not die from an automobile accident. He spontaneously erupted, bringing the total number of these events to six this year. I don't know how much longer we can keep the lid on. Once this gets out we can expect a firestorm. We don't know if it's a disease or a new form of terrorism. We have videos of two of the immolations. These will be issued on a locked disc. They are disturbing.

"I have instructed the NSA and HS to issue a heightened alert." He paused as if searching for words. "We're trying to find out how far back these go. I don't know if you remember—that radical cleric in Cairo two years ago, went down in flames? Al Qaeda took credit."

Yee raised her palm and let it fall to the table. She was a diminutive Asian woman and had served three Presidents. "Mr. President, I learned only moments before this meeting that Dmitri Yakovitch the oil magnate died in a sudden blaze at his dacha on the Black Sea. From the press blackout I assume he spontaneously erupted. That makes seven."

The President hunched as if expecting a blow. With his rugged face and mane of silver hair he looked like Pixar's idea of the ideal Commander in Chief. "Margaret will head up this task force. Anything you need, just ask. I want you to identify the source of these attacks and neutralize them. Not a word to anyone. If this gets out we will have panic."

No matter whom he named to head up the task force, some were bound to be disappointed. But there was no objection. Those seated at the table had all long ago learned to mask their feelings behind a diplomatic face.

The President turned to Hayley Gross. "Dr. Gross, is there anything in your experience that would explain this?"

The model-thin Gross, designer glasses perched on her ax-shaped nose, consulted her PowerBook. "John E. Heymer in his book *The Entrancing Flame* advanced the theory that the victims all suffered from depression and fell into a coma shortly before they combusted. Heymer believed that their subconscious released hydrogen and oxygen molecules within the body setting off a chain reaction.

"Arthur C. Clarke wrote, 'There's one mystery I'm asked about more than any other: spontaneous human combustion.' Some cases seem to defy explanation, and leave me with a creepy and very unscientific feeling. If there's anything more to SHC, I simply don't want to know." She closed the laptop.

"I have been interested in SHC my whole life, but I have yet to find any scientific evidence that the body itself can spontaneously combust. The human body is mostly water. Moreover if your source is correct, Sen. Darling was hardly depressed. Just the opposite."

The President turned to General Panny who seemed too small for his dress uniform. Pale gray stipple formed a skullcap on his narrow face. "Rolf?"

"What worries me, Mr. President, is that this seems to be some new kind of technology. There hasn't been enough left of the victims to fill a matchbox, much less provide for an autopsy. Human flesh is hard to burn. Crematoria require a sustained heat of 1,700 degrees Fahrenheit for up to three hours. These combustions appear to generate from the inside out and are complete inside ninety seconds. This requires an incredible source of energy."

Luther Brubaker cleared his throat. He might have played a kindly family doctor on television, but his reputation was of a no-nonsense take-no-prisoners executive who got things done while irritating as many people as possible. He'd been a field agent and had firsthand experience with black ops. "Mr. President, we have been conducting experiments with microwaves, as you know. We have been unable to achieve anything like this and we've been at it for twelve years."

"So have the Russians," Panny said.

"So have the Chinese," MacCauley said.

The President fixed his piercing green eyes on Lubitch. "Howard, could there be a connection between Darling's role as Chairman of the Energy Independence Committee and these attacks?"

"We've been looking into this since we got the directive," the FBI Director said.

"These other victims have only a peripheral relationship to the energy industry, if any. Petrovich—that's new. He was oil. The problem is there's nothing left after these immolations to autopsy. We're hoping to get a break on the next one."

"Mr. President," Yee said in her soft but perfect voice. "As you know, we employ the Project Genesis system to select the appropriate personnel. We initiated a search pursuant to your directive last night. This morning the program identified the contractor most likely to succeed with an 89 percent probability, Otto H. White, a retired CIA operative."

Brubaker's lips formed a grim line. "Aardvark White? Seriously?"

CHAPTER SEVEN
AN UNLIKELY CHOICE

The President turned to Brubaker. "What about him?"

"Otto White was given a medical discharge last year after displaying symptoms of paranoia and acute schizophrenia. He was part of a seven-man team inserted into Libya in April '11. Due to faulty intelligence, they walked into an ambush. White was one of four survivors and managed to escape into the desert where he survived eating ants.

"White had an excellent record. He'd been in the field for nine years—that's too long for anybody. We should have seen the signs. He never should have been sent into Libya." Brubaker would know. He had been in the field ten years.

"Was that Operation Firebrand?" the President said.

"Yes, sir," Brubaker replied.

"Mr. President," Yee said, "White has an uncanny ability to think outside the box and do the unexpected, often with very positive results. That's why he's the best man for the job. He's also an arson investigator. And lucky."

"What do you mean, lucky?"

"Just that. He's phenomenally lucky. He wins at slots. He wins at roulette. It's not something that can be taught. You've either got it or you don't."

The President turned to his right. "Rolf?"

"It's Margaret's call."

Chief of Staff Murray Compton said, "I'll have his casebook and profile on your desk this morning, Mr. President."

Brubaker pushed the bridge of his glasses up with a forefinger. "There's a good chance he'll turn us down. If we can find him. My understanding is that he went off the grid. Lives in the mountains somewhere like Liver Eater Johnson."

"After his return to the U.S. and until shortly after his discharge," Yee said, "White had an affair with Senator Darling's daughter Stella. I've been in contact with Stella and she's willing to bring him in."

"Stella Darling," the President said. "Why does that ring a bell?"

"She's defending the Below the Beltline Sniper, Mr. President," Yee said.

"That's right."

The sniper, so-dubbed because he'd committed most of his crimes just south of the 395, had murdered six people in a week-long shooting spree, most of them in their cars. The victims had all been persons of substance: lawyers, lobbyists, venture capitalists. Two of their vehicles had burst into flames and incinerated their occupants. The police believed shots had ignited the fuel tanks.

When apprehended, Lester Durant claimed that he had been aiming at "the spiders."

"Isn't she in the middle of a trial?" Brubaker said.

"Court's adjourned until next week."

"Do you know the daughter?" the President said.

Yee gave a tight little nod. "I've met her. I liked and admired Sen. Darling despite his rebarbative political predilections. I'll ask her today."

Compton, who resembled a dot-com millionaire with his Beatle hair and tinted glasses, cocked his head as his headset spoke softly. He looked up. All eyes were on the President. He caught the President's eye and tapped his headset twice.

"Murray?"

"Folks, if you'll tune your laptops to the in-house feed."

All turned their attention to their computers. Within seconds they had tuned to the Situation Room news feed. On screen: dozens of police and first responder vehicles arrayed in front of a nondescript office building in a commercial strip. One end was ablaze as firefighters maneuvered their hoses.

The news scroll along the bottom streamed: "Office attack leaves four dead ... building set on fire ... Volt Media President Lewis Stark allegedly pulled a gun and began shooting his employees ... developing ..."

CHAPTER EIGHT
A FAVOR

Sunday night.

Yee chose the restaurant at the Ritz-Carlton, The Brigadoon, for its anonymity. The intel meeting had gone well although she could feel the disdain rolling off Brubaker and MacCauley like cold off a glacier. The military mindset always wanted a military solution. Which was why terrorism existed—to deny the military solution.

Brubaker had lost his only son in the Gulf War, which conferred on him a certain moral dimension. He had also been black ops. He was not one of those men who jumped from desk to desk until they reached the top. MacCauley saw Red Chinese under his bed. Panny was a good soldier and had no dog in this fight. Lubitch was in over his head.

Yee had issued a memorandum last winter containing disinformation that eventually turned up on Wikileaks. Somewhere in the complicated cortex where NSA, FBI, CIA, and Homeland met there was a leak. Yee had taken it upon herself to track it down. The next couple of days would be interesting.

She was seated in the back in a corner banquette sipping Merlot when she saw the maitre d' escorting Stella Darling her way. An overweight tourist seated with his wife and two fidgety kids could not prevent his eyes from tracking Darling across the floor.

Tall and shapely in a gray Ralph Lauren skirted suit that complemented her figure and cover girl all American perfection, she wore her honey blond hair in a pageboy and carried an old-fashioned Gladstone by its strap over one shoulder. Darling never carried a purse. It was all in the Gladstone, including, Yee had heard, a .38 revolver. A gift from her daddy.

Yee rose to her full five one to greet the criminal defense attorney. "Thank you for coming, Stella."

Darling took her hand warmly. "Of course."

They both slid onto the red leather bench. A pale young man in black vest and white shirt appeared to take their drink orders. Yee ordered another Merlot. Darling ordered a Grey Goose vodka straight up with a twist. Darling's dark and puffy eyes were the only indication of the strain she was under. Darling pulled out a contact lens lubricant and dumped an ounce in each eye.

"These contacts."

"Don't wear them, dear. Eyeglasses look good on you."

Darling chuckled ruefully. "I know. Sam always insisted I wear contacts. 'Girls who wear glasses don't often get passes,' he told me. It's an old habit. I've been thinking of having my eyes lasered, but too many people tell me horror stories."

The waiter came with their drinks and discreetly withdrew. It was eight-thirty in the evening, the earliest Darling could get away after spending all day shepherding her client through the psychological evaluation procedure. It didn't help that Lester Durant was kept chained and shackled.

Yee held up her glass. "To Sam."

"To Sam." They clinked. Yee sipped. Darling drained half the glass.

She set it down and fixed her slightly bloodshot blue eyes on the NSA honcho. "How can I help?"

"We'd like you to bring Otto White in."

Darling blinked several times. "For what?"

"To head up a team to find and neutralize whatever it is that killed the Senator, and has killed at least twelve others of whom we know. I'm talking about spontaneous human combustion."

Darling lowered her voice, although nobody was around and they were speaking directly to one another. "There have been others?"

"This is top secret, Stella."

Darling flashed a nervous grin. "Why Otto?"

"He was a smoke jumper in college. He was a volunteer fire fighter for the Poudre Canyon district before he joined the Army where he was a military policeman and became a certified arson investigator. He has extensive counter-espionage experience, but most importantly, he has something we call the X-factor, the ability to do the totally unexpected and get results."

Darling smiled ruefully. "That's for sure. We were at St. Exupery one night and there's a foreign couple eating a table away. They looked Middle Eastern. Waiter brings their meal, Otto gets up, goes over, grabs the white linen tablecloth and yanks it out from under the dishes. Of course, not being a magician everything on the table went with it. Then he turns to the freaked out couple and says, 'I'm so sorry. I thought I could pull it off.'"

"I had to pay for their meal and the broken dishes. 'What the hell?!' I said to him as soon as we got out of there. Tells me the man was an Al Qaeda agent and they were listening in on us."

Yee's small black eyes sparkled. "I never heard that."

"I had to pay the staff a couple hundred to shut them up."

"You don't happen to know the name of the unfortunate diners he interrupted?"

"No, I'm sorry."

"Did he ever regard you with suspicion?"

Stella looked surprised. "Me? Never. That's one thing about Otto. 'An elephant's faithful one hundred per cent.' An old-fashioned Boy Scout. It killed me to break it off with him, but what could I do? He was hallucinating ninja out of the woodwork. Every time we met he dumped my purse upside down on the table."

Yee glanced at the Gladstone. "That thing?"

"Sam gave it to me. I call it my purse."

"This incident at St. Xupe. Was this before he was hospitalized?"

"Right before."

"You never visited him. Why was that?"

A crease marred Stella's forehead as she realized NSA would have access to the hospital's visitor logs. A tingle of paranoia zipped down her spine. Were they tracking her?

"I was afraid it was me who was causing him to act crazy. Otto never does anything halfway. When he fell in love with me, it was more *Othello* than *Love's Labors Lost*. I wanted him to get over me. I still do. I have no idea what would happen if I suddenly showed up out of nowhere. And believe me, it is nowhere. It might throw him into an emotional tailspin."

Yee trained her lasers on Stella. "It's the President who's asking. Will you go get him? Ask him to come in?"

Stella inhaled deeply and let it out. It had been over two years. "Of course."

Yee blinked revealing nothing. She smiled. "I knew we could count on you. When's the memorial service?"

"It's not a service, it's a wake, and don't come if you don't like drunk Irishmen. It's Saturday at two, at Chiklis, upstairs in the private dining room."

Yee signaled the waiter, caught his eye, and made a little writing motion with her hand in her palm. She turned back to Stella. "I'll bring a bottle of Irish Mist."

CHAPTER NINE
VISION QUEST

Monday.

Wiry juniper covered the ledge like steel wool, gin aroma stirring dark memories of Otto's youth. He smelled sage and water from the creek below. Otto hunkered just below the rim, right arm over Steve's neck, snugging the big dog close. Steve was part Alsatian, maybe some border collie and otter. Otto held a pair of Zeiss binoculars. He set them carefully on the rock shelf and looked sixty meters across the canyon to a ledge, ten meters above the gushing stream coming off the mountain. It was there, three weeks ago, he'd spotted Max.

He called the cougar Max out of respect. After maximum effort and Manfred Freiherr von Richthofen.

At least he thought it was a cougar. A flash of tawny fur and gone. Splintered bones and tufts of fur lay at the base of the ledge against the shadowed rock.

Steve growled deep in his throat, a soft electric vibration. Otto ruffled the dog's fur and whispered, "Whassup, homie? We gonna get lucky? Is Max coming back?"

Just give me some kind of sign, girl, oh my baby, show me that you care. Show me that you're mine girl, well all right ... played over and over in his head. In his gut he knew what he was really looking for: proof of the divine. Otto refused to believe that man was nothing more than a collection of molecules spewed forth from a random universe, as his father had said.

They'd been six hours on the mountain, including the hike from the trailhead. Three hours in the hot sun. An occasional breeze off the mountain brought the cool promise of fall. Otto had brought plenty of water and they could always dip into the stream, but that would spook the cat.

Otto had embarked on this vision quest after meditating for sixteen hours. The quest had led him and Steve to Mt. Smithback in the Never Summer Range. As befits a vision seeker, he hadn't eaten in forty-eight hours and had brought no food save for several Ralston Purina dog burgers for Steve. He felt light-headed but clear. He could see for a hundred miles over the snow-capped peaks to the ever-rising mountains to the southwest. At 11,000 feet they were just below the tree line.

"Here, kitty kitty," Otto crooned into Steve's ear. Steve jerked his muzzle skyward and growled, the hair on his back forming a dorsal ridge. Otto looked up. An aerial battle was in progress: four ravens dive-bombing a bald eagle.

The eagle banked and came in for a landing on Max's plateau jutting out over the canyon above the gushing stream. The ravens followed and took up position at the four points of the compass. The eagle extended its wings in a show of force. It was big— possibly seven feet. It advanced on one of the ravens like George St. Pierre throwing a feint and the raven darted back. The eagle turned facing each of the ravens in turn, giving each a little scare when suddenly, the raven behind the eagle exploded as the eagle's mate hurled into it at 150 mph, feathers flying in all directions.

Every ace needed a wingman.

As the mate hit, the first eagle rose in a widening gyre, the remaining ravens scrambling airborne and trying to flee. They never stood a chance. The male eagle executed a perfect Immelmann and struck the second raven like a dum-dum bullet. The raven fell in pieces to the earth, feathers trailing. The eagle's mate effortlessly grabbed big air, went into a barrel roll and hit the third raven like a bunker buster. The lone remaining raven was hell bent for leather to the east, but the male eagle zeroed in like a sidewinder missile and took it out in a little black explosion.

The female settled to the plateau and began to eat the first raven she'd killed.

Otto was thunderstruck. He instinctively touched the tiny cross tattooed above his sternum. Clearly God or the Great Spirit or Buddha or Gaia or maybe even John Denver had something important in mind, to bring him this far and show him this sign. Steve too seemed mesmerized by the aerial display and looked longingly after the departed birds, tongue lolling.

Otto trained his binocs on the eagle and watched her feed. Her mate soon joined her.

That's how you do it, he thought. You eat your fucking enemies.

Steve whined quizzically, rose and headed back the way they'd come barking furiously. Otto turned and looked. There was nothing that shouldn't have been there. The land lay the same, untouched by any human presence. There were no other people within a three-klick radius, possibly larger. There were no trails here in the Roosevelt National Forest and the casual hiker could soon find himself in trouble.

Steve stopped barking, looked back over his shoulder grinning and trotted down the mountain.

Otto was hungry enough to eat a raven. Maybe that's what the message was. Go home and eat. He rose to his feet.

"All right, Steve. All right!"

CHAPTER TEN
CRYSTAL

Monday afternoon.

Stella flew United to Denver, arriving at one-fifteen in the afternoon. Upon deplaning, she paused in the reception lounge to phone her stepmother, Crystal. Sam and Martha, Stella's mother, had divorced twenty-four years ago. Martha had remarried an automobile salesman. Martha and her husband died in a fiery car wreck while driving through Tennessee fifteen years ago. The bitter irony preyed upon Stella's mood.

"Hello, dear," Crystal said. "I am so looking forward to your visit. I'm only sorry it took a tragedy for us to get together."

Yeah. Right.

"I should be there in two hours, Crystal."

"Wonderful. We'll have dinner."

Stella blanched at the prospect. Crystal could barely follow the directions on a package of frozen food. She was probably already hitting the Chard. Hitting it hard.

Stella called her boyfriend Gabe Winner. She got his voice mail.

"Hey, Detonator. I just hit Denver and I'm about to beard the beast in her den. Give me a call when you get a chance."

After retrieving her luggage from the carousel Stella took the shuttle to Avis, passing the dreadful blue demon horse whose upraised hooves and blazing red eyes greeted visitors to the airport. Did no one consider the message it sent? It was like an upside-down cross or something. It was called "Mustang."

Stella rented a Mustang. She took the E-470 tollway to Interstate 25 and headed north past familiar landmarks: Furniture Row, RV World, the motocross field, Johnson's Corners. She turned west on Harmony, amazed at how the once barren landscape between the Interstate and College had filled with strip malls. They all subscribed to the same architectural school, semi-industrial support members, gently curving roofs, earth tones.

Harmony turned into 38E climbing the Front Range. Stella passed numerous cyclists, most clad in bespoke cycling clothes with streamlined helmets and camel backs, churning up the heart-breaking slope. As the road rose Stella could see all of Fort Collins stretching to the eastern plains.

She turned west at the top and then north on 23, a spectacular drive along the eastern edge of the seven mile long Horsetooth Reservoir. The res was filled to bursting for the first time in twelve years at this late date. The winter had deposited an epic snow pack and snow still clung to the mountains and canyons. It was eighty degrees outside and Stella kept the AC on. She turned left onto an impossibly steep concrete drive with a closed metal gate. A sign said, "PRIVATE DRIVE."

Stella lowered the window and punched a code into the keypad. The metal gate rolled smoothly out of the way. Holding the Mustang in first gear Stella drove up the steep drive, took a hairpin right at the top and pulled into the sloping concrete driveway of her ancestral home, a freaky-deaky new age design that looked like a lumberyard trying to take flight with spectacular views of the reservoir and the city below. As a child, Stella would huddle in her bed in winter fearing that the wind would tear their house off the ridge and fling it at Kansas.

The garage lay in shadow as the sun lowered in the west. Stella retrieved her Gladstone and the rolling suitcase from the trunk and dragged them up the winding flagstone stair to the front door that lay beneath an arched cutout. The house was sheathed in weather-resistant recycled barn siding and was on four levels, stepping up to the ridge, then down again toward the lake. It had a metal roof.

Stella tried the door. It was unlocked. She pulled her suitcase into the large foyer with its Spanish tile floor and softly burbling fountain, a water nymph in a lily pad. Cooking smells permeated the house.

"Crystal! I'm here!" she sang out.

A moment later the staccato sound of high heels approached from the hallway. Crystal appeared looking slightly flushed and glassy-eyed. She came up to Stella, hugged her and kissed her on both cheeks. Stella smelled Chard.

"I'm so glad you're here, dear. The radio and TV people have been hounding me non-stop."

Stella doubted that was the case.

"How are you, Crystal?"

Crystal waved a hand. "Oh, you know me. I'll get through. Come down to the living room. Would you like a glass of wine?"

"Have you got anything stronger?"

"You know where the bar is, dear. Just leave your suitcase there. Your old room is waiting."

Stella planned to do her duty by her stepmother before heading to Otto's place in the morning. He had taken her there once, before he started building. Told her his plans, where he planned to get the raw materials, how he would put them together. A home craftsman's dream. She hoped she could find it again.

There was no way to contact Otto. He had no telephone, no internet. Certainly no television or even a radio. Although he was conversant with all those tools, he chose to live like a nineteenth century mountain man.

Stella hit the half bath off the kitchen, washed her hands and went through the kitchen to the dining area. There were three place settings on the oak dining table. She went down two steps to the sunken living room looking west at the sun, a blazing orange ball sinking toward the jagged rocks of Horsetooth Mountain laying down a flickering stripe on the surface of the deep lake.

Stella went to the wet bar hidden behind an Oriental screen. She poured herself several fingers of Macallan, dropped in three ice cubes from the stainless steel Maytag and joined Crystal on the Italian leather sofa facing the sunset.

Crystal held up her glass of wine. "Well, here's to the senator, kiddo, he was quite a guy."

They clinked and drank. They suffered an awkward silence. Both spoke at once.

"Crystal,"

"Dear—"

Crystal giggled with nervousness. "You go ahead."

"Did you speak to Sam recently? Did he seem troubled about anything? Did he give any hint that something was about to happen?"

"No. As you know, we spoke once a week. If anything, he seemed more exuberant, more, you should excuse the expression, full of himself than ever. I feel sorry for that doxy he was banging."

"You don't know that."

Crystal sighed dramatically. "Oh dear. You're his daughter. Of course you believe him."

Stella sought a sharp retort then realized, what's the use? Crystal could no more help being Crystal than she could stop being Stella.

"Are you really going with that movie star?" Crystal said.

"Gabe is a very dear friend."

"When I go to King's Super, the women bring me the tabloids. There was even a photo of you two in *Us!* I'd love to meet him, wouldn't that be fun?"

"I'll see what I can do."

"I've been seeing somebody too and I took the liberty of asking him to join us for dinner."

"You're kidding," Stella said.

"Why no, dear."

The doorbell rang.

CHAPTER ELEVEN
THE BLASTER

Monday evening.

Crystal sprang to her feet and began rearranging her hair as she headed for the front door. Stella remained where she was and finished off her Scotch. She'd been hoping for a little quiet time with her stepmother whom she hadn't seen in over a year. Not that she craved Crystal's company. It just seemed like the right thing to do, and if there was one thing Sam taught her, it was to do the right thing.

Stella heard the front door open, exuberant greetings, a hushed exchange, an awkward silence and then Crystal returned with a man in tow. He was short, barely taller than Crystal, and thick, with the wide shoulders and rolling gait of a linebacker. He had a square head, small twinkly eyes, and a very short crew cut. He wore jeans, a black silk T-shirt that bulged over his belt like a feed sack and a gray sports jacket. She hoped he was not another used car salesman.

Stella rose.

"This is Tom Blaine, dear, a very dear friend of mine."

Blaine was careful not to crush her grip. "Crystal has told me so much about you. I'm only sorry we had to meet under these circumstances."

"Pleased to meet you, Tom."

Crystal went straight to the bar and mixed Tom a gin and tonic with a curl of lemon. Blaine took the Barcalounger at one end of the sofa, seated at a ninety-degree angle. He wore a diamond pinky ring and a gold chain.

"Crystal told me about your current client. I know you can't discuss it, but what a case, huh? Right up there with O.J."

Stella shrugged. "I didn't ask for it. A judge in Virginia requested me. One of Sam's cronies."

Crystal handed Blaine his drink, sat next to Stella and took her hand, which Stella found presumptuous. A little show of family solidarity for the boyfriend.

Stella could restrain herself no longer. "What do you do, Tom?"

"I install audio systems," he said.

"Tom's an inventor," Crystal declared proudly. "Do you know anyone who wants to invest in a surefire hit?"

Blaine blushed, took a slug of the gin. "Crystal, let's not bore Stella with my big ideas."

"Such as?" Stella said.

Blaine almost rubbed his hands in delight. "I've developed a tiny sound system that can literally replicate the feel, volume, and clarity of a stadium show, include making the earth move. It works on any concave or vibratable object. Would you like a demonstration?"

"Please," Stella said.

Blaine practically leaped to his feet. "I've installed a prototype here."

"Careful, boy," Crystal said. "Last time you demonstrated we got complaints from across the lake."

Blaine crossed to the credenza beneath an oil painting of buffalo and picked up a small gray device the size of a stick of gum. "This is the memory and amp—you can plug in your iPod or whatever." He pointed to two tiny metal blossoms in one corner, ground level and at two meters, the same in another corner. "These are your speakers. They use the ninety degree angle between walls to amplify sound."

He pushed a button on the unit and "Bohemian Rhapsody" poured forth like an avalanche.

"SCARAMOUCHE SCARAMOUCHE ..."

It was so loud Stella clapped her hands to her ears and watched the glass in the windows vibrate.

"TURN IT DOWN!" Crystal shrieked in a fight announcer's voice.

Grinning, Blaine turned it down to a throbbing pulse that Stella felt in her calves.

"Wow," she said. "I'm impressed."

"That's not all. What about the dog toys, Tom? He invested in that local company that makes dog toys out of recycled water bottles, oh what's their name?"

"Rubber Biscuit. I sold my shares last year, but yes, that's one example."

"Tom discovered that every health club and karate shop has literally hundreds of abandoned plastic water bottles. Tom recycles them into unbreakable dog toys. He's really quite ingenious."

Why the hard sell, Stella wondered. She must be planning to marry him.

"Tom was a star college quarterback, dear."

"I was a linebacker."

Crystal rose. "Excuse me, I've got to check on something in the kitchen. We'll eat soon."

"Do you need any help, Crystal?" Stella automatically asked.

"No. You two just sit and chat."

The sun dipped below the mountains.

"How much money do you need?" Stella said.

"A mil to get started."

"I was very impressed. I doubt you'll have any trouble finding the funds." He probably already found the funds, right in the house.

"Well, we'll see. Crystal tells me you're a shooter."

"Sam wanted a boy."

"I'm sorry I never met him," Blaine said.

Crystal bustled around the dining room in the background. They heard the clink of silverware and china.

"Come on, dears!" Crystal sang. "Dinner is served."

Stella and Blaine stepped up to the dining level. The table was covered with a white linen cloth. Three places had been set, each with a side salad and a steaming squab dead center on the big china plates. A bouquet of sunflowers occupied the center of the table between two sterling silver candlesticks with burning tapers.

Blaine held the chair for Crystal. Crystal and Stella sat at opposite ends with Blaine between them. Stella reached for one of several bottles of salad dressing, when Blaine folded his hands and bowed his head. Crystal did likewise. Stella sheepishly complied.

"Dear Lord," Blaine said, "for this food we are about to receive, we thank you. Amen."

"Amen."

Stella snagged the hot dish—it was the dreaded canned green bean and mushroom soup casserole. Stella dished a ceremonial amount onto her plate. Blaine refilled Crystal's glass from a wine bottle on the cabinet behind him. He got up to refresh his gin and tonic.

"Freshen your drink?" he said to Stella.

"No thanks. Alcohol interferes with my sleep. I've been on the go since four a.m."

"You poor dear," Crystal said. "You must be exhausted."

"I'm going to have to make a short night of it, folks," Stella said, secretly relieved. Now she wouldn't have to listen to Crystal's litany of complaints. Blaine had filled that position for which Stella was grateful.

The squab was underdone. Stella passed on the Sarah Lee Frozen Cheesecake and excused herself. She pecked Crystal on the cheek and shook Blaine's hand. Down the hall she went, leaving her stepmother and her beau to get on with the serious business of getting sloshed. Stella glanced out the front door. Blaine drove an older 911. She hoped it wouldn't be repossessed while he was visiting.

At the end of the hall Stella opened the door to Sam's home office and went down three steps to the burgundy pile rug. Man cave. Leather furniture, mahogany paneling, the inevitable hero wall bearing photos and testimonials. Sam with Bush the Elder. Sam with Clinton. Sam with Bush the Younger. Rustic/modern woodstove jutting from one corner. Expansive view of the lake. A stunning Jerry Bingham Western landscape. And of course the gun cabinet.

Certificates of Achievement from Rotary, The Boy Scouts of America, Benevolent Protective Order of Elk, Lions, Colorado Sheriffs' Association, Larimer County 4H. With the troops in Afghanistan.

Stella sat in the deep leather chair behind the desk. She loved the smell of leather, just a lingering touch of Sam's Brut. A wave of exhaustion rolled over her like a Greyhound bus. She had to get some sleep. There was a pamphlet on the desk. She picked it up.

A Guide to Pawnee Grove.

CHAPTER TWELVE
SAMISMS

Monday night.

Stella's Blackberry chirped. It was Gabe.

"How you doin', sweetheart? I just got back to LA. We were on location all day."

"Hi, Winner. I'm in Fort Collins at the family manse."

"Not too gruesome, I hope."

"Crystal's got a new boy toy. Come tomorrow morning, I'm outta here. Next week's Lester's competency hearing. They're going to find him crazier than a shit house rat."

"Wasn't he a war hero?"

"Bronze star. Survived a shot to the head which may have led to his actions."

"How much time do you have off? Want to come out here? I'll send you a ticket, pick you up at John Wayne."

"I'd love to, Winner, but I can't. I've only got three days and tomorrow I have to find a crazy man in the mountains and convince him to go back to work for the government."

"Otto?"

"Yes."

"Well good luck with that. Maybe you ought to take someone with you."

Stella trilled. "Oh, Winner. Otto would never hurt me. He's not psychotic."

"Good to know. Maybe you could make some time for me next weekend."

"Depends on who's traveling," Stella said.

"A-huh. Well, let me see how the week goes. I'm on location through Thursday but you can always reach me."

"Good night, Winner."

"Good night, babe."

They'd met at a fundraiser in Miami two months ago. Republican Congresswoman. Stella stood at the edge of the pool looking out on Biscayne Bay wondering what she was doing there. Favor for Sam. She hadn't the slightest clue who Winner was when he approached her, standing silently for a minute gazing out at the evening lights on the yachts and across the bay.

"Nice to be out there," he said after awhile.

"Boats are holes in the water into which you pour money," Stella replied by rote, one of many Samisms.

Beat.

"It's better to have a friend with a boat than a boat. Could I get you something to drink?"

"How about a Cuba Libre?"

He went for drinks and returned, expertly ferreting out Stella's work and where she was from. Finally it was her turn. "And what do you do?"

"I act."

"Really. Have I ever heard of you?"

"I doubt it," he said eyeing her with a gleam in his eye and an irresistible dimple in his cheek. "Perhaps you saw my Dinosaur Meat dog food ad?"

Stella bemusedly shook her head.

Winner found the fact that she'd never heard of him was a turn-on. An hour later she still wasn't sure he was telling the truth when a pack of teenage girls approached giggling with pens and cell phone cameras.

She ended up spending the weekend with him.

While other publicists flooded the media with breathless accounts of their clients' virtue, interviews, proof of good deeds, Winner kept a low profile and was extremely generous. Stella found out from an acquaintance that Winner regularly visited children's hospitals, signed photos, and went from room to room, bed to bed, joking, cheering and handing out comic books.

Maybe her luck was changing. But seriously. An actor?

She stretched in Sam's high zoot teak chair, leather and springs squeaking. How she would love to see Winner that very minute! If only her job weren't so demanding, but she had meetings with clients all day Tuesday and then she was in court for the rest of the week.

She rose, already snuggling between the sheets in her mind. As she was about to leave Sam's office she paused next to the vertical walnut and glass gun cabinet. It contained Sam's bird gun, a 12-guage Remington, his coyote gun, a .22 Ruger revolver, his elk gun, an RMEF X-Bolt Special Hunter, and his show gun, a commemorative edition Sharp's recreation with 24-carat gold scrolling, all visible through the quarter inch smash-proof glass.

Beneath the rifle section two deep drawers held Sam's handguns, ammo, cleaning kits, holsters and other accoutrements. A Schlage padlock kept it secure. Stella twirled it open. Sam had given her the numbers years ago.

Releasing the drawers via a catch, she pulled open the top drawer. The pistols were in their original boxes, some cardboard, some plastic. She reached for the Sig Sauer P-290, a nine small enough for a fanny pack or a pocket. Setting the box on Sam's desk she picked the pistol up, released the magazine into her hand and chambered it, insuring it was empty.

Samism #16: Always assume the weapon is loaded.

She took a box of Wolf nines, closed the drawer and locked the gun cabinet. Putting pistol and ammo in her Gladstone, she hefted the heavy bag and went down the hall and up the stairs to her room.

She hadn't been able to bring her .38 on the plane.

Before she went to bed she loaded and reinserted the magazine and placed the pistol beneath the pillow next to her.

It was the best sleep she'd had in weeks.

CHAPTER THIRTEEN
TANK TRAP

Tuesday.

Wiped on oxy and wine, Crystal slept long and deep. Stella was up at seven. The Porsche was gone. Stella hoped Blaine had survived the drive.

Fixing herself breakfast from muffins, cream cheese and fruit, Stella spread her *Colorado Atlas and Gazetteer* on the dining room table. Her finger traced the serpentine path of the Poudre northwest to Walden. Otto's place was southwest of Kinikinik, the trailhead, little more than two ruts following the jagged contours of the land.

Stella transferred her things from the Mustang to Sam's old Cherokee. Trying to reach Otto's place in a flatlander vehicle was futile. Only the most rugged four-wheel drives could make it. Or she could hike in. She used a tire gauge and a hand pump to bring tire pressure up to 35 psi. Samism #57: "Proper tire inflation is the key to good fuel economy and handling." A bumper sticker said, "SAVE THE POUDRE—STORE IT IN THE GLADE!"

Sam's positions had made life difficult for Stella in middle and high school. Her classmates had been taught in the womb that you can't hug a child with nuclear arms. And that we all must coexist.

And that hate is not a family value. That corporations weren't people until Texas executes one. It was a mystery to Stella how Sam ever got elected. Not that he was any of those things, but the press hated him.

It was no mystery. He was good with people. He had genuinely liked people. He kissed babies with gusto and petted dogs.

The bumper sticker was an invitation to vandalism. She used a putty knife to scrape it off. She found an old knapsack in the garage into which she stuffed bottled water, jerky and trail mix. She made herself a ham sandwich with deli fixings from the fridge and left Crystal a note thanking her for her hospitality and promising to get in touch soon.

By inviting Blaine, Crystal had instinctively avoided any intimate conversation about Sam or his death. Crystal wasn't fooled by the bullshit cover story, nor was she interested in what really happened. Crystal was interested in how it affected Crystal. Fine with Stella. She put the hand pump in the back with her knapsack and suitcase. She stopped in town to gas up. Gas was at an all-time high. It cost her sixty-five bucks to top off the Cherokee.

Up 287 to Ted's place where she turned west onto 14. Poudre Canyon wound up and through Cameron Pass, 10,276 feet above sea level. Radio reception was mostly nonexistent in the narrow canyon and the old Jeep lacked a CD player. The Poudre was unusually fast for this time of year due to the heavy snowfall of the previous winter. The narrow, serpentine blacktop clung to the canyon walls, occasionally opening up for the odd homestead. She passed vacationers in Winnebagos, bikers towing trailers with teddy bears bungeed to the sissy bars, huge trucks hauling wood and hay, pick-up trucks and bicyclists tricked out in primary colored spandex and teardrop-shaped helmets, all streaming up and down the mountain. The bicyclists rode with their heads down and their rumps in the air.

Mishiwaka, the notorious music bar that loomed over the rushing water, was still shuttered at this hour of the morning. Stella had been to the Mish often while attending UC Boulder. She'd dropped Ecstasy and grooved to Phish, Drag the River, Leftover Salmon. She smiled ruefully at the memory and a Samism popped into her head.

"Stella, you think about what you do now if you ever plan to run for public office. You don't want your opponent telling people you dealt grass or banged the Rams' starting line-up."

Her minor experimentation with drugs had ended long ago and she would have rather pulled her own teeth out with pliers than run for office. Even before he sought office, Sam hadn't been around much, to which he attributed the demands of his job as CSU fundraiser, but which Stella later realized were due to his relentless hound dogging.

Sam was great when he was there. He never bitched that God hadn't dealt him a son. He taught Stella how to ride horse, shoot a rifle, ride a bike and field-dress a deer. Martha appreciated none of these things, so father and daughter had time to themselves. Sam hadn't had the greatest taste in women. Stella loved Martha but Stella wasn't blind.

Like Crystal, Martha was a drunk and a pill popper. Stella had been made aware of various other poopsies and one-night stands through friends, gossip, the occasional tabloid, but Sam was beloved by his constituents and could do no ill. Sally Crandall, Pendragon's girl in D.C., had been the best of the bunch. Stella had met Sally at some soiree six months ago and liked her immediately. She instinctively knew that Sally was Sam's latest squeeze.

Well, who could blame him, with Crystal's wild mood-swings and days in bed for fibromyalgia. Stella was glad Sam had Sally. He should have married her in the first place. Oh well. Hindsight was 20/20, as Sam endlessly told her.

Samisms #1 and #2 were: Attitude is everything. Character is destiny.

"Yes, Sam," she said to the gray rock. Out of the city it was cooler and she had the windows open, noting the subtle change in the air itself with the first hint of pine sneaking in. On this sunny Tuesday in late June, the river was a rolling party, blue helmeted rafters battling rapids with yellow paddles, kayaks rushing by. Most of the riverside picnic grounds, Ouzel, Dutch George, had already begun to fill with fugitives from the city setting up their barbecue. Anglers stood knee deep in the furious water, casting flies.

Stella found the turn-off to Otto's place just past Pingree Park. A plank bridge lay over the river. On the other side was a line-up of seventeen mailboxes affixed to a stand made of two-by-fours, and a chain suspended between two steel poles sunk in concrete deep into the ground, held shut with a padlock.

Stella turned the engine off. She got out, took a drink of water, and looked at the mailboxes. Twelve of them had names. None said White. She looked around. The mountains rose steeply to the southwest, covered with a mottled mantle of Kelly green and bark beetle brown. The land retained enough moisture so that the fire level was moderate. Overhead an eagle circled pursued by several ravens. Otherwise not a soul.

Stella wondered what to do. She could leave the Jeep and hike in, but it was about six miles and none of it was easy. She wasn't certain she was up to that kind of challenge despite her daily rigorous workouts at Gold's in Silver Spring. She heard the sound of a transmission grinding gears and seconds later a blue Ford 150 with some kind of lab mix in the bed pulled around the curve up to the chain and stopped.

The gnarled homunculus who stepped out looked like a stick figure on whom someone had draped coveralls and a John Deere cap. The old dude went up to the padlock and looked at Stella.

"Mornin'. Help you?"

"I'm looking for Otto White. I'm Stella Darling."

The man proffered a hand that seemed to belong to a larger man. "Wayne Winslett. White. White. I know just about everybody on the mountain but our mystery man, drives some sort of Transformers truck, got a German shepherd. That him?"

"That's Otto."

"Never said word one to me. Friendly enough, but like many people up this way, they live up here for a reason. However, you don't look like a Fed or a lawyer."

Stella blushed and smiled. "I'd appreciate it if you'd let me in, Mr. Winslett. We're old friends. I would have contacted him if there were any way, but Otto doesn't have a phone. He doesn't have a computer. I don't think he even has electricity."

Winslett unlocked the padlock and let the chain fall to the ground with a clank. "Go on ahead. I'll lock up."

Stella gave Winslett her jury-winning smile. "Thank you."

She got in the Jeep and drove through the steel poles following the rutted rocky trail as it wound upwards. She shifted to lower case four-wheel drive, grateful for the seatbelt that prevented her from slamming her head into the headliner as she clambered over gully-wumpers and hassock-sized rocks. It was slow going. The trail switch-backed up the mountain and now the scent of pine was everywhere.

"You smell that, honey?" Sam asked her on one of their hikes. "That's the smell of money. That's what a rich neighborhood smells like."

It was true. In the water-starved west, only the wealthy or original settlers got the land with the trees. Uphill. The richer you were the further uphill you moved. By those standards, Otto was a millionaire. She remembered when he'd showed her around the place two years ago. His land was mostly flat rock snugged up against a red rock shelf, low ground cover of juniper, prickly pear, mountain rose, yucca, a stream, if you could call it that, winding through the rocks, several clumps of aspen. The remains of an old cabin with a stone foundation lay in shadow beneath the rock.

That was where he planned to build the main house, tucked under the shelf like an Anasazi dwelling. Where he'd put the rain basins and holding tanks, and where he planned to build a tank trap for anybody foolish enough to drive in uninvited.

Stella assumed the tank trap was hyperbole. Otto said a lot of things in an inflectionless voice that might lead people to think he was insane.

She was climbing now through ponderosa, stalks of brown kindling where the bark beetle had done its work. She came around a bend and a wall of meat filled the narrow space between the trees. The moose regarded her with disinterest and ambled off into the forest. Even from within the Jeep, she could feel the animal's bulk and power and it had made her afraid. This was not the park and concrete jungle she routinely roamed.

This was the wild. And as Sam always said, the wild could rear up and bite you in the ass when you least expected it.

Pikas scolded her from boulder tops. A coyote slinked across the trail. Through the trees she could hear the burble of the creek as it tumbled down the mountain. The air was rich now with the scent of pine. You could bottle that air and sell it by the quart, she thought. She checked the odometer. Coming up on six miles. Any second now. The entrance to Otto's land was unmistakably marked by a red pole gate swung shut and latched. There was no lock. There were no casual visitors up here.

She wallowed around a tight bend and there it was, jammed between two granite formations that looked like the aftermath of a giant baby's building block tantrum. She stopped the Jeep and got out. It was at least fifteen degrees cooler up here than back in the city. There were two signs affixed to the gate: "PRIVATE PROPERTY—STAY OUT" and "PROTECTED BY SMITH & WESSON." Although the gate was unlocked, Stella decided to leave the Cherokee there. She opened the tailgate and hoisted the backpack over her shoulders, cinching the belt tight around her waist. A water bottle hung from a carabiner affixed to her belt. She found a Water Valley ball cap in the rear seat and put it on over wrap-around shades, threading her hair into a ponytail through the back of the cap. She put a piece of jerky in her pocket. In her multi-pocketed khaki shorts, Adidas hiking boots and scout shirt she was indistinguishable from the Standard Issue Colorado Woman.

Stella climbed over the gate and followed the cratered trail which curved out of sight around another granite outcropping. Stella looked up. A few fluffy white clouds scudded overhead. The wind whistled through the pine. It felt good to be out here on the mountain, far removed from the pressure of her job and the tension from living in a pressure cooker with millions of others. She could feel her shoulder muscles relaxing.

Stella walked around the bend and paused to enjoy the view. Spreading her arms she inhaled deeply. Pure ambrosia. City stress exited with each exhalation. One minute she was looking at a red rock outcropping over a peculiar stone wall, the next she realized she was looking at Otto's house. True to his word he had built it out of stone and tucked it under the red rock shelf. It looked deserted.

Stella took a step and stumbled. The rock she stepped on rolled a few inches and disappeared. Disappeared into a hole in the ground.

Stella got down on her hands and knees and discovered the edge of a tarp stretched tightly across an excavation. "What the hell?" she said. In a rush of fury and disgust she realized what it was. Crouching, she found the corner, untied the concealed anchor rope, and bent it back enough to reveal an SUV-sized excavation with a series of metal spikes mounted at the bottom.

CHAPTER FOURTEEN

HOGAN

Excited barking cracked the silence. Loud, joyful barking, getting louder. Stella looked. A furred missile ran toward her, tail wagging. Stella sat on her heels, arms wide to receive 120 pounds of German shepherd. Steve knocked her over and furiously began licking her face. Stella laughed and laughed, half-heartedly warding the dog off with her arms.

"Well, hello," Otto said appearing minutes later. "What a surprise."

Stella pulled the chunk of jerky from her pocket and gave it to the dog. She stood, blushing and brushing the hair out of her face. What do you say to an old lover whom you last saw in the psychiatric ward?

"Otto."

Walking around the tank trap, Otto went up to Stella and hugged her and Stella found herself hugging back, remembering the warmth of his hard body, that aftershave he wore. Even here in the wilderness. A little flame flared. She tamped it down.

Business, girl.

She stepped back a little breathless and looked at Otto. He had a military haircut and the tanned lean body to go with it. He wore a fishing vest over a white T-shirt, blue jeans and heavy leather boots. He wore an Aussie bushman's hat with one brim pinned up and a pair of Foster Grant sunglasses. He looked like the host of some survival show.

"How long have you been here?" he said.

"Just got here."

"Well, come up to the house. I'll show you around. Steve and I just got back. I haven't even been in the house yet."

"Where were you?"

"Just walkin' around. We saw a pair of eagles wipe out an unkindness of ravens."

"An 'unkindness?'"

"That's what you call a bunch of ravens."

Steve running circles, they walked toward the long low structure. The horizontal windows looked like they'd been taken from a lab. In a clearing at the far end was Otto's Road Warrior Power wagon looming over the landscape on tractor-sized tires.

It was cooler inside the hogan-like structure. The hardwood floors were made of recycled bark beetle timber and bore that species' unique pattern. Otto had finished them himself and put them in using tongue and groove. Navajo rugs covered the floor. The east-facing side had all the windows. A great room combined kitchen, dining, and living, two skylights shining on the painting over the mantle. Beyond that a hall led to the master bedroom, a full bath, and a spare bedroom. There was dog hair everywhere. Tufts formed into balls along the baseboards. A set of kettlebells in increasing size were lined up on the floor like a set of Russian nesting dolls. A lava lamp blobbed red on an oak end table.

The back wall was mostly built-in bookshelves holding tons of books, miniature Egyptian sarcophagus, and a perfect 1/25th scale model of Otto's truck. Stella stared at the model from a half meter. A tiny gold crucifix hung from the truck's rear view. The hi-fi system consisted of a Transcriptors turntable, a Harmon Kardon amp, and Bose speakers, all ancient by modern standards. There was a Count Basie record on the turntable. Stella looked at the two-foot shelf of vinyl: Ellington, Basie, Miles, The Rascals. All retro as befitting a man digging his heels in against the future.

On the north wall, a crucifix hung above a framed print of Michelangelo's Madonna and Child. There were three framed Ansel

Adams black-and-white photographs of the mountains. Several cardboard boxes labeled EMERGENCY FOOD SUPPLIES were stacked in the corner.

Otto took off his hat and shades. He removed two Mason jars from his hand-built cabinet and opened the olive green refrigerator. "Would you like a glass of iced tea?"

"I'd love one. You have electricity?"

Otto nodded, closing the door. "Put the line in last fall. My requirements are nugatory. I've mounted 120 solar panels to a frame that goes up tomorrow. All my water comes from the sky or the mountain. I've got basins all over the place." He handed her a Mason jar filled with iced tea. Stella sat on the weathered brown leather sofa. The cushions creaked and something hard dug into her ass. Working her hand between the cushions she retrieved a Grendel P30 .22 automatic. She looked at it for a second as if it were a turd, then placed it carefully on the wood end table with a *thunk*.

Steve came over and licked her knee.

"Stop that," she said without conviction.

"Don't lick the knee, Steve," Otto said.

"Otto, when you said you would build a tank trap I thought you were joking."

Otto sat in a big leather creaker angled toward her around the free-form mahogany slab coffee table. He shrugged and the corners of his mouth turned down.

"This is private property. I can do whatever I want."

"Actually, you can't. Although it's private property, you would be responsible if someone trespassed and hurt themselves because you did not take reasonable precautions to remove an obvious hazard. What would have happened if I'd stepped on that thing?"

"Nothing. It's strong enough to support a few people."

"How would anybody even get a tank up here?"

"That's their problem. You didn't hike up here to give me grief about my tank trap."

"No. I don't suppose you know what's going on."

Otto smiled and stretched. "Not the slightest."

Stella was practiced at concealing her emotions, partly through Sam's example, partly through her work. She struggled to say it in an even tone. "Two days ago Sam died. He burst into flames at a rural Virginia resort."

Otto's demeanor did a U-turn as he leaned forward, arms on knees, face creased with concern. "Jesus, Mary and Joseph, Stella! I'm so sorry!"

He half raised himself to go to her, but something about Stella's demeanor—hostile pheromones perhaps—queered the deal. She looked drained, like she'd done all her crying beforehand. The motion failed and he sank back into the chair. "He burst into flames?"

"He's the sixth prominent American to die by spontaneous combustion this year. The FBI is trying to determine how far back they go."

"Okay."

"It's for real. The President wants you to take charge of the investigation."

Otto peered at her.

"Why me?" he said.

"They have a computer program that matches ops with jobs."

"Who was number two? Get him."

"Otto," Stella said quietly. "We're talking about Sam. You're an arson investigator. You're one of a handful of people who's actually seen this happen. You understand special ops. I'm asking you."

Otto sat perfectly still. He'd lied about his age to join the Army, partly to piss off his old man, a university professor who taught American history. Professor Jonathan White lectured on white privilege, institutional racism, and that the U.S. was the chief engine of war and poverty throughout the world.

As each generation rebels against its parents Otto rebelled against Jonathan's relentless America-bashing and contemptuous atheism. Even as a child Otto was fiercely independent. He looked at his father and thought here was a guy who couldn't pound a nail, hauling down big bucks to teach kids that the United States was the root of all evil.

Otto instinctively shunned his father's values. He came to doubt his father knew the value of hard work. Otto was a throwback to his Scots Irish forbears who fought for hearth and home. In Jonathan's house the *Federalist Papers* were considered seditious, so Otto read them. The *Declaration of Independence* and *Constitution* were considered outmoded and irrelevant, so Otto studied them. Thomas Jefferson was a slaveholder and libertine, so Otto eagerly sought out his biographies.

Jonathan gave Otto Noam Chomsky and Howard Zinn to read. It only reinforced his opinion that his father was out to lunch.

Otto's mother left when he was fourteen upon learning that the professor had been carrying on an affair with an undergrad. Otto credited Babs with instilling in him a love of the Church, or if not the Church, God. She'd let her faith lapse during the Jonathan years in the face of his aggressive and pedantic atheism. Once divorced, she began attending church again and Otto joined her. At first it was just to piss off the professor. But he gradually came to accept not only the need for faith, but faith itself. Who was he to second-guess the Founding Fathers?

Otto joined at the beginning of Desert Storm. The Army assigned him to the Army Engineers, who in turn taught him all they could about investigating explosive devices and the results, which included arson investigation. The CIA recruited him after he figured out he was too crazy to be in the regular Army.

He touched the crucifix tat above his heart. He thought about what he'd seen in Libya. He thought about what he'd seen on the mountain.

"Of course I'll come," he said. "On one condition."

"What?"

"Steve comes too."

CHAPTER FIFTEEN
IN FROM THE COOL

Stella waited while Otto battened the hatches. He spread an enormous tarp over his monster truck and tied it down to iron rings set in the rock. He came back in, grabbed the pistol off the end table and took it back to his gun safe. He fiddled with the model truck. Stella got up to refill her tea. She watched Otto strip off his shirt through the open bedroom door and noticed a tattoo on his left bicep too far to read.

She returned to the living room, sat down, and picked up a copy of *American History* from the walnut slab coffee table. Otto came out of the bedroom with a bulging black leather valise, which he set by the door. Stella looked around. There was no security system. Odd for a man who'd built a tank trap.

He disappeared into the spare bedroom and emerged moments later with a nine mm Ruger in a shoulder rig.

"Do you have a permit for that?" Stella said.

"Of course," he replied. Stella wondered if whoever had granted the permit had access to Otto's medical records. She doubted it. Those things were supposed to be classified.

It was three by the time they left the mountain, Steve filling the back seat. They would not reach Denver before six at the earliest. There was no point going to the FBI building where the agent in charge had prepared an ops center.

The old Cherokee jounced and rocked down the rutted trail. They pulled aside twice to let vehicles pass going upslope. Steve hung out the window.

"What have you been doing?" Otto said. "What's going on?"

"Have you heard of the Below the Beltline Sniper?"

"Nope."

"I'm defending him."

"Whom did he snipe?"

"My client is alleged to have killed seven people. He is currently undergoing psychiatric evaluation."

"Wow." Otto knew enough not to ask for details. "What else is going on?"

"The President is concerned that these spontaneous combustions are a new form of terrorism."

Otto looked out at the ponderosa and aspen, wind-blow pine crawling from nooks and crannies. "It takes a lot of energy to incinerate a human body. If I had to measure it in units I'd say it would take eight to ten thousand BTUs. You couldn't carry enough batteries. Where's that energy coming from?"

"The Army has been conducting experiments with microwaves. They're working on a weapons variation that would cook human flesh from up to a mile away. You'll be working under Director Yee."

Otto had heard the name. That's all.

At the bottom of the rustic trail Stella waited while Otto checked his mail and unlocked the gate, returning to the vehicle with a stack of magazines and letters. He flipped through them on his lap. "Gimme, gimme, gimme," he said, tossing the unopened envelopes on the floor. There was no phone bill. There was no gas bill. There was no cable bill. There was a credit card bill. The magazines included *Guns & Ammo*, *American Sportsman*, and *The American Spectator*.

They turned east on 14 and headed down the mountain. A pair of cycles passed them going the other way, straight pipes reverberating off the canyon walls. Otto turned into himself. He never was the life of the party. Stella turned on the radio, got lucky and found a Denver jazz station playing Sonny Criss. It waxed and waned with the canyon walls.

Stella drove the old Jeep with verve and precision, slowing down before the hairpins. She slowed way down at one hairpin and some flatlanders in a Toyota came around straddling the middle line. Stella waited patiently for them to pass.

As they passed Mishawaka, Otto turned in his seat to look at the American flag painted on the roof. "That's new."

"Yeah. Some artist gets five thou a pop to paint the American flag on roofs, barns."

"I'm just grateful it's not a picture of the Virgin Mary fellating Jesus," Otto said.

They stopped in Fort Collins where Stella exchanged the Jeep for her rental. Mercifully, Crystal was not at home.

"How'd it go with Crystal?" Otto said when they were underway.

"Same old, same old. She was pleasantly bombed by the time I arrived. She's got a new boyfriend. Tom Blaine the amplifier king. He's invented an amp/speaker combo the size of a cigarette pack that'll blast a stadium. Perfect for that garage band next door."

"You could mount one on the roof. HEY DOOFUS! GET OUT OF THE WAY!"

Stella laughed. It sounded like gold coins falling into Otto's hands.

"Tempting."

"So, Sam was seeing a lobbyist. You think Pendragon has anything to do with this?"

"I don't know."

They arrived in Stapleton at six-thirty. Stella booked two rooms at a pet-friendly Best Western several blocks from FBI HQ. They entered the Pike's Peak Lounge with Steve wearing a leather harness with a green banner that said Service Dog.

The young hostess cooed over Steve and showed them to a corner booth. Stella ordered red wine and Otto ordered a beer. Steve lay beneath the table out of sight.

Stella took out her iPhone and dialed someone. A few minutes later she said, "Margaret, it's Stella. I have him."

She listened, then handed the phone to Otto.

"Otto White," Otto said.

"Mr. White, this is National Security Director Margaret Yee. Thank you for serving your country."

"My pleasure, Madame Director."

"You will be operating directly under NSA auspices. You will report directly to me. Do you understand?"

"Yes, ma'am."

"You understand the mission?"

"Yes, ma'am."

"Good. We are calling this 'Operation Flameout.' Stella will give you my contact information. I look forward to meeting you soon. Let's talk again tomorrow after you're set up out there."

The director hung up. Otto handed the phone to Stella, who slid a piece of notepaper across the table containing the director's private number.

A sulfuric stench rose from beneath the table.

Stella covered her nose and mouth and turned away. "Oh my God I forgot about Steve's farts."

Otto removed a pack of matches from a pocket, lit several and waved them around.

"I have a seven-forty flight," Stella said, "so I probably won't see you in the morning. Can you get yourself to the Feds in the morning? It's two blocks west."

"I think so."

"Ask for Special Agent Lon Barnett."

Otto removed a small spiral pad and pen from his cargo pants pocket and made a note. "What's your number?"

Stella gave him both her numbers. Otto was not a talker. He ordered two buffalo burgers, gave one to Steve under the table. Occasionally Stella caught him looking at her with such longing, it was a stab to the heart. But one thing she could always count on with Otto. He was a practical man. He lived in the real world, at least in so far as having no illusions. She had often thought Otto would have been happier living two centuries ago where he could carve his destiny from an as-yet-untamed land.

Otto set down the remnants of his sandwich and finished off his second beer. "What's going on? Seeing anyone?"

"I'm seeing Gabe Winner."

"Not the actor," Otto said.

"That's the guy."

"No shit. He's one of the few actors I can stomach. He makes decent action flicks and he keeps his mouth shut off camera."

"I have all his films if you're interested.

"Did you buy them?"

"He gave them to me."

Otto grinned. "Maybe I'll get a DVD player. I did see *The Detonator*. What's that like, dating a Hollywood personality?"

"Gabe is very grounded. We've only been seeing each other three months."

"Enjoy it while it lasts," Otto said.

A sharp retort perched on Stella's lips but she held it back. Otto was probably right in his assessment that her affair with Gabe Winner would result in no long-term relationship. Just look at her record. Two separate careers in two different locations. Hollywood.

Stella insisted on paying. They paused awkwardly outside her room.

"You coming back out?" Otto said.

"I doubt it. I was lucky I could work this in. Thank you for doing this, Otto."

She unlocked her door.

"No problem," Otto said.

Stella gave him a peck on the cheek, went inside and shut the door thinking she might never see him again.

CHAPTER SIXTEEN
THINGS GO TO HELL

Tuesday evening.

Otto took Steve for a walk on the hotel grounds, cleaning up after the big dog with a plastic bag. They returned to Otto's ground-floor room, which opened onto the patio and pool area. Otto and Steve lay on the bed. Otto turned on the television using the remote and found a news channel.

Scenes of chaos: Fire trucks and police vehicles surrounding a smoking loft. Anxious residents huddling behind police barriers wrapped in blankets. Otto turned up the sound.

"The fire appears to have started on the top floor, home of Volt Media founder and COB Lewis Stark. It is unknown whether Stark was in the loft when the fire broke out. Fire fighters have not been able to get in there. Stark recently revealed he suffered from a heart defect and voluntarily gave up his position as CEO."

As Otto watched, a wall collapsed sending up a nuclear cloud. Pumper trucks plumed arcs of water onto the blazing building. Otto changed the channel. A giant transsexual dressed as Marilyn Monroe vogued across the *America's Got Talent* stage as Piers Morgan's buzzer sounded.

Click.

BMX boys doing double flips in a stadium.

Click.

A man pulling a prehistoric fish out of a river.

Otto turned the television off but remained staring at it, back against the headboard. Steve slowly rolled over on his back like a doomed freighter and stuck his paws in the air.

Otto had a bad feeling about what he had just seen, an atavistic sixth sense from the time man crawled on four legs. The fire didn't feel like a terrorist operation. There were no threats, no demands, no videos boasting of their great success.

Otto had been fascinated with spontaneous human combustion since reading a Jack Kirby comic when he was twelve years old. It was one of those recurring urban legends with just enough documentation to keep it alive.

Otto differed from other true believers in one respect.

He had seen it.

CHAPTER SEVENTEEN
BILLUPS

Tuesday evening and Wednesday morning.

The Canadians had delivered him to a U.S. "aid mission" in Zejtun from where he was airlifted to an aircraft carrier and from there to Ramstein where he was debriefed. A team of psychiatrists observed him, much as psychiatrists were now observing Stella's client Lester Durant, the Below the Beltline Sniper. All field ops were subject to psychological evaluation.

Otto insisted they'd been betrayed. The Agency conducted a thorough investigation and could find no evidence of a leak. When Otto asked if anyone else had survived they wouldn't respond.

In the end it was adios and thanks for your service. Don't let the screen door hit you on the way out.

Convinced he was about to get whacked, Otto disappeared. He melted away. He traveled the nation. He never approached the land he owned in Colorado. He spent the next six months underground frequently changing identities. He watched. He waited. He used library computers and cyber cafes. Despite not owning a computer he was thoroughly conversant with the technology, at least up until six months ago. He learned by clicking and doing. He learned to spot a certain type who also frequented these venues: hackers. He could spot a hacker a mile away. They were all men. They were all pierced and tatted and wore anti-conformist badges, wired on Red Bull and coffee.

The silence re: Operation Firebrand was unnerving. He searched for other members of the team but they seemed to have disappeared as well. As if someone were stalking them.

Whoever set them up must have deemed him no threat. He was damaged goods, not worth the hit. Discredited. A loon. He had no valuable intel.

He'd relived the mission a thousand times in his head.

Was Ghaddafi really the target, or was it the laptop? Was Hornbuckle in on it? He must have been. But Hornbuckle too had disappeared.

Lying in the Best Western, Otto used an old Jedi mind trick to turn his own off: he counted thylacines. Finally he fell asleep.

In the morning, Otto fed Steve a can of horse meat, put on khakis, a plain gray T-shirt and a gray sports coat, locked his pistol in the room safe, had breakfast in the cafe, put Steve in the service harness and walked the two blocks to FBI HQ at 8000 E. 36th St., across the street from Humberto Uribe Park. The foyer contained an information desk front and center, behind that a series of stanchions forming an aisle leading to a metal detector, and beyond that the elevators. An armed agent in a blue blazer sat in a folding chair next to the metal detector. The lobby was active at nine a.m. with agents coming and going.

The information officer was a no-nonsense middle-aged woman in a blue blazer with nametag Special Agent Maureen Fassbacht. Her eyes followed him across the foyer until he stood in front of her.

"Good morning. Otto White to see Special Agent Lon Barnett."

"One moment please." The woman picked up a telephone and spoke. She replaced the receiver and reached beneath the desk for a laminated card that said 'VISITOR' attached to a lanyard.

"Please put this on and step back through the metal detector."

The other agent had Otto and Steve step through the detector, then asked Otto to empty his pockets. Otto complied. Wallet, wintergreen Certs and a steel folding knife with a four-inch blade.

The man wanded Otto and the dog. He gestured for Otto to pick up his belongings, but held on to the knife.

"You can claim this on the way out. Wait here. Someone will come down and get you."

Otto sat on a marble bench against the wall. Eight elevators, four facing four, opened and closed. A man in a white long-sleeved shirt with the sleeves rolled up and a dark blue tie held in place with a tiny American flag clasp exited the elevator. His eyes fixed on Otto and he beelined over. He was stocky, middle aged, with a shaved muscular head.

Otto stood.

"Agent White?" he said offering his hand. "Lon Barnett. Who's this?"

"This is Steve."

"What kind of service dog is he?"

"Steve is a tracker. He goes where I go."

Barnett held the elevator door for them. A young woman with a briefcase cooed over Steve and petted him. They got out on the eighth floor.

"I'll be your liaison for both the FBI and Homeland Security," Barnett said leading them down a hushed hallway with offices on both sides. They entered a large foyer with "SPECIAL AGENT IN CHARGE NORMAN BILLUPS" etched in the glass. Beneath the blue and gold FBI symbol mounted on the oak wall sat an attractive young secretary. "Go right in. The director is expecting you."

The director had a big corner office overlooking the park and the Platte River. Billups was a big man with a full head of curly white hair and mustache who rose from behind his gunmetal desk and came around to greet them. He wore a banker's striped dark blue three-piece and had a grip like a lumberjack. He stooped to pet Steve.

"Mr. White, thank you for joining us. Please have a seat."

Otto and Barnett sat in upholstered oak chairs facing the desk. Steve sat at Otto's feet.

"We've set up a command center for you. You'll be working with Lon here and Gus Alvarez. Gus is a tech guy. Computers, special equipment, ask Gus. I understand you need to be brought up to speed. How much do you know?"

"Senator Darling died from spontaneous human combustion. He's the sixth case this year, and there is speculation that this is terrorism."

"That's true. Thus far we have been able to identify thirty-three possible cases of spontaneous human combustion since 1998. There may be others we don't know about. We know of a couple in Russia, a couple in the Middle East and one in Hong Kong. Do you have any preliminary thoughts?"

Otto spread his hands. "Only that it takes an enormous amount of energy to consume a human body down to ash. A modern crematorium must generate 1,700 degrees for three hours. These 'spontaneous' combustions occur in a matter of minutes. I'll need a physics guy to run simulations."

"That's Gus," Barnett said.

"Gus was instrumental in the development of the Army's long-range microwave weapon," Billups said.

"Dossiers on all the victims."

"In your computer," Billups said. "We have video on two of the combustions. They're disturbing. Anything you need, you let us know. You're being comped, by the way. Where are you staying?"

"Best Western up the street."

"Save all your receipts." Billups opened his top desk drawer and took out a small gray phone, which he passed to Otto. It looked like a compact. "This is called an Ocelot. Beryllium powered. You can send and receive from anywhere on earth without being traced or eavesdropped. We call them Ocelots because they use some kind of oscillating signal. This is your phone. Mine, Lon's and Gus' numbers have been preprogrammed. It cannot be tracked. So don't lose it. This will all go smoother if you're a federal agent, so if you don't mind, please stand."

Otto stood. Billups produced a Bible from his drawer and came around the desk. He set the Bible on the desk as he faced Otto. "Please place your hand on the Bible."

Otto did so, raising the other.

Billups held up a laminated eight by ten card. "Please recite the Oath of Office."

"I, Otto White, do solemnly swear that I will support and defend the Constitution of the United States against all enemies, foreign and domestic; that I will bear true faith and allegiance to the same; that I take this obligation freely, without any mental reservation or purpose of evasion; and that I will well and faithfully discharge the duties of the office on which I am about to enter. So help me God."

Billups held out his hand again. "Congratulations Agent White."

Barnett rose, shook Otto's hand and slapped him on the back. "Welcome to the shop."

Billups reached into his jacket pocket and withdrew a black leather badge holder bearing the bright gold shield-shaped badge with an eagle on top. Agent #32,677. Otto slipped it into his inside jacket pocket.

"Agent Barnett will take you through credentials, get you squared up. Did you bring a weapon?"

"I have one locked in the safe in my hotel room."

"I really don't think you'll have a need for it."

"That's fine."

"Again, Mr. White, on behalf of the agency and the country, thank you. Lon, will you show him the ropes?"

CHAPTER EIGHTEEN
BEADS OF SWEAT

Wednesday morning.

Barnett took Otto to a low-ceilinged, well-lit room with a half dozen agents at desks. An old-fashioned bulletin board on the wall was crammed with notices including the *Ten Most Wanted*. There was also a list for the *Ten Most Wanted Hackers*. Otto did a double take before he realized it wasn't his photo on the page. A trim little man with a hair-line mustache took Otto's photograph against a white background and presented him with a laminated FBI ID card.

Barnett used a magnetic key to unlock the stairwell door. They went down two floors to communications and logistics. In an open office area, Barnett led Otto and Steve toward three agents leaning against desks shooting the breeze. The agents turned to face them as they approached.

"Bob, Mel, Gus, this is Otto White, the agent in charge of the Darling investigation."

They shook hands. The men petted the dog. Gus Alvarez was a slight, balding man with rimless glasses, red suspenders and pale skin. He fell in behind Otto and Barnett as the latter led them out of the room, down the hall, to an office Barnett unlocked with a key card.

Barnett handed the key card to Otto. "This is your office. Gus is your tech support. Anything you need."

The windowless office contained a desk with two computers, a printer, a shredder, and a two-year-old *Sports Illustrated* swimsuit calendar on the wall. Fluorescent lights in a long hooded fixture cast cool light. The floor was a colorless rug with a couple telltale cigarette burns. A six pack of bottled water in a plastic yoke rested on the desk.

"I've loaded everything pertaining to the investigation into your computer," Alvarez said. "Under documents, the titles are self-explanatory."

He wrinkled his nose. "Jesus God."

"Steve's a little flatulent."

Alvarez pulled out his wallet and handed Otto his card. "Anything you need, call me. You want a laptop?"

"Sure. Steve needs water."

"I'll take care of it. I suggest you start by watching the videos. The first is Alan Froines, a senior partner of Atkins, Alley, and Ross with offices on Bedford Street and in Albuquerque. As you know, Atkins, Alley and Ross include Glass Systems among their clients. Glass Systems is a major defense contractor. This video was taken from a surveillance camera in the firm's underground parking lot in Albuquerque.

"The second is Cap and Trade lobbyist Jody Albrecht (Green Future, LLC), taken at Harrah's Casino in Reno, NV. The quality of the tapes is radically different. The Albuquerque tape was taken with old technology. The Harrah's tape was taken with the new Pelco, which use three exposures with different light values, refined for depth and shadow, and gives a very clear record of what occurred. I have to warn you that the videos are upsetting.

"You will find all the victims under VICTIMS. Each has a link to his file."

Otto sat at the desk. Steve curled up at his feet. "No women?"

"None of whom we know. It's just another odd wrinkle. We're baffled. That's why they're paying you the big bucks."

"Riiight," Otto said tapping the control key. The monitor sprang to life with the home page of the FBI. Two rows of icons marched vertically on the left in military ranks. Short cuts to VICAP, NCIC, and the Terrorist Watch List. The two videos had their own icons: Froines and Albrecht.

"You need me, I'll be right down the hall," Alvarez said. "I'll get your dog some water."

"Thanks, Gus."

Alvarez left shutting the door behind him. Otto was alone in the belly of the FBI, the only sound a faint hum from the hard-drive, a fluorescent buzz and Steve's ragged breath. Otto brought up the list of victims. Sixteen of these were confirmed instances of spontaneous human combustion. Seventeen were speculative. Most of the speculatives had occurred overseas. Sen. Darling was the latest addition. Otto began printing out each individual's history. He would study them in his hotel room.

There were two raps on the door. Otto scooted back on his smooth-gliding chair and opened it. Alvarez came in with a plastic hotel ice bucket filled with water that he set on the floor next to the wall and an Apple laptop, which he handed to Otto.

"I loaded this one too so don't lose it."

Steve got up and began to drink. Otto thanked Alvarez. Alvarez left.

Otto turned off the overhead lights. The only illumination came from the computer terminal, a cool blue reflecting the FBI home page. Otto brought up the first video, Allen Froines in Albuquerque.

The screen was black and white, a still life of a parking garage with pale gray pillars and expensive cars. The quality was surprisingly good. A heavyset man wearing a hat and a dark suit and carrying a briefcase entered the picture, back to viewers, from below the camera. A blinged-out Chrysler cruised slowly past and disappeared beneath the camera. Froines stared after it with distaste.

Froines was halfway across the floor to his car when he stopped, dropped the briefcase and took off his hat. Smoke wafted from his ears. He staggered, turning to face the camera, eyes blank, mouth. open, hands groping. Flame burst from his mouth and in a sudden blaze that turned the screen white he went nova. The blaze flared silently for over a minute. It faded revealing the blackened cinder of a man banging into a pillar and collapsing. He continued to burn long after he fell.

The video made Otto queasy. He'd seen too many burn victims, smelled the blackened flesh. The sight brought back those sensations. Once you've smelled burning flesh, it stays with you. The most disturbing aspect was sometimes the smell of cooked human flesh made him hungry, even as his belly was in full rebellion. Just before Froines burst into flames Otto thought he saw a gleam near his head, like a droplet of flung sweat.

He sat quietly while his equilibrium returned. He sipped bottled water. He cued the second video.

The second video was worse. There were others present. The quality was astonishing, as shot by Laszlo Kovacs. Cap and Trade lobbyist Jody Albrecht (Green Energy, LLC,) a slight, balding man with a diamond ear stud, regarded his cards at a blackjack table. The video was taken from over and behind the dealer. One player sat on Albrecht's left, two on his right. The men on Albrecht's right appeared to be Chinese, wearing identical black suits.

Albrecht shoved a stack of chips into the pot then flung his cards across the table, striking the dealer. Albrecht looked surprised. He lurched out of his chair, curling in pain. When a security guard stepped up to ask if he was all right, he shoved the bigger man away with enough strength to send the guard stumbling into the table. Albrecht spun around like a dog chasing its tail and burst into flame like a Roman candle. He became an indistinct white blaze. Players scrambled for the exits. Three casino personnel were on the scene within seconds emptying fire extinguishers on the writhing figure, to no avail.

Charred remains poked up through the white foam like the contents of a shark's stomach.

This one had witnesses. There were numerous articles in the Reno press about the incident. The police claimed that Albrecht's clothes caught fire. Grief and trauma counselors believed it was a mass hallucination. Some believed David Copperfield was behind the stunt.

ALBRECHT'S DEATH RULED A SUICIDE

People simply refused to believe what they'd seen, what the evidence supported. A U of N physics professor explained that Albrecht had made his clothes from a highly flammable synthetic fiber imbued with accelerants. Several of the witnesses claimed to have smelled a chemical aroma around him.

Otto sweated despite the chill temperature. He calmed himself ruffling Steve's fur. He watched both videos again. He watched the Albrecht video five more times, trying to isolate the incident where a minute gleam appeared in mid-air. Had he really seen it? After much back and forth the best he could do was a bright mote that lasted for a split second.

Like Froines' flung sweat.

CHAPTER NINETEEN
'Optical Illusion'

Otto sent the images with gleams to Alvarez, pushed himself away from the desk, and went to the door. Steve followed at his heel. They went down the hall to the bullpen where Alvarez huddled in his cubicle intent on the monitor, which displayed scrolling numbers. Otto stood silently as Steve thrust his snout over Alvarez' thigh. Alvarez looked down in surprise, then back at Otto. Alvarez removed a set of minute headphones.

"Gus, you've seen the Froines and Albrecht videos."

"We've all seen them."

"Did you notice a tiny gleam next to the heads of both victims?"

Alvarez stared. "No. Can you show me?"

"It's in your inbox."

Otto waited while Alvarez opened the file. He stared at it a long time before pointing to what might very well have been digital interference. "That?"

"Yeah."

"It could be any number of things. A drop of sweat."

"I thought so too. There's one in the Froines' video as well."

"Could be electronic interference, resistance, an impure chip."

"Both parties? At more or less the same time in each sequence? Do you have videos of any of the others?"

"The Russians have one. We're trying to get it."

"Might be interesting to see if that one has it too."

"I'll see what I can do to isolate that image, run some tests. Where did you study arson investigation?"

"I was a volunteer fireman when I was a kid. Then I was an MP at Fort Bragg. We had a series of arsons—mostly outbuildings, and I caught the guy. Pure luck. Naturally the Army assumed I was an expert."

Alvarez swiveled his chair and indicated a chair in the corner. Otto sat. Alvarez took off his glasses and rubbed his eyes.

"How did you catch him?"

"First one was a storage locker. Burned to the ground. I could tell the fire had been started inside by the carbon on the inside walls. Figured he piled up a bunch of rags, doused them with gasoline, tossed in a cigarette and ran like hell.

"I was the first one there, so I caught the job. That's the way the Army works. 'Son, from now on you're an arson investigator!' I started going through personnel files looking at criminal records. Technically, you can't join up if you have a record but we know how well that turned out.

"Week later, second fire. A gardening shed behind the base commander's house. This time the fire was set from the outside. Looked like he had walked the perimeter with an accelerant. But how did he set it off? I found a stain in the grass that looked like a long cigarette burn—like someone had set down a fuse and lit it.

"But it was all burnt up. Didn't know what it was. No cigarette butt, no matchbook, nada. A few days later another fire. Now he's reducing the period between episodes and we're getting worried that he might be building up to something. This was pre-9/11, year 2000.

"This one's on the obstacle course. He lit the Weaver, which is kind of like a wooden jungle gym, and there's that same black scar on a portion of timber. Only this time, it didn't entirely burn. Left a hardened, clearish lump. I scratched it. Smelled like Testors' plastic model cement. I know about that shit because I've been a model builder all my life. I remembered seeing an issue of *Military*

Modeler at the base PO. Only one guy on base gets it. Private Dennis Pratt. AWOL. We put out a bulletin.

"Month later he burns down a warehouse in San Diego with him in it. I was just in the right place at the right time. And that's how I became an arson investigator."

Alvarez grinned. "The Army's funny that way. Let me take a look at these videos."

Otto stood. "Thanks, Gus. Let's go big fella."

Otto and Steve stepped into the hall. A couple agents waved at Otto.

"Nice dog," one said.

Otto and Steve left the bullpen and turned left toward their office. Behind them the elevator door dinged open. Otto was about to swipe his key card.

"Excuse me," a voice rang out in the slightly querulous tone of someone who suspects malfeasance. Otto ignored it.

"Excuse me, sir," the man said approaching. Otto looked up. Stared.

The man stared back equally incredulous.

"Hornbuckle?" Otto said.

"White?" Hornbuckle croaked.

CHAPTER TWENTY

MISUNDERSTANDING

Wednesday afternoon.

Hornbuckle pasted a smile across his mug and stuck out his hand. "Good to see you. I'd heard you'd retired." It was the same pale white skull, wide-set eyes and razor slash mouth. Some guys shave their skulls, they look like an uncooked muffin. Others looked designed that way. Hornbuckle was of the latter.

Otto gaped. Steve growled. No one had ever said a word to him about whether any of the other members of the team had survived. When he asked, they told him it was need to know. Otto made his own inquiries, all of which led nowhere. The Agency would not confirm or deny Hornbuckle's death.

And he pops up here in the middle of an SHC investigation? Otto didn't believe in coincidence.

"Have you been recalled?" Hornbuckle said still gripping Otto's hand.

"I'm working on a national security matter with the Feds. Why did you hail me just now?"

Hornbuckle released Otto's hand and half-covered his involuntary smile. "You look remarkably like Top Ten hacker Randall Kleiser."

"How long have you been with the Denver FBI?" Otto said. "What happened to you after the mission?"

Why did you leave the room?

"Why don't you and me get together for a drink at five? Is this your office? I'll stop by."

"Sure," Otto said. What the hell.

"Nice dog," Hornbuckle said, backing away.

Otto went into his office, shut the door and phoned Alvarez.

"Gus, could you come down here a minute?"

Seconds later Alvarez knocked and entered. He took the spare chair and petted Steve who laid his head on the agent's knee. "What's up?"

"Do you know Agent Hornbuckle?"

"Not well. He's only been here a month. He's in charge of the cyber-tracking unit. Why?"

"He was on my last mission. We went in to tap Ghaddafi. I always thought the mission was FUBAR, the way they threw it together. Do you know what happened?"

"I've read the reports. You witnessed an SHC."

"Nice of you to say so. That's what led to the medical discharge. At that time somebody in the agency had to know about the combustions. They should have listened to me."

"We're listening to you now. What about Hornbuckle? Something queer there?"

"Once I mustered out, I tried to find him. The Agency wouldn't tell me if he were alive or dead. He and I are the only survivors of that mission and he shows up here? Doesn't that strike you as odd?"

"Nothing strikes me as odd. As long as Hornbuckle has a higher security clearance, there's nothing we can do about it. I see a lot of guys like Hornbuckle. Close-lipped, uptight. Doesn't mean he's sketchy. But I'll keep an eye out."

Otto felt foolish. Hornbuckle was probably legit. Well, he'd find out.

"Sorry to bother you, Gus."

"No bother. Bunch of the guys are meeting up at six at the Irish Public House."

"I'm meeting Hornbuckle, but maybe I'll see you."

Alvarez returned to his office. Otto watched the videos again. Each time the conflagrations appeared more divorced from time and space, otherworldly in their intensity. He felt the beginning of a headache and turned away from the computer to rub his temples.

Back to the glass teat.

FIRST IRISH CASE OF DEATH BY SPONTANEOUS COMBUSTION
(Sep. 23, 2011)

A man who burned to death in his home died as a result of spontaneous combustion, an Irish coroner has ruled. It is believed to be the first case of its kind in Ireland. West Galway coroner Dr. Ciaran McLoughlin said it was the first time in 25 years of investigating deaths that he had recorded such a verdict. Michael Faherty, 76, died at his home at Clareview Park, Ballybane, Galway on 22 December 2010.

Deaths attributed by some to 'spontaneous combustion' are when a living human body burns without an apparent external source of ignition. Typically police or fire investigators find burned corpses but no burned furniture. An inquest in Galway on Thursday heard how investigators had been baffled as to the cause of Mr. Faherty's death. Forensic experts found that the fire in the fireplace of the sitting room where the badly burnt body had not been the cause of the blaze that killed Mr. Faherty.

The court was told that no trace of an accelerant had been found and there had been nothing to suggest foul play. The court heard Mr. Faherty had been found lying on his back with his head closest to an open fireplace. The fire had been confined to the sitting room. The only damage was to the body, which was totally burnt, the ceiling above him and the floor underneath him.

Dr. McLoughlin said he had consulted medical textbooks and carried out other research in an attempt to find an explanation. He said Professor Bernard Knight, in his book on forensic pathology, had written about spontaneous combustion and noted that such reported cases were almost always near an open fireplace or chimney.

'This fire was thoroughly investigated and I'm left with the conclusion that this fits into the category of spontaneous human combustion, for which there is no adequate explanation," he said.

Retired professor of pathology Mike Green said he had examined one suspected case in his career. He said he would not use the term spontaneous combustion, as there had to be some source of ignition, possibly a lit match or cigarette. "There is a source of ignition somewhere, but because the body is so badly destroyed the source can't be found," he said.

He said the circumstances in the Galway case were very similar to other possible cases. "This is the picture that is described time and time again," he said.

"Even the most experienced rescue worker or forensic scientist takes a sharp intake of breath (when they come across the scene)." Mr. Green said he doubted explanations centered on divine intervention. "I think if the heavens were striking in cases of spontaneous combustion then there would be a lot more cases. I go for the practical, the mundane explanation," he said.

Otto recalled Dickens' words on the subject from *Bleak House*: "Here is a small burnt patch of flooring; here is the tinder from a little bundle of burnt paper, but not so light as usual, seeming to be steeped in something; and here is—is it the cinder of a small charred and broken log of wood sprinkled with white ashes, or is it coal? Oh, horror, he IS here!"

Otto turned his attention to Sen. Darling. He went over the Senator's schedule going back several years. Fact-finding mission to Iraq. Fact-finding mission to Afghanistan. Burnishing his foreign policy cred. Had Darling been planning on seeking higher office? He'd have to ask Stella.

But if Darling planned to seek the Presidency wouldn't Stella have mentioned it? And what was Pendragon's part in his death, if any? Pendragon was at the forefront of the new energy companies and had received a half billion-dollar government loan to develop solar resources. But Pendragon could cover the entire North American continent with solar panels and they wouldn't produce enough juice to light New York, let alone incinerate a man.

Besides. Darling was their honey boy. They had no reason to want him dead.

He'd read Sally Crandall's transcripts. He doubted she'd lied. She was as baffled as anyone.

Otto searched the vic list for other politicians. Jean-Jacque Fusillier, a member of the French Socialist Party went up in flames at his country cottage at a birthday celebration for his seventeen-year-old son. The investigation blamed the fire on birthday cake candles, but the whole thing smelled of cover-up.

Otto put in a RFI to the agency for Fusillier and Yakovitch. He phoned Stella. She was in court so he left a message. The dossier on Froines was thick and included a classified assessment of Glass Defense Industries. Glass was developing an infrared weapon for the Army for use in crowd situations. As near as Otto could tell, the Glass Infra-Red Crowd Control Initiative caused an unpleasant tingling sensation on the skin but didn't actually cook anybody.

Find the source of the energy and you solve the mystery. If it were a battery it would solve the earth's energy needs. It wasn't a battery. Technology like that could not remain secret for long.

Steve licked Otto's pants.

"Don't lick the pants, Steve."

The Ocelot buzzed. It was Yee.

"Mr. White, please activate the video link on your computer."

CHAPTER
TWENTY-ONE
FIRST CONTACT

Otto found the link and turned it on. Secretary Yee blinked into view wearing a Kelly green blazer, white shirt, and cat's eye glasses. He could tell from her delicate features she was a small woman.

"Can you hear me, Mr. White?"

"Yes, ma'am."

"I have reviewed your history and I know Stella as a good friend. Thank you again for agreeing to do this. In addition to the attributes we sought through Project Genesis, you possess another quality that I find essential. You're loyal."

Otto didn't know what to say so he said nothing.

"There are people who will stop at nothing to gain the technology behind these assassinations. There is no question in my mind that this is not a natural phenomenon, but the work of our enemies. There are strategic issues here that go far beyond mere assassination. If these immolations are the result of technology, how do they store the energy? Where is it coming from? Is it a new source of energy? The nation that solves the riddle will have a huge head-start."

"I know that, ma'am."

"Any thoughts?"

"Just to keep an open mind."

The director's lip curved up at one end. "It is possible that a foreign power, learning of your mission, will try to steal anything you uncover. It is also possible that we have a traitor in our midst."

"Do you suspect someone, ma'am?"

"I have long suspected a leak within the intelligence community, which has now spread out among so many agencies it's virtually impossible to keep track of who knows what. I first suspected we had a leak when internal agency memoranda began turning up on Wikileaks. Several years ago, to test my hypothesis I released some disinformation as an internal memo. Sure enough, it showed up on Wikileaks within seventy-six hours."

"I see."

"It is even possible they will try to stop you. I can assign you some minders if you like."

"No, thank you, ma'am. I prefer to work alone. Ma'am, I ran into a guy I last saw in the Libyan desert. Ryan Hornbuckle. He's out here in charge of the cyber crime unit. He was there that day I saw Malik self-combust."

"I will look into Mr. Hornbuckle. You have my number. Don't hesitate to call if there's anything you need. God bless you for doing this."

"Thank you, ma'am. I'll do my best."

CHAPTER TWENTY-TWO
PALLIES

W ednesday evening.

White and Hornbuckle went to the Irish Public House and took a booth at the rear. Cops and firemen sat at the bar. Otto ordered a beer and Hornbuckle ordered a Gray Goose vodka straight up with an olive from the young ponytailed waitress whose badge said Linda. Otto ordered a bowl of water for Steve.

"What kind of service dog is he?" the waitress asked petting Steve on the top of his head.

"He's a pant licker. He licks your pants and can tell whether you've committed a crime or not."

"Really?" she asked incredulous.

"No. He's a tracker."

The waitress left. Lady Gaga—or Katy Perry—played on the sound system.

Otto and Hornbuckle stared at one another for a second. Otto spoke first. "What happened at the raid? Why'd you leave the room?"

"That's classified."

"Bullshit, Hornbuckle. Bullshit. I was there. You nearly got me killed. I have a right to know."

"I had nothing to do with whatever happened in that room after I left. I had my orders and you had yours."

"Who else got out of the building?" Otto said. It had been less than five minutes after Hornbuckle left him with Malik that the sidewinder hit the building.

Hornbuckle stared unblinking.

"What about that freak, Benson?"

"He was killed in the missile strike."

"What was on the laptop?"

The waitress returned with their drinks, stopped several feet short of the booth and stared. Otto unclenched his shoulders and sat back. Hornbuckle leaned back and smoothed his tie. It was dark blue, held in place with a tiny ceramic pig. The agent turned toward her and smiled.

Reassured, the waitress set down the drinks. They waited until she left. Hornbuckle hoisted his.

"Cheers."

Otto felt like throwing his beer in Hornbuckle's face but he hoisted his glass and drank. He wasn't going to get anywhere being surly.

"What was on the laptop?"

"I don't know. I turned it in. Those were my orders."

"I tried to find you when I got out," Otto said. "You fell off the edge of the earth."

Hornbuckle shrugged. "You know how it is. My last assignment ended a year and a half ago. I joined the FBI in March."

And already agent in charge of the cyber crime unit. It was an unusual career move. Federal agents held most agency guys in contempt. Elliot Ness vs. Frank Nitti.

"You know why I'm here?" Otto said.

"We were informed that you were investigating Senator Darling's death. I thought he died in a car accident."

"Darling self-combusted. Moment after you left Malik and me, he self-combusted."

Hornbuckle nodded. "I see. They didn't believe you at the time."

So Hornbuckle had been privy to his debriefing.

But you did, didn't you?

"Naturally, if there's anything I can do …" Hornbuckle said.

"So you're cyber crime," Otto said. He didn't know what else to say.

Hornbuckle reached into his briefcase. "Let me show you something." He took out a manila folder and slid it across the bar. Otto opened it. It was BOLF for Randall Kleiser wanted for criminal tampering, smishing and vishing and mail fraud. The black-and-white mug shot showed a young man with a shaved skull glowering at the camera. Save for the tats and piercings he looked remarkably like Otto.

"You see why I mistook you for Kleiser?"

Otto shrugged and slid the file back. "Perfectly understandable."

"Kleiser lives in Arvada and boasts that he's going to walk into FBI HQ and personally erase our hard drives. He's head of a group of cyber-hackers, call themselves Black Widow. They're going to smash the capitalist structure blah blah blah. They have a website but don't go there—they'll come back at you. I think they're dealing meth too."

"Is DEA involved?"

"I have no evidence. Just a hunch."

"What's his problem?"

"In 2008, his girlfriend Patty Ivan died aboard a SW flight from Denver to Austin. Kleiser blames the TSA and the whole federal apparatus in fact for her loss."

"Really," Otto said. "Why would he do that?"

Hornbuckle shrugged. "Maybe meth has turned his brain to mush?"

"You met Kleiser?"

"Not yet. But I will. So you're the go-to guy on spontaneous human combustion. There must be other cases."

"I'm not at liberty to discuss that."

"So you married? Got kids?"

"No and no. You?"

"Not me. I have bad luck with the ladies. I'd rather pay for it."

"Good for you."

Hornbuckle laughed, drained his martini and looked around for the waitress.

"What's funny?"

"They throw us together on some clusterfuck deal that goes ass end up, and you and I are the only survivors. We'd never met until Cairo, right? And here we are years later getting to know one another."

Steve whined and nudged Otto's leg. "'Scuse me while I walk Steve."

"Sure."

Otto held the door for an elderly couple entering, then he and Steve walked outside into the warm Denver evening. They walked around the corner to Palmer Street where Steve relieved himself on a construction site. When Otto and Steve went back inside, Hornbuckle was at the bar with some other agents and a fresh martini in front of him.

Otto quietly retrieved his backpack, put money on the table and left.

CHAPTER

TWENTY-THREE

THE WRONG ROOM

Wednesday night.

Quinn the Eskimo knelt in his motel room, ground floor end, stripped to the waist wearing black sweat pants. His lean torso glistened with sweat, veins and muscles popping after a forty-five minute work-out. His black hair was cut short, pale blue eyes fixed on some point in the mid-Pacific, miles from Indio, where he was.

Five years. It had taken him five years to catch up with Master Gunnery Sergeant Alec Hathaway who saw something at Surir he should not have seen and had been running ever since. Hathaway was no fool and had that survivalist mind-set so that when the time came, he was ready. Benson never could figure how Hathaway got out of the Mideast. He intended to ask the sergeant about that. It was Benson's own fault he'd spent the past five years tracking Hathaway. Benson had come along to insure that there were only two survivors.

Hathaway had looked in the wrong room; he ran into the desert puking. It was just bad luck. At the time Benson had his hands full with the other members.

Not that he'd spent the entire five years on Hathaway. He had also performed scores of minor ops from drop-offs to security to intel. He'd performed four sanctions, slightly less than one a year.

Quinn rose silently and turned toward the nightstand on which lay his Old Testament. Why did the motels only have the New Testament and the Book of Mormon? Quinn was grateful there was no Koran.

He picked the Bible up and opened it to the ribboned bookmark. "The people that walked in darkness have seen a great light: they that dwell in the land of the shadow of death, upon them hath the light shined."

He set the Bible down, went into the bathroom, stripped and took a shower. He toweled off and slipped into olive green cargo pants, black Adidas, black turtleneck and a black watch cap he could pull down over his face. He grabbed his gear, locked the door and got into his battered '88 Ford F-150 that he'd bought from a Mexican for $250 one week ago, sans license or title. Quinn had his own license and title.

He got on the 111 and headed southeast toward the Salton Sea. It was ten p.m. and the highway was feverish with vehicles heading west, heading east. Quinn wondered who they were, what series of events had brought them to this place, driving across one of the bleakest stretches of America, a sort of American Negev complete with its own Dead Sea. He saw illegals, coyotes, dope dealers, gangbangers, and mercenaries. He never saw people, only hustlers or marks.

When Quinn's father made the difficult transition from the Yukon to Detroit to build a better life for his family, he plunked Quinn down in the middle of an inner city school where he was bullied on a daily basis by the mostly black student body for his looks, his hair, his strange manner of speech. He got beat on a lot. One day he discovered Bruce Lee at the Roxy, Special Matinee: *The Big Boss* and *The Chinese Connection*, one dollar. Quinn remained in his seat long after the credits had rolled and they'd turned up the light, mesmerized by what he'd seen.

Thereafter he spent every day at the dojo, turning his scrawny body into an anatomy lesson. He was a black belt at sixteen. He was ungodly fast. He fucked up a couple star athletes and word began to get around.

Don't mess with the Eskimo. They sang "Quinn the Eskimo" behind his back but not so he could hear it. Quinn studied pre-law at Michigan State, which he attended on a gymnastics scholarship. The Agency recruited him when he was a sophomore. He could pass for white, Asian or Latino. He had a gift for languages. English was his second.

And here he was driving to Slab City to perform a sanction. He never really wanted to be a lawyer.

How low did a man have to fall to end up at Slab City, the sad remains of a failed subdivision at the north end of the Salton Sea, now a campground of last resort for losers, fugitives, or those who simply wanted to be left alone?

Hathaway knew how to forge documents and disappear. He'd slipped up when he ordered his favorite cigars from Tobacco Imports in Miami and had them delivered to a post office box in Indio. Quinn had been tracking the company's orders for years. For five years he'd chased down one false lead after another. Fortunately there weren't too many as the cigars were very exclusive and very expensive. Quinn figured Hathaway was out of the country for a lot of that time, probably in Costa Rica.

But Quinn had been unable to find him in Costa Rica. So he staked out the PO box in Indio and one day a Mexican kid driving a rattle-trap pick-up stopped in and emptied the box. Quinn intercepted him in the parking lot, showed him a badge and a photo.

"You know this guy?"

The kid was scared shitless. Hathaway, who called himself Meeks, had paid the kid twenty bucks to go and get his 'gars. Quinn paid him a hundred to show where "Meeks" lived, and to keep his mouth shut. Quinn promised another hundred the following day.

There would be no following day.

Quinn saw the sprawling encampment from the highway, glowing low and softly like a phosphorescent swamp. Hathaway was living in a run-down Grand Courier that he'd taken over from an old drunk whom he paid cash. It was still in the last owner's name, not that anybody gave a shit. Nobody at Slab City paid federal taxes. The only taxes they paid was when they bought food or booze.

Quinn despised them.

He parked his battered truck on cracked concrete near a pile of rubble consisting mostly of concrete with rebars. Plastic grocery bags tumbled gracefully past in the steady breeze. Even at this hour of night it was warm. Quinn got out and looked up. He saw a million stars. There was something to be said for living in the country.

Just not this country.

Quinn carried a 9 mm Sig with a suppressor made from a plastic liter Pepsi bottle and duct tape. There was no moon, but a million stars cast a glow on the desert. Quinn jogged silently through streets with names like Lilac Lane, and Moon View Court, heading toward the far fringes of the settlement and Hathaway's trailer.

It was two-thirty. A faint amber glow emanated from the living room window of the trailer, which rested on concrete blocks with a propane tank at one end. The nearest trailer was ten meters. The old pick-up truck was parked next to the front door. Quinn crouched by a dumpster and surveilled the trailer. He looked beneath the trailer, between the concrete blocks and saw several lawn chairs on the opposite side, and a pair of legs.

The faintest whiff of a Cohiba wafted his way, filling him with rage. What kind of patriot buys Cuban cigars? If Quinn weren't intent on killing Hathaway, he would have arrested him for trafficking in illegal materials.

"And the Lord said unto Satan, Whence comest thou?" Quinn mouthed silently to himself. "Then Satan answered the Lord, and said: From going to and fro in the earth, and from walking up and down in it."

Silent as the grave, Quinn dashed to the propane end of the trailer and slunk around with his back to it. From a crouching position he saw Hathaway, now with a gut, sitting in his lawn chair, the faint red glare of his cigar flaring. Quinn brought the Sig up and approached Hathaway from his left side, no more than a shadow.

Two big hands reached out from beneath the trailer, grabbed Quinn by the ankles and jerked savagely, causing him to slam onto the concrete slab and lose his pistol. The real Hathaway, who had been hiding beneath the trailer ever since Miguel had told him of his strange encounter, was on top of Quinn in an instant, straddling him and beating the shit out of him.

Quinn reached for the eye gouge, creating a little room that he used to buck off the much heavier Hathaway, then draw back and slam his heel into Hathaway's crotch. Hathaway was wearing a cup! It provided little protection from Quinn's dragon stomp and Hathaway folded gasping. Quinn sprang to his feet like a pop-up frog and scooped his pistol.

Both men were breathing hard.

That little prick Miguel.

"I knew … you'd come …" Hathaway rasped.

"Why … why'd you come back?" Quinn said keeping his voice low.

"I just got tired of running. You nearly got me in Sao Paulo. Freelancers in Belize. I thought I was through with the killing."

For a second both men gasped for breath.

"It was the lab, wasn't it?" Hathaway said at last.

"Yes," Quinn confirmed.

"Did you know it was there?"

"We knew something was there. We didn't know what it was."

"A lab where they burned people to death. I haven't had a good night's sleep since."

"'He giveth his beloved sleep,'" Quinn said, putting two in Hathaway's head.

CHAPTER

TWENTY-FOUR

SPREADS

Wednesday night.

Otto and Steve walked two blocks back to the Best Western. Otto let himself into his room from the patio, never passing through the hotel lobby. The little red light on the house phone blinked rapidly.

Otto filled the ice bucket with water for Steve, sat down on the bed, opened a notepad, took out a pen and listened to his messages. First was Stella.

"Just checking to see if everything went okay. Call me."

The front desk wanted to know if he needed anything.

Otto took off his shoes, got on the bed and pulled out the laptop. He brought up the vic files. Forty-five minutes later he learned that in '09, Froines had been a guest at Pawnee Grove, a think tank/campground outside Estes Park.

It rang a bell. Otto set down the file and gazed unfocused at the wall, hearing the whoosh of traffic on nearby Stout Street, faint television chatter through the walls, the clink of dishes in the corridor.

Pawnee Grove. Sen. Darling had also been a guest.

Otto glanced at the clock—nine-thirty. He was usually asleep by now.

But Otto couldn't sleep. His mind was a roiling sea of conjecture, apprehension and anticipation. Uneasy. He thought about the last time he'd been to confession. Five years ago, was it? Just before the Libya mission. He made the sign of the cross.

He thought about the things he'd done since then. Surely he was damned.

Steve jumped on the bed jolting Otto from his reverie. He automatically ruffled the big dog's fur, reached for the remote and turned on the TV. He ran through channels until he came to CNN. Fire fighters and pumper trucks arcing water into an Atlanta office building. An unctuous young thing appeared in front of the image.

"Firefighters believe the blaze started on the top floor. We are trying to confirm if Boogie Down Productions President and CEO Fonzelle Armstrong is still in the building. Chet?"

The image switched to the anchor desk, a middle-aged man of serious mien. "Thank you, Charlotte. Please keep us updated."

Otto hit the mute. Fonzelle Armstrong had come up from Atlanta's hard streets to forge a career as a rapper and a record mogul, signing Los Negativos, Darius Strange, and Little Miss Money Maker. He had signed the bizarre and diminutive Korean hip-hopper Sis Boom Ba, whose eerie wail had even penetrated Otto's skull during the long wet spring whenever he ventured into town or turned on the truck's radio. Her noxious ditty "Boom-Ba Style" was everywhere like a jackhammer.

May I please have your atencio! My plan is reprehencio!
Won't keep you in suspencio, BOOM-Ba BOOM-Ba BOOM-Ba!

Armstrong had since branched out into clothing and become unlikely friends with Richard Branson.

Bad juju.

Otto sensed impending crisis. He'd sensed it all his life and tried not to let it dictate his actions or personality. As the senator once told him, attitude is everything. Paranoids may be right but they were miserable. The history of mankind was one crisis after another.

But something new was in the air—something vile, gelid and unnatural. Otto felt it gathering force in his blood. His instinctive reaction was to stock up on ammo and ready meals and head for the hills. He'd been convinced mankind was on the brink of extinction since he was twelve years old. The Professor was big on Toffler, Malthus, Ehrlich. The sky was always falling. On this, Otto and the Prof saw eye to eye. The Prof installed a bomb shelter the year Reagan was elected, convinced of imminent nuclear conflagration. Otto used to sneak down with his pals to get high.

He got up, let Steve out for a tinkle, stripped off his clothes and got in bed.

Otto tossed and turned. Hornbuckle's appearance was upsetting. Otto worked his way through a jungle of maybes and might-have-beens before finally vowing to go to confession. Get it off his chest. Come clean. Eventually he fell asleep.

CHAPTER
TWENTY-FIVE
WITHERSPOON

Thursday morning.

After breakfast in their room, Otto and Steve walked to a nearby Habitat for Humanity thrift store. Using his credit card, Otto bought pants, shirts, underwear and a nice set of BK running shoes with hardly any mileage. He wore a tan sport jacket over a black tee and new jeans. They arrived at FBI HQ at ten. The receptionist and wand operator waved them through without a check.

Otto and Steve went to their cubicle. Otto googled Fonzelle Armstrong. The CEO was believed to have died in the blaze. It was too early to determine what caused the fire or where it had started.

Otto googled Pawnee Grove. *Wikipedia* came up. "Founded in 1912 by Theodore Roosevelt and John D. Rockefeller, Pawnee Grove is an exclusive camp for movers and shakers occupying its own mountain top outside Estes Park, Colorado. Originally conceived as a weekend getaway and hunting lodge, over the years

Pawnee Grove has been transformed into a social and business-networking event of far-reaching implications.

"As a measure of the club's exclusivity, it is reported the waiting list for membership is from fifteen to twenty years. While a fast track, three-year membership process is possible, two current members must sponsor the prospective member. A non-refundable initiation fee of $25,000 (as of 2006) is required in addition to yearly membership dues. New members are allowed to prorate the initiation fee into annual payments until they reach the age of 55.

"Members may invite guests to the Grove although those guests are subject to a screening procedure. A guest's first glimpse of the Grove is typically during the "Spring Jinks" in June, preceding the main July encampment. Pawnee Grove club members can schedule private use events at the Grove any time it isn't being used for club activities. Its exact membership is a closely guarded secret.

"Pawnee Grove has come under criticism in recent years for its refusal to admit women.

"The Grove has long served as a launching pad for ideas. Although no records are available, attendees claim that everything from the internet to the rail gun was discussed at Pawnee Grove years before they became reality.

"Emil Witherspoon has been camp director since 1972. He lives on the property year-round with a skeleton staff. During peak season, the staff swells to thirty-five, all former military." There was a link to Witherspoon, which Otto tapped. The photo showed a tall, taciturn man with jowls and a widow's peak. It was taken in 2004 at Ronald Reagan's funeral.

Otto returned to the main page and scrolled down. The single aerial photograph showed a cluster of tiny buildings next to an ovoid lake.

Otto returned to Witherspoon. *Wikipedia*: Born on April 14, 1941 in Cleveland, Ohio, Emil was the sixth of seven children ... Served two years in the Army, graduated cum laude with a business degree from Princeton. Witherspoon joined the Chicago law firm Totleben and Bissette in 1965, became a partner two years later. He served on President Johnson's Advisory Committee on Foreign Affairs. In 1972, the Pawnee Grove Institute offered him the directorship.

Witherspoon's decision to abandon a promising law career baffled friends and family, but it must have been a good fit because he'd been with them ever since.

Or could it be, Otto thought, that as director of the Institute Witherspoon exercised far greater power than he would have as a lawyer?

By one p.m. Otto had established that fifteen of the victims, including Fonzelle Armstrong, had visited Pawnee Grove over a span of twelve years. That left eighteen who appeared to have no connection to the think tank. However, two of the latter had contact with Grove attendees. One was the personal assistant of the head of a multi-national communications conglomerate. The other was a Hollywood lawyer whose client list included celebrities who had attended the Grove.

Whatever was causing the immolations was highly selective. Big shots only. No women. And now this tentative connection to an old boys' club in the mountains.

Malik had never been to Pawnee Grove, but he had met with the American Secretary of State who worked closely with the Undersecretary of State who had attended the Grove in '08. Six Degrees of Kevin Bacon.

Otto began a new file. Former Undersecretary of State Norman Rushfield was the first name. At the top he wrote, "Carrier?"

The Grove was not on the net. The earliest confirmed SHC had occurred on Sep. 11, 2001. Because of other events it did not receive much press coverage.

Steve licked Otto's pants.

"Don't lick the pants, Steve."

It was one-thirty. They needed a break. Otto locked his office, took Steve with him to the men's room, then down the elevator out the front door and across the street to Humberto Uribe Park, a swatch of green rimmed by blue spruce with a playset and a sandbox at one end. A series of benches occupied the rim. Otto sat on a bench gazing at the gleaming mountains beneath the cerulean sky. On such a day it was difficult to fathom the nature of evil. Even for Otto.

They returned to the building. Otto stopped at Alvarez' bullpen. The tech had on a pair of ear buds and watched a series of numbers scroll across his screen. Steve laid his snout on Alvarez' leg.

"How's it going?" Alvarez said, swiveling to face Otto and patting Steve on the head.

"Fine. Fifteen of the vics attended Pawnee Grove. You've heard of it?"

Alvarez nodded. "Up by Estes."

"I need a vehicle."

"Barnett will get you one. You have a driver's license?"

Otto nodded. He went down the hall, let himself into his office and phoned Stella. Going straight to voice mail he asked her to call him back.

Two hours later he had written software that would locate similarities among the victims. All male, all over thirty-five, all successful. Seven Americans, three French, four Russians, five Chinese. Six each from Singapore, Australia, Taiwan, Canada, Brazil and Argentina. Nineteen whites, six blacks, seven Asians. One Aborigine.

When he looked at the clock, it was after five. Otto phoned Barnett about a vehicle.

"Sure," the agent answered. "Come on down to the motor pool."

CHAPTER TWENTY-SIX

BLACK WIDOW

Wednesday evening.

When Hornbuckle saw White and his dog in the corridor, Hornbuckle's first thought was, *He's done it. That bastard Kleiser got in the house.*

When Hornbuckle realized it was not Kleiser but that aardvark from the Libyan goatfuck he was incredulous. Couldn't they see the man was mental?

The first time Hornbuckle saw White, in a villa in Cairo, the veteran agent was mortified. White's hair looked like a goddamned hippy's and he had a diamond stud in one ear. In Hornbuckle's opinion, personal vanity had no place in the agency. Operatives were supposed to blend in, not stand out. White's ear stud represented two years' salary to the average Egyptian. It was a breach of protocol.

At the briefing White kept asking questions—about sand density and Operation Eagle Claw, the disastrous Carter era effort to rescue Iranian hostages.

Hornbuckle's mission had been twofold: collect the laptop and insure that no other ops survived except Benson, who was in on it. In this, he had failed due to White's phenomenal luck. What happened to White was a freak occurrence and would never happen again no matter how many times you tried to recreate the circumstances.

Hornbuckle lost track of Hathaway and Benson in the melee. Control told him not to worry about Hathaway and Benson. That was already taken care of.

White's debriefing and subsequent behavior were enough to render him harmless in Control's eyes. White dropped out of sight with his disability pension and that was the end of it.

Or so Hornbuckle had thought. Now White was back like a hard drive you tried to dump in the municipal landfill. Darling's whip-smart lawyer daughter Stella had no doubt used her influence to get White the job.

Love made you stupid. White might get results, but he was a loose cannon. He could blow up in their faces at any minute. He was unpredictable. And this affected Hornbuckle's assignment.

Unlike those stooges in Washington, Hornbuckle had compete faith in the utter incompetence of the U.S. intelligent establishment.

There were still men of vision scattered throughout the services. There were still patriots who vowed the U.S. would never slip militarily to anything less than *numero uno*. Men whose mild outward demeanor and ability to get along masked a deep love of American traditions and a commitment to insure U.S. military supremacy.

Military men. Under secretaries at State and Defense who had been there for years. Private contractors. These men had dealt with administration after administration, constantly adjusting their positions to ensure their longevity.

They called themselves *Kagemusha*—the Shadow Warriors after the Kurosawa film and they aggressively pursued the technology behind the SHCs.

Hornbuckle noticed White leaving the bar last night. Fine with Hornbuckle. An agent with no social skills was worthless.

Hornbuckle sat at his desk in the office he shared with three other agents (and this irked him no end—that they'd give White a private office) and read the memos coming in from all over the world; the latest NSC reports on computer security breaches, police reports of stolen credit cards and PIN numbers, the latest appalling figures from financial institutions on how their data banks had been hacked, online threats, the latest in viruses and malware.

Number One with a bullet was Alexi Grigorivich Kornilov:

Alexi Grigorivich Kornilov was indicted in the Southern District of New York on November 26, 2011, on one count of conspiracy to commit wire fraud and one count of conspiracy to commit money laundering. Kornilov was indicted for his alleged participation in a money-laundering scheme involving unauthorized access to the accounts of a major provider of investment services. Kornilov allegedly accessed compromised accounts and wire transferred funds out of these accounts to money mules in the United States. These mules were then responsible for transferring the money back to Kornilov. Between June of 2007 and August of 2007, Kornilov allegedly wired or attempted to wire over $350,000 from compromised accounts. He is believed to have ties to the Chechen terrorist group Black September, responsible for the 1994 Rome International Airport terrorist bombing in which sixteen people died, including four Americans.

Number two was Anonymous, a loose confederation of hackers with branches in every major country. Anonymous launched one successful attack on the Federal Reserve Board that resulted in shutting down the NYSE for six hours. They had hacked the Los Angeles, New York, and Chicago Police Departments.

Number three was Black Widow, aka Randall Kleiser. Kleiser had successfully tapped into Quickbird 3, the spy satellite network, and programmed it to transmit Weird Al Yankovic's "Like a Surgeon" video over and over. It took Langley twelve hours to get him out. NSA feared Kleiser more than Tehran. Since the security breach eighteen months ago, Black Widow had kept a relatively low profile.

That wouldn't last.

Fish gotta swim, birds gotta fly. And a hacker has to hack. Hornbuckle knew Kleiser wanted nothing more than to break into a secure system—government or the banks—he was an equal opportunity hater and either tried to bring down their hard drive or install malware.

Kleiser had been born in Arvada, graduated Arvada HS in '04, spent two years at Denver Poly-Tech studying computer sciences. He should have been teaching. Dropped out '07, went underground, moved from place to place staying with sympathizers or other members of the group.

Kleiser was around. Hornbuckle could smell him. Hornbuckle had to get out in the field.

He had to know what White knew.

Kleiser was the key.

CHAPTER
TWENTY-SEVEN
KLEISER

W ednesday evening.

Barnett took Otto to the basement-parking garage where Otto signed for a black Denali with mags, spinners and twenty-two inch wheels that had been confiscated from a Jamaican-born money launderer who was now serving life in Florence. The Denali had tinted windows and a sound system that could trigger a seismic event.

"Billups wants a report Friday," Barnett said.

Otto nodded, opening the door for Steve who leaped into the shotgun seat. Otto turned on the radio as they exited the garage. Gangsta rap scoured his brain like a belt sander. He used the seek feature to find KUVO the jazz station playing some old Philly Joe Jones. "Blues for Dracula."

Otto drove from Stapleton to Schenk Avenue in Arvada where he found several blocks of trendy shops lined with upscale cars, many sporting university symbols or stickers. The streets were chock-a-bloc with bicyclists, skaters and board punks weaving around nuisance pedestrians. Otto found a place at an angle to the curb and eased the big SUV in between a Subaru plastered with testaments to skiing and a Mini-Cooper S painted like a Union Jack.

As Otto looked his car out of the corner of his eye, he registered a violent incident, fast movement and the smack of impact. He turned. A guy in a mullet and wife beater had just clotheslined a board punk skating by. The board punk lay on his ass all sticks and angles, pierced and inked, looking up in bewilderment. Mullet rounded on him prepared to kick ass.

Otto was no fan of board punks, but he didn't like bullies either. He fronted the mullet, who had him by three inches and sixty pounds. Up close, the man had little pig eyes set close and deep, illegible Celtic script inked on his bulging neck.

"You want to try that with me?" Otto said. Steve growled menacingly in a crouch, hair a stiff mohawk.

The mullet stared hard, saw something he didn't like. His eyes fell. He walked away.

"Just havin' a bad day is all," he said over his shoulder.

Otto helped the punk to his feet. He retrieved his Hellboy-painted longboard.

"Thanks, man."

"Maybe you shouldn't ride on the sidewalk."

The corner Full Throttle Coffee Bar offered free Wi-Fi. The bike rack out front was jammed with expensive mountain bikes. The joint's open doors radiated steaming energy. Students flopped about on a wide-selection of mismatched furniture or sat at the numerous small square tables staring at laptops. With Steve by his side Otto stood in line behind three students. When his turn came Otto ordered a mocha java and two poppy seed muffins. He snagged a table in the corner and fed Steve one of the muffins.

He had come here on a whim. The last time Otto had visited Arvada was when Rocky Mountain HS had battled the Arvada Warriors for the State Class B High School Basketball Championship a lifetime ago.

Otto never went to high school reunions. He retained no close friends from childhood.

Otto brought out his laptop. For forty-five minutes he delved into victim files trying to find others who had some link to

Pawnee Grove or any other common characteristic. He knew that commonality was not necessarily causality. He also knew how to gather evidence and build a case. He had learned that in high school in math and science.

He hit *Drudge*. Bad news. Fire at a popular nightclub in Los Angeles had killed sixty-five people including Schnauza Powa, the headliner. Among the dead and missing: Dash Karenga, star running back for the Los Angeles Rams.

He hit Stratfor, MMRI and a few others out of habit.

Steve pressed his muzzle against Otto's leg. Otto looked down. Steve pointed. Otto looked up. A man standing at the espresso dispenser stared at him. Otto got a weird sense of *déjà vu*. It was like staring in a mirror. The man had a shaved skull and a diamond earring stud. He wore a Denver Nuggets hat, bill turned sideways.

The man brought his large brown ceramic cup over to the table. He wore a backpack, blue jeans, Doc Martens and a Rage Against the Machine T-shirt. Tribal tats descended from his left shoulder to his wrist. Up close his eyes revealed a hidden grief. His smile was all mouth.

"Dude, how weird is this?"

"They say everybody has a doppelganger. Have a seat." Otto closed his laptop and put it on his lap.

Otto stuck out his hand. "Otto."

The dude flopped, bopped and clasped. "Randy."

"Randy Kleiser."

Kleiser turned white.

"Relax. We're cool."

Kleiser leaned forward and lowered his voice. He seemed a little jumpy. "How do you know who I am?"

Otto leaned forward. "I'm a federal agent. Relax. I'm not going to arrest you."

Kleiser looked startled.

"A G-man. I sit down with a fucking G-man. Have you been following me?"

"No. Sheer coincidence." Otto held both his hands up. "I'm not phoning anyone. I'm not recording. I'm sipping coffee and cruising S&M sites."

"Well are you going to take me in?"

"No. I told you."

Kleiser eased out of his backpack and set it on the ground between his knees. "How come?"

"Are you as good as they say?"

"You want Scarlett Johansen's private e-mail? Want to know how much Nic Cage has left in the bank? Not a fuck of a lot."

"Are you trying to crash the defense network?"

"No, G-man. Right now I gotta make some shekels."

"Here's the deal. I might need your help. How can I reach you?"

"I ain't no snitch, G-man."

"No snitching. I'm talking about your technical expertise."

Kleiser shrugged. "Leave word for me at Time Warp in Boulder. It's a comic store."

Otto wrote the phone number of his new phone down on a slip of paper and slid it across the table. "Be a lot easier if you just give me a phone number."

"Dude, I get a new phone every day. How'm I gonna know the number tomorrow?"

"Randall, we never met, *capice*? Tell no one."

Kleiser nodded.

"You renege, or don't get back to me in twenty-four hours I'm coming after you. Steve. Take a whiff."

The big dog parked his snout in Kleiser's crotch and sniffed. Steve licked Kleiser's pants.

"See?" Otto said, scratching Steve's ears. "He's got your scent."

Kleiser's face twisted. "Miracle this dog can smell anything over his own stink."

Otto leaned down to sniff Steve's fur. "Really?"

Kleiser scooped up his backpack and stood. "See you around."

CHAPTER TWENTY-EIGHT
Time Out

W ednesday evening and night.

Hornbuckle needed a 4X4. Leaving his four-year-old Corvette in the parking lot, he signed out a Jeep Cherokee that had been confiscated from a Chinese restaurant owner who secretly had an enormous indoor-grow operation. It was six p.m. when Hornbuckle left the building and drove to a luxury condominium in Englewood, seized from a man who had been convicted of securities fraud. The high-ceilinged condo's enormous windows looked across Clarkson Street to a park in Cherry Hills Village.

It was furnished as the thief had left it, with eight foot speaker towers, hardwood floors, and pictures of babes on bikes. A mirror clung to the ceiling over the bed in the master bedroom. Hornbuckle slept in another room. The place was cleaner than an operating theater. Hornbuckle had brought nothing but his gun, clothes and personal electronics.

Hornbuckle carefully hung his gray silk Calvin Klein sports jacket on a wooden hanger. He went into the kitchen, opened the large vertical freezer, dug around behind the frozen entrees and retrieved his Ocelot. Tucking it under his arm, absorbing the cold the way a sponge absorbs water, he walked into the living room and sprawled in one of the Danish-designed teak chairs that skidded backwards an inch on the oak parquet floor.

Hornbuckle put his feet up on an ottoman, enabled the encryption device and entered an eleven digit code. His call pinged a Raytheon comsat in synchronous orbit over the equator. The satellite redirected the call to an unoccupied safe house in Stuttgart from whence it bounced to the basement of the Ministry of Justice in San Pedro, San Salvador. From San Salvador the message once again leapt into the heavens to the French-owned, Surinam-launched Pericles Commercial Network, from whence it sprang to its final destination, a rural Virginia farm.

As Hornbuckle waited for his party to pick up, he plucked several dog hairs distastefully from his sharply creased Dockers. Filthy animal. He took out the folded slip of paper he had carried every day since Libya. He looked at the numbers. Control had run those numbers a thousand times and they still didn't know what they meant.

The numbers were the key.

The Ocelot rang.

A dry male voice answered on the second ring. "Yes, Hornbuckle."

"Sir, Otto White's out here in charge of the Darling investigation."

"This complicates things, but it offers us an opportunity as well. What was his reaction upon seeing you?"

"I think he was surprised. He's hard to read. I'll let you know as soon as I learn something."

"Do what you gotta do."

"Yes sir."

"Our friends in Moscow are also interested."

"I'll keep an eye out."

The voice on the other end hung up. Outside an emergency vehicle wailed by siren screaming, reminding Hornbuckle of his stint in the Green Zone where the sirens never stopped. He had slept with ear plugs and a white noise maker running at top volume. Once the power went out but the thrum of explosives more than compensated and Hornbuckle slept right through.

Hornbuckle stood, went into his bedroom and changed into sweats. Barefoot, he went back into the living room, moved aside a coffee table and a Persian rug, and went down in nearly complete side splits. Bouncing up he did some more stretching. He went to the wall-mounted Samsung and cued up some Anthrax and Deep Purple. Hornbuckle inhaled deeply, sank into horse stance and began the first of fourteen Tae Kwon Do forms as interpreted by Jhoon Rhee.

Forty-five minutes later, drenched with sweat, Hornbuckle stripped, showered, and dressed in blue jeans and a Navy blue cotton pullover. Dropping a .25 Beretta in his pocket, he left the condo, took the stairs to the basement-parking garage, and drove to the Landau Gentlemen's Club and Turkish Bath on West Colfax. Hornbuckle parked the Jeep in shadow across the street and down a half block as a hooker languidly detached herself from the open front seat of a '69 Buick low-rider with tiger-striped upholster and wheels the size of bottle caps.

She aged fast as she approached until she was in her mid-thirties by the time she reached Hornbuckle. She was Mexican. She leaned on Hornbuckle's open window and blew the scent of jasmine and cigarettes.

"You lookin' to party baby?"

"I am, darlin', and no offense, but you got any white meat?"

The hooker rolled her eyes and gave Hornbuckle the finger. "Wait here."

Hornbuckle watched her sashay back to the Buick, booty swinging. She leaned in the open passenger window. Seconds later the door opened and a thin girl with straight white hair got out. She wore a baby doll dress and pink, heart-shaped glasses. This one got younger as she approached so that by the time she reached the car she was seventeen.

Hornbuckle had a seventeen-year-old daughter he hadn't seen in nine years.

His fucking bitch of an ex-wife had turned his own daughter against him. Painted him as some kind of monster.

"You want to party?" the girl said trailing off into that self-satisfied glottal purr all girls seemed to do these days.

"Sure do, Darling. Why don't you get in the car."

"Are you a cop?"

"Nope."

"So what are we talkin' here? You want to go to a nice hotel? I got a room nearby."

"What I have in mind wouldn't take that long. We can even do it right here with your manager watching."

"Okay, so what do you have in mind?"

"You know. A blow job."

"That'll be a hundred bucks, cash in advance."

"A hundred bucks for a blow job?! Jesus! I can get one in Lodo for twenty."

"You ain't in Lodo, honey. Come on, baby. Look at these luscious lips of mine." She pouted and minced.

Hornbuckle dug in his wallet and pulled out a hundred dollar bill. The girl quickly ran around the front and got in the passenger seat. They were parked in front of a single-family dwelling that looked like something you'd find in a migrant camp, gray wood, sagging porch, dim light way in back. Pedestrian traffic was light.

The girl vanished the bill down the front of her dress. She wasn't wearing a bra. Didn't need one. "My name's Kimberly," she said.

"Pleased to meet you," Hornbuckle said unbuckling his pants. Kimberly helped him and by the time he got them down Hornbuckle Jr. was standing at attention. With one hand on the back of Kimberly's head Hornbuckle scanned the street, eyes gradually becoming unfocused.

Kimberly sat up and wiped her mouth with a paper towel she had picked up off the Jeep's floor. She opened the door. Hornbuckle's big hand closed around her bicep. She looked back with a flash of fright that quickly turned to anger.

"If I scream Carlos is going to come back here. You don't want that."

With his free hand, Hornbuckle flipped open his badge showing only the badge itself and not the ID. "Give me the hundred or you and me are going to take a little ride."

Sullenly the girl reached down the front of her dress and withdrew the c-note. She threw it on the floor as Hornbuckle released her and she sprang out the door.

"I hope you rot in hell, you motherfuckin' pig!" Kimberly screamed. The valley girl drawl was gone. "I hope you get fucking cancer and die screaming!"

The low-rider's driver door opened and a pair of Tony Llamas hit the street.

"Move along, darling, before we take that ride."

Kimberly slammed the door hard and stalked back toward her pimp. Hornbuckle started the car, pulled out past the glaring pimp, returned to Englewood and went to bed.

Tomorrow he had a lot of driving to do.

CHAPTER
TWENTY-NINE
A Vow

Wednesday night.

Otto and Steve returned to the motel at eight fifteen. Otto took Steve for a short walk and let himself into his room off the pool area. A couple of teenagers were splashing around in the blue-lit pool.

In his room, Otto checked his phone. Stella had called. He called her back.

"Otto," she said. "What's going on?"

"What do you know about Sam's visit to Pawnee Grove outside Estes?"

"He was a guest two years ago. I just came across the brochure they gave him."

"Really? Could I see that?"

"Well, it's up at the house. Crystal has it. I'll phone her and ask her to send it to you at FBI HQ."

"Have her Fed-ex it," Otto said. "Use this account number." He read a number off the back of the card Barnett had given him. "We'll pay."

"I'll do the best I can. You know Crystal."

"Do you know anybody who can get me in as a guest?"

Stella thought for a minute. "Let me ask Gabe."

"That would be great. How's that case you're working on?"

"It's in the hands of the shrinks. I'll bet you dollars to doughnuts they'll find him crazier than a shit house rat."

Otto barked.

"Good night, Otto. Love you."

"Love you too."

The phone beeped as soon as he put it down. Alvarez.

"What's up, Gus?"

"I've obtained satellite photos of Pawnee Grove. I can't send it to your laptop but it will be here in the morning."

"Do you have spectrograph readings?"

"Yes. They're somewhat surprising."

Otto was tempted to put his shoes back on and head to the building but a wave of exhaustion rolled over him from the toes up.

"Thanks, Gus. See you in the morning."

Otto spread out on the bed, switched on the television and found CNN. Scenes of firefighters again, this time outside an industrial building on the outskirts of Madrid. The newscaster identified the building as headquarters for Meridian Properties International, the brainchild of Hilario Salvo, playboy industrialist whose Formula One Team won the world championship in '10. The newscaster attributed the fire to arson set by a mob of "demonstrators" who had been camping out in the park across the street protesting austerity measures.

Otto went back online. Salvo had been in the U.S. for two months in '08 during which he had addressed the Aspen Institute at their Aspen campus. It was quite possible he had visited Pawnee Grove as well although Otto could find no hard evidence.

The conflagrations were increasing. How long before even the supine media began to look into the phenomenon?

Otto turned off the lights and lay in bed tossing and turning. The shrink had prescribed paroxetine and Otto had taken it for a couple of months, but it made him lethargic and he stopped taking it. It was for depression anyway. Otto wasn't depressed. Sure, he thought about killing himself but what intelligent being didn't? He had never told anyone, not even Stella, because he knew that wasn't the way to go.

It was a mortal sin.

His secret fear was that he would start taking down others, like Stella's client. He started making a mental list of all the people he would take out. Hundreds. Thousands. Stop. He would never get to sleep this way.

God, please forgive me for even thinking about killing people. I will go to confession this week.

Eventually, he fell asleep.

CHAPTER THIRTY
FANCY COLORS

Thursday morning.

Otto and Steve rose early and went for a run along the creek that ran through the park across the street. Returning to the motel, Otto showered and shaved. He and Steve were at FBI HQ by seven forty-five. Alvarez was already at work at his cubicle in the bull pen. He looked like he'd spent the night there.

They were the only people in the big room. Otto sat in a folding chair. Pictures of Alvarez's two kids, dogs and wife were tacked to the carpet-surface partitions. Smiling and hugging in the back yard. Decked out in puffy ski duds at Vail.

Alvarez reached into his briefcase and withdrew a white manila envelope with 'TOP SECRET' stamped in red, held shut by red string wound around a button. Alvarez had obviously kept the file with him since obtaining it. Otto unwrapped the string and shook out five eight and a half by ten glossies shot from a comsat twenty-six klicks above the Earth. The first photograph was black and white, taken in winter, a high-res image of the institute detailed enough that Otto could see the lake, the main lodge and the individual cabins.

"The first image is straight down, establishing shot, as close in as they could get it. You're looking at about three square klicks."

Otto stared at the photo for several seconds before sliding it onto the bottom. The next photo encompassed approximately ten times the area and was in color, from faded brick to black with pale blues and greens. "This was taken with hyper-spectral last November, after the camp had closed. The red regions indicate electro-magnetic activity slightly above normal, which can be attributed to any number of factors including heat, composition, humidity and time of day."

Otto examined the photo. The three brick-colored dots formed a triangle enclosing the camp and the lake, which was approximately eight klicks around.

"What am I looking at?" Otto said.

"Look at the next picture."

Otto slipped the top onto the bottom and stared. It was the same perspective but this photo looked like a psychedelic poster from sixties San Francisco, bursting with eye-searing magenta, day-glo greens and purples.

"Wow," Otto said.

"That was taken on June 22 of last year while camp was in session."

"Why has nobody noticed this before?"

"The comsats take literally hundreds of thousands of images every day. No one was looking for it. The program wasn't set up to recognize it. Rockwell's sending us real time updates from now on. They'll be in your in-box."

Otto traced a triangle from one crimson point to the next. "Can you translate this into what's going on? Like, does this represent a million kilowatts or what?"

"Good question. I'm waiting for the lab report. Hope to have it this week."

"This week? Why not today?"

Alvarez shrugged. "We're moving as fast as we can."

"You see about the Spanish billionaire?"

"No," Alvarez said. "Enlighten me."

Otto ran through the conflagrations of the past week. Alvarez pulled an iPad from his cargo pants and made notes.

"I'll get in touch with local PDs and work with them on the investigations."

Otto scratched Steve's head and tapped his foot.

"What?" Alvarez said.

"Suppose they're doing something to these guys up in the mountains."

"Like what? You don't just grab a Senator and subject him to an operation. There hasn't been a hint of scandal associated with Pawnee Grove since JFK brought a mistress in '61."

"I'm just saying. Some of the victims never visited Pawnee Grove, but at least one that I know of interacted with someone who had."

"So like it's contagious? It's a disease?"

"I don't know. Can I take these?"

"They're yours."

Otto and Steve went to their office. Otto brought up Kleiser's file. The mug shot showed a defiant skinhead with a hint of a smirk, diamond stud, tribal tat crawling up his arm.

My brother from another mother.

Kleiser was wanted for wire fraud and conspiracy in connection with a Black Widow hack into Bank America's system. BFD. Hadn't even made the news. And Kleiser was number one on Hornbuckle's Shit Parade? It didn't make sense.

Kleiser had his own Wikipedia entry.

On June 6, 2006, Kleiser's longtime girlfriend Patty Ivan boarded SW Flight #467 from Denver to Austin, TX. Ivan was subjected to a full body search. Four Muslim clerics in robes were not. The flight exploded upon landing killing all 183 people on board. Al Qaeda later claimed credit for the bombing. This was a dramatic turning point for Kleiser who heretofore had been content with hacking as political theater and anarchist entertainment.

Otto immersed himself in the investigation until Steve licked his pants. It was eleven. He took Steve across the street to the park.

Otto's phone buzzed. He took it out. Stella.

"Gabe's going to ask his agent, Ralston Goldfarb. He's pretty sure he can wangle an invite and bring you along as his personal trainer."

CHAPTER
THIRTY-ONE
INTERLOPER

Thursday morning.

Hornbuckle was on the road by seven. White had given his address as Fire Road 219 just north of the Joe Wright Reservoir. Hornbuckle had studied county plat maps and a satellite photo to determine which of several homesteads belonged to White. Some homes were not visible due to heavy tree cover, primarily ponderosa pine and aspen. Others were in deep shadow due to the peculiar light characteristics of the canyon. Hornbuckle had determined which homestead belonged to White by studying the infra-red photos and comparing them to those taken in daylight.

Hornbuckle's was the only homestead with no heat signature.

The old Jeep's radio was AM only and all Hornbuckle could find were farm reports and come to Jesus meetings. The vehicle was so old it didn't have a CD player. Hornbuckle hoped it was up to the task. A gym bag on the seat next to him held the tools of his trade.

Traffic up the Poudre was light, a few early risers in motor homes towing 4X4s with kayaks on the roof and bicycles cantilevered over the rear bumper. Beat-up Jap econoboxes, backlights plastered with bumper stickers. Lots of pick-ups. It had been warm out on the plains but it was cooler up the canyon. Hornbuckle drove with the windows open, elbow in the wind.

Joe Wright slid by on the left, mirror surface reflecting the chill blue sky. Fire Road 219 was readily apparent due to the platoon of mailboxes standing at attention. The chain was down. Hornbuckle shifted into four wheel drive and headed up the canyon.

Twice SUVs coming down the mountain pulled over to let him pass. He waved and smiled. The old Jeep managed to jounce up the rutted road. Hornbuckle had programmed his GPS to lead him to the site. He pulled a Payday from the bag, peeled it and tossed the wrapper out the window. He passed several private drives but glimpsed no dwellings through the forest. At times the grade approached forty per cent.

The GPS settled into a flat hum as he came around a rock outcropping and saw the pole gate and the warning signs.

The steel pole gate was held shut by a massive laminated Master padlock. Hornbuckle had bolt cutters in the Jeep but he elected to work the car off the road so that it was nearly concealed in a stand of alder and juniper. He grabbed his gym bag and squeezed out, car door compressing the wiry shrubs.

He carried a John Wayne commemorative .45 that his father had given him and was the subject of much ridicule at Quantico. He hung a half gallon water bottle over his head and squeezed around the concrete-mounted pole that formed one end of the gate. Like a salesman making a call he walked up the rutted dirt road carrying his gym bag.

The bag contained micro-recorders and transmitters, a hand-held metal detector, gloves, wire-cutters, glass-cutters, evidence bags and a half pound ground beef spiked with ketamine in case there were dogs.

Hornbuckle sauntered around another giant granite molar, his ankle-over Nevados silent as he stepped from rock to rock. As he rounded the huge rock he caught his first glimpse of chez White, a dark horizontal shape beneath a red rock ridge. Hornbuckle walked toward it. The ground beneath his feet shifted.

Hornbuckle froze for an instant, wondering if it were an earthquake, and then he saw a depression near his foot through which sand ran. As he watched the depression yawned into a black maw as the tarp's supports began to give rapidly, lowering Hornbuckle into the pit. Hornbuckle watched in slo-mo horror as a rusty metal spike jammed up through the tarp and seared into his right leg just above the ankle.

"SHIT!" Hornbuckle howled. The fucking spike was buried an inch deep. Slowly, painfully, Hornbuckle lifted his leg free of the spike. They were all over the bottom of the pit forming dozens of tiny tents where the tarp had settled.

What kind of lunatic built a tank trap in his driveway?

And this was the man they had chosen to head an investigation?

What if the fucking spikes were coated with human feces?

The wound throbbed and bled. Sucking air through his teeth, Hornbuckle leaned against the side of the pit—how had he done it without a backhoe? Even with a backhoe? Hornbuckle raised his right leg, pulled down the sock and looked at the bloody wound. Nasty. He tried to remember the last time he had had a tetanus booster.

Naturally, he'd neglected to bring a first-aid kit. Maybe there was something in the house he could use. But first he had to get out. The hole was seven feet deep. Hornbuckle ran four miles every morning. He tossed his gym bag over the edge. Using a small boulder as a base Hornbuckle boosted himself up and out of the pit.

He walked back a few paces and sat on a rock, breathing heavily. Sweat popped on his forehead and he felt damp beneath the arms. Not that cool on the mountain after all. He squeezed his wound to make the blood flow.

Hornbuckle rummaged around in the gym bag and found a bandana that he used to stanch the blood. He drew the sock up over the wound and wrapped duct tape around it to hold it in place. Now he had to re-rig the tarp to hide any evidence of his visit. Hornbuckle stripped off his sweat shirt and went to work. It took forty-five minutes to restore the tank trap to its previous condition, by which time it was past two. He covered the hole the spike had made with dried leaves and sprinkled dust on it.

Sweating and covered with dust, ankle throbbing, Hornbuckle limped up the trail to the long-low structure built of native rock and mortar with a green metal roof hunkered beneath a massive red rock overhang. Hornbuckle paused ten meters from the sturdy oak door.

White was an explosives expert. Any man who would build a tank trap in his front yard wouldn't stop there. Hornbuckle used his eyes. He couldn't see any cameras or obvious alarms, but that meant nothing. Cautiously he approached the house. He ignored the front door and did a three-sixty counter-clockwise, examining the windows for wires or tape. There was a propane tank at the north end. The house stretched back beneath the overhang, but stopped short of the cliff, leaving a six-foot wide alleyway in perpetual twilight. Here, there was door off the kitchen and a hot tub. Hornbuckle lifted the lid. It was turned off—the water was cold. Hornbuckle peered through the windows at the still interior. The back door provided ingress and egress in complete privacy.

A single power line entered the house on the south side, descending from a series of poles.

Hornbuckle emerged from the gloom at the south end of the house behind the massive 4X4 covered with a tarp. Bungee cords extended from grommets in the tarp to steel rings sunk in the rock. Big winds up here.

Using a flashlight, Hornbuckle shimmied under the tarp. There was enough ground clearance beneath the old Dodge power wagon to race a go-cart. Hauling the gym bag beneath the tarp, he selected a motion-activated Honeywell GPS transmitter the size of a playing card, which he epoxied to the inside of the frame and smeared with axle grease.

A breeze stirred the tarp, refreshing Hornbuckle. He crawled out from under the truck, grabbed his gym bag and walked around to the front of the house. He put on latex gloves and examined the lock. Schlage deadbolt. He tried the door.

It was open.

CHAPTER
THIRTY-TWO
ALLERGIES

The heavy oak door swung silently inward on oiled hinges. Hornbuckle threw a handful of talcum powder over the frame to check for lasers. He stepped into the house. It was cool inside with a faint aroma of sage. Within seconds Hornbuckle began sneezing. He pulled out a bandana and fired off sneeze after sneeze until he jammed a forefinger up beneath his nostrils and held it there for thirty seconds.

He was allergic to dogs.

Hornbuckle quietly closed the door behind him and stood just inside the entrance, allowing his senses to adjust. First impression: hand-made sailing ship. The way the tongue and groove wooden floor was put together, the walnut cabinets and bookshelves built into the back wall, all very compact and ship-shape.

Hornbuckle admired White's carpentry. The man knew his way around a hammer. If only he'd pursued carpentry as a career.

Hornbuckle set his gym bag down on the sofa, lofting a puff of dog hair into the air. Dog hair swirled with every step, attaching itself to his khakis. Hornbuckle's sinuses backed up for a full-frontal assault. Tufts of dog hair stuck to the walls.

A portrait of Jesus, one of the Madonna and Child and a wall crucifix confirmed what Hornbuckle had suspected, that White was a mackerel snapper. Man cannot serve his country and the Pope too. The U.S. should have learned that lesson after the election of Moscow's puppet Kennedy.

Hornbuckle was too young to remember, but his father, a minor official at State, taught him well. Religion was for suckers. Religion was the oldest scam in the world after "I love you." His father taught him that you could learn a lot about a person if you look at what he reads. Hornbuckle padded over to the built-in bookshelves, every step sending tiny puffs of dog hair scurrying.

The Bible. The Federalist Papers. A bunch of sci-fi shit. The freakin' *Boy Scout Handbook. Satan is Real* by Charlie Louvin. Hornbuckle pulled it out and looked at the cover: two country singers in white suits shuckin' and jivin' before a lurid red image of Satan as flames consume the cover. He put it back.

Most shelf space was taken up with stacks of magazines: *Road & Track, Field & Stream, Guns & Hunting.*

A 1/25th scale model of White's monster truck on the shelf. Hornbuckle examined the exquisitely detailed model up close. Everything was perfect down to the valve stems, brake lines and tiny Colorado license plates spattered with mud. He checked the numbers on the plate just in case. He withdrew a tiny spiral note pad and wrote them down. They did not match any of the numbers he'd obtained in Libya. The patience and craft that had gone into the model reinforced Hornbuckle's image of White as obsessive/compulsive.

Obviously that did not apply to his housekeeping.

On another shelf, Hornbuckle found a Mason jar stuffed with feathers. He was pretty sure they were eagle feathers, possession of which was a federal crime. There were enough that Hornbuckle took a chance on sealing one in an evidence bag. Next to the feathers were several flint arrowheads and carving tools, also federally protected artifacts that belonged in no private collection. Hornbuckle photographed everything with his Ocelot.

A bonsai tree on the window ledge.

Hornbuckle went into the kitchen. White wasn't completely irrational. He had electricity. Hornbuckle checked the refrigerator. Moldy cheese, a six-pack of Fat Tire, an open box of baking soda and some summer sausage. He opened the freezer. Five frozen pizzas and some ice trays. Hornbuckle removed the pizzas but there was nothing hidden in the freezer. He replaced everything exactly as he'd found it.

Down the hall to the bathroom, flurries of dog hair hovering around his ankles. The bathroom was big enough to contain a shower, a Jacuzzi, a clothes washer and drier and the Rinnai tankless hot water system. Horizontal east facing window, tiny potted cacti on the sill. A cardboard box next to the toilet overflowed with magazines, mostly cars, guns and nature.

Hornbuckle checked the medicine cabinet. Aspirin, Right Guard, Axe Body Spray, toothbrush, floss, toothpaste, and little amber bottles containing paroxetine, clonazepam, and trazodone. Each had more than three refills on the scrip and had been issued six months ago. The doctor's and pharmacy names did not appear on the generic labels.

Hornbuckle lifted the lid off the top of the old-fashioned five gallon flush tank. Nothing. Opposite the bath was more shelving built into the wall containing neatly folded ranks of towels and wash cloths. The next door opened on a small dark bedroom backed under the cliff. Hornbuckle found the switch and turned on a table lamp on a slab of wood resting on two three drawer file cabinets that White used for a desk.

A half-built model truck lay on the desk next to modeler tools, tubes of glue, filler, sandpaper and a French curve.

No computer.

No television.

No numbers.

How the *fuck* did anyone hope to go through life without a friggin' computer?

This alone disqualified White in Hornbuckle's eyes.

One wall was entirely covered in shelving made of pine boards resting on red bricks. Kierkegaard, Nietzsche, Dostoevsky, Pasternak, Solzhenitsyn. No fiction, lots of magazines. Again, nothing out of the ordinary. Hornbuckle checked the closet and found a Patriot gun safe with a combination lock.

Fuggedaboudit.

Finally only the master bedroom at the end of the hall remained. No ceiling mirrors for White. A simple king-sized futon rested on a plywood frame, which in turn sat on cinder blocks. A discarded cable company wooden spool served as a nightstand on which sat a cordless alarm clock/radio, a hairbrush, another Bible, and a photograph in a frame that had been placed face down.

Hornbuckle knew there'd be another Jesus on the wall before he looked. The bed was made and covered with a gray wool blanket that was rife with dog fur. Hornbuckle whipped the bandanna out of his pocket and let fly.

He went around to the side table, sat on the bed and picked up the photo. It showed White and a good-looking blond in a bikini leaning back grinning in a catamaran with blue ocean, white beach and palm trees in the background.

Stella Darling.

But White was no careerist! From what Hornbuckle understood, White wanted only to be left alone. Only the entreaties of his one true love could bring him back.

Hornbuckle searched the closet and the home-made five-drawer dresser. He found a stack of *Penthouses* and a jar of Vaseline. So White was normal after all. More significantly, Hornbuckle found nothing on spontaneous human combustion. Wherever White kept his notes it wasn't here.

Hornbuckle put a voice-activated recorder inside the center cinderblock beneath the bed. He put one in the living room underneath the sofa. From the looks of things the man never swept up. He put one in the kitchen behind the refrigerator. Hornbuckle would have preferred transmitters, but they were too easy to locate with a simple tracking device.

From the looks of things, White was still living in the 19th century but Hornbuckle couldn't take the chance. Retracing his footsteps, he looked to see that everything was as he'd found it.

As quietly as he came he let himself out the front door.

CHAPTER THIRTY-THREE
BROCHURE

Thursday afternoon.

In 1901, having recently established the Standard Oil Trust, John D. Rockefeller invited his friend President Theodore Roosevelt to join him on a hunting expedition in the Rockies. Roosevelt, then running for Vice President on the McKinley ticket, enthusiastically joined Rockefeller for one week in July. Their venue was then known as "Pawnee Park," a wilderness area northwest of Estes Park, Colorado. The area is defined by a triangle of peaks: Mt. Isosceles, Mt. Pythagoras, and Mt. Archimedes, all in the 13,000 foot range.

In the course of bagging four bull elk, two black bears and a cougar, Roosevelt suggested to Rockefeller that the site would make an excellent nature retreat, a place where men could shed the pressure and stress of the workaday world to relax with their peers in an atmosphere of rustic comfort and comity. Rockefeller concurred. In July 1903, two months prior to McKinley's assassination, which made Roosevelt the youngest president in American history, the then-VP caused a bill to be introduced in the House of

Representatives through his friend and protégé, U.S. Representative from New York's 17th district Aaron Burpee.

The bill caused Pawnee Park to become part of Federal lands and preserved in perpetuity as a retreat and place of learning under the Aegis of the Dept. of the Interior, helmed by longtime Roosevelt associate Harmon G. Entwhistle.

Pawnee Park encompasses approximately twenty-two square miles in what is now known as the Roosevelt National Forest. It is bordered on the northwest by Mt. Archimedes and on the northeast by Mt. Pythagoras with Mt. Isosceles forming the lower point. Lake Pawnee covers approximately five and a half acres.

Construction on the main lodge began in 1904, paid for entirely with donations from Rockefeller and wealthy businessmen he invited to join. The first annual Pawnee Grove meeting took place in Cleveland, June 24, 1904. No minutes survive, but it is believed the group included both Thomas Edison and Nikolai Tesla.

Rockefeller chaired the meeting during which the group, at least twelve men but possibly as many as nineteen, agreed to a Constitution and By-Laws. Their contents remain secret to this day. Members swear to keep these matters secret. There have been rumors that membership requires a blood oath.

The first annual meeting at Pawnee Grove took place amid snowdrifts on June 1, 1904. Pawnee Grove now serves as a retreat for members and a Petri dish for new ideas. In an interview with The Cleveland Plains Dealer *Rockefeller said, "Our mission is to foster values-based leadership, encouraging individuals to reflect on the ideals and ideas that define a good society, and to provide a neutral and balanced venue for discussing and acting on critical issues."*

Otto set the brochure down on his desk, leaned back and stretched. The brochure had arrived by courier a little after one. The 15x20 centimeter leaflet was printed in black and white on coated card stock. The cover said *Welcome to Pawnee Grove* above an ink drawing of the main lodge, the lake, the mountains in the background.

The inside cover listed the Director Emil Witherspoon and contact information. No website. The first page showed black-and-white photos of Rockefeller and Roosevelt, standing side by side in their hunting togs, rifles at parade rest, over a mound of Canadian geese.

The center spread of the eight page pamphlet provided a map of Pawnee Park and the Grove, showing the locations of all buildings including twenty-eight separate cabins, nature trails around the lake and through the surrounding mountains. No mention of the many controversies the Grove had engendered merely by existing in the PC age.

No women. There were rumors that JFK was the only exception. Only by maintaining a low profile and greasing the right media wheels had Pawnee Grove survived a mass feminist attack in the media.

Otto's phone buzzed. He picked it up.

"White."

"Mr. White, will you hold for Mr. Gabe Winner?"

CHAPTER
THIRTY-FOUR
:DETONATOR

Otto went blotto. *Gabe Who?* The tether snapped and he realized where he was. "Sure."

A moment later a man came on the line. "Otto? Gabe Winner. Stella's told me quite a lot about you."

"I'm sure she has, Mr. Winner."

"Call me Gabe."

It was a bit unnerving to hear the famous voice coming over his phone, as if Otto too were an actor in a play.

"Gabe, did Stella tell you what's going on?"

"She said it had to do with an investigation into the Senator's death. Naturally I'll do whatever I can to help, but I never met the Senator. Wish I had."

Being a lawyer, Stella would not have mentioned the specifics of why she called.

Otto put his feet up on the desk and leaned back. Steve farted.

"Can you get me into Pawnee Grove?"

Beat.

"I don't know. I've never been, but my agent Ralston is on their board of directors. Can you tell me what this is about?"

"I'll tell you when I see you. Of course our goal is to discover what really happened to the Senator."

"He didn't die in a car crash?"

"I'm sorry to be so mysterious, Gabe. The sooner we can get together, the sooner I can talk."

"I'll get back to you."

Otto turned his attention to Army experiments with infra-red weapons.

The ADS works by firing a high-powered beam of electromagnetic radiation in the form of high-frequency millimeter waves at 95 GHz (a wavelength of 3.2 mm). Similar to the same way that a microwave oven heats food, the millimeter waves excite the water and fat molecules in the body, instantly heating it and causing intense pain. (Note that while microwaves will penetrate human tissue and remove the water to "cook" the flesh, the millimeter waves used in ADS are blocked by cell density and only penetrate the top layers of skin, so it will not damage human flesh. Such is the nature of dielectric heating that the temperature of a target will continue to rise so long as the beam is applied, at a rate dictated by the target's material and distance, along with the beam's frequency and power level set by the operator. Like all focused energy, the beam will irradiate all matter in the targeted area, including everything beyond/behind it that is not shielded, with no possible discrimination between individuals, objects or materials, although highly conductive materials such as aluminum cooking foil should reflect this radiation and could be used to make clothing that would be protective against this.

A spokesman for the Air Force Research Laboratory described his experience as a test subject for the system:

"For the first millisecond, it just felt like the skin was warming up. Then it got warmer and warmer and you felt like it was on fire.... As soon as you're away from that beam your skin returns to normal and there is no pain."

This was different from the sustained intense heat necessary to reduce a body to ashes. Tests with animal carcasses caused them to wither and smoke but not to burst into flame, much less sustain intense heat long enough to be incinerated.

There was a knock on the door.

"Come in," Otto said.

Alvarez pushed the door open. "You want to grab a beer?"

Otto looked at his watch. It was five-thirty.

"Sure."

With Steve in harness, Otto donned a pair of sunglasses and carried a cane. Alvarez didn't comment. They rode in the black Denali to O'Leary's Pub, maps of the Emerald Isle, pictures of Dublin and Belfast on the wall. They took a booth in the dark back, Steve curled up at Otto's feet. A middle aged waitress in a tight black skirt, frilly white shirt and Tam O'Shanter took their order.

When she returned with their beers, they ordered dinner. Otto ordered two cheeseburgers. After the waitress left, he emptied a white ceramic bowl containing packets of sugar, poured half his beer into it and set it on the floor. Steve slithered his tongue over the rim and lapped without getting up.

Otto held the glass up toward Alvarez. "Skål!"

Alvarez clinked and drank. He opened his briefcase on the bench next to him and withdrew a manila binder. The binder held a half-inch wad of papers including many graphs.

"Spectrographic analysis of Pawnee Park indicates anomalous electromagnetic spike activity when camp is in session."

Otto took the graphs and examined them. Activity versus time and date. Maybe all that brain power was causing them to spike.

"Has no one ever noticed this before?"

"No one was looking. We don't have the resources to process all the petabytes we record."

Their cheeseburgers came. As the waitress left, Otto set one cheeseburger on the floor next to Steve.

"I saw that," the waitress said, but did not return.

They ate in silence. Otto set down a half cheeseburger.

"Could we obtain a warrant on the basis of these graphs?"

Alvarez chewed and swallowed. "Doubt it. There's no crime involved, not unless we find causality between these readings and some glitch in the system. You sure you want to go that way?"

"No, I'm just thinking."

"On the other hand, there's nothing stopping us from asking their permission. Given the Club's history, I don't see how they can turn us down."

Otto shook his head. "That's not the way to go. I need to get up there and do a little digging without disrupting their normal functions. We don't want to tip our hand."

"I see," Alvarez said.

Otto told him about Gabe Winner. They went over the latest data. There were now thirty-four confirmed cases of SHC and twelve possibles. Twenty of the confirmed had visited Pawnee Grove. Of the remaining fourteen, all had interaction either with a Park attendee, or someone who was close to someone who was close to an attendee.

"If I go up there," Otto said, "can you take care of Steve?"

Alvarez looked up surprised. "Not a prob if he can get along with Molly and Barkley."

"Steve's a sweetheart," Otto said ruffling the dog's hair.

At the bar, their waitress talked to a short, bald-headed man in a polo shirt who kept glancing over. He came out from behind the bar and approached.

"Gentlemen, can I see a license for that service dog?"

Alvarez reached for his wallet. "We were just leaving."

CHAPTER THIRTY-FIVE
A NEW ELEMENT

Friday morning.

After their run through the park, Otto and Steve returned to the motel. Otto showered and they drove to the Full Throttle in Arvada where Otto bought coffee, bottled water and two blueberry scones and took a prime location at a round metal table on the sidewalk beneath a Barclay's umbrella.

What did he know about Gabe Winner? Very little, save for having enjoyed the actor's performance in *The Detonator*. Since then, there had been two highly successful sequels, neither of which Otto had seen. He rarely went to movies. Maybe once a year. The last time had been with Stella. They'd seen the re-release of Disney's *Beauty and the Beast*.

The only reason Otto knew about Winner was because *The Detonator* was playing in the rec room aboard the USN Enterprise a few years ago in the Persian Gulf. *The Detonator* was just the latest in a long line of tough guy franchises including James Bond, Jason Bourne, and Rambo. In the movie, Winner played an ex-Special

Forces demolition expert who finds himself the lone force for freedom during a communist purge of a small Caribbean island.

The Detonator cobbled bombs out of chemical fertilizer, bleach, baking soda, gasoline, even a grain elevator at one point, taking out the bad guys in spectacular fashion. Before that, Winner had been nominated for a Best Supporting Oscar for his role as quadriplegic Vietnam veteran Lt. Stan in *Little Orville*. That movie really put him on the map.

Winner shunned the Hollywood scene, lived in Santa Barbara, and spent considerable time playing rock and roll for the troops. The more Otto learned, the more he liked him.

Otto's phone buzzed. Barnett. He picked it up. "White."

"Lon Barnett. We got the autopsy back on the Senator."

"I'm on my way."

Twenty minutes later, Otto wheeled the Denali into the underground parking garage. He showed his badge to the agent inside who consulted a clipboard and waved them through. Barnett was waiting on the sixth floor landing. They shook hands.

"Let's go. We're meeting with Billups."

Billups' secretary waved them through. Alvarez was already there with his laptop open on the coffee table before him. Billups rose from behind his desk, came out and shook their hands. He picked up a manila envelope from his desk and sat on the leather sofa next to Alvarez. Otto and Barnett sat in upholstered captain's chairs facing them over the coffee table.

"You boys need anything?" Billups said. "Coffee? Water?"

Otto held a hand up. "I'm good."

Billups tossed the folder on the table with a slap. "They recovered twelve grams of charcoal at the scene. That's what they autopsied. Nothing surprising, except traces of some unidentifiable element."

Otto picked up the folder and opened it. He flipped through graphs and charts until he came to a geometric construct of a molecule over a big question mark.

"What is it?" Otto said.

"No idea," Billups said. "They're trying to recover the remains from some of the previous burn-outs. This was found through spectrographic analysis, which is not a normal autopsy procedure."

Otto and Alvarez exchanged glances. Steve got up and licked Billups' leg.

"Steve. Lie down."

The dog obeyed.

"What does that mean, an unidentifiable element?" Otto said.

"It means it may be a new element," Billups said. "To add to the 118 we already know."

CHAPTER
THIRTY-SIX
THE PAWNEE CONNECTION

F riday afternoon.

The President met with his national security team in the Situation Room.

On the President's left sat National Security Advisor Margaret Yee, FBI Director Howard Lubitch, and CIA Director Luther Brubaker. On his right sat Homeland Security Director General Rolf Panny and Joint Chiefs Chair General Arthur MacCauley. At the far end of the table sat WH Chief of Staff Murray Compton.

"You've seen the autopsy report," the President said. "What about the others?"

"We've recovered Froines' remains from his widow," Lubitch said. "About fourteen grams. We should have the results sometime today."

"The question is," the President said, "whether we share this information with other countries, particularly Russia. Margaret?"

"Deputy Minister Sokolov has been less than forthcoming, Mr. President. We know that Dmitri Yakovitch, an oil millionaire, self-combusted in his dacha on the Black Sea. There's allegedly video but they're not confirming or denying. My sense is that they've made a similar discovery and don't want to share it."

The President steepled his fingers. "But you don't know for sure."

"No, sir. That is just my gut feeling. I expect fresh intel shortly."

"Can you expand on that?"

"Not yet, Mr. President."

Brubaker, the *éminence grise* of the intelligence community, raised his hand. The President nodded toward him.

"Luther."

"Mr. President, we're inclined to believe this is some type of weapon that can be trained on a person from a distance, possibly through walls. The Army's microwave program cooks your skin from a distance."

"Yes, but Luther," Lubitch said, "the microwaves can't cause combustion and lack the amount of energy necessary ..."

"I offer the microwave merely as an example of what can be done from distance. The Army is conducting experiments with different wavelengths, I believe. It is possible to broadcast energy through the air."

"Through walls?" Lubitch said. "That would require a tightly focused beam, like a laser. If anything came between the source and its target, it would be instantly obliterated."

"We are looking into the possibility," Brubaker said, "that whoever is doing this is above their victims directing the beam down."

"Do we have people in Russia?" MacCauley said.

"There are agents in place."

"Can you explain that?" MacCauley said. "We only put the pieces together a week ago."

Brubaker rolled a fifty cent piece expertly down his knuckles. "A good scout is always prepared. Five years ago we didn't know what we were looking for. Now we do."

"No we don't," Lubitch said.

The President cleared his throat. "What about the parking garage, Luther? How would someone on the next level up even know where their victim was through a foot of concrete?"

"They didn't need to shoot down in the garage. It was deserted. They could have targeted Froines from behind a pillar or vehicle. I have a team working on this. They have discovered irregular waves."

"Excuse me?" said Yee.

"A type of wave that only appears in solids as it passes. Sort of a wave within a wave."

"How long have you known about this?" Murray Compton said softly.

"The team first discovered the solid wave in September of '10 during Ventriloquist, which as you know is a program to develop secure communications. We've been conducting experiments ever since. It's all in the intel report."

The President had majored in physics. "Can the wave transmit energy?"

"Minute amounts, but the team believes if they can tune it, it would open up enormous possibilities."

"And how far are they away from doing that?" the President asked.

Brubaker shrugged. "Could be days, could be years."

"Margaret?" the President said turning his face like an arrow in her direction.

"Twenty of the victims visited Pawnee Grove in the past six years. The remaining sixteen interacted with those who did or with someone who knew someone who had been a guest. As you know, President Gilman was a guest." Gilman was the President's predecessor.

She had their attention.

"I've already assigned extra Secret Service personnel to President Gilman," the President said. "Mr. Lubitch, what is your take on these escalating incidences?"

"They appear unrelated save for the unbelievable odds of a handful of fairly important people suddenly going berserk and bursting into flames. Al Qaeda has taken credit for the Perrignon immolation, by the way. They claim to have invented a virus that only infects infidels."

Brubaker snorted. The President turned his hand. "What do we do?"

Silence hung in the air.

Finally Lubitch cleared his throat. "If we make an announcement there will be panic."

"The public isn't stupid," Yee said. "Sooner or later they'll catch on, if they haven't already. The internet is foaming with conspiracy theories."

"And?" the President said.

"Otto White is going up to Pawnee Grove and should have some answers for us shortly."

Brubaker frowned. "I hope he doesn't cause an incident."

CHAPTER
THIRTY-SEVEN
DENIAL OF SERVICE

Friday afternoon.

In his windowless office Otto pored over the Secret Service dossiers on Emil Witherspoon and his crew. Witherspoon appeared to be sexless. There was no mention of wives or girlfriends, no children, nor any hint of scandal. His Head of Security was an ex-CIA spook named Bob Casey. The fifty-five year old Casey was a fire-hardened veteran of Afghanistan with an outstanding service record including a Bronze Star. He came highly recommended by the Board of Directors.

Casey supervised a staff of fifteen, all men, all ex-military, all thoroughly vetted by the Secret Service. All with nearly spotless records. They included five African-Americans, four Hispanics and two Asians.

The Board consisted of twelve good men and true, chosen by vote every twelve years. As Pawnee Grove was a conservative institution, board members remained ensconced until they passed. It was an interesting list: four CEOs, four former diplomats and

Cabinet secretaries, a boxer, a talent agent and two scholars, all notable figures with lavish biographies. The board included two Nobel Prize winners, two National Book Award winners, and the former heavyweight champion of the world. The youngest was sixty-two.

Not the type of people you interrogated.

There were no SHC victims among the board members who were often in attendance throughout the summer. Otto worked the list of board members like a Rubik's Cube searching for patterns and connections. There were many. Four were Yalies. Nine were veterans. Four had been Rhodes Scholars. Eight had been Boy Scouts. Five had played college football. All twelve subscribed to the *NYT* and the *Wall Street Journal*. But nothing sinister, nothing to indicate a pattern of deceit.

Otto put in an RFI for the board members.

He switched to *Drudge* to cleanse his palette. A box of flame appeared front and center over the flashing red/blue crisis strobe and 32 pica red lettering:

TERROR ATTACK?

Otto clicked the link.

"A source close to Brainiac founder Bryan Ayres claims that he recently began to behave in a paranoid manner. He appeared jumpy and started carrying a gun. I was shocked. I mean here's a guy who was a life-long progressive ... he hated guns. And then he started wearing baggy pants and hoodies."

At GENCON 2003, Brainiac came out of nowhere to take the computer gaming world by storm with *Untamed Savagery*, a sword and sorcery fantasy so real, People For the American Way wanted it banned due to its addictive qualities. The First Lady inveighed against it on *The View.*

Brainiac made computer games: *Tear the Roof Off the Sucker*, *Lourdes' Landing, Kill Or Be Killed*, and *Marine Sniper. Marine Sniper* had been made with the cooperation of the USMC and was used as a training tool at numerous ROTCs and in basic training.

Lester Durant had used it.

Even Otto had played it.

It was scare o' the day, freak of the week.

Otto's phone vibrated. Winner.

"Can you meet us in Estes Park Sunday? Ralston and I are flying into Denver tomorrow to go up to Estes. We should make it to the park by noon."

"That's quick, Gabe," Otto said.

"Well, I'm off this weekend and it so happens that the next Pawnee Grove Chautauqua starts Monday. I don't know how Ralston did it, but he got me an invite. You're a screen writer with whom I'm collaborating."

Otto was secretly relieved that Winner wasn't spending the weekend with Stella followed almost instantly by shame that showed itself as a creeping red tide on his neck.

"Okay."

"No sweat. I'll teach you how to fake it. Can you meet us at one at the Stanley?"

"I'll be there."

Otto called Stella, got her machine.

"Hey. Winner just called. I'm meeting him and his agent Sunday."

Otto was online when the screen went blank. The gray nothing. Seconds later a white dot appeared in the center of the screen and expanded into a black screen with a black stylized black widow spider, red hourglass on its back. And below in the type of gothic lettering you'd find on a Hell's Angel, THIS DISRUPTION IN SERVICE BROUGHT TO YOU BY BLACK WIDOW!

CHAPTER

THIRTY-EIGHT

BLACK WIDOW

F riday afternoon.

Present in Billups' office were Otto, Steve, Barnett, Alvarez and Hornbuckle. It was six-fifteen, two hours and nineteen minutes since their computers went down. The IT guys working with the central office and the Strategic Initiative's Internet Emergency Response team succeeded in restoring service after forty-five frantic minutes.

Billups had come out from behind his desk to take a seat on one of the two leather sofas. They sat in a circle sipping coffee from plastic cups and water from plastic bottles.

"Ryan?" Billups said.

Hornbuckle consulted his clipboard. "We traced the attack to a computer in Esfahan. Needless to say, we can expect no cooperation from the Iranians, but this is a smart operator. He probably bounced it all around the globe."

"As you gentlemen know," Billups said, "Black Widow began right here in our back yard." Billups raised his eyebrows in unspoken accusation.

"It's just a matter of time, chief," Hornbuckle said. "I'm closing in on him. I can feel it. I know how this guy thinks. He likes to hang around and view his handiwork."

"Him would be Randall Kleiser," Billups said flipping an eight and a half by ten glossy black and white mug shot on the table.

Alvarez grinned toothily. "Looks like Otto."

"He's my brother from another mother," Otto said. He could be fired and worse for withholding what he knew. But there was something in his nature that clung fast to Kleiser. It was the pain he saw in Kleiser's eyes, that sick at heart feeling you get when you've lost your reason for living. Otto often felt it circling just beyond the firelight.

"You all know why he calls himself Black Widow, right?" Otto looked around. Blank faces.

"In 2006 his girlfriend, Patty Ivan," Hornbuckle recited, "boarded a Southwest flight from Denver to Austin. TSA searched her, but did not search four Muslim clerics traveling in traditional garb. The plane blew up on landing ..."

Billups nodded solemnly. "I remember. It might give us some insight as to his motives, and maybe we can use that to get close to him." Billups lifted his coffee mug with his pinkie extended. The mug bore a glowering picture of Billups above the slogan, "It's your mug!" and was undoubtedly given to him by one of his two daughters. He sipped and set the cup down with a minute clink.

"As you all know, Agent White's in charge of the investigation into Senator Darling's death, as well as other instances of spontaneous human combustion. Hornbuckle's in charge of the investigation into Black Widow. Is it possible, gentlemen, that whoever is perpetrating these attacks is using the internet?"

"Do you mean as in transmitting enormous amounts of energy through the net?" Alvarez said.

"For starters," Billups said.

"I don't see how that's possible. It would fry the system."

"How would the internet come into play in a parking garage?" Otto said.

"Didn't he have a laptop with him?" Billups said. "A smart phone?"

Otto took out a spiral pad and made a note silently kicking himself for not having thought of it in the first place. The idea of working with Hornbuckle again made him ill.

"What about Albrecht?" Alvarez said. "He was seated at a blackjack table. He didn't have a laptop with him."

"No," Billups said, "but he was surrounded with computers. At the bar behind him. At the chip-cashing booth. And surveillance up the yib-yob. You could enter a tracking program and follow him from room to room."

"He would have had a phone," Hornbuckle said.

Barnett leaned forward. Since he seldom spoke, everyone stopped talking. "Is it possible Black Widow is receiving Iranian support?"

Billups turned toward Hornbuckle. "Ryan?"

Hornbuckle shrugged. "It's possible, but Widow's mission statement condemns all organized government. Maybe he got tired of running credit card scams for a living."

Billups was placid as a Buddha. "And?"

You could see Hornbuckle's face working, chewing a rubbery idea. "I'll alert State and Intelligence."

Billups nodded imperceptibly and shifted his gaze to Otto. "Otto?"

Otto brought them up to speed re: the Pawnee Grove connection. "I'll be going up Monday. You're all aware of the accelerating pace of these incidents. My fear is that we're approaching a point where they'll become obvious and there will be a general panic."

"It may be," Billups said, "that people with no connection to Pawnee Grove have nothing to fear."

Otto scratched Steve's head. "Possibly."

"Boys," Billups said, "what about a Firestarter scenario?"

"Sir," Otto said, "I'm familiar with that program and they haven't been able to ignite a match."

"We know," Barnett said, "that the Russians are far more along in this than the West. They claim they have telepaths, but nothing about telekinetics."

Two sharp raps and the door opened, admitting Billups' cute blond secretary.

"What is it, Rose?"

Rose walked across the thick carpet around the back of the sofa, leaned down and whispered in Billups' ear. Everyone waited in tense expectation.

"Thank you, Rose."

The secretary left quietly shutting the door behind her.

"Undersecretary of Foreign Intelligence Angelo Rio shot two Agency employees, barricaded himself in his office and either set a fire or combusted. They're battling the fire right now."

CHAPTER
THIRTY-NINE
UP IN FLAMES

Saturday morning.

Otto rose at dawn, put on his sweats and Nikes, opened the safe, put his pistol and his phone in his kangaroo pouch, looped Steve's leash around his neck and headed out. They ran down the creek side path, Steve trotting unerringly at Otto's right side. Other runners passed going the other way, some with dogs. Steve paid no attention to other dogs. They passed bicyclists and bicyclists passed them.

At three klicks, they turned around and ran back.

Just outside the patio entrance to the motel, Otto pointed to a patch of lawn.

"Sit," he commanded.

Steve sat.

"Stay."

Otto went to the lobby for his complimentary breakfast: a bowl of oatmeal, two bananas, two apples, a platter of scrambled eggs and sausage, orange juice and coffee arranged on a plastic tray he'd commandeered from the bar,

Balancing the tray expertly on one palm, Otto let himself out, and into his own room, holding the door for Steve. Steve sat dutifully while Otto divvied up the goods. He sliced an apple and a banana for Steve and gave him half the scrambled eggs and two sausages.

They slurped for five minutes. Otto took a shower, wrapped the towel around his waist, sat on the bed and opened his laptop.

UP IN FLAMES! read the 36-point flashing red and blue type on *Drudge* and linked to an AP story that Secretary Rio was the third prominent American to burn to death inside a week and hinted at terrorist involvement.

Rio's name had not come up in a search of Pawnee guests, but Rio had worked with several men who had attended including CIA Director Brubaker.

The President planned to address the nation at two.

At seven minutes of noon, Otto's Ocelot buzzed.

"White."

"Mr. White, please hold for the National Security Director."

Seconds later Yee came on the line. "How are you, Mr. White?"

"I'm fine."

"Your report was a real eye opener. I'm afraid to guess how many government officials and important people have visited Pawnee Grove. I'm sure it has occurred to you that the victims might have had something implanted in their bodies like a homing device."

"It occurred to me, Miss Yee, but it seems unlikely. Operating on a bunch of big shots without their knowledge? Like they wouldn't notice? There are problems. We've requested a manifest from their quarter master. They said they'd take it under consideration. I also queried all the regional medical supply companies and FedEx. No special orders for Pawnee Grove. Nothing out of the ordinary. I'll know more after my visit."

"Will you stay the entire week?"

"As long as it takes."

"The President knows what you're doing and is deeply appreciative."

"It's an honor to serve my country, ma'am."

"All right. Good luck and God speed."

"Thank you, ma'am."

Otto phoned Time Warp in Boulder and left a message for Randy.

Kleiser phoned back fifteen minutes later. "What?"

"We gotta meet. How's your afternoon shaping up?"

"Man, I got shit to do."

"This isn't optional, Kleiser. Meet me at four. You choose a place."

Silence while Kleiser mulled it over. "Casa Bonita on Colfax. You know it?"

"See you then."

CHAPTER FORTY
CASA BONITA

Saturday afternoon.

Casa Bonita was a four-story Mexican restaurant with an open atrium, a pool at the bottom, and a fake rock cliff from which waiters dove. The parking lot was almost full when Otto pulled in. He took Steve for a walk and left him in the car with the windows cracked. He went into the foyer and sat on a bench. The interior was decorated with garish colors, fake fruit and toucans, Spanish tile and wrought iron balconies.

Kleiser ambled in at ten after four wearing a Tapout hoodie with the hood up and carrying a backpack. A waiter led them to a booth in an alcove on the second floor. Otto ordered a beer. Kleiser ordered a margarita. The waiter left.

"Did you attack our system today?" Otto said.

"Not me. I warned those guys not to fuck with the Fed, but they wouldn't listen."

Otto stared hard at Kleiser. Kleiser looked away. "Come on, man. I'd have to be three kinds of stupid to pull that shit right after I meet you. And forget about me naming names. That ain't part of our deal."

Otto wondered how long Kleiser would hold his tongue if Otto stuck him in a cell. But that was cop think. Otto never wanted to be a cop. He only wanted to serve his country.

The ambient noise in the restaurant was that of a boiler factory. Kleiser had chosen this venue because it was virtually impossible to bug and there were no clear sightlines to their lips.

The waiter brought their drinks. Kleiser sucked half down. "What do you want?"

"Are you aware of these fires that keep burning people up?"

Kleiser leaned forward and his eyes glittered. "Apocalyptic shit, dude! Some motherfucker has figured out how to throw fire."

"Do you know that?"

"Nah. I'm guessing."

"Could someone use the internet to cause these fires?"

Kleiser leaned back with a bemused expression. He finished his margarita and looked around for the waiter. He ordered another drink.

"You got this, right?"

Otto nodded.

"Wireless energy transmission. Nikola Tesla was said to have developed it not far from where we're sitting. I've been thinking about this. There are basically two ways: microwave and laser. The problem with microwave is you need a huge transmitting surface and a huge reception surface. We're talking giant arrays here. Laser is more likely since both transmitter and receiver are tightly focused. But you lose about 50% in transmission and conversion. Both methods require line of sight. I'm not aware of any desktop or personal computers that could handle that kind of energy without burning out. The other problem with a tightly-focused laser beam is you're not gonna get the body burning up evenly like they seem to do. It's gonna focus on one tight little spot. You'd have to train it on every part of the body in turn to burn it all up."

"See what you can find out about this shit, wouldja?" Otto said.

"Whoa, dude. You want me to help the FBI?"

"Randall. I know about Patty. Deepest condolences. But this is still a good country."

The waiter brought Kleiser's margarita. He drained half, rested his elbows on the table and leaned forward with feverish intensity.

"The federal government is a grotesque cancer crushing the life out of this country. Look at the national debt. Every person in America, legal or illegal, owes the government $55,000 just to pay it off! Your kids, my kids ..."

Kleiser ran out of steam. He looked down. "Patty was pregnant. No one knows that. She was going to tell her parents. I was gonna follow in a couple days—I was in the middle of a project."

"I'm so sorry."

"There's a lot of guys in government I wouldn't mind if they burst into flames."

"Believe me," Otto said, "I understand how you feel."

Kleiser looked up. "Do you? Ever lost someone close to you?"

"Not in that way."

"So screw the fuckin' FBI, no offense."

"Randall. The FBI is not the USA. The country faces a frightening new weapon. This goes beyond politics. Right now, you're facing federal charges. Do you know what the inside of a federal pen is like? Help me and I can make those charges go away."

Kleiser drummed his fingers on the table top. He opened his backpack and took out his laptop. It was covered with band stickers: Nautical Mile, Blind Strike, Dead Kennedys, Rage Against the Machine. He opened her up and cruised using a wireless mouse he pulled from his pocket. Otto waited patiently. He could sit motionless for hours.

"Sixty five stories on Google about spontaneous human combustion," Kleiser said.

"Fuck."

"This other shit, I can't do that here. Ahmina have to go deep into my spider hole."

"I need it as soon as possible," Otto said.

"Dude, you are fuckin' up my weekend."

"This is a matter of national security. You'll be a hero."

Kleiser shut down the laptop and put it away. "If you say so."

CHAPTER

FORTY-ONE

CONFESSION

Sunday morning.

Otto went to mass at our Lady of the Redeemer on Felton Avenue, a gray stone gothic monster with a sharply steepled tower and gargoyles. Otto told Steve to stay on a grassy patch just outside the door. Steve settled down to people watch.

The congregation only filled a third of the benches and most of the parishioners were elderly. Where were the young? Were they raising a generation of feckless seculars who never thought about the nature of life, the hereafter and their place in the cosmos? How was that even possible?

Otto knew how it was possible. Look at his old man. If the family failed to instill spiritual values, the state cannot impose them.

He took communion and waited for other parishioners to confess. He brought Steve a paper cup of water. An old man with flaxen hair shot him a dirty look over the dog.

"Bless the beasts and children, sir," Otto said.

The last elderly woman left the confession booth. Otto waited a minute to allow the priest to compose himself and slipped inside. The dark booth contained a hint of human warmth, the smell of lilacs, leather and dust. Through the slats, Otto saw that the priest was an old man and he wondered whether the Church was dying, whether they had enough acolytes lined up to man the confession booths.

And when all faith had disappeared, then what? Would man finally declare himself the god he'd been waiting for?

Everywhere Otto looked, faith was on the rout.

"How are you, my son?" the priest said in a wheezy voice.

"Forgive me Father for I have sinned."

"How long since your last confession?"

"Five years."

A raspy intake of breath. "Why so long?"

"I took an oath. I was duty bound. Confession wasn't on the table."

"You harm no one but yourself by not confessing."

"I'm here, aren't I?"

"So you are," the elderly priest said and cleared his throat with a moist gurgling sound. "Proceed."

Otto was out of practice. His natural reticence had always been at odds with his faith. He didn't need the Church to feel contrition. He needed the Church to forgive him. He went blotto, blinked several times and it snapped back into place.

"I, uh, lust after my ex-girlfriend and wish she'd dump the guy she's dating."

"Pretty venal, my son."

"I fantasize about getting him out of the picture. I don't know—sometimes in a car wreck, sometimes throwing him off a cliff."

"But you would never act on these fantasies, would you?"

"Of course not. When I have them I feel ashamed."

"That's how you should feel until such time as you are able to rise above. What else?"

"I killed four men."

Silence.

"Did you murder them?" the priest said at last.

"That's a gray area, Father. I was working for my country."

"Were you in the military?"

"Not exactly. Two of them were bad men. Their crimes would gag a dog off a gut wagon. The others were self-defense."

"How do you feel about it now?"

"I have nightmares. I see those guys ... sometimes I'm stalking them. Sometimes they're stalking me. Always, always overwhelming anxiety. I can't find my unit. I can't find my gun. I see a blazing man. He leaves an after-image on my retina, even when I wake. When I wake, I'm so relieved it's just a dream, but then I remember it was all real and it makes me feel like—it makes me angry. I have the stink of burning flesh in my nostrils ..."

I have these fantasies. These fantasies of mowing everybody down.

"My son, all your sins can be washed away in the blood of our Savior. Do you feel remorse?"

"Of course I do. Some of them had families. Sometimes I dream about their kids—naked and starving, their little ribs showing and distended bellies—and huge eyes, holding out their hands ..."

"Have you made any effort to reach out to those children?"

"That's against the rules, Father."

"Mmm. What about this blazing man?"

"He was real, Father. Ghaddafi's son Malik. I saw him burn. That's why I'm on the job now."

"It's just that ... the image of the burning man is also biblical. Some scholars say that the reference to God's burning bush could also be interpreted as a burning man, or an angel."

"This guy was no angel."

"My son, if you truly seek forgiveness, it is yours."

Otto's throat was bone-dry. He swallowed. His voice cracked. "I dream sometimes about shooting people."

"Did you shoot those men you killed?"

"All but one."

"Do you fear you're in danger of acting on this impulse?"

"No! Never. But I have these dreams. What bothers me is that evil is real and good isn't. I've seen so much evil, Father. I've tried to understand it but sometimes ..."

"Evil exists because God exists. Evil exists because good exists. If you believe in Satan, you must believe in God."

"I don't know what to believe, Father."

"I shall pray for you, my son."

CHAPTER
FORTY-TWO
THE STANLEY

Sunday morning and afternoon.

Alvarez lived near the Botanical Gardens in an old Victorian with a fenced-in back yard. Steve and Alvarez' two English pointers raced around the yard.

"I really appreciate this, Gus," Otto said.

"No problem. We love dogs. And Steve's a sweetheart. Wish I could go with you."

"I don't know how long this will take—I might be up there the whole week."

"That's fine. There's always someone here. Good luck."

Otto took the interstate to Baseline and turned west toward Boulder. From Boulder, he took 36 north and west through Lyons, winding up through the mountains to Estes Park. It was cooler in the mountains. Topping a rise, Otto saw Estes spread out before him, a gleaming little valley with a lake and a golf course in the middle, snow-capped peaks all around. The Stanley

Hotel was immediately apparent at twelve o'clock, the wedding cake on the town's crowded lace.

Otto paid five bucks to park the big Denali behind the hotel. He was early, so he took a self-guided tour. The Stanley wasn't that big. It was built by Freelan Stanley, co-inventor of the Stanley Steamer automobile, and its greatest claim to fame was having served as the inspiration for horror writer Stephen King's *The Shining*. Otto meandered through the leather and brass-hued bar, paused at the broad display of King memorabilia just off the lobby, went out front onto the broad veranda from which he had an excellent view of the Rockies including Long's Peak.

Otto watched children cavort in the swimming pool that looked out over the town. He sat in a white Adirondack chair. A black Infiniti SUV prowled up the hill heading for the parking lot. Otto relaxed in the warm sun, giving them time to park the car and enter. He got up and sauntered into the lobby. He did not have long to wait.

Two men appeared from the corridor leading to the bar and walked toward him. Winner was a trim five-ten with the confident gait of a movie star, thick, close-cropped hair. Ralston Goldfarb rolled like a sailor on thick thighs. He wore a purple and green Hawaiian shirt over creased white slacks, a straw hat and dark shades. A hefty gold chain dangled on his hairy chest and a cigar jutted from his black beard. A ruby the size of a hummingbird egg clung to a massive gold ring on his right hand. He looked like a narco-gangster.

Winner also wore sunglasses. He smiled and extended his hand. "White?"

Otto shook Winner's hand. "Thanks for coming. You too, Mr. Goldfarb."

"Call me Ralston," the agent growled giving Otto the old crusheroo. The back of Goldfarb's hands were covered with black hair. He wore a gold diamond ring the size of a lug nut on his left hand. "Let's eat."

Otto followed them back the way they'd come, through the restaurant out onto the patio behind the hotel. A waiter led them to a white-cloth draped table beneath a Bacardi umbrella in the shadow of the mountains.

There were perhaps a dozen other diners on the patio. Nobody gave Winner a tumble. The waiter took their drink orders and went inside.

"I really appreciate this, gentlemen," Otto said.

Winner waved a hand. "Not a problem."

Goldfarb twirled his cigar over a blue flame from a gold Dunhill. "In life, timing is everything, Otto. I had been planning to attend this conclave anyway and the boy here gets a week off from shooting while they find a new leading lady."

"What happened to the first one?" Otto found himself asking.

"She claims she has food poisoning. What she's really got is a psycho boyfriend telling her this movie is a career killer."

"Be kind, Ralston," Winner said.

"Kind my ass. That bitch has already cost the production 200 grand just fucking around with the lighting. This is the best part she's had in years." Goldfarb pointed his stogie at Otto. "You're a G-man, huh? Mind if I see some ID?"

Bemused, Otto removed his badge holder, flipped it open and handed it to Goldfarb who took it and examined it like a jeweler. "So what's this all about, Elliot Ness? The last time the Feds asked for my help was never."

Otto looked at Winner. "What did Stella tell you?"

"She said you were investigating her father's death. That's it."

"That's right," Otto said.

Goldfarb stared at him, the stogie once more lodged between his thick lips. "That's all you're gonna say? What's it got to do with the Grove? This is my fifth trip, by the way. The Grove is invitation only. Every camper must receive a unanimous vote from the board of directors. Every camper is entitled to bring one guest. When Gabe asked if he could bring a guest I about shit my pants. You stir up any kind of ruckus there, or cause me any embarrassment whatsoever and I'll make you wish you'd never been born."

"I assure you," Otto said, "I'm the soul of discretion. I'm here to observe."

"Don't go 'round asking any questions. They caught a reporter once sneakin' around the mountain. Took his clothes and boots and sent him bare-ass back down the mountain. These are not people you want to piss off."

"I understand, Ralston."

Goldfarb grinned. He had a gold tooth. "I like you, Otto. You're a no-bullshit kinda guy. So you're collaborating with this *schmendrick* on the screenplay to *Detonator 4*."

"That's our story," Winner said.

"And why not. He could hardly do worse than what's-his-name, the Oscar winner. Oscar my rosy red patootie! Where's the waiter? I could eat a buffalo."

CHAPTER FORTY-THREE
FRIED

Sunday night.

Over crab cakes and antelope steaks, Goldfarb regaled them with scurrilous anecdotes about the rich and famous. Otto waited until Goldfarb had downed his third bourbon.

"So, Ralston. What do you do up there all week?"

Goldfarb looked around for the waiter, who was right there. He ordered another drink. "Whoa—the whole week? No way. I have to be back on Wednesday. They have activities, a lot of discussion panels. Last time it was sustainable this and sustainable that. Pedestrian friendly communities. Like Brussels. These geniuses, these *schmendricks*, always trying to be the smartest person in the room. Always telling us how to live. I'm going to give up my four acre estate in Santa Rosa, my Mercedes SLS to live in a condo and walk to the butcher shop?! My ancestors would crawl from their graves and poke my eyes out with their finger bones."

"What's your impression of Witherspoon?"

"Emil's one cool customer. Mr. Everything's Under Control. One year Harry What's His Name, the linoleum prince, had a heart attack. Emil's got an ambulance and EMT team there in twenty minutes. Twenty minutes! In the fucking mountains!"

"Guy's got no wife, no kids, no girlfriends, what's up with that?"

Goldfarb shrugged and picked at his dessert. "You could say the same thing about Jodie Foster. Doesn't mean he's queer …"

"Not that there's anything wrong with that," Goldfarb and Winner simultaneously recited.

"Hobbies? Interests?"

"Emil's an avid hunter. Several of the trophies are his. A fucking moose for Chrissake. All shot on the grounds."

"You hunt?"

"Can you see me in my camo outfit crouching in a duck blind at four a.m.? Neither can I. But a lot of guests do hunt. The lodge even provides guns."

"How many guns do they have?"

Goldfarb stared into his bourbon. He sipped. Winner laid back, still as a fawn taking it all in.

"Well there are two gun cabinets in the great room and each has at least a half dozen rifles and shotguns. Nobody hunts with a pistol although I suppose you could …"

"A Desert Eagle .50 will stop a grizzly bear," Winner said.

Otto took out his little spiral pad and made notes.

"Good to know, Gabe," Goldfarb said. "Good to know. The staff have pistols although you don't generally see them."

"All of them?" Otto said.

"I don't know, but I've seen Bob Casey carrying a pistol. He's head of security."

"What's he like?"

"Bob? Quiet professional. Movie buff. I'm pretty sure Casey was positive on Gabe's invite. They're not gonna invite some meshuga asshole like Sean Penn. We brought *Detonator* DVDs for everybody. Want a set?"

"Sure."

"Seen any of Gabe's movies?"

"I caught *Detonator* a couple years ago. Good movie."

Goldfarb nodded in satisfaction as he removed a gold-foil wrapped cigar from his breast pocket. "What else you want to know? The food's terrific. They got a French chef. Jean-Marc— been there for years. Studied at the Sorbonne."

"What does that even mean, Ralston?" Winner said. "What is the Sorbonne and where is it?"

"Fuck if I know. The food's good."

"What can we expect when we arrive?" Otto said.

"First night is a big megillah. Big ceremony down by the lake."

"Walk me through it. We drive up to the lodge. Who's the first person we see?"

"Emil or Bob, probably. Emil likes to greet each visitor, especially newcomers. He'll come out front. Staff will take your bags to your cabin. You go into the main lobby and sign in at the desk. You pose with a stuffed bear shot by Teddy Roosevelt. They usually have the evening's events posted on a bulletin board.

"Emil will assign you a cabin and staff will take you there in a golf cart. You're pretty much on your own until dinner. First night's always barbecue on the veranda overlooking the lake. After coffee, everybody gathers on the great lawn for the convocation and the evening's 'impromptus.'"

"'Impromptus.' What are those?"

"Emil hands you the club and it's your turn to speak."

"What club?" Otto said.

"I forgot about the club," Goldfarb said. "It's like an Indian thing. Whoever holds the war club has the floor. Emil appears in a full Cheyenne war bonnet. We drink the blood of the white man. Hell, I'm always glad to do that!"

"Okay, so Emil hands you the club."

"I get up there, there's a podium, and I give 'em my sure-fire plan to rule the world. Whatever you want to talk about. Me, I do enough talking. Last time I was up, Richard Branson talked about commercial space flight. Some other guy talked about urban farming. Sustainable this and sustainable that ..."

Goldfarb ran out of words, his mouth slightly open, his gaze unfocused. Winner leaned forward and moved his hand up and down six inches from the agent's face. "Ralston's fried. Help me get him to his room."

CHAPTER

FORTY-FOUR

KAGEMUSHA

Sunday night.

Hornbuckle stretched in his Barcalounger waiting for the call to go through. The gash in his ankle had prevented him from working out and he was bored and frustrated. His attempts to track the source of the cyber-attack had led nowhere. Whoever was behind it—and Hornbuckle was convinced it was Black Widow—was two steps ahead of him.

His APB on Kleiser had produced zip and he was too new to Denver to have developed a network of informants. He suspected that cyber-cafes who had received the APB were either ignoring it or telling Kleiser.

They'd never met, but Hornbuckle knew Kleiser was aware of him. He'd made his presence felt. Two months ago, when he'd still been based in Virginia, he'd come this close to nailing Black Widow, but by the time the local feds had obtained a search warrant for the artists' collective housing the server, the spider had moved on.

Hornbuckle listened to clicks and beeps through his headset. Secure lines had their drawbacks. His gaze fell on the photo on the wall, the one with him and his older brother Pete, shirtless, tanned, lithe bodies by the lake, arm in arm. Hornbuckle had worshiped Pete. Pete had been an Army sergeant. He'd died during Desert Storm. The Army posthumously awarded him a bronze star. Now they were trying to jew his widow Deborah out of her pension benefits.

God love ya, bro. Wish you were here.

The ear unit snapped and the weirdly transmogrified voice of control entered Hornbuckle's skull, dry as the Serengeti. "What's happening."

"White's up at Pawnee Grove."

"Do you think there's anything there?"

"It's a connection we hadn't noticed, but as for this thing being developed and deployed from there, I don't believe it. It's contrary to what they stand for. The whole thing's a red-herring."

Hornbuckle listened to Control thinking, which came across as a series of light crackles.

"Have you seen the spectrographic charts?"

"No. I didn't even know there were any."

"Mmm. There appears to be a lot of unusual electro-magnetic activity up there.

"There are rumors they've got a Cray up there."

"Cray can account for every unit."

"Or worse—not a Cray. Something we don't know about."

"You'd never know it from their electric bills."

"We got the autopsy report from New Mexico. Froines' remains contained the same unknown element as Senator Darling's."

"Can you send that to me?"

"It's there. What about Kleiser?"

"I'm closing in on him," he lied.

"You have one week. We ran an extrapolation. If the immolations continue at the present rate, they will become self-evident and we'll suffer a worldwide panic. Millions will die. Apocalyptics are already citing them."

Hornbuckle clenched his jaw and sucked air in through his teeth. "Okay."

The line went dead.

Hornbuckle's heart pounded. Why did talking to Control exact such a toll? It was simply an electronically-altered voice. He brought the chair to full upright and rubbed his knuckles into his eyes seeing an Escher-like world of Mobius stairs and moiré patterns.

Finally, there were no options left save Farouk.

CHAPTER FORTY-FIVE
ARRIVAL

Sunday night and Monday morning.

Goldfarb had reserved a room for Otto.

Otto opened his laptop. The icon for his home surveillance unit was blinking. Otto downloaded the file. Through the tiny camera concealed in the headlight of his model monster truck, he observed Hornbuckle enter his home and look around, including the extreme close-up when Hornbuckle admired the model.

Otto smiled grimly. He composed a short note and forwarded the file to Margaret Yee. He took a shower and hit the sheets.

Otto dreamt he was back in the palace, Malik approaching, smiling beatifically, surrounded by a heavenly nimbus, holding out his hand. The hand of Brotherhood. The hand of Peace. But his other hand was behind his back and Otto was terrified of what it held.

Malik came closer and closer until his perfect grin seemed to fill Otto's vision. He burst into flames.

For an instant Otto felt an overwhelming rush of heat. His skin melted like wax and the fat crackled.

He woke up. It was too warm in the room. He got out of bed and opened the window, admitting cold mountain air. It took him a long time to fall back to sleep.

Otto woke at seven—late for him—feeling exhausted. Putting on sweats, he went for a long, loping run down the road to a shopping mall, through the mall and back up. His room phone was blinking when he returned. Winner had left a message to meet them for breakfast at ten. They met outside at the Cascades where the morning sun had breached the mountain and was rapidly warming up.

Winner was already seated, wearing white shorts, a polo shirt and sunglasses, a copy of the *Denver Post* and what looked like a script in front of him. The headline was about the burnings. As Otto sat, a young waitress with a Scandinavian accent came over with a fresh pot of coffee. Otto nodded enthusiastically as she poured. Winner waited until Otto had doctored his coffee and taken his first sip.

"I talked to Stella last night," Winner said. "She sends her love."

Otto grunted and studied the menu.

Goldfarb appeared in a purple and yellow Hawaiian shirt, cargo shorts and Birkenstocks wearing sunglasses, an unlit cigar jutting from his jaw like the 20 mm cannon on the *USS Ticonderoga*, designer bag slung over one shoulder. He pulled out a cast iron chair with a nerve-scraping sound and plopped down. The waitress appeared immediately to pour coffee.

"Whassup, boys? Everybody sleep all right?"

Otto grunted in assent.

"Said on the news this morning there's a big fire in Aspen."

Otto looked up sharply, reached for his laptop. "Do you know where in Aspen?"

"Yeah. At the Institute. Probably some nut doesn't like their position papers."

Otto wrote a note to cross-check Aspen Institute guests that week with those who had visited Pawnee Grove. They ordered, they ate, Goldfarb picked up the bill. Otto reminded him to forward his hotel room receipts for reimbursement. They agreed to meet in the lobby for a noon departure.

Otto returned to his room and began cross-checking Aspen Institute guests who had also visited Pawnee Grove. There were three: a physicist from UCLA Berkeley, an economist from the Freedom Foundation and a playwright. The playwright had been invited to speak at the current Aspen Institute event. It was he, Otto thought, who had burst into flame.

A playwright? If this were terrorism, why attack a playwright? Otto researched the playwright's works but there was nothing risible.

Internet news was sketchy as authorities did not know whether anyone was in the building when it burst into flame. Simply, those three fire departments were battling the flames and there was fear it would spread to the surrounding mountains. When Otto looked up, it was time to go.

They checked out as valets brought their cars around. Winner slid into the black Infiniti's driver's seat. Goldfarb took shotgun. Otto tipped the valet a buck and got in his Denali. The two big black vehicles looked like a diplomatic convey as they wound away from the Stanley and headed north on Devil's Gulch Road toward Glen Haven. The road curved around exclusive condos and resorts, free-form log cabins on odd lots and pink granite boulders. Several miles out of town they came to Pawnee Grove Drive, a shut gate and a gentleman in a blue blazer and sunglasses lounging against the front fender of a forest green Jeep Cherokee. "Pawnee Grove" appeared in gold letters on the hood.

The smiling watchman approached Winner. They talked, Goldfarb leaning to fork over a letter and pointing to Otto behind them. The man examined the letter, had a brief conversation. Goldfarb retrieved a box from his luggage, Winner signed it and handed it to the watchman.

The watchman opened the gate, waved them through followed by Otto. As Otto passed, he saw that the watchman was holding the boxed Complete *Detonator* DVD set. In his rearview Otto saw the man shut the gate and go back to his Jeep.

The road was smooth and black as a licorice whip. Soon they were surrounded by towering Ponderosas and the sound and scent of the breeze through the open car windows. Two miles down, the trees fell away and they entered an open area in front of the main lodge, a three-story log cabin with a great peaked gable looming over the main entrance like the prow of an ocean liner. The logs were massive. An apron of flawless blacktop flowed from the main structure, fresh yellow paint demarking parking spots gleaming in the sun. The big lot was largely empty save for a half dozen pick-ups, vans, and 4X4s parked in the far corner, obviously those of the staff.

Otto pulled up behind the black Infiniti that had come to a stop in front of the main entrance. Otto shut the engine off and stepped out. He wore a Broncos ball cap he'd found in the Denali, sunglasses, short-sleeved knit sport shirt and khakis. Before Goldfarb could reach the broad stairs the double front doors burst open followed by a human tank—blue blazer, tan slacks, sunglasses, crew cut, broad as an ox. Bob Casey.

Witherspoon followed gliding on long legs, arm extended, wearing black knit wool trousers, a white dress shirt and a dark green sport jacket with a theatrically long tail and "Pawnee Grove" embroidered in gold over the breast pocket.

"Ralston," the caretaker boomed. "So good to see you again! And this is the famous Gabe Winner."

Otto hung back. Witherspoon appeared simultaneously vigorous and withered, in that way some thin men achieve in their later years. His skin was taut over high cheekbones, a hooked nose, thin lips, lank hair falling straight down from a balding skull, a cross between Ebenezer Scrooge and Uncle Creepy. He and Winner shook hands and exchanged small talk. Witherspoon used the Double Hand Clasp to signify special meaning. Winner turned to Otto and motioned him forward.

"Otto, Emil Witherspoon. Otto's a retired Special Agent who's helping me write a screenplay."

Witherspoon's spade-sized mitt completely enclosed Otto's hand. Up close, Otto saw that Witherspoon's eyes were close together and deeply set, an arctic blue that made him feel there was something behind them watching, something that couldn't or shouldn't be revealed. "Very pleased to meet you," the caretaker said. "Why don't you come inside, we'll have coffee, or something stronger if you prefer. The boys know where to take your luggage."

The tall man turned and led them into the lodge.

CHAPTER FORTY-SIX
FAROUK

Monday morning.

Farouk Ben Fakir had been born Robert Weinstein in Evanston, IL. While attending Northwestern he had become radicalized by the Muslim Student Society, dropped out of school, went to Pakistan to attend a terrorist-training camp, and changed his name to Farouk Ben Fakir.

Farouk had majored in computer science. He was an autodidact who could build his own computer out of the bits and pieces of others. Al Qaeda set him up in Pakistan with a network and urged him to wage cyber-war on the Great Satan. Three years ago Farouk succeeded in invading the computer-run coolant pumping station at the Birch Bay Nuclear Power Plant in Upper Michigan.

Fortunately, the redundant safety system noticed the intrusion long before the reactor was in any danger of meltdown. Civilians wearing radiation-proof suits manually corrected the pumps while the Cyber Warfare Unit tried in vain to track the source.

But.

A high-level Libyan minister defected during the first week of the insurrection, supplying intel that led directly to Operation Firebrand. Farouk was fast friends with Malik Ghaddafi whom he met at a meeting of the Pan Arab Conference.

Hornbuckle had set up the sting operation that lured Farouk to Abu Dhabi, leading to his arrest. He'd baited his trap with a totally fictitious twelve-year-old Arab beauty named Farrah, complete with photos, who promised to fuck Farouk's feathers off.

Hornbuckle made the arrest and conducted the initial interrogation. Farouk copped to the cyber-attack but knew nothing about the other matter for which Hornbuckle was tasked.

White had been in the right place at the right time. For anyone else it would have been the wrong place and the wrong time. But White had damnable luck. His survival of the missile attack was one in a million.

It was nine-thirty when Hornbuckle turned his Jeep into the entrance to the Florence Supermax, a long, low beige structure on the high plains east of Colorado Springs and the repository of the worst of the worst. It was here Farouk was serving his thirty-six year sentence. Hornbuckle would have come earlier, but for the past six weeks Farouk had hovered between life and death in the hospital due to some bug he'd brought back with him. A bug with a delayed reaction time.

Finally Farouk was well enough to answer questions.

Two massive concrete silos with gun turrets on top framed the main gate, flanked on each side by a ten foot double hurricane fence topped with concertina wire. The guard examined Hornbuckle's badge and picture ID and waved him through. Hornbuckle drove to the administration building and parked the Jeep next to a series of bland sedans belonging to prison guards and administrators.

Inside the main entrance he surrendered his cuffs and pistol and submitted to a pat-down and a wand search.

"You know the way to the Warden's office, Agent Hornbuckle?" a guard the size of a dumpster said.

"Yes, thank you."

Hornbuckle followed a green linoleum trail down the disinfectant-smelling hall and turned into a suite of offices with a secretary seated at a desk in front of a wall bearing the Seal of the Great State of Colorado and flanked by American and Colorado flags. She was young enough and good looking enough to remind Hornbuckle that people made bad decisions everyday.

"Agent Hornbuckle?" she chirped, indicating a door to the left. "Go right in. He's expecting you."

Hornbuckle pushed the heavy walnut door open and stepped into Warden Cruz' commodious office. Cruz was putting into a plastic hole. He was a stocky man in gray slacks, white shirt and gray and red argyle vest sweater with a full head of black hair and a dust mop mustache. He leaned the putter against his desk and shook Hornbuckle's hand.

"Thanks for setting this up," Hornbuckle said.

"No prob. Anything for our friends at the Bureau. What's it about?"

"I need Farouk's expertise in ferreting out another cyber-terrorist."

"Good luck with that. Let me walk you back and if you don't mind, stop in before you go."

They entered the prison through a steel portal similar to those used in old-fashioned photography studios, a fat cylinder with a revolving door. Cruz accompanied Hornbuckle to the unit's desk, manned by two uniformed guards.

"Bring Farouk up, would you boys?" Cruz said. He slapped Hornbuckle on the shoulder. "Good luck."

The guard unlocked the interrogation room, a cold white cubicle with a beige linoleum floor, a stainless steel counter bisecting the room. Another door behind the barrier led to the cells. The steel chairs were bolted to the floor. Seconds later the inner door opened and the prisoner entered wearing a day-glo orange jumpsuit, legs and wrists shackled to a chain that went around his waist. Farouk Ben Fakir wore a buzz-cut and round steel-rim glasses. He looked pale and thin with dark circles and red dots. He had learned to keep his face immobile, betraying no emotion. It was very un-Arab.

Farouk sat in the chair opposite, chains jingling.

"Good morning," Hornbuckle said. "I need your help."

Farouk stared at the wall.

"If you cooperate, it may result in a reduced sentence."

Farouk barked mirthlessly.

"I'm trying to catch a right-wing hacker. A white supremacist."

For the first time Farouk looked at him, his gray eyes bereft of hope but not without interest. "Who?"

"Black Widow."

There was no recognition in Farouk's eyes. He'd been in Supermax for eighteen months. No TV. No newspapers. No internet. Let out of his cell one hour every twenty-four when he was permitted to work out beneath the sky in solitary.

"What did they do?"

"First off, this is mostly one guy. Randall Kleiser from Arvada. I have every reason to believe he's in the area. He invaded the FBI's central computer system and shut it down for forty-five minutes."

"How did he do it?"

"He used robot computers to overload the system."

"You have domain names for the rogue computers?"

"We're on top of that. What I need from you is insight."

"Tell me about this guy. What's his tag?"

"Calls himself Black Widow. Blames the government because his girlfriend died in a terrorist incident."

"What happened?"

Hornbuckle gave him the rundown.

Farouk's eyes focused on the far distance on the other side of the wall. "I know that guy ... Spider ... met him in a chat room in '09 ..." Hornbuckle's heart raced.

"Hangs out in cyber-cafes ..." Farouk trailed off, his mouth open.

"Anything you can remember," Hornbuckle prompted.

Farouk gazed into infinity. His chains jingled. "Yeah. Big basketball fan. What's the team here?"

"The Nuggets."

"Yeah. Spider loves him some Nuggets. Goes to their games, the whole nine yards. He doesn't like one of their players. Caramel Something."

"Carmello Anthony."

"Yeah. Says Anthony sucks dead squirrel meat."

"They traded Anthony."

Unfortunately the basketball season was months away but it was more intel than Hornbuckle had been able to gather since his arrival.

"What else?"

"Sci-fi ... plays *Halo* ... loves movies ... *Star Wars*, *Matrix*, he loves that *Nexus* series. He waited in line for twelve hours to see *Nexus II* at midnight. That's all I remember. You gonna be able to help me?"

"I said I would."

Hornbuckle stood and signaled for the guard to unlock the door. He looked back. Farouk stared at the wall.

CHAPTER
FORTY-SEVEN
A WALK IN THE WOODS

P awnee Grove's lobby had a soaring, open-beam ceiling, a fieldstone floor, a chandelier fashioned from elk antlers, knotty pine paneling and Teddy Roosevelt's bear upright and pawing. Other trophies glowered from the wall behind the registration desk. Witherspoon went behind the counter and brought out a heavy leather ledger and a bespoke pen, which he handed to Goldfarb.

"Gentlemen, if you would register please, and we'll need a credit card for incidentals and room service."

While Goldfarb registered Witherspoon sipped at a can of Mountain Dew and produced pamphlets similar to the one Otto had obtained from Crystal, giving a history of the Grove with a map in the center spread showing hiking trails. The trails dead-ended well short of the mountain tops.

Otto registered.

"Gentlemen," Witherspoon said, "you're our first guests today. We will be meeting at five on the veranda for drinks and hors d'oeuvres followed by our welcoming ceremony down by the lake. Dinner will be served at seven. The pamphlet contains a list of activities for the week. Please familiarize yourselves with the rules and by-laws."

Witherspoon consulted a laminated map of the property. "I'm going to put you in Zachary Taylor. It's farthest from the main building so you should have no trouble sleeping. Burt will take you to your cabin." Witherspoon picked up an old-fashioned telephone receiver and pushed some buttons.

"Burt, I need you."

Winner went up to the bear and read the plaque. "Colorado black bear shot by Theodore Roosevelt, Aug. 19, 1902. Height: Five feet two inches. Weight: 185 lbs."

Otto examined old black and white photographs, sepia-toned rustics of manly men in hunting togs glad-handing each other or standing over their trophies. A minute later a man wearing a corduroy jacket with leather shoulder inserts, white shirt and khakis entered.

"Burt, will you take Mr. Winner and Mr. White to Taylor?"

Otto looked at Goldfarb.

"I always stay in the main building. Not so much walking."

"We have a dozen rooms but most guests prefer the cottages," Witherspoon said.

Burt introduced himself. They shook hands.

Minutes later, they were dashing through the fragrant pine forest in a silent golf cart atop buttery blacktop. A series of cottages lay on both sides of the road partially concealed by the forest.

"Welcome to the Grove, Mr. Winner," Burt said, eyes on the road. "I'm a great admirer of your films."

"Thanks, Burt. Call me Gabe."

"You were with the agency, Mr. White?" Burt said.

"That's right. Retired a couple years ago."

Burt slowed way down and then stopped as a fawn wandered from one side of the road accompanied by its mother. Otto looked at a nearby cabin. James Polk. All the cabins were named after presidents.

"Me too," Burt said softly, so as not to startle the deer. "Retired six years ago. Been with the Grove ever since."

"What do you do in the winter?" Winner said.

Burt laughed. "I ski. Between the Grove and my pension I'm pretty much free."

The stocky crew-cut Burt looked to be in his mid-forties.

Taylor was a metal-roofed cabin tucked in among the pine with a winding flagstone path connecting it to the smooth blacktop, which ended ten meters on. Winner signed a boxed *Detonator* set and gave it to Burt.

"My kid is gonna love this. See you tonight then."

Otto opened the unlocked door. The interior resembled an upscale bunkhouse with bedrooms off the main room, two metal-frame beds in each, a separate bath, hardwood floor covered with Indian scatter rugs and a stuffed wolf head over the stone fireplace. Their luggage had already been placed inside.

It took them less than five minutes to sort their gear. Otto waited until Winner visited the head. He quietly shut the door to his bedroom, pulled out the Ocelot, opened it and put it to his ear. No problem. The Ocelot relied on comsats, not radio towers.

Otto slipped it into his pants, went into the living room, sat on the cloth sofa beneath a mounted deer's head and traded his loafers for hiking boots.

"Up for a little hike?" he said.

"One minute," Winner said from the bedroom.

He emerged in hiking boots, cargo shorts, short-sleeved shirt and a Chargers cap carrying a small backpack and a big canteen. He tossed Otto a tube of sun screen.

"Slather up. You got water bottles?"

Otto nodded, smearing sun screen on his face with special attention to the nose and beneath the jaw. Otto filled his plastic water bottle at the kitchenette sink and looped it over his shoulder. He wore olive-colored cargo pants, a *Raiders of the Lost Ark* T-shirt and a ball cap, bill forward. He stood in Winner's door.

Winner took out his Blackberry in Otterbox and set it on the dresser in his room. "Guess I won't need this."

Armed with their map, they left the cabin and headed counter-clockwise through the forest around the lake. Through the trees, the lake was the color of amethyst, butting up against the gray granite cliffs on the far side. In breaks in the rock, they could see snow-capped peaks gleaming like diamonds in the sun. Awed by their surroundings they proceeded in silence. Winner pointed at a big buck picking its way through the trees. A trout broke the perfect surface of the lake and slapped back in, faint echoes whispering across the valley. It was difficult to believe land so beautiful could have anything to do with the killings.

Within a kilometer, the trail left the woods and followed a granite ridge toward Mt. Pythagoras. They paused at an overlook to take the view and drink. The scenery stunned them into silence.

Above the azure lake, Mt. Pythagoras gleamed phosphorescent where the sun struck snow. Winner pointed again. A curved-horn mountain ram plucked greens from a ledge 200 meters above the water.

The air was redolent of pine and sage. Winner inhaled deeply.

"If you could bottle this air you'd make a fortune."

They picked their way past juniper and prickly pear until they topped a small rise and saw rocks piled in a berm blocking the path and a big black on white sign:

DO NOT PROCEED BEYOND THIS POINT

It was accompanied by a red skull and cross bones.

Winner and Otto exchanged glances. Without a word, they squeezed around the barrier and continued up the trail.

CHAPTER
FORTY-EIGHT
RED BALL

T he trail was precipitous but not technical. The jagged granite provided plenty of handholds. As they rose, the land began to stretch before them until they could see across the lake to the lodge where tiny, ant-sized figures were setting up chairs on the lawn. Above and beyond the camp lay the Rockies, with Long's Peak prominent. Despite the altitude, it was a warm, sunny day and both men were sweating. From time to time Winner would whip out a bandanna and mop his face.

Halfway up it turned into real work. They were now well above the tree line.

They paused at a granite escarpment leaning back against the sun-warm rock. Winner pointed to an eagle circling high overhead. He Who Spots the Wildlife. As they watched, the eagle dropped like a javelin, piercing the mirror surface of the lake and emerging with a trout in its claws. As the eagle rose, the trout flashed its rainbow, a startling beauty born of nature's cruel struggle.

Winner stood with his back to the mountain smiling at the sun. It would be so easy, Otto thought. One good shove. A tragic accident in the mountains. It happened all the time. Otto would have an unobstructed path to Stella.

He was immediately suffused with a deep shame.

God forgive me.

He couldn't stop the thoughts from coming. All he could do was handle them as a person of integrity.

They resumed their climb. Neither had breath for conversation. A pika emerged on top of a boulder and furiously scolded them. The final hundred meters were virtually vertical. Otto was glad he'd brought gloves to deal with the jagged shards. Winner was first to hoist himself over the top followed by Otto minutes later. Otto found Winner sitting with his legs splayed, panting, drinking water and staring at the spectacular view. Mountains marched away in waves to the west as far as the eye could see, many of them gleaming with snow. High above, a pair of dissipating contrails crossed in the azure sky.

"Quite the view," Winner said.

The top of the mountain was gently domed, sloping up to a center point that glowed carmine in the afternoon light. Winner got to his feet.

"Let's check it out."

"Be right with you," Otto replied, squinting back the way they had come. The tiny figures on the lawn seemed agitated, the tall figure of Witherspoon unmistakable. Otto removed his binoculars from his backpack and zeroed in. Witherspoon appeared even taller in a black beaver skin hat, something a mountain man might wear. He was planted on the veranda behind a telescope trained on the mountain. On Otto. Witherspoon pointed toward the mountain, made an emphatic gesture, and a figure who stood close to the house went back inside.

Uh-oh, Otto thought. He got to his feet, turned and climbed the final dozen meters to the summit where Winner stood with his legs spread, hands on hips.

"Look at this."

Otto joined Winner and stared at the unnaturally smooth surface of what appeared to be a red globe, approximately forty centimeters in diameter, buried in rock to its northern latitudes.

For a moment neither spoke.

"What is it?" Winner said, kneeling and extending his hand.

"Careful ..."

Winner touched the rock with his index finger, then splayed his fingers across the surface. "It's warm—probably from the sun."

"We're in deep shit," Otto said. "Witherspoon pointed at us and pitched a fit."

Winner looked up. "Really? What do you suppose they don't want us to see? This?"

Otto cautiously extended his own hand until it rested on the red stone. He rapped it with his knuckles. It felt like rock. He removed his pocket knife and tried to make a scratch. The rock was impervious. He picked up a shard of granite and tried that. Otto had never seen anything like it. It looked artificial, but why would anybody make such a thing, come up here and bury it? It looked like a bowling ball. And how had they done it? The top third of the stone protruded from gray granite as if it had broken surface from below. Just eased on through as if the rock were porridge.

Were there similar rocks atop Mounts Archimedes and Isosceles?

Winner saw what Otto was doing, picked up a jagged rock tooth and wanged it against the red stone. No mark.

"I wonder if it's some kind of monument," Winner said.

"To what? By whom? And how did they sink it in the rock like that?"

"Ancient cultures had a lot of knowledge which unfortunately just got lost. I believe that at one time Atlantis was the center of civilization, and their technology was far more advanced than ours. But all of it was lost, unfortunately, in some kind of cataclysm we can't even imagine."

Otto thought that was a lot of speculation but said nothing and reminded himself that although Winner seemed normal, he was still a movie star and they believed all sorts of crazy shit.

Let the brain waves wave. Think outside the box. He could use all the help he could get. Otto turned and looked south toward Mt. Isosceles where the snow gleamed in the lowering sun. He knelt, steadying his binocs on a natural cairn. Did he see a gleam of red at the summit or was it his imagination?

Otto rotated 110 degrees toward Mt. Pythagoras, its summit was lost in a fluff of cotton candy. The eagle was back, circling over the lake. Winner tapped him on the shoulder and handed him a sandwich wrapped in foil.

"Had the Stanley make up lunch."

They ate in companionable silence approached by several fearless pika to whom Winner tossed crumbs. When they finished Winner gathered the trash and jammed it in a paper bag, which he put in his knapsack.

They returned to the red dome like moths drawn to flame. Otto removed his cell phone and used the camera function to take several pictures of the rock from various angles. He immediately uploaded the image to the National Security Director.

"Gentlemen!" a man shouted. Otto quickly shoved the phone in his pocket.

Bob Casey and another man, a giant with a black beard who might have been Paul Bunyan strode toward them in camo outfits. Both men were red-faced and sweating heavily.

Otto and Winner waited like guilty school boys.

CHAPTER
FORTY-NINE
BLOOD OATH

Monday afternoon.

There was a road, if you could call it that, up the backside of the mountain. You could wrest a 4X4 to within two klicks of the top. The two employees said nothing as they led their chastened guests grimly down the back slope, rocks skittering with every step, to their bashed, ancient Toyota Land Cruiser.

"Put on those seatbelts, gentlemen," Casey said. "It's a matter of liability. You should understand that, Mr. Winner."

"I'm very sorry," the actor said hanging his head.

"There's a reason we have rules, gentlemen," Casey said pedantically. Otto braced himself for a lecture but Casey fell into silence.

The road had a forty degree grade in places. Casey proceeded at a dead crawl. Several times Otto feared the old SUV would tip over.

Below the timberline the rutted path gave way to a gravel road that wound through the forest. It took a half hour to work its way back to where the pavement ended, by Otto's and Winner's cabin. The parking lot was now more than half full and men were heading toward the lodge trailing rolling suitcases or hefting backpacks. Casey pulled up beneath the log porte-cochère. "Mr. Witherspoon is waiting for you in his office. Arthur, would you show them the way?"

The lumberjack got out and led them into the lobby, which contained a dozen men waiting to check in. They looked distinguished, semi-famous. Otto spotted a popular radio talk show host. The lumberjack hustled the boys through the lobby, walked down the hall and motioned with a ham-like hand to Witherspoon's open door.

Witherspoon waited primly behind his desk, hands folded before him. He gestured for Otto and Winner to sit in captain's chairs. The lumberjack quietly but firmly shut the door. Otto felt like a schoolboy called before the principal.

Witherspoon reached into his pocket and put on a pair of *pince nez*, resembling Uncle Creepy more than ever. "Gentlemen, there's a reason we have rules. It's a matter of liability. Did you read the by-laws as I requested?"

"We're very sorry," Winner said with genuine contrition.

"Several men have lost their lives attempting to scale those peaks."

"I understand. It won't happen again."

"I hope not, Mr. Winner. It took some persuasion to get certain board members to approve your visit. The last actor we invited to the Grove was Ronald Reagan."

Otto had been looking at Witherspoon the whole time. "I'm sorry too."

"Look," Winner said. "If you're worried we'll talk about what we saw up there, don't."

Witherspoon shifted his gaze back to Winner. "What did you see?"

"That red sphere buried in the rock. Come on. That's why you don't want people going up there. Let's not pretend it's not there."

Witherspoon clasped his hands again and leaned back, weighing his words carefully. "Gentlemen, that sphere is believed to be an Anasazi artifact dating back six thousand years. It wasn't discovered until after Pawnee Grove was established. We are an institution that puts a high premium on privacy. We choose not to make that artifact known to the scientific world not only to preserve our privacy, but to preserve this area which is virtually untouched since the founding of the Grove."

Otto was unaware the Anasazi had ever crossed the Rockies, but he said nothing. It was a plausible story. He badly wanted to ask about the other two peaks but he forced himself to remain silent.

Winner felt no such reticence. "What kind of ancient artifact has a perfectly smooth surface like that? It looked like a bowling ball!"

"Ancient peoples had far more skills than we credit them. Look at the Mayan calendar, accurate two millennia into the future. Look at the pyramids. A Mayan pyramid was recently discovered in Georgia. It's entirely reasonable to suppose the Anasazi quarried the rock elsewhere, chipped away at it until it was spherical and then polished the surface until it was smooth."

"Very possible," Otto said. Left unsaid was how the stones had been sunk into the rock.

"Mr. Witherspoon, once again, we apologize. I appreciate the invitation and I will do nothing to jeopardize our stay here."

Witherspoon smiled grimly. "Gentlemen, Pawnee Grove has always looked to our Native American heritage for guidance."

He opened his top desk drawer and withdrew a sheathed hunting knife with a sheep's horn handle. "Gentlemen, are you prepared to take a blood oath?"

Winner giggled. "You're kidding."

Witherspoon reached into a side desk drawer and withdrew a brass candle holder with a pan-like base and a three inch fat white stub. He set it on the desk and lit it with a kitchen match. He ran the edge of the blade back and forth across the flame, waved it around until it cooled and handed it to Winner.

"If you want to stay you'll swear on the blood of your ancestors and the blood of your children that you will say nothing about the mountain top now, or ever."

Winner ran the blade across the palm and held it up to show Witherspoon the bleeding cut. "I so swear."

Witherspoon took the knife and handed it to Otto.

"Mind if I sterilize that first?" Otto said. "Not that I think my good friend Gabe has AIDS or anything."

Witherspoon produced a bottle of rubbing alcohol and a box of tissues, which Winner used to clean his palm, and Otto used to clean the blade. Otto drew the blade across his left palm, feeling the razor-sharp steel brutally slice the flesh. He held up his hand. A drop of blood fell on Witherspoon's desk.

"I so swear."

"Well then, gentlemen, you may want to freshen up. We meet for cocktails in fifteen minutes."

CHAPTER FIFTY
THE BLOOD OF THE WHITE MAN

Monday evening.

Light fell early in the mountains even in summer. By the time Otto and Winner showered and put on fresh clothes, guests had already begun to gather on the broad stone veranda overlooking the lake. From the veranda, a verdant lawn descended fifty meters to the rock where the trucked-in soil stopped and nature began. Efficient-looking men in blue blazers and tan slacks were setting up folding chairs facing the lake and a wooden dais that had been carried out. Citronella torches surrounded the seating area.

On the veranda white-liveried attendants dispensed drinks from a portable bar. A buffet table contained cold cuts, buns, salads and condiments. Otto wore cargo pants and a yellow knit golf shirt with a tiny golfer embossed in red. Winner wore sharply creased gray Dockers and a red and blue Hawaiian shirt with the tails out. They made their way through the murmuring crowd to the bar. Otto got a beer and a bottled water. Winner got a gin and tonic. People acknowledged the famous face with smiles and nods. They saw Goldfarb across the way glad-handing a well-known producer.

A tall man with graying hair came up and stuck out his hand. "Mel Tyler, Tyler Aeronautics. Say, my boy thinks you rule the world, Mr. Winner."

"Please call me Gabe."

They shook hands. Winner promised to give Tyler a signed copy of his boxed DVDs. The ringing of a cook's triangle cut through the conversation. Everyone looked to Bob Casey who was banging on the gong with a soup tureen. "If I may have your attention, people, please take your seats on the lawn for the invocation and impromptus."

The sun was a burnt macaroni strip over the mountains as Otto and Winner took seats on the end of the third row. A quick head count showed at least fifty campers. Amidst the quiet rustling and clinking of ice, Witherspoon emerged from the main lodge wearing an Indian war bonnet that made him seem even taller and carrying a war club/pipe. As he walked toward the podium a half dozen employees as well as a half dozen campers seated in the first row began to bang on pots and pans and even a set of bongo clubs that someone had brought while chanting "Hey na na na ... hey na na na ..."

Against the majestic backdrop of Mt. Pythagoras, to which a narrow band of gold clung to the very top, Witherspoon took his place behind the dais. Gripping the sides of the oak dais, which bore a bas relief carving of a bonneted warrior astride his horse above the Grove logo, Witherspoon waited for the murmur of conversation to die down. Men in blue blazers wheeled out carts loaded with Thermoses and red Solo cups.

Witherspoon held the club toward the lodge. "Dog brothers!" he thundered in a sonorous voice. The valley was a natural amphitheater, his words bouncing off the rocks and pinging back. "Welcome to the 118th annual gathering of the tribes and celebration of our father the sun and our mother the moon!"

Applause, war whoops, whistles. Otto looked around. Fortune 500 CEOs stomped their feet and stuck fingers in their mouths. Some of them looked soused already.

Witherspoon fixed the audience with a steely glare and a twinkle in his eye. "Tonight we honor those brave warriors who have gone to the valley of eternal spring, those who walk among us, and those yet to come. I hold in my hand the speaker's pipe. Whomsoever holds the speaker's pipe must be listened to."

"Bad grammar!" someone yelled.

The attendants began filling solo cups and passing them down the rows.

"As we weep for those needlessly slaughtered, we pray for the souls of their killers, for we are but mud following in the Great Father's image. The world was once a garden of Eden riding on the back of a great turtle! Then the white man came, he raped, he pillaged, and he took!"

Boos and hisses. Witherspoon tamped it down. "Kind of like you, Bill," he said looking at the software billionaire in the first row. The billionaire laughed along with the rest of the crowd.

"My ghost warriors are now handing out the blood of the white man, which we drink in atonement and to mark the passing of another year in which we have all grown wiser!"

Laughter and jokes.

Witherspoon held up a cup. "Wankantanka hear our prayer! Thank you for the rain and air! Thank you for the food we eat— the corn, the schnapps, the buffalo meat ..."

Someone muttered, "The ostrich roams the great Sahara ..."

Otto surreptitiously upended his bottled water, emptying it. While all eyes were on Witherspoon, he carefully poured half his drink into the bottle, screwed the cap back on and slipped it into a pant pocket. It was full dark now and nobody paid him the slightest attention.

"Drink up, dog brothers!" Witherspoon cried. The tribe needed no urging.

Otto put a hand on Winner's arm and sniffed what remained of his own drink. He dipped the tip of his tongue in the red mixture and concluded it was a Bloody Mary with an odd, subtle undertone. He quietly poured the remainder of his drink beneath the chair.

Winner followed suit, but he had already taken a sip.

"As you know," Witherspoon boomed, "we have a serious side. Pawnee Grove was always intended to be a modern Chautauqua, a place where the foremost thinkers of the day could present new ideas. It was here Henry Ford first articulated the idea of the automobile assembly line. Mark Twain outlined what he believed to be the future of the newspaper business. In recent years the subjects have ranged from faster-than-light travel to new ways of extracting natural gas.

"A record number of you have requested the pipe tonight so we may not get you all in, but there's always tomorrow night. It's first come, first serve. Mel, the speaker's pipe is yours."

The tall aeronautics executive stood and approached the podium, accepting the ceremonial pipe with a grin. Witherspoon stepped down, sat in the front and removed his war bonnet. Sis Boom Ba's eerie wail drifted faintly from the kitchen.

"Dog brothers!" Tyler began brandishing the pipe. "It was in 1994 that Konstantin Tsiolkovsky first proposed an orbital elevator to carry men beyond earth's gravitational boundary. The geostationary orbital tether would have to be a minimum thirty-five kilometers in length. That's twenty-three miles. Until recently, such a project was deemed unfeasible because we lacked the knowledge and materials. Could such a thing support its own weight without crashing back to earth? Where is the best place to build such a thing?

"I am pleased to announce that Tyler Aeronautics has developed a carbon nanotube that meets all the requirements of the geostationary orbital tether ..."

The engineer paused gripping the sides of the podium. He grinned. An orange glow gleamed behind his eyes. He opened his mouth to speak and a tiny cloud of vapor escaped. Otto bolted from his seat and before anyone could stop him, leaped onto the podium, ducked, hefted Tyler in a fireman's carry and ran toward the lake.

CHAPTER FIFTY-ONE BONFIRE

Monday night.

The water was shockingly cold. Within seconds, Otto's toes had gone numb. He staggered in up to his waist and dropped the bigger man into the lake. Vibration transferred through the water. Otto felt the explosion and staggered back, falling, turning over and swimming away beneath the surface as the engineer erupted in flame. A wash of super-heated water rolled over Otto. He stood, shielding his eyes from the boiling conflagration, dimly aware of a stirring and muttering on the lawn, chairs overturned, tables upended, men running for the trees.

His legs were numb from the knee down.

The lawn was lit up like day from the ball of flame in the lake, a blazing nova whose strobing light illuminated the herky-jerk motion of movers and shakers abandoning their seats and running for their cars like the zombie apocalypse.

"Come out of the water now!" someone yelled. Otto tried to catch his bearings.

"Come out of the water now! Put your hands behind your head!"

At first Otto was blinded by the patio spotlights that had all been turned on. It took him a minute for his eyes to adjust. Bob Casey stood in a shooter's stance at the shore with his pistol trained on Otto's middle, luridly lit like a scene in a Roger Corman movie. From behind the spotlights. In front, the blazing ball.

"I didn't kill him!" Otto said. "I tried to save him!"

Witherspoon joined Casey. "Why'd you kill him, White?"

Two other staff stood nearby, pistols in their hands. The last guest hot-footed it toward his cabin. Most of the lawn chairs had been tipped over in the mad scramble and red solo cups dotted the yard.

Otto shuffled out of the water hands out, palms up.

"Down on your knees!" Casey yelled. "Hands behind the head!"

Otto did as he was instructed. While Casey held a gun on him, Burt approached with handcuffs.

"Hey, wait a minute! One cotton pickin' minute!"

All eyes save Caseys', which were glued on Otto, turned to Gabe Winner who stood to the side with his hands visible. "What's the matter with you guys? You all know about the spontaneous human combustions, right? Otto was trying to save Tyler's life!"

There was a moment of stunned silence. Who did he think he was? The Detonator?

"What spontaneous human combustions?" one of the crew said.

"I'm a federal agent," Otto said. "My badge is in my right front pocket."

Casey motioned for Otto to pull it out. Burt stepped back. Otto slowly withdrew his badge holder, flipped it open and handed it to Burt who looked at it and handed it to Casey.

"Are you armed?" Casey said.

"No," Otto replied, still on his knees. "And what has that got to do with anything. I thought you encouraged visitors to pack."

Casey conferred with Witherspoon. Otto couldn't hear what they said.

Casey holstered his weapon. "Apparently the police are on their way. You'll have to stay here and talk to them."

Otto got to his feet. "I intend to. First I have to get out of these clothes."

Casey handed Otto his badge back. "You might have informed us."

"Need to know, Mr. Casey. I'm sure you understand that."

A minute later Winner zipped up in one of the golf carts. Otto got in and they whirred up the lawn, onto the blacktop and into the forest, the cart's weak lights barely showing the way. The cool evening air and wet clothes chilled Otto to his marrow. At the cabin Otto hurriedly stripped and took a hot shower. He locked the "blood of the white man" in the cabin safe next to his Ruger.

In his room with the door shut Otto used the Ocelot to phone Gus Alvarez.

"Alvarez," the agent answered.

Behind him, Otto heard dogs barking, kids laughing, other voices. "Gus, very sorry to interrupt your evening."

"Go ahead."

Otto told Alvarez what had happened.

"I'm on my way," Alvarez said without hesitation. "Don't let anyone touch the body."

Otto phoned Margaret Yee and left a brief message describing what had happened.

Winner was smoking a joint when Otto came out of the bathroom.

He offered the joint to Otto. Otto shook his head.

"Helps me relax."

"What just happened?" Otto said. "What did you see?"

"At first I thought you'd just gone nuts. I didn't catch the signals until you were almost up there. Then I understood instantly."

"Did you notice any unusual activity among the campers?"

Winner shook his head. "Everybody stood up when you ran to the water. Most of them must have thought it was part of the show. Nobody realized what was going on until he burst into flame."

"Why now?" Otto said. "There's never been an SHC at the Grove before. Whatever it is, it's happening faster. Like somebody's losing control."

"I know. Like, all of a sudden they're everywhere."

By the time they returned to the main lodge, an ambulance and a Larimer County Deputy had arrived. Otto found the deputy on the veranda talking to Burt. Otto looked around for Witherspoon and Casey. They were nowhere to be seen.

Otto pulled out his badge. "Officer, I'm Agent White."

The deputy took the badge and examined it. "You want to tell me what happened, Agent White?"

Otto gave him the rundown. "Where are Witherspoon and Casey? They were just here."

The deputy looked around. "Haven't seen them."

A team of EMTs went up the log steps, through the lobby and the back door with a folding gurney. At the shore they popped it into shape and waded into the lake. They fished around for the cadaver and placed it on the gurney. They wheeled it out of the lake.

Otto ran after them.

"Leave it there, boys!" he called waving his badge. "We've got this one."

One of the EMTs came out of the water in hip waders, walked up to Otto and snatched the badge from his hand, looked at it, handed it back and walked away muttering.

Otto went up to the patio. The deputy had come out back.

"Right now, it's just me," the deputy said, "but in the next twenty minutes this place is going to be crawling with cops. We'd better make sure that the remaining witnesses stick around."

The deputy turned to greet two more Larimer County cruisers as they pulled into the lot.

Otto walked into the lodge up to the desk and looked for the big leather ledger. It was missing. He checked Witherspoon's office. He went out onto the deck and watched the EMTs retrieve something that looked like a withered black branch and set it on the gurney.

The deputy returned with a Larimer County Sheriff. Like every sheriff and deputy Otto had ever seen, he was a very big man with the shoulders of an ox. He and Otto shook hands.

"Did you know Tyler was going to light up like that?"

"Of course not. I never expected it to take place here but when I realized what was happening I tried to get him into the lake to put out the fire."

"Walk with me," the sheriff said, stepping off the veranda onto the lawn and heading toward the gurney. The thing that lay on the gurney looked like a Giacometti sculpture. One limb—an arm or a leg—had been separated. Some hair and skin still clung to the skull.

"A federal team will arrive shortly. We'll take possession of the body. I'll be happy to sign for it."

The sheriff stood with his arms crossed staring at Tyler's grotesque remains. "That's fine. This one's a little outside our purview."

Otto saw the red and blue lights reflecting off the tall pine on the other side of the lodge. More cops. He looked around. Winner was gone. Probably went back to the cabin or using a lodge phone to talk to Stella.

Gus Alvarez and a young agent arrived in a van at seven forty-five followed by a plain brown Crown Vic with Lon Barnett and another agent. Witherspoon's and Casey's cars remained in the parking lot, but there was no sign of the two men.

CHAPTER FIFTY-TWO
CHEYENNE MOUNTAIN

Monday night.

Otto left the Denali at the lodge and rode with Alvarez and Tyler's body sealed in a rubber bag down the mountain. The Junior G-Man drove.

"How's Steve?" Otto said. Alvarez turned around in the shotgun seat. "Steve's fine. Carrie loves him. We're taking the body to Cheyenne Mountain where we've set up an autopsy lab with the help of the Air Force." Alvarez brought Otto up to speed regarding the other autopsies. There had been no progress in analyzing the unknown compound. The Russians were not cooperating.

Otto pulled the blood of the white man from his pocket. "They had everybody drinking this. I'm thinking there's something in it."

Alvarez took the clear plastic bottle and sealed it in a zip-lock evidence bag that he placed in a gym bag open on the seat next to Otto. By now it was nine p.m. Barnett and the other agent remained at camp to interview the employees. The guests had fled like a mass jail break. No one wanted to be associated with the incident.

Otto related everything that had happened since he and Winner had arrived at the camp. Alvarez waited until he was finished.

"You think this red stone on top of the mountain has something to do with it?"

"They've gone to a lot of trouble to prevent people from looking at it. And those spectrographs don't lie. There's some kind of extreme energy sloshing around between the three summits."

The driver turned on the lights and siren when they hit the interstate. Otto removed his spiral pad and pen and wrote down the names of every guest he could remember. They could all be at risk. There had been no new conflagrations since Otto went up the mountain but word was spreading on the internet that it was some kind of disease, worse than AIDS, cooked up by the CIA or Al Qaeda or North Korea.

As they passed through Denver, Otto dozed off. He woke as they drove up the winding road to Cheyenne Mountain outside Colorado Springs. The former NORAD HQ had been converted into the ultimate survival bunker.

Otto sat up and looked out at the sodium-lit tarmac. The van stopped at a checkpoint. A soldier asked the agent to turn off the engine and for everyone to produce ID. A second soldier opened the rear of the van, flashed a light inside and looked. He got inside and unzipped the body bag, wincing and turning away. A third got down on his back and scooted beneath the van with a flashlight. The first soldier checked their names off against a list and waved them through.

They passed through another checkpoint, this one manned by soldiers carrying automatic weapons. The entrance to the tunnel itself was lined with ten foot hurricane fence topped with concertina wire and looked like the entrance to the Holland Tunnel. The soldiers waved them through and they drove inside the mountain through meter-thick, twenty-five ton blast doors. Twenty meters in the van stopped and the driver hopped out. Alvarez and Otto got out as well. It was warm inside the cave. Otto was surprised. He looked around.

The inside of the mountain had been hollowed out to create an enormous room the length of a football field. Christ-like shrouds had been affixed to the ceiling and walls to catch any falling debris. A series of prefab modules rested on giant coil springs that served as shock absorbers in event of a direct strike. Cables crisscrossed the interior, lights gleaming at every intersection. The modules were laid out on either side of Main Street, which ran down the center of the cavern and had its own green street sign.

Alvarez spoke briefly with an Air Force captain.

"You look about spent, Holmes, Captain has an apartment for you to crash in."

That seemed like a good idea. Otto was exhausted from the hike and the swim. From the sheer pressure of trying to remember every little detail.

The captain wore fatigues and introduced himself. "Captain Jack Warren."

"Otto White. Just call me Otto."

The captain walked down Main Street. "The modules are sound-proof so if atomic war busts out while you're sleeping, I'll come and wake you."

"Thank you, Captain Jack."

The captain paused in front of a big, off-white prefab box with square windows and rounded corners. Otto stumbled into the unit and pulled the door shut. The only sound came from the subdued whoosh of the air transfer. Inside a small bedroom was a metal-framed cot with an olive drab blanket. Otto peeled off his clothes and pulled up the covers. He was asleep within minutes.

He was on an airplane. First, it was military transport, then civilian. They were flying right down Main Street of a major city with skyscrapers on either side, ten feet above the asphalt. The wings did not catch on the buildings for some reason, but it was evident to every passenger that the flight was in trouble and there was a good deal of anxiety.

Otto could not take his eyes off the cockpit door. It swung open and a blazing man stepped out—burning from toes to scalp. Alarms went off. Oxygen masks fell. The cabin filled with smoke. The burning figure said, "Folks, we're about to experience a little turbulence."

The whole plane shook violently.

Otto woke up. A wild-eyed Alvarez shook him by the shoulder.

"What?"

"Get up. You have to see this."

CHAPTER
FIFTY-THREE
HOLY SHIT!

Tuesday morning.

Otto swung his legs over the cot and sat up, rubbing his eyes. He glanced at the digital clock on the nightstand. Five-thirty. He'd been asleep for six hours. It would be early morning outside. He pulled on his pants, socks and sneakers.

Otto followed Alvarez out of the module where an Air Force cadet waited at the wheel of an electric golf cart. "What?"

"You have to see it."

The cart zoomed silently down Main Street and took a right turn into a side tunnel with "MASSACHUSETTS AVENUE" stenciled in white on the cave wall, passing through another set of massive steel doors. At the end of this sub chamber was a large white trailer guarded by two military police clutching H&K automatic pistols. An air conditioning unit crouched on the roof growling. Thick crenellated tubes jutted from the roof connected to flexible couplers like giant drinking straws. Next to the door hung several metal boxes containing a telephone, a keypad, and various meters and dials.

"Get your ID out" Alvarez advised.

One MP checked Otto's photo ID against a detailed sheet on a clipboard that also bore Otto's likeness. He waved them through. The stairs were made of pine planking on cinderblocks. Three steps up. Alvarez shut the door behind them. It was so cold in the trailer, Otto could see his breath. The interior was one big room with an autopsy table covered with a white sheet through which disturbing black stains had crept. There were cadaver drawers turned lengthwise to accommodate the space and there were several work stations with computers. An old man in a stained gray suit and twisted purple tie sat in front of one of the monitors transfixed.

"Otto, Larimer County Coroner Abel Roth. Dr. Roth, Otto White."

The old man turned and stood and shook Otto's hand on autopilot. "Never seen anything like it."

"Your quick action," Alvarez said, "led to partial preservation of the head. Interestingly, the brain appears to be cooked. We took a routine X-ray and this is what showed up."

Otto sat at the monitor and looked at the picture on the screen. At first he had difficulty making sense of what he was seeing. He saw the telltale ghost X-ray outline of the skull. Alvarez pointed. Otto followed Alvarez' finger to the point where the spine meets skull.

"Holy shit," he said

Nestled atop the spinal column was a tiny space ship.

CHAPTER
FIFTY-FOUR
The Missing

It looked like a sewing spindle with stubby little wings. It was blacker than the blackest night—as if a negative had been burned onto the image. According to the scroll across the bottom of the screen, it was one millimeter long—smaller than a grain of rice.

"Is there anything alive in there?" Otto said voice breaking.

"Not of which we're aware. Of course, we've tried signaling but there was no response. I think it's cooked."

"Can we extract it?" Otto said.

"That's the plan."

Dr. Roth cleared his throat. "I'm not the man to do this."

"Thank you, Doctor," Alvarez said, turning to the tall man and shaking his hand. "We appreciate you're coming down here on such short notice to help us."

"Anything to help the boys in blue."

Roth hefted a little black bag and left the module where a soldier waited to take him outside the complex.

"Aren't you concerned he'll talk about this?" Otto said.

Alvarez waved a sheet of paper. "Non-disclosure agreement. He's a veteran. We have nothing to worry about. Not from him. Unfortunately the cat's ass is out of the bag."

Alvarez sat at the terminal and with a few strokes brought up the *Drudge Report*, whose illustration was the money shot from *Wicker Man* over the screaming red headline: *TERRORISTS BURNING US ALIVE?*

Below that in mere red type: *TYLER RAPE VICTIM COMES FORTH.*

Otto grimaced. He needed to call Yee, but not even the Ocelot could transmit from inside the mountain. There was a phone on the wall, but who knew where that led.

"Who's doing the extraction?" Otto said.

"Surgeon from St. Jude's in Denver. He'll be here this afternoon."

"What about the blood of the white man?"

"Absolut vodka, Spicy V8 and an unknown element identical to that identified in Darling's remains. It has a polycarbonate-like structure but we believe it's metal."

"I've got to report," Otto said. "To do that I have to go outside."

Alvarez motioned toward the door. "Let's go."

Otto had lost all track of time and was surprised when the sun hit him in the face as their jitney exited the mountain. Otto got out and walked to the end of the parking lot, from there he could see all the way down the valley to Colorado Springs and the plains beyond.

He pressed his uplink and listened while his call pinged around the cosmos. Ten seconds later, it rang.

Yee answered. "What's going on?"

"You know about Tyler?"

"Yes."

"We found some kind of projectile above his spinal column. It looks like a tiny spaceship."

A long pause followed.

"A tiny spaceship?"

"Yes, ma'am. Unfortunately it appears to be crisped."

"Is this for real, Mr. White?"

"Yes, ma'am. I know it sounds crazy. It might be a projectile shot with some kind of air gun or something."

"Who knows about this?"

"Gus Alvarez, the Larimer County Coroner and me. The coroner signed the secrecy act. He's ex Air Force."

"Keep it that way. Anything you need," Yee said.

"Did you receive the video?"

"Yes. This is very troubling. However, for the time being, we're going to keep this among ourselves. I want to give Hornbuckle enough rope to hang himself, and there are bigger fish to fry."

"I understand."

"You are doing an excellent job, Mr. White. Goodbye."

Yee hung up. The jitney driver watched Otto from fifteen meters. It was six-thirty. It would be five in L.A. Otto phoned Winner. He got Winner's voice mail.

"Gabe, just wanted to thank you for your service to your country. I'll be in touch when this winds down. You have my number."

He wanted to call Stella, but for what? He couldn't tell her what was going on. He really had nothing to say to her except I love you, I was wrong, please come back. He'd tried it and it hadn't worked.

Alvarez walked toward him pocketing his own cell phone.

"Still no sign of Witherspoon and Casey. They identified a vehicle rented to Ralston Goldfarb. If the car's still there, where's Goldfarb?"

"They must all still be up there," Otto said.

"Come on. Let's go find them."

CHAPTER
FIFTY-FIVE
BY REASON OF INSANITY

Monday afternoon and evening.

Stella accompanied Lester Durant from the Harriet Kramer Detention Facility in Manassas to the Clempson County Courthouse in Alexandria. The state-appointed board of forensic psychiatrists was about to deliver their verdict.

Durant looked younger than his twenty-six years, as if a high school kid caught up in events he didn't understand. His curly black hair was cut to the nub. A bullet crease formed a puckered pink valley over his right eye. His prison-issue day-glo green jumpsuit hung on his thin frame like a tent. He was shackled at the wrists to a chain around his waist. His legs were chained together. They rode in a Virginia Dept. of Corrections van with an armed guard and the driver.

"How you doing, Lester?" Stella asked.

"I'm good, ma'am," he said in a soft southern drawl. "Whatever happens I can deal with it."

For Durant, this was a major speech.

Stella had kept Durant off the stand to prevent him from talking about the spiders. A bolus of dread crouched in her gut that they would find him sane and ready to stand trial. There was a free-floating consensus that far too many mass murderers were escaping justice via the insanity defense. It would become a media circus. Durant had already inspired countless internet chat groups and pages, disturbed individuals genetically prone to conspiracy theories as well as late-night comics. The van stuttered through traffic to the courthouse, a Georgian revival with Doric columns and a marble floor.

The carnival waited. Four major networks, Fresh Young Faces pushing forward pushing microphones. Stella and Durant circumvented this by entering the underground garage guarded by federal marshals.

Accompanied by an armed guard they took the elevator from the basement parking garage to the fourth floor and entered the Miriam C. Rosenkranz Courtroom. The board of experts were already seated in the jury box: four men, two women and at least two dozen doctorates. Stella and Durant took their seats at the defendant's table, chains jingling. The seal of the Commonwealth of Virginia hung on the bench. Behind the judge's seat, flanked by American and Virginian flags, was a gilt-framed painting of early settlers fighting savage Indians. Many groups had tried unsuccessfully over the years to have it removed for "insensitivity."

"All rise for the right honorable Justice William Graves."

A squat black man in judicial robes with white hair and glasses emerged from his chambers and took his place behind the bench.

"Judge," the bailiff said, "this is Case 43,209, Commonwealth of Virginia versus Lester Durant."

The judge peered over his specs. "Will the defendant please approach the bench."

Stella and Durant stood in front of the judge.

"Ladies and gentlemen, have you reached a decision regarding the defendant's ability to stand trial?"

The head of the committee, a tall woman in a navy pantsuit, stood. "We have your honor. We find the defendant incompetent to stand trial and recommend that he be remanded to the state for a period of observation until such time that he is ready to stand trial, if ever."

"Thank you ladies and gentlemen of the jury. You are dismissed."

The judge turned to Stella. "Does the defendant have anything to say before I issue my ruling?"

"No, your honor," Stella said.

"Very well. The defendant is remanded to Tuscadero State Hospital for the Criminally Insane until such time as he is either judged competent to stand trial or no longer deemed a threat to society. Thank you all. You're free to go."

Durant remained unaffected by the ruling as if he'd already checked out. Stella squeezed his arm.

"Lester—this is good news!"

Stella and Durant rode the elevator in silence, each with their own thoughts. They reached the basement parking level. Stella walked with Durant to the van. They had little in common. He was a black boy from the South. She was a princess from the West.

"Lester, I'll be checking in with you in a few days when you get settled. If you need me for any reason you have my numbers."

No response. Lester was on another planet.

Stella turned to go. As Lester was getting into the van, he turned. "Mizz Darling, there were spiders in the courtroom."

Stella was relieved he hadn't spoken up, not that it would have affected the judge's decision. Normally when she won a big case like this—and getting Lester ruled insane was a big deal—she celebrated. But there was no one with whom to celebrate. She hadn't heard from Gabe since he'd gone up to Pawnee Grove. Winner hadn't answered her calls.

She didn't have any girlfriends. It bothered her. She wondered what was wrong with her. It wasn't that she was unlikable. She just hadn't gotten to know anybody well enough in the ten years she'd been in D.C. How pathetic was that? The women she met were either obsessively career-oriented or married or both.

Her sixty hour work week precluded hanging out at athletic facilities or bars, the two biggest meet and greet venues in the city. Business-related parties usually involved the same old corporate clients and the unlovely Washington criminal defense corps.

Lawyers. *Brrrrr!*

As long as her job was her life, she was unlikely to develop any strong friendships here. She pined for Gabe even as she told herself it couldn't last. They were two ships passing in the night. Their worlds were mutually exclusive. Stella knew a few show biz lawyers and they were even creepier than criminal defense attorneys.

Stella took a taxi to her offices at Bing, Adolfo and Thompson in the Gerhardt Building on K Street. She met with two clients. At six fifteen, Stella left the office and had dinner by herself at the Husun Grill. She tried Gabe again and went straight to voice mail. He'd warned her that there would be no reception in the mountains, but she couldn't stifle a jagged little shard of worry.

She over tipped the waitress and took a taxi to her condo at 2020 12th St. NW.

She took a hot bath, cracked open a bottle of Coppola Chardonnay, and tilted back in her Barcalounger in her living room to watch the news.

A stern-faced male reader informed her that astrospace genius Mel Tyler had disappeared while hiking alone in the Rockies. When they mentioned the location, she put the pieces together. She didn't believe the cover story for one second, more likely Tyler was another burn victim.

She felt profoundly uneasy. Two men with whom she was close were up there and she hadn't heard from either of them all weekend. She had that edge-of-your-seat anxiety knowing she would be unable to sleep. She checked the TV listings—it was all shit as far as the eye could see. Two hundred and twelve channels and nothing to watch.

Stella debated taking a Nembutal given her by a client but they sometimes left her groggy in the morning. Fortunately, she had a light schedule that week—that meant she was only working fifty hours or so. She turned off the TV, went into her bedroom, sat on the bed, and took the Nembutal from her side table drawer, weighing the little capsule in her hand.

She was exhausted. What the hell. She reached for the glass of water she kept bedside. Her phone chirped. She glanced at the little window. Her heart went pitter-pat.

"Gabe! They found Durant crazier than a shit house rat! How are you?"

"Can you come up here?"

"I don't know. Why?"

"Have you seen a newspaper?"

"What, about Tyler? I saw it on the news."

Winner told her about the aerospace engineer's immolation. "The police are here now. I think you should take a look at what we found. I think Otto's gonna need a lawyer."

"Gabe, you sound funny. Are you all right?"

"Frankly, I'm gob-smacked by what we found. Besides. I miss you."

"I miss you too. I'll fly out tomorrow."

At last she was able to sleep.

CHAPTER FIFTY-SIX
RABBIT

Tuesday afternoon.

Hornbuckle had been haunting the Nuggets chat rooms for two days. Spider was all over the place offering advice to players and coaches, calling games, arguing with other fans. But was it the right Spider? There were spiders on the football, hockey and baseball chat rooms as well. He was monitoring a discussion on the NBA site when the following exchange occurred:

Quizguts: Hey—26 points—not too shabby!

Spider: Afflalo still sucks dead squirrel meat.

Spider appeared to be friends with one Quizguts, sex and age unknown. Spider and Quizguts had been going back and forth for days about man-on-man vs. zone. Finally, they agreed to meet at three p.m. Tuesday. Code language indicated they might be making a transaction.

Now that Colorado had legalized medical marijuana, dispensaries had sprung up on the fringes of every town that didn't specifically ban them. Fort Collins had recently booted all their MMJ shops, many of which moved to Boulder.

Boulder would *never* boot its MMJ shops.

The MMJ situation made Hornbuckle sick to his stomach. Everybody knew that the medical part was a load of horse shit. Too many people in Colorado enjoyed getting high. Too many people were making big bucks off home grows. Once the state got a taste of the tax revenue, Katy bar the door.

Kleiser was meeting Quizguts at the Full Throttle Coffee and Internet Bar in Arvada. Kleiser was a child of the suburbs. Strip malls and internet cafes were his native habitat. Hornbuckle tied a blue bandanna around the top of his head and wore mirrored gargoyles and baggy saggy cargo pants. He looked like a gang banger. He wore an Avalanche hoodie with a voluminous front pocket in which he stashed a .25 automatic.

He carried his laptop in an REI backpack. He went through a McDonald's on the way, stuffing two double cheeseburgers down his gullet while he drove. Hornbuckle cruised the Full Throttle on Schenk Boulevard, a bistro-bright coffee shop with blinding yellow trim and a number of round black tables on the sidewalk, separated from the hoi polloi by a wrought-iron fence.

Hornbuckle parked around the corner in front of a tattoo parlor. His ankle throbbed with every step. Punks rolled by on bikes and boards. A gangly youth on a long board headed his way with a cig dangling from his lower lip. Hornbuckle walked straight at him, daring the kid to run into him. The pierced and inked punk jumped off his Hellboy board at the last minute, executing a crude twist and bonk that brought the board down on the edge and sent him stumbling into the wall of an insurance agency. That punk was pissed. He rounded on Hornbuckle.

"Hey asshole!"

Hornbuckle stopped and turned. The punk took one look into his fathomless gray eyes, lowered his eyesight, grabbed his board and pedaled away like a one-legged soap box derby car. Halfway down the block he turned, raised his middle finger and fired his Carpathian shot: "Fuck you!"

It put a spring in Hornbuckle's step and a smile on his face. A half dozen students and punks occupied the outdoor tables. Hornbuckle went inside, stood in line behind a girl with a nice ass, ordered a double cappuccino with whipped cream and retreated to the corner table in the back from where he could see the entire cafe and out into the street. Above him hung a framed Toulouse-Lautrec print of a woman riding an old-fashioned bicycle with an enormous front wheel.

Typical socialist watering hole. Stacks of *Westword* and other seditious free newspapers sat on the cold fireplace mantle. Hornbuckle picked one up. It was filled with ads for marijuana dispensaries and sex services.

Framed quotes from Gandhi and Chairman Mao hung on the wall, as if the joint had been preserved since the sixties. Of course, the wireless, iPads, Blackberries, Nooks and laptops were new. Hornbuckle brought out his own laptop and spooled up, switching quickly from its FBI home page although he was in no one's line of sight.

Behind his hunter's blind Hornbuckle scanned the patrons dropping them into slots. Earnest pre-med. Junkie/musician. Eco-activist. Hornbuckle hit his hot spots: stratfor.com, MEMRI.com, hackersanonymous.com. *Drudge* and *Huffpo*. The horse had left the barn. Americans now lived in fear that anyone at any time could burst into flames. An editorial on one of the left wing hate sites said that the plague of spontaneous human combustions was Gaia's Revenge. All the victims were white heterosexual males except for two conservative black men reviled by the black community, and in that sense the burnings were to be welcomed.

BURN BABY BURN! read the headline.

Another site theorized that it was a sexually-transmitted disease.

The over-all consensus favored terrorists.

According to *Drudge*, hardware stores and Walmart were selling out of fire extinguishers and couldn't keep up with demand.

Hornbuckle looked up. A strapping young man in a Nuggets hoodie, wearing wrap-around shades and carrying a backpack stood at the counter. The afternoon sun hung in the window behind the man whose face was hidden in shadow inside the hood. Hornbuckle's pulse quickened. He quickly closed his laptop, slipped it into the backpack and hitched the backpack over one shoulder.

Hoodie took his drink and went outside taking a seat at a table against the window. It was either Spider or Quizguts, and the other would be along in a minute. Hornbuckle dawdled at the magazine rack, one eye out front. And here came the other, cruising up an on long board like the Silver Surfer. Hornbuckle was glad he waited, because the board punk was Kleiser, skull gleaming. Kleiser wore a wife beater exposing the extensive tribal tattoo on his left arm.

Easy as pie.

Hornbuckle sauntered toward the door as Kleiser entered. Hornbuckle put a hand on his shoulder. "Black Widow?"

Kleiser looked at him with an expression of shock. Gripping Kleiser by the arm, Hornbuckle turned him around and marched him out of the coffee shop. The man in the Nuggets hoodie stared.

"Special Agent Hornbuckle, FBI. Let's take a walk."

With a Vulcan death grip on Kleiser, Hornbuckle marched him out of the wrought iron enclosure and steered him down the sidewalk toward his car.

"How do I know you're a federal agent?" Kleiser whined.

Hornbuckle reached into his front pant pocket for his badge. He had a split second adumbration of disaster before his backpack was ripped savagely from his shoulder throwing him off-balance and breaking the strap.

The board punk whom Hornbuckle had stopped sprinted diagonally across the street between traffic. The laptop contained highly classified information.

"Shit!" shouted Hornbuckle giving chase.

CHAPTER
FIFTY-SEVEN
THE ANTISEPTIC CRIB

Tuesday afternoon and evening.

Alvarez drove to his home across the street from the Botanical Gardens in his Ford Explorer. Otto rode shotgun. Alvarez had three kids. The two older boys were out, but fourteen-year-old Carrie was home on the broad veranda tweeting, texting and Facebooking in a chain-supported rocker. Like the window surrounds and details, the balustrade and rocker were painted forest green. A kidney of perfect lawn surrounded a mound of small fir and a couple aspen.

Alvarez spent a few minutes with his daughter while Otto fetched Steve. In the backyard, Steve was trying to hump one of the English setters, who turned on him and snarled. Steve was fixed but he tried to hump other dogs. Otto wondered if Steve could achieve orgasm, and whether it was wrong for him to think of jacking off his dog.

He put Steve in the vehicle. Alvarez came out the front door with a bulging gym bag. They stopped at Petco where Otto picked up a bag of Science Diet for Dogs. They drove up through Lyons and Estes Park, through a brief rain shower. It was three-thirty when they arrived at the lodge. A Larimer County Deputy waited at the gate to check their identification. He phoned the lodge to let them know.

The parking lot contained an FBI crime lab and several unmarked vehicles. Three expensive luxury vehicles including Goldfarb's rented Infiniti remained cordoned off with yellow tape.

Lon Barnett was happy to cede control of the operation to Otto.

"Any sign of Goldfarb, Witherspoon or Casey?" Otto asked.

"Nada," Barnett said.

"What about Gabe Winner?"

"I think he got a ride down with one of the other campers," Barnett said.

Otto went inside, Steve at his heels. Alvarez and Barnett remained on the front deck comparing notes. Otto used the land-line behind the counter to call Winner. It went straight to voice mail. He phoned Stella and it went straight to voice mail. Otto left a message to call him back.

Alvarez and Barnett entered the lodge. Barnett motioned for Otto to join them at some overstuffed furniture in front of the massive fireplace. Otto filled a plastic ice bucket with water and set it down next to his chair. Barnett pulled out an iPad and brought them up to speed.

"I've talked to the ten staff members who were here when I arrived last night. They all pretty much describe the same thing, which is what Otto told us. We have not yet entered Witherspoon's or Casey's private quarters. Figured I'd leave that to you."

"What about his computer?" Otto said.

"Haven't touched it."

"Will the employees submit to X-rays or EMR scans?" Alvarez said.

"I imagine they would."

"Can we arrange that ASAP? Lon, can you think of a facility that could do this for us?" Otto said.

"We have a good working relationship with St. Mary's. They have state-of-the-art equipment."

"Are the employees still here?" Alvarez asked.

"No. We let them go last night."

Steve licked Barnett's pants.

"Steve! Don't lick the pants."

Barnett pushed the dog gently away. "Is he a tracker?"

"He can track a snowflake through a blizzard. I have a feeling Witherspoon, at least, is still on the property."

"We checked every cabin," Barnett said, "and every guest room in the main house. We checked the outbuildings too. If they're here, they're well hidden."

"It's a big place," Otto said. "Plenty of room to hide."

"I'll show you to Witherspoon's quarters and you can take it from there."

"Otto," Alvarez said. "you take the apartment. I'll take the computer."

The caretaker's apartment was on the third floor of the three-story lodge overlooking the lake. Otto bade Steve sit while he examined the room from the open door, seeking telltale signs of improvised explosive devices through long habit. He entered the apartment followed by Steve. It consisted of a living room/kitchenette, a separate bathroom and a bedroom.

The living room was ten by twelve with a picture window overlooking the lake. Mt. Archimedes gleamed gold in the late afternoon sun. An old plaid fabric sofa faced a wall-mounted LCD HD TV. Otto recalled seeing the dish on the roof. The old coffee table in front of the sofa held several issues of *Reader's Digest* and *National Geographic* from the sixties. There was also one recent issue of *Vibe*. The place was immaculate. The walls were decorated with historic photos of the Grove from the beginning: Teddy Roosevelt, John D. Rockefeller, Harry Houdini, Nicola Tesla, Charles Lindbergh, all the way up to Bill Gates and Steve Jobs. Witherspoon began appearing in the photos in the early seventies.

There was nothing else of a personal nature. No photos of loved ones or Witherspoon's childhood. The room had a peculiar antiseptic quality as if it had been preserved for future generations.

Steve roamed the apartment sniffing.

Otto looked in the refrigerator. It contained a bottle of quinine water and a box of baking soda. That was all. The freezer contained a pair of desiccated ice trays. The kitchen cupboards held a few mismatched dishes, but the stove was spotless as was the floor. Witherspoon must have taken all his meals in the main kitchen or dining hall. Otto checked beneath the sink and found cleanser, Pine sol, window cleaning liquid and a half dozen other cleaning agents as well as a neatly stacked pile of clean rags.

The bed in the small bedroom was tightly made in military fashion with an olive drab blanket and white sheets. The bedroom closet held a number of suits and smelled of moth balls. The cheap laminate dresser contained dozens of identical black socks, boxer shorts and T-shirts. Nothing out of the ordinary. No pictures of family or friends, no porno, not even a radio. No books or magazines. It was a monk's quarters.

Otto carefully searched the closet shelves, opening the shoe boxes, going through the pockets in all the suits, shirts, and pants. Not even stray pennies. He went into the bathroom and opened the mirrored cabinet over the sink. It contained toothbrush, toothpaste, and floss. That was it. No aspirin, no cold remedies, none of the prescription drugs one would expect to find in a man of Witherspoon's age. Otto lifted the lid of the toilet tank. Nothing but water and float. He got on his knees and looked up underneath the sink counter for anything that might have been affixed to the underside. A wicker laundry hamper contained clothing. Otto chose a pair of boxer shorts and held it for Steve to sniff. Steve sniffed. Steve barooed. He had the scent.

On hands and knees, Otto looked beneath the bed. Nothing—not even dust bunnies. The lack of books and personal items was troubling, as if Witherspoon was only alive when he stood in front of others. Otto lay on the bed and slowly took in everything the caretaker saw. He stood on the bed and unscrewed the overhead lamp shade.

Satisfied that the room had given up its secrets, Otto and Steve took the stairway down to the first floor, opening a door onto the corridor. Alvarez was intent on Witherspoon's computer, spiral notepad at hand. Half the valley lay in shadow, including the lodge, as the sun sank.

"Room's clean," Otto said. "Find anything?"

"Mr. Witherspoon was well-versed on world affairs, which is damned odd considering that he was apolitical."

"We don't know that. This place tilts right."

"If he had strong beliefs he kept them to himself. I'm still trying to crack the e-mail. I'm about ready to knock off for the day. What say you?"

Otto shrugged. "Might as well. We're not going to find them at night."

CHAPTER

FIFTY-EIGHT

OTTERBOX

Tuesday evening.

The larder contained enough food to last all summer. Otto searched the walk-in freezer on the off chance it contained bodies. One of the sheriff's deputies had been a cook in the army and made chili to feed the two FBI agents and the two Larimer County Deputies who remained. They ate in the voluminous mess hall beneath glass-eyed trophies. Someone started a fire in the massive fieldstone fireplace and the diners congregated toward that end of the hall on picnic tables.

It reminded Otto of the Boy Scouts, which he'd joined over his father's objections.

After supper, Otto and Steve visited the bunkhouse, a pole-barn dormitory with monastic cells for the employees, a communal bath, and a rec room equipped with a flat screen, an Xbox, and a copious supply of DVDs. Otto flipped through the titles, which included the first three *Detonators* as well as *Mamacitas I through VI*. The Xbox held *Call of Duty: Modern Warfare 4*, a busman's holiday. Otto had played the original *Call of Duty* at Quantico waiting to be shipped out.

Casey's room overlooked the parking lot and was the size of a college dorm. On the wall was a framed poster of a surfer riding a monster wave, the only decoration. A clock/radio sat on the small bed stand. Otto picked it up, removed the battery panel and checked inside. He went through the night stand's drawer and found an antihistamine, some rubber bands, a paperback copy of *Great Expectations* and a set of car keys with a remote Honda fob. Underneath the bed was a slide out drawer. Inside were combat fatigues. One corner of the drawer remained blank as if something had recently been removed. He smelled gun oil.

Otto searched the closet, finding nothing of interest. Casey's discarded socks lay in a heap on the closet floor, but Otto had no interest in muddying Steve's clear scent of Witherspoon. Steve at his heels, he left the bunkhouse and walked out to the middle of the parking lot. He squeezed the key fob. A Honda Pilot beeped and flashed its lights.

Otto opened the driver's door and eased into the seat. Steve sat on the tarmac and watched, tail wagging. Otto searched under the seats and through the center console bin. He found Casey's registration in the glove compartment listing his home address at a condo in Colorado Springs.

Otto put the key in the ignition and started the vehicle. He looked at the digital odometer—it was in the nine hundreds. Casey wasn't one of those guys who carefully reset their trip odometers. Otto turned the engine off and opened the hood. Using a pocket flashlight, he poked around in the engine compartment, pulling up the windshield washer basin to see if anything was hidden inside.

The back of the vehicle contained snow shoes and heavy weather gear. The sunken tire bin held no surprises. There was a disturbing lack of personality in both Casey's and Witherspoon's quarters, almost as if they were only alive in front of others. As Otto and Steve headed back to the main lodge, he paused in the middle of the parking lot and looked up. Stars glinted like tiny lasers in the velvet dark. A sliver of moon peeked over the mountains to the northeast. Otto paused to inhale the dry, pine-scented air.

Thank you God for bringing me this far. Thank you for my health and loved ones.

Otto did not pray to God to help him with his assignment because such a prayer would have been frivolous if not blasphemous considering what God had on his plate.

They found Alvarez in Witherspoon's office still trying to find the password. It was nine-thirty.

"Gus—we have a lot of ground to cover tomorrow. You ought to knock off. I'm in Taylor—it's the last cabin toward the lake. You can take the other room."

Alvarez stretched and pushed himself back from the computer.

"Let's go," he said.

They walked in companionable silence beneath the ponderosa hearing the occasional call of a pika. The cabin had not been touched since Otto and Winner had used it twenty-four hours ago.

Otto said goodnight and went into his room. Steve hopped up on the bed.

A moment later Alvarez knocked on his door.

"It's open."

Alvarez walked in holding a flat plastic device with the word Otterbox on it. "What's this?"

CHAPTER
FIFTY-NINE
A JOG IN THE PARK

Tuesday afternoon.

Hornbuckle's ankle shot a bolt of pain with every impact as he ran after the punk. Kid had long legs and was a sprinter, but Hornbuckle had been a distance runner and still ran several miles a day. The punk led by twenty meters but you could tell he was flagging the way he gripped the backpack. He'd gas out from all the dope he smoked.

The punk dashed across six-lane Monroe Blvd. eliciting horn blasts, curses and middle fingers. Hornbuckle closed the gap as traffic prevented the punk from cutting straight across. Astonishingly, the punk leaped on the hood of a sedan causing it to sink with his weight. By the time the outraged driver was out of his vehicle, the punk had leaped atop a slow-moving Lincoln Town Car, onto a parked Prius, over the hedge-border and into Ghirardelli Park, a green space with bike lanes, picnic tables, and a fast-moving stream tumbling down from the Rockies.

The suspect rabbited past surprised picnickers and strollers heading upstream toward the mountains. He pounded on the bike trail, infuriating cyclists who pointed at the perfectly good adjacent dirt groove. Hornbuckle found his rhythm, stretching out in long, easy lopes, ignoring the stabbing pain in his right calf. Blood trickled into his sock. Maybe he should have seen a doctor, but it was too late for that now, not with his security clearance on the line.

The perp no longer bothered to look as he stretched his long legs for seven league leaps. Maybe he didn't smoke dope. Maybe he was one of those fitness freaks who liked to skate. Fifty meters on lay an oval tunnel over which ran Colorado Boulevard. Hornbuckle fingered the tiny automatic in his belt pouch. The tunnel was long and dark—if he found himself alone with the perp, he might risk a shot. But the .25 was notoriously inaccurate beyond six or seven meters.

Hornbuckle followed the perp into the tunnel. The temperature dropped ten degrees. Ahead he could see several bicyclists riding his way including a couple illegally riding side by side. They must not have seen the black clad punk because they were blocking his way as he came upon them. The punk shoved the girl's bike into the boy's causing both to go down, leaped over the tangled mess and pounded on.

The girl squealed in pain. The boy shouted, "HEY MOTHER-FUCKER!"

Hornbuckle leaped the girl like Jeremiah Johnson catapulting into the end zone, the bottom of his shoe scraping the top of her head. He emerged into bright sunlight on the other side of the tunnel just in time to see the perp disappear beneath a crest in the path. Hornbuckle redoubled his efforts, gritting his teeth and ignoring the pain that now shot all the way to his knee.

A stitch developed in his side as he topped the low hill. And then he caught a break. Twenty-five meters on, the perp stood in the middle of the bike lane, back to Hornbuckle, staring at a dense squadron of bicycles that not only covered the bike lane but spread out onto the narrow dirt paths on either side. No way could he get around that bunch. The mutant bikers, already stoked on numbers and Red Bull, screamed at him to get out of the way.

The perp looked back into the face of death. He unhooked the backpack and twirled it around his head—once, twice, three times—and hurled it out over the fast moving creek.

"FUCK!"

Hornbuckle didn't hesitate. He leaped the gorse and alder growing through the rocks, landed in the icy cold water and sank to his crotch. It took his breath away and shriveled his testicles. Hornbuckle waded out into the middle of the stream—his backpack was caught in the current heading his way fast. He had one chance to snag it. Feeling cautiously along the bottom, which was lined with slippery rocks, he waded out to where the water was over his bellybutton and grabbed his backpack.

The cycle mob hooted and honked as they flowed by. By the time Hornbuckle had crawled out of the stream and sat on the grass, the perp was long gone. Hornbuckle prayed his laptop hadn't been ruined. At least he'd prevented it from falling into enemy hands. He opened the backpack and upended the contents onto the dry grass. The laptop slipped out in its nylon sheath. He held the sheath over his lap, opened the laptop and booted up.

Much to his relief the FBI home page appeared. He'd saved it.

But he'd lost Kleiser.

He was too exhausted even to curse. Joggers and cyclists tooled by without interest. His cell phone chirped startling him. He reached into his soggy front pocket surprised that it still worked until he remembered that the agency-issue phones were waterproof. The source was blocked. He knew who it was.

"Hornbuckle."

Hiss and crackle.

At last, Control spoke in an eerily modified voice. "Where is Kleiser?"

Hornbuckle gritted his teeth. "Sir, I had him under observation and he slipped away from me in a crowd."

An unspoken rebuke accompanied the hiss and crackle.

"Forget Kleiser. White's onto something. Get up there and find out what."

CHAPTER SIXTY
UPHILL STROLL

W ednesday morning.

Otto woke first. He fed Steve and they went for a walk. Winner's empty Otterbox bothered him. Why would the actor take his phone but leave the box, which cost almost as much as the phone?

Alvarez was smearing on sun screen when they returned to the cabin. He handed the tube to Otto. Otto slipped a paracord bracelet around his left wrist. Otto, Alvarez and Steve went to the main lodge and ate a quick meal of fruit and cereal. Otto gave Steve two all-beef Kosher hot dogs. Otto and Alvarez each had a backpack filled with supplies. They sat at a picnic table on which Otto had spread an NGS map of the area. He traced a line clockwise around the lake.

"Notice how the Grove map shows this to be an impassable wilderness. See how the ridge rises from about fifty meters west of the grove and continues all the way to the top of Mt. Pythagoras? If they have some kind of hideout it would make more sense to place it over here."

"Yeah," Alvarez said. "And I'd like to see what's on top of that mountain."

"You up for this? Looks about six klicks to the summit."

"Been hiking all my life," Alvarez assured him.

It was eight when they left the main lodge. They both wore ball caps. Walking clockwise around the lake, they encountered first the dormitory and then a big pole-barn garage with a concrete base in which the camp stored golf carts and other vehicles. Lon Barnett had gone through it yesterday.

Past the garage, a dirt path began its gradual ascent amid the boulders, prickly pear, mountain mahogany and juniper. At the start of the trail Otto took Witherspoon's boxer shorts, knelt, and held it out for Steve.

"Steve, find!"

Tail wagging the big dog trotted up the trail.

"Don't try to keep up with him," Otto said. "He's not going anywhere."

Alvarez followed Otto up the trail. It was already in the seventies and both men had brought plenty of water. They climbed in a companionable silence for forty-five minutes, Steve's tail a semaphore beckoning them on. They paused on a natural rock shelf a half klick above the lake. An eagle gyred overhead and Otto was reminded of his vision.

God could still paint a beautiful picture.

They resumed their climb. Alvarez sweated through his shirt and used a bandana to mop his face. The climb became precipitous and Otto worried that Alvarez would not be able to keep up, but the slight agent didn't complain. They emerged above the tree line. From here to the top was all jutting granite.

Otto gained a flat shelf after a particularly grueling session and stood leaning against a rock jutting out over the canyon waiting for Alvarez to arrive. Something whizzed past his ear. A second later, he heard the crack of a high-powered rifle.

CHAPTER
SIXTY-ONE
THE BEAR WENT OVER THE
MOUNTAIN

The shot bounced around the valley, over and over, getting more distant until it disappeared like a freight train in the night. Otto flattened himself against the near vertical rock opposite the boulder on which he'd been leaning.

"Steve come!" he called.

Seconds later the big dog scrambled onto the ledge tail-wagging. Otto stooped, beckoned him over and held on to his collar.

"What the fuck?!" Alvarez exclaimed out of sight beneath the ledge. "Was that what I thought it was?"

"Yeah," Otto said just loud enough to reach the ledge and drop over. "Somebody took a shot at me from up there."

"What do you want to do? I can get the Air National Guard up here with a chopper."

"Let's not do that. I think I see a way to circle around and come up behind him."

"You sure you want to do that? What if they're both up there?"

"Give me an hour, Gus. You're packing, aren't you?"

"Yeah."

"I'm pretty good at creeping around. You want to go back down and form a posse, that's gonna take hours."

"No way. I'm sticking."

Otto eased out of his backpack and set it in the shade against the sheer cliff wall. He pointed at Steve. "Sit. Stay."

He unscrewed the fat lid from one of his canteens and poured Steve some water in a natural depression. Looping the canteen over his shoulder Otto took off. He carried his Ruger in a pancake holster on his left hip. Otto had studied the topographical map closely and saw that each of the mountains was accessible by two routes: the obvious one facing the lodge and the lesser known one up the backside.

Back to cliff, Otto inched himself clockwise around the ledge. It dropped off abruptly to a boulder field shielded from the summit by a towering abutment. Otto eased himself down onto the boulder field and began the laborious process of traversing it, climbing over rocks the size of house trailers. Frigid rivulets ran between the rocks.

Some thirty minutes later Otto emerged from the boulder field on the northwest face of the mountain. A natural chimney formed by some antediluvian eruption provided a concealed route to the top. Otto crouched by the rock and drank deeply from his canteen. He pulled on a pair of leather gloves and approached the chimney. He wasn't aware of the rattlesnake until it started shaking its maraca. Spying the coiled reptile sunning itself on a rock Otto calmly stepped out of range and waited. The rattler undulated off the rock and away.

What is the message? Does everything have to have a message?

Otto jammed himself into the crudely rectangular chimney and climbed using natural toe and hand-holds caused by flaking granite. He moved his pancake holster around so it nestled against his belly and looked up. The chimney grooved out of sight some fifty meters up. It was almost like climbing a ladder. He climbed in shade most of the time keeping an eye out for snakes. Gray/green lichen covered the granite surfaces and tough little vines grew in the cracks.

A sudden wind whistled down the chimney chilling him. He was almost at 4,000 meters. Colorado had fifty-two peaks over 4,267 meters, or "fourteeners" as the locals called them. There was ice wedged deep in the granite that never saw the sun. He pulled himself out of the chimney and crouched on the gently rounded sloping summit. The actual summit lay thirty meters up. Otto approached carefully, pistol in hand. From the summit, he would have a better idea where the shooter was. A deep drift of snow remained on the north side.

Otto scrambled up a twenty-five degree grade studded with boulders and looked up. A flash of red glinted. The red sphere was three quarters buried in the rock. How had they done it? Did they heat the rock to liquid and insert the sphere? Did the sphere grow from within the rock like a pimple? Otto crouched and laid his gloved hand on the smooth red surface. It was warm to the touch, about the size of a bowling ball.

Otto had no doubt what he'd find on the third peak.

He carefully traversed the dome until he was above the shooter. Inching forward on his belly he cleared the rim and looked down. A series of ledges jutted out like stacked shelves concealing those below.

Seeing no obvious path, Otto unwrapped the paracord bracelet around his wrist. He fixed one end of the super strong fiber around a jutting tooth of granite and let it fall over the ledge. Quickly he shinnied over and down to the topmost ledge. He lay on his belly and crawled to the lip of the ledge, which extended about five meters from the sheer cliff face.

The sun was still climbing and would not cast his shadow. Ever so carefully, he eased his head over the rim and looked down. A black tube projected from the ledge four meters below. The protruding rifle barrel looked like the appendage of some poisonous insect, like the scorpion in the Libyan desert that appeared from time to time in his dreams. The rifle barrel twitched from side to side like a scorpion's tail.

Dude was using a telescopic sight.

Otto withdrew and examined his surroundings. Where the ledge met the cliff, a tumble of boulders formed a cobby surface running down the mountain. The rocks were big and looked like they hadn't moved in millennia. But you never knew. If Otto tried to climb down and popped something loose the shooter could easily get the drop on him.

Or he could be crushed in an avalanche.

Same story on the other side. Otto inched over and looked at the rocks. They weren't going anywhere. Like a spider, he climbed down belly up and reached a precarious perch where three spindle-shaped boulders leaned together like tent poles. He crouched as the wind whipped around. An eerie howling sound issued from below.

Otto realized it was caused by the wind striking the rifle barrel, which, from the sound, was mere meters away. Balanced precariously on crystalline granite, Otto eased around the abutment, pistol in hand, until he could see a portion of the shooter's shelf.

Hairy hands and a rifle. He couldn't see more without stepping off into air.

Steve's barks ascended followed by their echo. Fool dog must have spied a pika. The shooter inched forward and sighted sharply down. Triangulating the shooter's position with his eyes and his hand, Otto held the pistol around the rim and squeezed off two shots.

The rifle clattered over the edge. Using one hand, Otto swung free of his perch into full view of the ledge, pistol extended. Ralston Goldfarb lay in his loud Hawaiian shirt, blood pooling beneath his whale-like body.

Vapor poured from his ears, nose and mouth.

Otto just had time to scramble back behind the abutment before Goldfarb erupted into a fireball.

CHAPTER SIXTY-TWO

THE SUMMIT

Wednesday noon.

The heat through the rock felt good, which was obscene. Otto flattened himself against the side of the abutment and let the heat enter his body. After a few minutes it died down and Otto once again inched around the natural buttress until he was looking at the shelf. Goldfarb had been reduced to ashes, which the wind whipped away so that there was little left of him save a black stain on the rock and a lump of gold with a ruby in it.

Otto went to the edge of the ledge and shouted, "GUS!"

Seconds later, the agent responded. "WHAT?"

"Come on up! Bring my backpack."

Otto turned his attention to Goldfarb's remains. His skull looked like a used charcoal briquette. There would be no X-rays on this one. The underside of the ledge above was stained with soot. Where did Goldfarb get a rifle? Where did he learn to shoot? Otto had a feeling Winner would be unable to answer those questions if they could find him, but now Otto worried that whatever had possessed Goldfarb had taken the actor as well.

Where was Winner?

Otto perched at the lip of the ledge and scanned a slow one-eighty. Across the valley on the slopes of Mt. Archimedes, a long-horned Rocky Mountain sheep grazed, sticking to the mountain through sheer animal magnetism. Below in the Ponderosa, which reminded Otto of a bad case of hair plugs, there was no human activity. From here he could just make out the main lodge, tiny in the distance. He'd left his binocs with Alvarez and had no way of knowing if anyone at the lodge was reacting to the shot.

People heard gunfire in the mountains all the time. Canyons and wadis could conduct sound through dozens of dog legs and over great distances. From his perch Otto could see north to the Mummy Range and the Never Summer Mountains, close to his own spread.

He looked down at the bright blue lake, the tiny lodge. Could a sniper have fired the projectile they found in Tyler's skull from up here? The projectile was too small to have sufficient mass to cover the distance with any sort of accuracy, assuming it would fly that far. Unless it was made out of some unknown compound, heavier than plutonium. Or was intelligent and self-propelled. Many of the flame-outs occurred inside buildings. The shooter analogy didn't hold water when you considered victims like Senator Darling. Certainly Sally hadn't shot him.

Froines had erupted in an underground parking garage, a place where someone could easily conceal himself and fire from cover. Albrecht had been in a crowded casino where the constant razzle-dazzle would distract from a shooter. But the casino was always under close observation by operatives trained to note deviant behavior. A canvas of the rest of the casino's security tapes revealed nothing suspicious.

Otto heard the scrape of steel on rock and stuck his head over the ledge. Alvarez had just picked up Goldfarb's rifle—a Remington with an attached scope. Steve scrambled up the steep embankment and ran grinning to his master. Otto endured furious face licking.

Alvarez flopped Otto's backpack, heaved himself over the edge and lay there for a moment panting.

"That's a little harder than I thought," he said lying on his back and staring up at fluffy white cumulus clouds scudding east. "I saw the fire. Know who it is?"

"Goldfarb," Otto said.

Alvarez sat up abruptly. He stood and looked at the man-sized burn scar. "How can you tell?"

Otto pointed to the melted ring.

"There's his pinky ring. His gold necklace is probably fused together under that soot."

Steve sniffed around the edges, eyes darting nervously. He licked the rock.

"Steve! Don't lick the rock!"

Looking chagrined Steve ran around to Otto. Alvarez took out a small digital camera and took pictures.

Steve stuck his nose in the air, sniffed a few times, and zoomed toward the back of the ledge that lay in shadow. Otto peered into the depths and for the first time realized how deep the shelf ran under the mountain. It was a cave that daylight barely penetrated. The ceiling lowered as he entered so that Otto had to crouch to see where Steve stood, apparently barking at the cliff face.

"What is it, Steve?"

Steve barked, turning to look at Otto then back to the wall.

That's when Otto saw the door.

CHAPTER
SIXTY-THREE
INSIDE THE MOUNTAIN

The ceiling narrowed to two meters at the back. The door was one and a half meters by a half meter and oval on the top and bottom like the hatch in a submarine. It appeared to be made of smooth gray metal set in a frame sunk smoothly into the wall like the red spheres. Gabe and Alvarez duck-walked back and crouched before the door. It had a black handle.

"Ho-lee shit," Alvarez said.

Otto reached out with a gloved hand and touched the door. It felt like metal. He rapped on it causing a faint thud. It didn't sound like metal. Steve pawed at the door and whined.

"He's got a scent," Otto said.

The question lay between them unspoken. Should they barge on in or wait for reinforcements? Otto turned the handle and pulled. The door swung silently, smoothly open emitting a whiff of cool dampness tinged with creosote and gun grease.

Otto had a disturbing flashback to his anti-terrorist training at Quantico, when they were simulating urban warfare. Entering a hostile environment.

"Gus, can you find me some kind of stick?"

Gus duckwalked out of the cave and disappeared. Moments later he reappeared with the remains of Goldfarb's rifle, perhaps a half meter ending in molten slag. Gripping the barrel in one hand and his flashlight in the other Otto jammed the barrel into the room's airspace.

There was no response.

Holding gun and flashlight together, Otto shined through the door and discovered a chamber the size of a three car garage with a floor as flat and smooth as an operating room. There was a meter drop off from the door's rim.

"Hang on to my belt," he said. Alvarez grabbed the back of Otto's belt as he eased himself into the space, slowly shining the flashlight all around. He started at six o'clock, directly below and circumvented the chamber laterally and longitudinally.

He eased back, turned around, and lowered himself through the opening.

As soon as his feet hit the ground, the entire ceiling glowed softly like a phosphorescent reef. Brackets on the inside and a metal bar could be used to seal it shut. Otto swung his gun around the room. Piled against three walls, sitting on wooden plats were hundreds of wooden cases, many marked with a red warning diamond and the name of a factory in Azerbaijan. One of the boxes had been opened leaving a gun-shaped depression in the straw. The interior reeked of creosote and contained five AK-47s. Other boxes contained ammo and grenades.

Steve leaped onto the smooth stone floor followed by Alvarez.

"Fuck me runnin'," Alvarez exclaimed. "This is a terrorist stockpile."

"Wait a minute, Gus," Otto said while scanning the back wall. "If they were going to use this for terrorist purposes, why would they store it in this inaccessible place? You can't even land a helo around here."

"Well who would think to look here? Maybe there's another way into this room."

"Bingo," Otto said watching Steve growl at the back wall from ten centimeters. On closer inspection, Otto made out the outline of a door, a minute crack that was arched on top. No handle was visible. Otto placed his gloved hand flat against the door and with a subdued hiss, it pulled back and slid noiselessly to the side. Beyond lay a vast darkness.

Otto looked at Alvarez.

"Freaky," Alvarez said.

Otto pulled a whining and pent-up Steve away from the opening. "Stay." Gripping flashlight and pistol together, Otto shined a light through the door. It dissipated before delineating the cave's dimensions. This was not a prepared room but a system of caverns that probably permeated the whole mountain. And it was enormous.

Pulling to the side so he was not visible through the opening Otto flicked off his light and said, "Witherspoon and Casey are inside the mountain."

"Let's go," Alvarez said.

Otto snapped his fingers and Steve fell in beside him.

Quietly they stepped through the door onto the smooth sloping floor of the cave. The door slid back into place with a safe-like *thunk* leaving them in complete darkness.

"Wait," Otto whispered, half expecting Charon to appear with his boat. Perhaps it was from sitting through too many fire and brimstone sermons. Every time Otto entered a cave, he felt he was in hell's outer circles. He believed in heaven. He believed in hell. Could hell exist at 4,700 meters above sea level?

They waited. Gradually they could make out a faint glow somewhere in the distance. Otto flicked on his light and shined it on the ground in front of Steve. "Let's go," he whispered. Steve trotted cautiously as he'd been taught. Alvarez followed gripping his Sig Sauer in both hands.

They had gone perhaps a hundred meters when they came around a bend into a chamber with a bedroom-sized pond. Light emanated coolly from the water showing a soaring ceiling draped with dramatic stalactites. Steve surged to the edge of the pool and stuck in his snout. Otto crouched and shined his light in the water. Hundreds of tiny nearly transparent fish veered in unison like a pack of starlings.

What did they eat?

What ate them?

Steve led Otto and Alvarez clockwise around the pond to another passage, which descended in a tight spiral with a rippled surface like frozen waves of Saharan sand. The temperature was a steady fourteen centigrade. They heard the drip of condensation falling into water.

The walls narrowed then opened into an expansive chamber with columns the size of redwoods stretching from the cave floor to the ceiling. Natural phosphorescence swirled through the walls like the Milky Way, casting just enough light to see, a perpetual twilight.

Cautiously they approached the "forest."

Steve growled deep in his throat and the hair on the nape of his neck stood up.

"Drop!" Otto spat a split second before the bullets flew.

CHAPTER SIXTY-FOUR

SPIDER HOLE

W ednesday afternoon.

Hornbuckle put the pedal to the metal and felt the tall Jeep lean in the corners. He was a lead foot who attracted tickets that he fended off with his badge and some bullshit. He'd had a hard-on for White ever since Firebrand. He was deeply resentful that a flake like Aardvark should be placed in charge of the combustion squad in the first place.

It should have been Hornbuckle's job. He'd been tracking the immolations for years before White ever learned about them. Had been since Control had brought him into the loop, back when they learned that Libya planned to deploy SHC as a weapon. And that Malik was in charge. The agent slowed way down to permit some backpackers to cross the highway—college students with multi-colored knit caps. Probably going to smoke dope on the mountain, maybe start a fire.

Control was convinced that the combustions were connected to the internet. Hornbuckle's actual goal was to recruit Kleiser in a crash mission to find out how they did it—whoever they were. No question it was a foreign power, probably Iran.

Estes Park was chock-a-block with gawkers and bikers. It took twenty minutes to work his way through the center of the crowded little village before he turned north on Devils Gulch Road. A half hour later he arrived at the locked gate to the Grove. Hornbuckle pulled off the highway and got out of the car. The aluminum gate had been closed with a Master padlock. There was no one else around.

Hornbuckle returned to his vehicle and withdrew a massive bolt cutter with which he cut the lock. He pushed the gate open with a hair-raising screech, drove through, and shut the gate behind him.

Highly unusual. Where were the police? A hot investigation and no one was controlling access?

On the other hand they wouldn't know he was coming, which gave him an advantage. He emerged from the forest into the parking lot which held a handful of vehicles including Gus Alvarez' car with its federal license plate. Hornbuckle parked in the handicapped spot next to the front door and got out. No one.

The place felt deserted. Hornbuckle had a bad feeling as he went up the steps. Somebody should have been there to greet him, and why didn't Control know that there was nobody at the lodge? There were supposed to be agents on site 24/7 until the fugitives were apprehended.

Hornbuckle entered the lodge and stopped cold, worst fears realized. A Larimer County Deputy lay on the hardwood floor sightless eyes staring at the ceiling, a pool of blood under his head. He'd been shot through the forehead.

Hornbuckle drew his Glock and did a slow three-sixty. The big lodge was eerily quiet, a heavy blanket of hush which Hornbuckle dared not disturb. He quickly searched the main floor, going through the massive lobby, the dining hall, the kitchen, the rest room and the offices.

Protocol demanded that he notify HQ immediately. Their security was breached with at least one dead. Hornbuckle had no intention of honoring protocol. He was a spook first and an agent second. He had to find White and fast. He had no doubt the other deputy was somewhere on the property dead. He systematically searched the lodge's second and third floors. There were also twenty-eight cabins to search. On the other side of the lodge lay the bunkhouse and the garage. For some reason he couldn't explain, Hornbuckle was drawn toward those buildings.

Gun drawn Hornbuckle searched the bunkhouse. Empty.

Hornbuckle checked the rec room and casually flipped through the DVDs on the table. The *Detonator*. Pussy. Today's movie stars couldn't hold a candle to real men like John Wayne and Lee Marvin.

Out the back door facing the lake and down the tarmac trail thirty meters to the garage, a big pole-barn with two sliding garage doors facing the parking lot and one facing the lake. Hornbuckle entered through a side door and found himself in the garage office, a one-windowed cubicle with a gun metal gray desk, a computer, a Rigid Tool calendar on the wall along with a hanging clipboard and a big bulletin board on which every Grove vehicle was listed and placed in its proper spot. Rows of keys hung from a key rack, each with a grimy cardboard tag identifying the vehicle.

There were ten electric golf carts, two all-terrain vehicles and two 4X4s. Hornbuckle sat at the desk and cued up the computer, which had been left on. The Homepage belonged to the *Denver Post*. He scanned the headlines. *FEDS LAUNCH TASK FORCE.* Every government agency with a toe in security was cooperating with a new task force charged with identifying and neutralizing the spontaneous combustions. NSA Director Margaret Yee was in charge.

Hornbuckle went into the guts of the machine searching for links to other computers. He went into the hard drive and searched for hidden files. Nothing.

Hornbuckle went through the drawers. Aside from several issues of *Hustler,* there was little of interest. He went through the door into the garage. The electric golf carts were painted forest green with beige canopies. Two were plugged into a docking station on the near wall. Hornbuckle looked up. Massive ducts and steel beams crisscrossed overhead. Hornbuckle traced the ducts to a furnace room.

The electric golf carts were lined up on opposite sides of the garage with the all-terrain vehicles and SUVs near the parking lot entrance. Hornbuckle methodically examined every golf cart finding a little over three dollars in change, two forgotten cell phones and a number of hats.

He approached the vehicles parked just inside the parking lot entrance. First was a massive GMC suburban. It was unlocked with a clipboard on the passenger's seat holding forms regarding mileage and service. Next to it was an ancient Toyota square backed Land Cruiser, similarly accoutered.

The second deputy lay between the two all-terrain vehicles. He lay flat on his back with his legs splayed as if he'd been struck in the face with a two-by-four. It was a large-caliber round judging from the hole in his chin. Another lake of blood lay beneath his head.

Hornbuckle looked from the deputy to where the shooter must have stood. He turned around and traced the splatter on the cement floor and ATV. The blood stretched an enormous distance into the middle of the garage. Hornbuckle looked up. There was blood on the underside of the duct. The deputy had been shot at an upward angle, as if the shooter had been lying on the floor.

Hornbuckle walked five paces and saw where the dust had been disturbed. Scrape marks that abruptly stopped, erased along a perfectly flat line. Hornbuckle crouched and examined the floor closely. He saw a hairline crack with a tiny slot chink right before him.

Hornbuckle got up, walked to the work bench and found a flathead screwdriver. Inserting it in the chink, he levered up a square trap door that was 15 cm thick and canted inward at the bottom so the door could be opened and closed without binding. A whiff of strange cool air exploded in Hornbuckle's face. He pulled a penlight and shined it down.

Steps led into the darkness.

CHAPTER
SIXTY-FIVE
SCOOBY SNACK

W ednesday afternoon.

The crash of gunfire filled the cave as slugs careened off millennia-old stalagmites, off the limestone flow and caromed around the chamber like a pack of livid hornets. Otto and Alvarez sought shelter beneath a limestone ledge, Otto hanging onto Steve's collar and pulling him close.

The fusillade lasted four seconds but it seemed like forever. The gunman stopped firing and a roaring filled the chamber along with the smell of cordite. Otto's ears rang with tinnitus. Every time this happened, he feared he would suffer permanent hearing loss, but gradually the ringing subsided and he heard Steve's rasping breath.

Alvarez was prone on his belly with pistol in hands. Otto scoped the terrain. The cave floor undulated like a frozen sea with water in some of the depressions. Otto whispered "stay" in Steve's ear and crawled to his left into a depression that surfaced five meters away behind a fat stalagmite. Water seeped into his shirt chilling him.

He crawled up behind the pillar tearing his shirt and peeked around the base from the left. The chamber was the size of an aircraft hangar with numerous protuberances caused by dripping lime. The shooter could be behind any one of them. He thought about sending Steve but he didn't want to lose his dog.

He could retrace his steps to the ordnance room and grab a couple of grenades, but he wasn't certain he could find the right route, it would take too long, and who knew what effect grenades would have down here? Images of the mountain crashing in on them clouded his brain. He had vivid memories of a *Li'l Abner* adventure wherein the hapless hillbilly was sealed inside a mine for a month with nothing to eat but mushrooms. He had gained a great deal of weight.

Otto had known a tunnel rat who used to get drunk and tell Otto the most harrowing stories of soldiers trapped underground, skewered with punji sticks dipped in human feces, rabid foxes and monkeys turned loose in the tunnels.

Those tunnels had been barely big enough for a man to squeeze through. The cave was enormous. But the atavistic fear was the same.

Otto looked back. Lying behind a ridge Alvarez signaled that he was going to try and circle behind the shooter moving counterclockwise. Otto gave him the thumb's up.

Otto inched clockwise keeping stalagmites and columns between him and the shooter. He heard a ka-chunk. The shooter was reloading. Otto ran up a smooth slope and hunkered behind a series of stalagmites that resembled a dog's lower jaw. He looked through the gaps and there was Casey crouched in a natural bunker scanning the cave to Otto's right. Casey was ten meters away. Otto was confident he could nail him with the Ruger.

A minute glimpse of Alvarez's tan shirt alerted Otto to the agent's presence at 160 degrees from where Otto stood. They had Casey in a crossfire without endangering themselves.

When all else fails, follow the rules.

"Casey!" Otto shouted. "Federal agents! Throw your weapons over the ridge and lie prone on the ground with your hands behind your head!"

Casey swiveled and squeezed the trigger. Three-oh-eight slugs slammed all around Otto sending cave chips flying. Alvarez fired three times striking Casey twice in the back. Casey staggered and went down. Vapor spewed from his mouth.

"Shit!" Otto exclaimed popping his head up and looking around. The nearest man-sized pond was twenty meters back. They'd never make it in time.

"GET DOWN GUS!" Otto shouted through cupped hands. Alvarez moved out of sight. They waited. A minute passed, then another. Otto was about to get to his feet when Casey went nova like one of those secondary IED bombs designed to catch first responders. An inner sun erupted, turning the cavern into a dazzling light globe, blinding Otto who stupidly looked. A wave of heat washed over him growing in intensity. There was a fat crackling sound as the flames consumed flesh and sinew.

Then came the disturbing smell. Otto's stomach rumbled. Steve growled and his hackles rose.

"You okay?" Otto shouted.

"I'm good!" Alvarez responded.

Otto dug his fists into his eyes as the intense combustion blazed once more and faded down to a glowing white worm. Otto stood and carefully made his way over the slippery rock toward the smoking remains. Alvarez approached from the other direction holding his pistol in both hands.

They stared at the blackened cave floor. The flames had not entirely eradicated Casey. His right leg from the knee down looked perfectly normal, except for the blackened point of bone protruding from the cauterized flesh. The remaining pant leg looked clean and creased.

"Steve, come!" Otto said.

The big dog loped up, gave Otto a courtesy lick, seized Casey's leg in his jaws and retreated behind a stalagmite.

CHAPTER SIXTY-SIX
THE END OF THE AFFAIR

Wednesday afternoon.

Stella landed at DIA at eleven-thirty. At the airport, she went to the bottom level where the storage lockers were and retrieved her pistol and a box of nine mm shells. By the time she'd picked up her rental and headed north on the Interstate it was twelve-thirty. She'd tried calling back the number in her phone several times and each time it went to Pawnee Grove's voice mail.

A very dry voice saying, "You have reached Pawnee Grove. We are unable to take your call right now so please leave a brief message and a number where you can be reached." It sounded like a Shakespearean actor. Ian McKellan or somebody.

She took Baseline to Boulder, cut through town on Broadway and headed north through Lyons on 36. She found a Clear Channel station and listened to the news, recognizing the fiction surrounding Tyler's death.

Fall my peach-shaped ass, she thought. *He burned.*

An anti-terrorism expert spoke about the frightening phenomenon spreading among the world's wealthiest nations: The U.S., Russia, China. Professional rabble-rousers parroted eschatological soothsayers in that whoever was incinerating capitalists and politicians was delivering justice on nature's despoilers and exploiters of the poor.

Stickin' it to the man!

Up against the wall, motherfucker!

Less sophisticated cultures went boogie bullshit. Uganda, Kenya, Nigeria Zimbabwe declared states of national emergency sending thugs swarming through villages and tenements looking for witches, seers, shamans and Satanists. Lynch mobs sprouted in Bangladesh, Pakistan, and the Philippines. The specter of a new Dark Age loomed, driven by fear, superstition, and black magic.

That's what we're up against, Stella realized, Black magic. What was magic but technology you didn't understand?

It was the shape of the thing that frightened the most. Death by burning, traditionally reserved for heretics, warlocks, and witches, exploded throughout the third world. Only the Arab world seemed to escape the scourge.

What if they apprehended the perpetrators? Could she defend them?

Would she defend them?

Stella smiled ruefully. No, of course not. And she wouldn't be asked, thank God.

Sam's death had left a Colorado-sized hole in her heart. She was not unaware of the shady deals, back-slapping and outright lies that were the stock in trade of every politician, but Sam had never personally short-changed her. He had always been honest about what he did and what he thought.

"Honey, I'd rather see you become a crack whore than a politician. 'He brings disaster upon his nation who never sows a seed, or lays a brick, or weaves a garment, but makes politics his occupation.' Khalil Gibran. He was one smart A-rab."

She saw with her own eyes the ever-revolving door of women in and out of Sam's life, but he had left her standing tall and unafraid. She patted the purse on the passenger's seat feeling the hard metal inside. Otto had been predicting the collapse of civilization since they'd met. She wondered if he secretly longed for it. Men like Otto were no good in peace and times of plenty. They only rose when society fell.

At least Otto wasn't the jealous type. She looked forward to seeing both her boys.

Estes was a clusterfuck. It took longer to get through town than it had to drive from Lyons. Eventually she turned north on Devils Gulch, the site of the grove circled in red magic marker on the map next to her. She hadn't trusted GPS since it had directed her to a Baltimore neighborhood that looked like the aftermath of Dresden. She'd barely escaped with her life and a cracked back light.

It was three o'clock by the time she reached the Grove. She drove past the closed gate once without stopping and had to turn around. Yes, there was the gate and the correct mileage fencepost, but there was no one guarding it. She pulled off the narrow road and pulled up to the closed aluminum gate. She took out her cell phone to call Director Yee and alert her to the lack of security, but of course there was no service in the mountains. There would be a land line at the lodge.

Stella got out of the car and looked around. "Hello?" she called. Her words echoed back to her faintly. Something glinted in the grass. She saw the clipped padlock. She pushed the gate all the way open, drove through and put the vehicle in park. Shutting the gate behind her Stella got back in her car and drove through the pine.

She came around the bend and saw the lodge glowing gold in late afternoon sun against the blue lake, a postcard of how the world ought to be. There were a handful of official vehicles in the lot and a couple unmarked. Stella drove slowly toward the main lodge noting the Jeep in the handicapped spot. Seeing healthy people park in handicapped spots had always irritated her.

Gabe came out on the deck in blue jeans and a blue knit shirt with Pawnee Grove stitched on the breast in gold, grinning with his hands on his hips. He appeared to be the only one there. He stood at the top of the stair while she parked the car in a visitor's spot, slung her purse over her shoulder and got out.

Why didn't he come down the stairs?

She stood by her car for a minute. "Gabe!"

"Lookin' good, babe! Come on up here!"

Something in his voice, a false note of bonhomie made the hairs on the back of her neck stand up. She'd dealt with enough psychopaths to identify unnatural inflections, a certain glibness.

Gabe was a better actor than that.

She stayed where she was, "What's going on?"

"Come on up here and I'll show you," Gabe breezily replied.

"Where is everybody? Where's Otto?"

"Otto's up the mountain! That's what I've been trying to tell you. Come around to the veranda, you can see him through the telescope."

"Okay—let me grab my purse." She slid back into the car, slipped her hand into the purse and found the Sig.

Stella went up the stairs eyes fixed on Gabe. As soon as she gained the veranda, Gabe wrapped her in his arms, drew her close and kissed her passionately, his erection obvious, hands slipping to her ass.

"Come on, beautiful," he whispered huskily. "We have to make up for lost time."

He took her arm and steered her toward a corridor. Stella twisted free.

This wasn't Gabe.

"What's the matter with you? Where is everybody?" she said calmly, slipping her hand into the purse.

Anger flashed behind the actor's blue eyes and he grabbed Stella's left wrist in both hands, dragging her down the corridor. Stella choked up on the purse strap and swung it at Gabe's head as hard as she could. The pistol made a dull bonking sound on impact. Gabe staggered and let go.

Stella's hand slipped into the purse, seized the Sig and thumbed off the safety.

Gabe stared at her as if she were an alien creature. His eyes flared yellow from within.

He charged.

Stella kicked him in the nuts and backed up several feet. An expression of shock appeared on Gabe's face and he froze. Stella brought the pistol up and jacked a shell into the chamber. Gabe snarled. Vapor issued from his mouth.

He lunged.

Stella shot him five times in the chest.

CHAPTER SIXTY-SEVEN : DOWN THE RABBIT HOLE

G abe flipped backward exploding into flame. Something sharp zinged across Stella's scalp drawing blood. She sagged and put a hand to her head. The fireball filled the corridor and physically shoved Stella down the hall, and for an instant time stood still and she felt as if she were floating near the ceiling looking down from above. The blast knocked her four meters through the air and rolled over her, leaving behind a rancid pong of burning flesh and a layer of slimy soot.

Gagging, she crawled on hands and knees through blinding smoke. The sprinkler system rained water. Gasping, she dragged herself into the lobby, pulled herself up the side of an overstuffed leather chair and collapsed coughing. The sprinkler system was site specific and did not affect the rest of the hotel.

She still had her purse. She opened it up and took out a tissue she used to rub the grit from her eyes.

Gabe, Gabe, Gabe. What have they done to you?

Stella was numb. She was sick at heart—beyond crying, in a state of shock. She ran a hand through her savaged hair and it came back red. Shrapnel. Her skin was sticky with Gabe's incinerated remains. The gorge began to rise and she barely made it to the big bathroom off the lobby where she knelt before the porcelain god and heaved and heaved until there was nothing left but a bilious yellow fluid.

Stella got up coughing, went to the counter and looked at herself in the mirror. She looked like Baba Yaga after her cook pot explodes in her face. She'd seen enough of the corridor to know there were private rooms and she had to get out of those clothes.

There had to be a shower.

When she emerged from the restroom, the sprinkler system had shut down leaving a soggy mess in the hall.

She went to the front desk and tried the land line. Dead. Likewise the phone in the administrator's office. She found the dead deputy dragged behind the portable bar in the big living room, blood trail cursorily wiped away.

Focusing her gaze on the wall, she went back down the corridor, through the black ring of Gabe's death. Why hadn't Gabe set the lodge on fire? Seventeen hundred degrees should have done the job, but it was as if the fire focused itself into a tiny sun.

On the other side of the blackened corridor, she found a room with the door open.

Inside was a typical hotel room with a made-up king-size and a private bath. Stella stripped off her filthy garb and took a shower turning the temperature as hot as she could stand it. She dumped an entire hotel shampoo on her head and worked it like pizza dough.

She toweled herself off, wrapping a green and gold Pawnee Grove towel around her head. She checked the dresser. It was filled with men's clothes. She'd brought a change of clothing, but it was still in the car. Salvaging only her bra, Stella put on jockey shorts, a loose-fitting pair of carpenter's pants, a Pawnee Grove T-shirt and a Pawnee Grove sweatshirt. The Sig fit neatly in a front pocket. She found a beaded belt in the closet and threaded it through the loops. It was so long she had to tie the ends together.

Seeing that her room opened directly on the back deck, Stella went outside and put her arms on the rail. God it was beautiful. She inhaled deeply feeling her lungs swoon with relief. Under any other circumstances she would have been awestruck. She inhaled deeply again, holding it in to cleanse her lungs of any memory of that awful cloud. A few meters to her right a white telescope had been set up on a tripod aimed at the mountain at two o'clock.

Stella had no idea which mountain Otto had climbed or even if the false Gabe had been telling the truth.

What had taken over Gabe's body and why? Had it summoned her from Washington so it could rape her? That didn't make sense. None of it made sense.

Girl, you're thinking too small.

It was terrorism. Why else would it only target big shots?

Stella pulled up an Adirondack, perched on the end and peered through the telescope. The mountain gleamed gold, violet and white in the afternoon light. She saw two Rocky Mountain longhorns grazing on a ledge, but no people. She moved her eye slowly, the way Sam had taught her, leaving no visible part of the mountain unobserved. She trained the telescope on the mountain at ten o'clock and worked it top to bottom. No sign there either.

Where was everybody?

Sam whispered in her ear. "Get back in your car and beat ass out of there, girl!"

But she couldn't. Not until she had some answers. Sam had also told her to question fiercely and fearlessly.

Pawnee Grove was a land of dread. The dead deputy, the absence of personnel was unnerving and uncanny. There were supposed to be two FBI agents on the scene and at least two Larimer County Deputies. She stood and her scalp pulsed where the shrapnel had struck. She went into the lodge, into the kitchen in search of a First Aid kit. There was a wall bracket for one but it was empty.

Stella went out to the lobby and looked behind the desk finding a stack of maps of the property. She placed one on the desk and looked at it. Certainly, the garage/workshop would have a first aid kid. She went back through the lobby to the broad veranda facing the lake, turned left and down three steps to the ground. A black asphalt trail circled the lake and stopped at the garage/workshop, a large pole-barn building painted beige.

She entered the building through a side door that took her into an office. She tried the phone, but of course it was dead. She went from there into the garage proper, scanning the walls for the familiar red cross. And there it was, across the big garage at the workbench, clamped to the wall.

As she reached the bench, she looked left and saw the second deputy.

CHAPTER SIXTY-EIGHT
STRANGE CONTRAPTION

Otto spotted a slag of metal in the ashes and kicked it free. It was a partially melted federal agent's badge. He picked it up in a gloved hand and showed it to Alvarez. Next to the agent's remains were three empty Red Bulls and a fourth unopened. Behind him, the cavern descended in broad galleries like the Moscow subway.

"Steve," Otto said.

Steve growled.

"Steve, come!"

Steve whined.

"Drop the leg and come!"

The big dog slunk out from behind its cover head hung in shame.

"Great," Alvarez said. "Now he's got a taste for human meat."

"I can always give him Spam," Otto said. "Dogs can't tell the difference."

Alvarez took lead shining his flashlight on the phosphorescent stairs before him. "You know why the people of the South Pacific love Spam above all other meats, don't you? It most closely resembles the taste of human flesh."

Overcome with awe they proceeded in silence. It seemed to Otto that joking about cannibalism inside nature's tabernacle was blasphemous. Only God could create such a place. On the other hand, you had to laugh. What else could you do? Otto wished he had a cross to light the way, automatically touched the tat on his chest and turned it into a genuflection. He caught Alvarez looking at him oddly before turning away.

Yea though I walk through the valley of the shadow of death.

Steve growled and Otto grabbed him by the collar and held him back. "Heel."

Steve had the scent. If they had to retrace their steps, Steve would know the way.

The cavern floor tilted downward precipitously and they had to scramble down to the next gallery on their butts, Steve skittering down on four legs. They descended for perhaps twenty minutes when up ahead they saw yellow light, electric light. Otto held a hand up and Alvarez paused. He looked at his watch. They had been in the cave for almost an hour.

Steve at his heel, Otto led Alvarez across a vast gallery with an undulating floor marked with stalagmites and columns. It was like tracking a fugitive through a ghost Disney World. It was almost impossible not to become distracted by the spectacular formations around them.

As they approached the light, they saw it reflected off a smooth cave wall veering to the right until it disappeared around the bend. Otto pointed at Steve. "Stay."

Steve sat, tongue lolling, smacking his lips.

Pistol in both hands, Otto crouched and edged around the corner moving clockwise. Ten meters on he came upon a natural barrier, a knife-edge limestone ledge caused by steady seepage from the ceiling high above. Otto crept to this natural bulwark and peeked between limestone teeth. He was both shocked to his soul and deeply reassured.

He always knew he would find something like this. His whole life had been a preparation for this moment.

Twenty meters into another vast chamber with a hemispherical ceiling, Emil Witherspoon sat in a gimbals-mounted chair in the center of two massive metal rings, joined at the north and south pole to form the outline of a sphere approximately five meters in diameter. The apparatus rested on a stout wooden deck, obviously tailored to the terrain. Three large cones that looked like pyramidal Daleks surrounded the platform. The chair appeared to be made of metal and plastic. In front of Witherspoon, a thick black wand extended from the base, flowing into a triangle with handlebars at the end. A red and white Igloo ice chest rested on the platform.

On top of the Igloo was the lodge ledger.

Witherspoon gripped the T-top device with both hands and stared into space, motionless.

Otto felt Alvarez creep up behind him. They looked in silence.

"What is it?" Alvarez whispered.

"Fuck if I know," Otto replied. "It's Witherspoon in some kind of freakin' Jack Kirby machine."

They again lapsed into silence as their eyes swept the rest of the chamber. There was a substantial lake on the other side of the device, perhaps ten meters across. Light came from a series of metal clamp lamps affixed to planks drilled into the wall with cords running up to and beneath Witherspoon's platform.

The bulbs were curly energy savers. A low electric thrum filled the chamber. Otto gestured for Alvarez to take up position behind Witherspoon's left shoulder while Otto took the right. Pistol gripped in both hands Otto circled counter-clockwise until he was well within Witherspoon's view.

"Mr. Witherspoon!" he said, shattering the silence.

There was no response. Otto approached, pistol trained on the caretaker's chest. Now he saw that Witherspoon was attached to the machine via a black stripe across his forehead. A tiny wire led from the stripe into the control unit, which Witherspoon gripped in both hands.

Two cans of Mountain Dew lay at the caretaker's feet.

Witherspoon was not entirely frozen. His fingers strained and squeezed as if he were performing ninja power focusing techniques. A *frisson* ran up Otto's spine. He didn't like this. He didn't like what Witherspoon was doing.

Otto was wearing gloves. Keeping the pistol trained on Witherspoon he ran up to the platform, grabbed the tape where it stuck to the caretaker's head and yanked it loose. It fell limply to one side.

Witherspoon's eyes popped into focus. He looked around as if seeing the place for the first time before his gaze settled on Otto.

"Mr. White. I thought we agreed the mountains were off-limits."

Alvarez circled around from the other side so that both men now confronted the caretaker with their guns, at four and seven.

"What are you doing, Mr. Witherspoon?"

Witherspoon released the control stalk, crossed his arms and offered a chilly smile. "Well, this day had to come sooner or later. It appears we are at a stand-off."

"Where's the stand-off?" Otto said. "I could blow you away right now."

"Without learning anything? I don't think so, Mr. White. You have questions. I have answers."

"Okay. Who are you?"

The frosty smile. "That's for me to know and you to find out."

"He's stalling," Alvarez said.

A flame flickered behind one chilly blue eye.

Otto stuffed his gun in his pants and leaped onto the platform. "He's gonna blow! Help me get him into the lake!"

Alvarez joined him, quickly and efficiently cutting through a shoulder strap with a pocket knife. They each took Witherspoon by an armpit—he offered no resistance, dragged him off the platform and into the gelid lake.

CHAPTER SIXTY-NINE
ICE CHEST

Wednesday evening.

Otto and Alvarez dragged Witherspoon, tasseled loafers scraping, until they stood waist-high in the numbing water. Smoke seeped from Witherspoon's nose as Otto pushed his head beneath the surface gripping the caretaker by his collar. Witherspoon didn't struggle. He'd gone limp, a line of tiny bubbles escaping from one corner of his mouth.

Abruptly the caretaker's right rear leg cleared the water and smacked Alvarez in the face. Alvarez stepped back cupping his chin. The back of Witherspoon's calf sizzled then burst into a line of improbably yellow flame, burning through the soaked fabric.

"Get back!" Alvarez said wading for shore. "He's gonna blow!"

Otto felt heat building through the water, but maintained his grip on the caretaker's collar. Witherspoon went wild, arms and legs thrashing with all his might as if he were trying to stave off drowning. Otto pushed his head deeper. A gout of flame burst through the surface of the lake beginning at Witherspoon's heels. A column of fire, smoke and water danced and collapsed. The smell of burning flesh filled the air along with a gray cloud that quickly dissipated in the cave's internal winds.

The water hissed and boiled for an instant then went silent. Otto realized he'd been holding his breath. Dragging Witherspoon by the collar, he backed out of the lake. The caretaker's torso and head appeared intact. His eyes had turned red.

Otto pulled the caretaker out of the lake and left him lying flat like a set of winter long johns. Alvarez stared at the body. Witherspoon's mouth had pulled into a rictus grin. Steve approached tentatively and sniffed.

"Leave it!" Otto said.

"Jesus," Alvarez said. He closed Witherspoon's eyes. They popped open. He closed them again. They popped open again.

"Now what do we do?" Alvarez said.

"Get that ice chest. Take out whatever's in there but keep the ice."

"Oh man …"

"It just makes sense. We've got to get this head to Cheyenne as soon as possible."

Alvarez went to the ice chest and removed three cans of Mountain Dew and two Red Bulls. He popped one of the Mountain Dews.

"You want a Dew?"

"No, thanks. Come over here and help me hold him steady."

Alvarez brought the ice chest and set it down on the cave floor. Otto took out a wicked-looking black knife with a serrated edge.

"Hold his head steady. This could get messy."

As Alvarez gripped the caretaker's head with both hands Otto sawed through the neck. Surprisingly there wasn't much blood. It seemed oddly congealed and reluctant to flow. It was hard slippery work. Otto kept losing his grip in what blood there was and having to rinse it off in the lake.

His knife made a moist vibrating sound as he cut through the spine that traveled up his arm and got into his head causing a sharp pain to bloom in his right temple. Even in the chill of the cave and water he began to sweat. Steve crossed his forepaws and laid his muzzle down looking longingly at the corpse. He whined.

"Shut up!" Otto snarled.

The head came loose. Otto placed it in the ice chest on a bed of ice and closed the lid. They went to the device. The wooden platform had obviously been built there but the rest of it looked alien.

Alien.

Otto had an instant of gut-clenching terror. An invisible repellant urged him to flee. He stifled a scream.

Alien.

As in from another world, another galaxy, another universe rife with infinite wonder and terror. Otto felt the weight of history pressing down on him as if the earth itself were balanced on one spiked stiletto. There should have been an Army Division present along with the President and Secretary of State. Ray Bradbury should have been there. Not he who didn't know his ass from a hole in the ground.

"Hey."

Otto felt a hand on his shoulder.

"Hey, are you all right?"

Otto physically shook himself and blew a raspberry. *Snap out of it!* He had a job to do.

"I'm good."

Otto went to one of three two-meter tall pyramidal black towers surrounding the platform. The top had a lattice frame like an oil derrick. Otto removed his pen light and shined it into the lattice. A red sphere the size of a ping-pong ball lay on a black metal base.

"Red balls," Otto said.

Alvarez went to another of the towers and looked. "Here too."

"I think we're looking at some kind of receiving station for a teleportation device," Otto said.

Alvarez looked at him in astonishment. "You're not serious."

"I'm deadly serious. Just because we don't know what it is doesn't mean it isn't happening. Looks like it's been happening for some time."

"What's been happening?"

"Alien fuckin' invasion. I believe we will find a microscopic vehicle at the top of Witherspoon's spine. I believe the three red spheres atop Mts. Archimedes, Pythagoras and Isosceles are some kind of transceiver that focuses right here on this platform. It's a teleportation device."

Alvarez palmed his face. "I have a headache just thinking about it. Where's this power coming from?"

Both men looked at the platform into which the cables ran.

Steve got to his feet and went ballistic. Sharp yelps and wild ululations ricocheted around the cavern like a hail storm. Steve took off like a shot deeper into the cave.

"Steve! Stop!" Otto yelled.

For an instant there was only the click-clatter of Steve's claws on stone.

The piercing retort of a bullet struck like a cold slap to the face. Steve yelped and went silent.

Seconds later Ryan Hornbuckle approached holding his smoking pistol.

CHAPTER SEVENTY
:DOWN AND OUT

"OTTO NO!" Alvarez shouted reaching for his friend. Otto drew his pistol and put three in Hornbuckle's chest. Alvarez collided with Otto sweeping his gun arm down. Too late. Hornbuckle was dead before he hit the ground. Otto looked at the gun in his hand, jammed it in his pants and ran toward Steve, leaping over Hornbuckle's body.

The big dog was barely alive. Otto took Steve's head in his lap and cooed at him while his eyes dimmed. "Who's the greatest dog who ever lived?" Otto sobbed.

Alvarez held back, unwilling to intrude on Otto's grief. At the same time, Alvarez drew his pistol.

For long moments, Otto held the dog. The silence stretched to the snapping point.

"You just killed a federal agent."

Otto looked up with red swollen eyes. "I know."

"I should put you under arrest."

"Not until we get to the bottom of this, Gus. You have nothing to fear from me."

Alvarez put his pistol up. "Do you promise you'll work with me until it's done and not try to bolt?"

"I give you my word."

"Shit," Alvarez said. "Shit shit shit. SHIT!"

The word buzzed around their heads and faded away.

Otto stood, Steve's blood on his clothes and hands. He went over to Hornbuckle's dead body, knelt, and pulled the agent's wallet. He flipped through the wallet. There were several hundred dollars in cash, numerous credit cards. No pictures of loved ones. Nothing personal. In a hidden pocket Otto found a folded piece of foolscap. He took it out and opened it. It contained six numbers. All were three digits. Five of them surrounded a central number on a pentagon pattern. The central number was 666. He showed it to Alvarez.

"What the fuck," the agent said.

Otto refolded the piece of paper and put it in his vest pocket where it wouldn't get wet. "Let's go. There's got to be another entrance on the property."

Each hoisted one side of the ice chest.

"Otto!" Stella cried, running forward, almost slipping on the rocks. Otto dropped the ice chest and took her in his arms as she slammed into him. She trembled in his grip.

"Gabe's dead," she choked "I shot him. It wasn't Gabe."

"What? Slow down!"

Stepping back and wiping the tears from her face Stella told them about Gabe's phone call and her encounter with the un-Gabe. "I don't understand what's happening!"

Otto looked at Alvarez who nodded imperceptibly. Stella noticed Hornbuckle's body for the first time.

"What happened to him?"

"I shot him," Otto said. "He killed Steve."

"Oh, Otto, no." She hugged him. "I'm so sorry."

Otto introduced Stella to Alvarez. She shook his hand and turned to Otto.

"Did you believe you were in danger from Agent Hornbuckle?"

Otto looked into her brown eyes and saw what was happening. "Absolutely. I was in fear for our lives. He had no reason to shoot Steve. He looked like a madman."

Alvarez shook his head and turned away. Otto touched Stella's head. His hand came away with a dab of blood. He raised his eyebrows.

"Something struck me when I shot Gabe. Like a piece of shrapnel or something."

Otto pulled a bandana from his backpack, dipped it in the lake and used it to swab the cut. He showed Stella the staging platform and told her all that had transpired since they'd headed up the mountain that morning.

"All right," she said when he was finished. "Let's get this head down the mountain."

"Why did the un-Gabe call Stella?" Otto said, holding onto one end of the ice chest.

"He must have been infected and taken over," Alvarez said. "If this really is an alien race it may be impossible for us to ever understand their motives."

That sense of vertigo came rushing back as if Otto had suddenly stepped off the edge of the earth. It was his greatest fear—an unknown implacable enemy whose very existence called into question everything he believed.

He pushed it away through sheer force of will.

"All living things subscribe to a list of hierarchies," Otto said. "First, self-preservation. Second, food. Third, to reproduce."

"It's not reasonable or rational to think an alien would want to mate with a human being," Alvarez said.

"Reasonable and rational are out the window," Otto said. "How do we know what they want? Can a fish comprehend what a man wants?"

They slid down a steep embankment on their butts holding the ice chest between them.

"Apples and oranges," Alvarez said. "We're self-aware and never discount the power of imagination. The SETI Institute has been preparing for this moment for decades."

"The most important question," Stella said, "is what are they doing here in the first place?"

Phosphorescent walls provided enough illumination to make their way steadily down the cave until they came to a flat floor with a perfectly rectangular corridor cut into the living granite. The corridor was about ten meters in length. A steel ladder clung to the wall at the far end.

How had the *aliens* managed to create this geometrically perfect tunnel?

They knew nothing about the enemy.

"This opens up into the garage," Stella said. "Let me go first."

Otto and Alvarez set the ice chest down on the ground and swung their arms. It had become increasingly heavy as they had descended. Otto couldn't keep his eyes off Stella's round ass as she climbed the ladder. It took his mind off Steve.

Stella paused at the top trying to remember which way the door swung. She felt along the edges and found a slight depression. She pushed it open and stepped up so that from inside the garage she was visible from the shoulders. Automatic pistols ratcheted as soldiers chambered their rounds.

A semi-circle of SWAT types wearing FBI flak jackets surrounded her.

CHAPTER
SEVENTY-ONE
ALONE TOGETHER

Wednesday evening and night.

Lon Barnett had set up HQ in the lobby, a map of the area spread out on a broad table the men had moved in from the conference room. He had chairs brought up for Stella, Alvarez and Otto who were only permitted to make a lavatory stop.

Otto looked at Alvarez and Stella. Both were covered with dust and scuffed. He imagined how he must look with Steve's blood on his pants and jacket. The ice chest rested on the table holding down one end of the map.

Barnett stood, opened the ice chest, looked, closed it and sat down.

Otto told Barnett everything that happened since he and Alvarez had gone up the mountain that morning. He turned over the slip of paper bearing the numbers. Barnett asked a few questions and took notes.

"What's next?" Barnett said.

"Get the head to Cheyenne and hope that we've preserved the projectile."

"Why didn't Witherspoon combust completely like the others?"

Otto shrugged. "Sir, we don't know. We're operating completely in the dark here. We won't know why they're here until and unless we establish contact with someone. Or something."

"There was mention of SETI's involvement," Alvarez said.

Barnett sat back, his bald dome reflecting afternoon light.

"Let me get this straight. Is this a first contact situation?"

"Yes, sir," Otto replied. "I believe it is."

Barnett rubbed his bristly jaw. He looked like he hadn't slept in days. "All right. I'll notify Cheyenne that you're coming." Barnett looked around. "Sawaya!" he called.

A man in SWAT togs including a fiberglass helmet with infrared glasses trotted over. "Sir?"

"I need guards at the bottom and top of the cave systems. Nobody gets in there without my permission. We're going to retrieve two bodies. You've had crime scene training, right?"

"Yes, sir!" The young agent was gung ho. He had freckles.

"Very good. Meet me at the bottom entrance in twenty minutes." Barnett stood and headed toward the front door. "Let's go, folks."

Otto and Alvarez hoisted the ice chest and followed. Barnett held the door for them.

"Did you have to shoot Hornbuckle?" he said quietly as Otto passed.

"Yes, sir, I did," Otto said looking straight ahead.

They got into a black GMC Yukon. The driver introduced herself as Yolanda Pike and was in her mid-thirties. Alvarez took shotgun with Otto and Stella in the back seat.

"What about your rental?" Otto asked Stella.

"I'll send someone for it."

She took his hand in the dark and didn't let go. Pike put the lights on as they went through Estes, kept them on all the way to Cheyenne Mountain. It was eight-thirty p.m. when they arrived and the entrance lurked in shadow. The guards waved them through after face recognition.

One cave to another, Otto thought.

The van took them directly to the lab. Two armed MPs arrived to escort the ice chest into the lab. Alvarez looked at Otto and Stella.

"You two look exhausted. Why don't you catch some kip and I'll inform you if anything happens."

"What about you, Gus?" Otto said.

"I'm way too keyed up to sleep. I want to be there when we establish contact. By the way—ix-nay on the brain surgeon. Witherspoon is dead. We don't need a surgeon. Plus I have to check all the equipment I ordered. I pray to God we're prepared for what we find."

"Me too," Otto said, signaling to a soldier at the wheel of a golf cart. The golf cart took them back to the same unit in which Otto had spent the previous night. He thanked the soldier and they got out. Hand in hand, he and Stella faced the unit. Stella noticed the giant springs.

"What are those for?"

"To withstand nuclear shock," Otto said opening the door to the unit. The interior smelled faintly of Lysol floral spray. A fat old color television confronted the threadbare sofa. Someone had come in and made up his bed. There were two bedrooms.

"I have to shower," Otto said heading for the bath and stripping off his clothes. "You take whichever room you like."

Otto reveled in the high-pressure hot water. He toweled himself off, put on his jockey shorts and jeans and stepped out of the bath. The door to the room Stella had chosen was closed. Otto felt as if he'd been put through a meat grinder. His neck and arms were stiff in ways he'd never experienced.

He went into the other bedroom, collapsed on the king-sized bed, reached over and switched off the lamp. The room felt incomplete. Steve had always slept on the bed at Otto's feet. How he missed that lump of fur. God he hated to lose a dog. Despite gospel, he knew dogs had souls and that Steve was up there somewhere in doggie heaven looking down on him. At least he hoped so.

He was almost asleep when his door opened silently and Stella padded in, sliding onto the bed and reaching for him.

"I don't think either of us should be alone tonight," she whispered as he turned toward her.

CHAPTER SEVENTY-TWO
: Down to the Nitty Gritty

Wednesday night and Thursday morning.

Otto lay awake with Stella's arm splayed across his chest, her finger unconsciously tracing the tattoo she'd noticed at Otto's hogan. "Stella" intertwined with a heart. A ten centimeter furrow creased the top of her head near the hairline leaving a line of dried blood.

The aliens couldn't penetrate women. Not in their little spacecraft.

Never in his wildest imaginings did he think Stella would return to him. It was a miracle. His prayer of gratitude shamed him, so unworthy was he of the blessings bestowed upon him.

Not even the prospect of being charged with Hornbuckle's death could dim the gratitude in his heart. If he died, then he would die fulfilled because Stella had come back to him. Nothing else mattered. Not Steve's loss nor the imminent collapse of civilization.

Duty crawled out of his guts like a sewer rat displacing the afterglow of love with grim reality. What the Japanese called *giri*. Obligation. He'd sworn an oath. So much remained to be done.

They may have discovered the cause of the self-immolations, but they were completely in the dark as to the purpose, or the technical knowledge of how they were achieved.

What if the mastermind remained hidden in the mountains or worse, someplace they would never think to look? A place they could not go? What if Americans had discovered a portal to another universe? Would they boil through and exploit that land in the name of eminent domain? Might not these *aliens* do the same thing?

Were the immolations the result of a plan or was their purpose so far beyond human understanding that the truth would drive men mad?

What significance did the numbers hold? Were they even related to the case?

Karma was a motherfucker.

As a kid, Otto had devoured *Watchmen*. In *Watchmen*, the smartest superheroes contrived to present a false alien threat as a means of uniting the world and ending war.

This wasn't like that. The killings were obviously designed to hide their actual cause by destroying any trace of the visitors once their host bodies—for whatever reason—ceased to function. Like an army using slash and burn to destroy occupied land. The killings could hardly be more terrifying. They struck at one of man's greatest fears—fear of burning alive.

Why were all the victims men? Was it simply because only men could attend Pawnee Grove? Or were women for some reason impervious? Otto recognized the gash in Stella's scalp as the result of one of the tiny darts trying to penetrate her skull. Did it fail because it struck the hard skull instead of soft tissue in the nose, mouth, ears or eye? Or was there something in female DNA that formed an impenetrable force field, or killed the aliens on contact?

What lay beneath the other two peaks? Would he have the opportunity to investigate or would they slap the cuffs on as soon as he'd outlived his usefulness?

Why had the entity chosen Winner? What did it hope to gain? Was each victim an outpost unto himself or were they somehow all linked to a central intelligence?

No one knew how many existed. Grove visitors interacted with thousands of others and those people in turn interacted with more thousands. If the plague jumped from person to person like the flu, there could be many thousands of these zombies. If they were somehow all interconnected, they could summon quite a mob.

As CEOs, senators, stars and athletes, they would be more difficult for authorities to control. No matter how you worked it, it was a brilliant plan.

There remained only one question. *What did they want?*

Before she fell asleep, Stella had told him about Durant seeing "spiders." Three of the sniper victims were among the expanded list of people who had contact with persons who had visited the Grove. Two of the sniper victims' cars had "burst into flame."

Was Durant able to 'see' the aliens?

Otto finally drifted into a shallow sleep in the early hours of the morning and dreamt a kaleidoscope version of his descent through the mountain. At first Alvarez was with him, but then it was Gabe. Flashing a million dollar smile, Gabe tried to kill Otto with a rock. Otto struck Gabe in the head with a big copper soup tureen that made a satisfying bong. Gabe's eyes began to glow.

Otto tried to run but he couldn't get any traction. It was like running on a treadmill through Jell-O. Five numbers circled his head like tiny moons. He felt exhausted and could hardly move his legs. Gabe blew up and the cavern cracked and shuddered, stalactites striking the ground like cannon fire.

He was wakened by persistent knocking on the front door. He glanced at the bedside clock. It was five-thirty in the morning. Otto swung his legs out, padded through the living room to the front door and opened it. Alvarez stood outside with an MP in a golf cart behind him. Alvarez' thick lenses were covered with grease and his shirt was hopelessly rumpled. His tie trailed carelessly from a hip pocket. What little hair he had stood out above his ears like clown wings.

Alvarez looked drained of blood.

"We've established contact," he croaked.

Stella appeared behind Otto in a robe. She took his arm. "Give me a minute to throw on some clothes."

Otto went inside and put on a shirt and an Air Force Academy sweatshirt he found in a drawer. He was out front first. Alvarez remained mute, his mouth a horizontal line. He got in the front seat next to the driver. Otto and Stella got in the back. The golf cart whizzed down the center-line toward the lab, faint thrum felt rather than heard through the frame. The loudest sound in the cave was the steady whoosh of the air circulation system shunting warm air outside.

Alvarez twisted in his seat. "The head somehow maintains vital activity. We placed it in a saline solution in a sealed tank and fitted it with a direct feed into Lovins, which is air-gapped. All the computers are. We used that lead he already had in his head.

"Two hours ago it began transmitting signals. Nearly crashed the system, but I was able to shut the feed down and reboot. It was trying different frequencies, possibly some type transmission of which we're ignorant. They started making sense …"

Alvarez barked ruefully. "They started making 'sense …'" He added quote marks with his fingers. "about an hour ago."

Otto leaned forward and put a hand on Alvarez' shoulder. "Who are they? What did they say?"

"Massive feedback—babies screaming, nails on a chalkboard, hands to ears and then quite distinctly, 'six two four' in a normal voice. Then back to screaming and we had to shut down the audio. Fed everything into the database waiting for results."

"Six two four," Otto said, taking out his spiral pad in which he'd copied Hornbuckle's numbers. "That's one of the numbers Hornbuckle had."

"Don't know. Don't know shit. Twenty minutes ago, we made visual contact. I must warn you it's disturbing."

The golf cart stopped in front of the lab door. The armed guard stepped aside as Alvarez led Otto and Stella into the brightly-lit lab. It was still freezing inside. Stella zipped up her windbreaker. An armed guard stepped out and closed the door behind him. A large cylindrical Plexiglas aquarium rested on a stack of wood pallets that brought it to eye level. The cylinder's bullet-proof wall was five centimeters thick. Within the cylinder Witherspoon's ghastly head tilted toward the ceiling, a minute lead running from his forehead to a transceiver attached to the Plexiglas wall. His eyes bulged like thousand-year-old eggs. No longer red, they were now nicotine-stained yellow. The cylinder was completely encircled by curving, overlapping seven-foot Plexiglas screens, some bearing extensive scratch marks.

Otto spotted three cameras in the ceiling.

A computer station had been set up facing the cylinder, a bean-shaped desk with several monitors. Alvarez slid in. Otto and Stella stood behind him, his arm around her shoulder. Alvarez tapped the computer. The screen turned gray and showed a bewildering scroll of numbers. He tapped some more and abruptly the image changed.

Stella clutched Otto's arm so hard she left indentations with her nails. "*The spiders*," she hissed.

CHAPTER

SEVENTY-THREE

CONTACT

Thursday morning.

The image had a disturbing grainy quality like WW II footage except for the coloring, a wet gutter reflecting lurid yellow. Neon lights reflecting off alley ponds. In contrast, the three creatures were so black they seemed to be a glimpse into the screaming void. So black they sucked the light in around them.

Each had three bulging red eyes forming a triangle: two on top, one on the bottom. The stark contrast between the red eyes and black background caused them to pop like a 3-D effect. It was difficult to tell exactly how many limbs they had since they appeared to be equal parts chitin, tentacles, and fur. The triangular heads bobbed on top of long, beetle-like bodies. The bulging spherical eyes splashed and flowed a disturbingly blood-like fluid. Everything about them was alien. Otto's first instinct was to turn and run.

Get away from them.

"They're watching us too," Alvarez said softly. "I've sent them greetings in English, a Mozart concerto, and using the SETI manual—a series of geometric designs intended to establish a base line."

"Have they responded?" Otto said.

Alvarez reached out and twisted a dial on a free-standing Bose speaker. An electrical crackle issued. "The radio lines are open. Operators are standing by to take their calls."

"Have you notified National Security?" Otto said softly.

"No. I figure that's your job."

They stared in silence.

"Why do they twitch like that?" Otto said.

"I know. At first I thought there was a glitch in the digital feed before I realized that's their natural motion."

Otto looked at the wall clock. It would be eight o'clock in the nation's capital. His instructions called for him to notify the Director if there were any significant breaks in the case, but at the same time he was reluctant to tear himself away from the lab for fear of missing an historic moment.

The aliens' herky-jerk motion was mesmerizing, like that of a mustelid. Perhaps it was meant to be. Otto yanked himself out of a near-trance. "Is there a secure line?"

Alvarez pushed himself back from the computer in his wheeled chair and pointed to a black wall unit near the door. "Hooked up an hour ago. It's encoded, encrypted and air-gapped. Only feeds the comsat."

Otto crossed the linoleum floor and reached for the phone.

"GREETINGS!"

The word crackled thickly from numerous speakers trailing weird harmonic undertones that scraped the inside of the skull like a rasp.

An atavistic chill shook Otto's spine like a flag in a tornado. His forearms prickled as he returned to the screen. Stella dug her nails into his arm and clung. The three aliens twitched like bobbleheads.

They waited for something to happen.

"Maybe we should answer them," Alvarez suggested.

"Yes," Otto said.

Alvarez spoke into a little desk mike. "Greetings. Welcome to Earth. Who are you?"

Bob, twitch.

"*WE ARE THE SKORZH.*"

Alvarez winced and adjusted the modulator.

"Sounded like 'Scourge,'" Otto said.

Stella put her lips to Otto's ear. "There's a protocol for first contact. Shouldn't you notify National Security?"

"Not yet."

Otto reached over and picked up the mike. "Why are you here?"

The aliens flickered like bad reception. It was impossible to read their body language. Nothing changed. The silence stretched until Otto thought they had lost communication.

"*We were able to affect a transfer from our universe to yours.*" The volume was lower, but the voice still sounded like demonic possession—wheezy with disturbing sonics at both ends of the spectrum, as if several people were speaking at once.

Perhaps they didn't understand the question. "But why have you come?"

"*First we transferred the stones. We followed and brought more stones.*"

"The red spheres," Otto whispered.

"They're not answering your question," Alvarez said.

Again, Otto spoke into the mike. "Why have you come?"

Crackles and hiss.

"*It is our destiny.*"

An industrial sewing machine worked its way down Otto's spine. He looked at Stella with alarm. It was like looking into a mirror—the same heart-sick expression.

Manifest destiny.

The statement left no room for humanity.

"You're killing our people. Is it your intention to anger us?"

Snaps, hisses and pops. A faint babble of voices veered in and out of the loop like a passing comet. A stream of bubbles trickled up from the corner of Witherspoon's mouth like a string of pearls.

"*First we transferred the stones. We followed and brought more stones.*"

"Oh great," Alvarez muttered.

"You've committed acts of war," Otto said. "Do you understand that?"

Stella put a hand on his arm but said nothing. He knew he was exceeding his authority but hell, somebody had to represent the human race.

More hissing and pops. That strange loop of multiple voices curved through the room. Otto heard it moving from speaker to speaker like Dolby sound, something Frank Zappa might have cooked up.

"Who's in charge?" he said.

Hissing, crackling, giggling.

"What is six-two-four?"

Hiss crack pop.

"Where are you from?"

"*From the land of sky blue waters,*" sang the speakers like a long lost radio commercial coming home at last, which is exactly what it was. Otto only recognized the ancient jingle because his grandmother used to croon that, and other old commercials to him when he slept over at her house, a welcome respite from his grimly instructive father. "See the USA in your Chevrolet." "Brylcreem, a little dab'll do ya."

If they'd intercepted a radio signal from the fifties, it meant they were in the same universe. The earth had been polluting the universe with signals since the invention of the wireless. A century and a half of screaming detritus.

It was a big universe. The earliest signals, traveling at the speed of light, formed a sphere of ever expanding radio noise. After 150 years, it was a big sphere.

After five minutes of silence, Otto went to the phone on the wall and entered his fourteen digit code. He would have preferred the Ocelot, but it couldn't transmit through a mile of rock. Last night, after they'd made love, Stella's hand came out from under the pillow with the Ocelot in her hands.

"What's this?" she'd asked.

Now the Ocelot was in his pocket, inert.

He listened to the pings and whirrs as his connection bounced off the comsat and around the world. He looked around. The lab had a sickly cast with a yellowing linoleum floor and flickering fluorescents in aluminum shrouds.

Six minutes later the National Security Director picked up the phone. "Hang on," she said. The phone went silent.

Thirty seconds later she was back on. "What's happening?"

"Madame Director you may want to be alone before I speak."

"That bad, eh? Just a minute."

Another thirty seconds passed. She came back on the line. "What?"

"We have a Close Encounters scenario."

This time the silence was different, like waiting for a stone to hit water.

CHAPTER SEVENTY-FOUR
BON APP III

Thursday.

Otto told Yee everything that had happened since discovering the cave yesterday.

"What's your feeling about these visitors?" she said. "Do they come in peace?"

Their voices made his flesh warp. Their image triggered panic and flight. "No. Like hell. If they came in peace, would they be burning up our people?"

"That's my feeling too. See if you can find out how long they've been here and how many of their teams are ensconced in human skulls."

"I'll try but they seem to ignore any question they don't like."

"Will they respond to an existential threat?"

Will we?

"Ma'am, they seem to have no problem going down with the ship, so to speak."

"Are they secure? Is there any chance they'll escape?"

"I don't see how. If they could have done so, they would have done it already. It's my belief that their system was damaged when we dragged Witherspoon into the pond. This could be new technology to them as well."

But there were six numbers.

"Keep on it. A SETI xenologist will arrive this afternoon. How do you surmise they enter the body?"

"I believe that this thing that looks like a spaceship is in fact a spaceship. They pilot them manually, so to speak. I believe they enter the body through soft tissue—the eyes, ears, nose and mouth. Same thing happened to Winner and when he erupted, the team targeted Stella. Only grazed her, thank God."

"That would make her the first woman so targeted."

"We don't know that."

"True."

"But they failed. Maybe that's why they don't target women. Their skulls are too thick."

Yee chuckled. "Did you get the intel on Yakovitch?"

"Yes. I wish we had video. Or a body."

"Is Stella there?"

"Yes she is. Would you like me to put her on?"

"Please."

Otto gestured Stella over and handed her the phone. "It's Yee."

"Hello Margaret," Stella said softly. She listened. "I arrived right after that happened. Yes, I understand."

Beat.

"That's nonsense, Margaret. It's exactly as he said."

She handed the phone back.

"Hello?" Otto said.

"Why did you shoot Agent Hornbuckle?"

"I have no excuse. He shot my dog."

"Well, either you have an excuse or you don't."

"It was a complete breakdown on my part. I'll have to live with it for the rest of my life."

"I may not be able to get you out of this, Otto."

"I understand, Madame Director."

"It's good you have a criminal attorney out there."

"Yes'm."

"Can you route that feed to me?"

"I don't think so. This is an air-gapped system but we're recording everything."

"Okay. Very good work by the way. Keep me appraised."

"Yes'm."

Otto hung up and turned to Stella. "What did she ask you?"

"She asked me if you were out of your freakin' mind."

The lights flickered.

"There's something going on," Alvarez said with an edge in his voice. The terminal showed a spike graph, the neon green on black line gyrating wildly.

Otto focused on the head in the jar. A trickle of bubbles fell upward from one nostril, orange eyes bulging from internal pressure until they looked as if they would burst. The head slowly turned from side to side as if taking in the scene, the pinpoint black pupils drifting apart.

The head shook violently causing the Plexiglas cylinder to bump and jive on the wooden pallets with a weird clattering sound. The whole lab vibrated, beakers and soda cans dancing off counter tops and crashing to the floor, giant springs groaning like hell's hinges. Otto ran to the door and tried to open it, but it was fused shut from pressure. He could hear the guards outside shouting.

The room jounced and rocked on its enormous springs creating a nerve-grating shriek that penetrated to the marrow. Stella reached out and took Otto's hand. He pulled her close.

The lights went out.

It was black as a cave.

No. Not entirely black. There was one source of light: Witherspoon's orange glowing eyes.

"SHIT!" Alvarez said. A match flared.

A deep thrum added to the din and the lights went back on. An emergency generator had kicked in.

Stella pointed at Witherspoon's head.

The caretaker's left eye erupted from within releasing a plume of coagulated blood. The tiny dart zipped through the solution to the outer wall. Otto stepped away from Stella's grip, bent at the knees and heaved the massive Plexiglas screen just enough to squeeze through. He raced to the cylinder as the tiny dart began to drill through with a high-pitched whine adding to a sonic storm that incited madness.

With astonishing speed, the miniscule vehicle powered through the space-age plastic. Otto watched from five centimeters, fascinated. It looked just like an ant.

Like those ants he'd eaten in the desert.

"With a donkey's jawbone I have made donkeys of them. With a donkey's jawbone I have killed a thousand men."

The vehicle had almost reached the outer surface. It's black needle nose broke through. In an instant, it would be gone, or would burrow successfully into Otto or Alvarez.

Otto laid his cheek against the cool smooth plastic and opened his mouth. As the vehicle emerged he bit down, crushing it between his molars.

That's how you do it, he thought. You eat your fucking enemies.

There was a white flash and the world blew up.

CHAPTER SEVENTY-FIVE
GRAFT

Sunday afternoon.

His first realization that he was still alive was the feeling of having a concrete block lodged in his cheek. Otto's jaw felt stiff, immobile. He opened his left eye. The light dazzled him, bringing tears. His right eye was covered with a bandage. The room was blindingly white. The ceiling was white, and the bed clothes and walls. Sunlight streamed through the Venetian blinds. Stella slept in a chair, long hair concealing most of her face.

An IV drip had been inserted in Otto's wrist. Tentatively he used his left hand to feel his chin. The lower right half of his face was constricted by some kind of device using metal screws inserted in the jawbone. He tried to sit up. A wave of dizziness overcame him and he lay on his back staring at the white ceiling, noticing the myriad tiny acoustical holes, the inset fluorescent lighting. He stared at the ceiling so long it began to flow.

He was in a hospital. The room smelled of disinfectant and clean linen. His mind was a blank. How did he get here? What happened to his face? Then he remembered—Cheyenne Mountain, the spiders. Everything came back in a rush.

"Stella," he tried to say. It came out flat and weak.

Stella opened her eyes and brushed the hair out of her face revealing a flesh-colored bandage on her forehead.

"Otto!"

She came over to the bed looking down at him with worshipful eyes blotting out all doubt. Stella had come back to him. That was the true miracle. Everything else was secondary. He tried to smile but it hurt too much.

Stella laid a palm on his chest, leaned over and kissed him on the cheek.

"Don't try to talk. It blew off half your jaw. The doctors did a bone graft. They're going to take skin from your ass and paste it on your face. I told them you look like an ass anyway …"

Stella smiled as a tear drop rolled off her check onto Otto's nose. He tried to sit up. Stella firmly, but gently, pushed him back.

"Don't. Give it some time."

Otto tried to speak. Stella held up her hand.

"Don't. I'll get you a pad and a pen in a minute. The federal district court is indicting you for the killing of Agent Hornbuckle. I contacted John Bullis at Camacho, Anderson and Bullis. He's one of the best criminal defense attorneys in the world. I can't be your attorney for obvious reasons." She held up a business card and placed it in the drawer of the nightstand next to his bed. "Call them."

Otto didn't care about that. She loved him again. He pointed to his wrist as if there were a watch.

"How long? You've been out for seventy-two hours. The FBI and federal marshals are rounding up every recent Pawnee Grove attendee for CAT scans. The Russians and Chinese are doing the same. There have been no immolations since you took control of the Witherspoon team."

Otto pointed to her bandage.

"I got hit with some junk. When you chomped the rocket it was a directed explosion. One of the servers exploded. Gus is fine."

Otto reached for a red Solo cup with a straw in it on the cantilevered table to his left. Stella reached over and snagged it, her breasts brushing his chest. She held it for him while he sipped.

"I have to get back to D.C. but I wanted to be here when you woke up to tell you I love you and I'll be waiting for you. I'll stay for the indictment. They found files at Hornbuckle's that never should have left the building. Now there's a full-scale investigation into his background."

Otto shrugged and made a 'what me worry' expression with his hands. It's what he'd wanted all along.

There was a knock at the door followed by the appearance of a tall middle-aged nurse in white slacks and blouse. "Mr. White, you're awake!" Otto caught a glimpse of a Denver police officer seated outside his room on a chair.

The nurse consulted an electronic monitor above and behind Otto, then timed his pulse with her index and middle fingers on his neck beneath the brace. "Excellent, excellent. Dr. Haas will be in in a minute. He's your reconstructive surgeon and he says that the chances are excellent he can restore full activity. Of course, you've suffered nerve damage and it will never be the same. It might even be numb. How do you feel?"

Otto made the thumbs up.

The nurse said to Stella, "Shouldn't be much longer" and left.

Moments later Dr. Haas entered. He was tall and broad with a full head of wavy hair and a mustache. "How's the jaw?" he said.

Otto made the thumb's up.

"We're using a printing technique called laser melting to construct your new jaw. We take an X-ray for CAD and build it up with metallic titanium, then we coat it with a type of ceramic designed with your own DNA. I'll install the new jaw tomorrow."

Otto made a writing gesture with his hands. Stella opened the night table drawer and withdrew a pad of note paper and a pen. She handed these to Otto. He scribbled, handed the pad to Haas. Stella looked over his arm.

How long before I can talk?

"Hard to say," the surgeon said. "Possibly within a week if the graft holds."

Otto nodded. The surgeon patted him on the leg. "We'll have another look tomorrow."

The surgeon left the room.

Lon Barnett was waiting.

CHAPTER SEVENTY-SIX

Horrifying Events

Barnett knocked on the door and entered looking grim, holding some white papers folded in half lengthwise. He wore a two-piece gray suit, white shirt, blue tie, gold clasp. He nodded at Stella.

"Is this a good time?"

"It's as good a time as any," Stella said.

Barnett went to the foot of the bed. "Otto, this gives me no great pleasure. The entire team is proud of what you've been able to accomplish and I'm sure the court will keep that in mind."

Barnett cleared his throat. "Otto White, you're under arrest for the murder of Agent Hornbuckle. Anything you say can and will be used against you in a court of law. You have the right to an attorney. If you cannot afford an attorney the court will provide one for you. Do you understand these rights?"

Otto nodded.

Barnett flattened out the papers, handed them to Otto with a pen. "Please sign at the bottom."

"What charge did you settle on?" Stella said.

"Manslaughter. Not even the DA had the heart to charge him with first degree murder. Plus there's his service and medical discharge to consider."

Not guilty by reason of insanity. Just like Lester Durant.

Stella held her hand out. "May I?"

She read the indictment and handed it back.

"Again," Barnett said, "I'd like to shake your hand."

Otto stuck out his hand and they shook.

"Good luck," Barnett said. "Say, the chief wants that Ocelot back. Do you have it?"

Otto shook his head. He hadn't seen it since the lab.

"If it shows up I'd appreciate a call," Barnett said and left.

Stella lingered a few minutes fussing over the pillows, making sure Otto had water close at hand. She took something out of her purse and slipped it under the covers into his hand. "In case you need to call somebody," she whispered.

She kissed him again on the forehead, gathered her things and left.

Otto found the TV remote in the nightstand and turned it to the all news channel. The President was about to address the nation from the East Room. A hushed reporter announced his imminent arrival and then there he was, walking up to the podium shaking hands and exchanging greets. He squared off behind the big podium, which bristled with a half dozen mikes. The Presidential Seal hung on the front of the wooden lectern.

The President wore a gray three-piece pin-stripe, a light blue shirt, and a red, white and blue tie. With his silver hair neatly parted, he looked like a man you could trust with your infant daughter while heading down to the corner bar for a drink. If you looked up "president" in the dictionary, you would see this man.

The press secretary sang, "Ladies and gentlemen, the President of the United States." There was a smattering of applause in keeping with the solemnity of the event.

President Reynolds faced the camera with a serious expression. "Good evening, my fellow Americans. I appear before you tonight to announce significant developments in a problem that has recently plagued many nations including our own, spontaneous human combustion.

"Although some authorities have known about this frightening phenomenon for years, it has only become public knowledge in the last few days. There have been countless rumors as to the source of these horrifying events from terrorism to God's wrath. Yesterday, American scientists working in conjunction with their counterparts in Russia, China, France, Japan, the United Kingdom, Abu Dhabi and Brazil, pinpointed the cause, if not the method of these events.

"We have annihilated the leaders behind this wave of terror and expect that from now on, instances of spontaneous human combustion will be drastically reduced, if not stop altogether. I am not at liberty to divulge the perpetrators' identities for reasons of national security, but I can assure you that your government is doing its utmost to protect you from this threat.

"Fellow citizens—do not be afraid. Do not let these incidents disrupt your daily lives. Those behind these heinous crimes have paid with their lives. I want to thank our brave men and women in uniform and in particular the FBI and CIA for their contributions. I wish I could call out every single patriot who contributed to this case but again, for reasons of national security, I cannot.

"In the days and weeks to come, we will release the details as they become available. Thank you and good night."

People shouted "Mr. President!"

Reynolds had turned to go but now he turned back, gripping the sides of the podium in both hands. "What is it, Jack?"

"Can you tell us what country or countries are behind the attacks?"

The President stared.

"What is it, Jack," the President said. He began to sweat. A puff of smoke escaped the corner of his mouth. His eyes flared yellow and the screen went white accompanied by screaming, the sounds of furniture being shoved aside and Secret Service personnel shouting.

CHAPTER
SEVENTY-SEVEN
LOCKDOWN

Monday through the following Monday.

Within two hours, the Vice President took the oath of office and issued a no-fly order for the entire country. National Guard patrolled the streets around the capitol in armored personnel characters. Anti-aircraft batteries were mounted on the roof of the White House. The concrete barriers went back up. Rail traffic ground to a halt as TSA inspectors swarmed the trains. Manic bureaucrats took precautions that had absolutely nothing to do with the danger at hand.

All top government officials including cabinet secretaries, the White House staff and heads of intelligence agencies voluntarily submitted to MRI scans. They found three officials, including the Secretary of Energy, hosting the parasite. The Secretary of Energy flared out in the MRI machine, causing a massive explosion that destroyed the Dr. Bartholomew and Elizabeth Chandler Wing at Bethesda Naval Medical Center, killing twenty-two and injuring fourteen.

The other two were taken into custody and isolated, raising civil liberty questions. The WH reached out to brain surgeons to extract the pellets of death.

Both Al Qaeda and the Anarchist Brotherhood claimed credit for the President's death.

Riots broke out in Detroit, Los Angeles and Miami. The governors of those states called in the National Guard. It looked to Otto like martial law. Only in small town America did life proceed with any semblance of normality. The mood at St. Mary's Hospital in Denver was grim. Formerly cheerful and joking nurses made closed zippers of their mouths and went about their duties like sleepwalkers.

Otto's personal guard increased to two. A young FBI agent joined the cop in the hall. Otto was out of bed walking around on the second day and made a point to keep his door shut.

The new President hadn't said a word about aliens.

How did they expect to pull it off?

Otto had a Grade 6 security rating. Stella was an attorney—she knew how to keep her mouth shut. But a secret this explosive would not stay buried. People would notice the takeover of Pawnee Grove by government troops and scientists. They would note the flame-outs associated with the Grove and start asking the hard questions. Some minor bureaucrat at the National Geodetic Survey would recall an unusual request for magnetic resonance imaging in the mountains north of Estes Park.

The rumors would grow attracting more bloggers, more citizen journalists, and perhaps even a few disinterested members of what passed for the press these days until one day *The National Enquirer* would shriek, "TARGET EARTH—ALIENS BEHIND BURNINGS!"

Mass hysteria roiled beneath the surface. People were already stressed out about the lousy economy, the terrible schools, the price of gas, the inevitable cry for more taxes and increasing commercial blocks on television. Food, insurance sales skyrocketed as did ready meals, distillers, batteries, generators, guns and ammo.

The world entered the heretofore unknown zone of shock overload. It was a matter of degree. Never had so many things gone wrong at once: the world economy, tribal warfare, global warming, global cooling, the dissatisfaction that had been building since the eighties. Since the dawn of time. There were more people now, less chance to get away, to let off steam, to enjoy some blessed privacy, unless you were rich. Social media exacerbated the difficulties exponentially as bloggers, periodicals and journalists clung to the hoary adage, "If it bleeds, it leads." Moral scolds dueled with sneering progressives. God's wrath! Gaia's revenge!

Riots broke out in Athens, Paris, Moscow, Marseilles, Stockholm, London, Belarus, the Ukraine, you name it. Millions of people screaming *Stop the world I want to get off!*

President Hamish Burke declared wage and price controls.

At least a dozen Grove attendees could not be located.

Was it even a matter for national security?

Was it the state's job to grapple with theological evil? What about the separation of church and state? Otto had his own views. He knew he was in the minority.

All Otto had to do was claim God told him to shoot Hornbuckle and the state would happily classify him insane. He could hang out with the Below the Beltline Sniper. But Otto had no intention of avoiding his duty. He would not, he could not allow himself to be incarcerated.

If God exists so does Satan. The *Skorzh* were an incomprehensible evil. If that wasn't satanic, what was? What if the *Skorzh* had been created in Satan's own image? What did that say about humanity?

Ever since Libya, Otto felt that he'd been spared for a purpose and now that purpose had been revealed to him.

He wished he could speak. He badly wanted to talk to that priest.

The cast came off a week later, Dr. Haas pleased with the results. Otto looked at himself in the mirror. He looked like a Steve Bissette drawing, normal from the nose up, but with a jaw that looked like it had been pasted together from cardboard and ass meat. Half his teeth were missing. Haas intended to replace them with synthetics sunk into the new jawbone he'd made.

The jawbone of an ass.

Otto spoke out of the left side of his mouth sounding like a hare lip. Bullis had been unable to visit due to the no fly order, but they finally spoke, ten days after Otto had been admitted.

"Mr. White," Bullis said via phone. "We usually avoid insanity pleas due to the difficulty of convincing a jury, but in your case it's the way to go. I've obtained classified medical reports regarding your service prior to your call-back. You should never have been called back in the first place."

Otto knew this was bullshit, but it was lawyer think so he let it go.

"The President's going to lift the no-fly order this evening. I can come out and meet with you on Friday, if that's convenient."

"Not going anywhere," Otto mumbled into the bedside phone. He kept the Ocelot concealed and charged every night. When he'd finished with Bullis, Otto went into the bathroom, shut the door and locked it, turned on the fan and sat on the toilet. He assumed that either the Bureau or the Agency had bugged his room. He crouched, concealing his mouth with the Ocelot in case there was a tiny camera linked to a computer with lip-read technology.

He dialed the Time Warp in Boulder and left a message for Kleiser.

Kleiser called back an hour later.

They spoke for an hour.

CHAPTER SEVENTY-EIGHT
COPY CATS

Monday morning.

President Hamish Burke met with CIA Director Luther Brubaker, National Security Advisor Margaret Yee, FBI Director Howard Lubitch, and Homeland Security Director General Rolf Panny. Chief of Staff Murray Compton had agreed to stay on to assist the new President in transition. They met in the Situation Room with the lights turned low, the wall of monitors reflecting the continuing disintegration of civilization, conflagrations and the odd flaming man.

If Burke were resentful about initially being kept out of the loop, he didn't show it. Yee had brought him up to speed with the developments at Pawnee Grove and Cheyenne Mountain.

"Gentlemen, Lady," the President began. "The Russkies finally agreed to share data with us. We'll be getting their videos and autopsy results this afternoon."

"Rolf, what have you discovered about the secret sauce?"

The secret sauce—the unknown ingredient detected in the remains of several victims and in the "Blood of the White Man."

"Dr. Ellen Jo Taylor, Head of Microbiology at Stanford believes it's a form of organic hydrocarbon. This appears to be an oxymoron, but as Dr. Taylor points out, we're dealing with an unknown element. They're still mapping its magnetic properties. She plans to subject the substance to the Martin Mass Spectroscope within the next couple of days. We'll know more then.

"In the meantime she's developed a blood test to find the element that gives us an alternative to the MRI scans. Dr. Hayley Gross has the test and is forwarding details to every hospital and emergency clinic in the country. It's called the BWM test."

"BWM?" Brubaker bristled.

"Blood of the white man," Panny explained.

The President turned his bland face to Yee. "Doctor?"

"Rich white men are experiencing loneliness right now. Not even their wives and mistresses want to get too close. Everybody who even knows somebody who's been to the grove are lining up for MRIs. Two staff doctors at St. Mary's in Denver where White is being treated have been put on administrative leave until they complete their scans. Every scanner in the nation has been pressed into use. Creeps are coming out of the woodwork to claim they'd been to the Grove. A lot more claim they've been invaded or possessed. It's like try-outs for American Exorcism. Here's where that blood test will save us time and money."

"Can't we simply eliminate the more outré individuals with an interview?" the President asked. "If some bum comes into an ER with needle tracks up and down his arm and claims to have a chip in his skull, I think we can safely eliminate him."

"Sir," Yee said, "we do not yet know the extent of the invasion. We have no enemy with whom to negotiate except for three men who tested positive and are in protective custody. We can't just go in there and remove the ship. That requires the finest brain surgeons in the country, if we want to keep these men alive. The operations can take hours. And what happens if the aliens power up during the operation and fly out? And leave their little calling card?"

The President shrugged. "I don't see where we have a choice. The future of civilization is at stake. I want those men operated on as soon as possible and I don't want the ships damaged. We must have someone with whom to negotiate."

The President turned. "Rolf, Howard, how close are we to understanding how that teleportation device works?"

Panny held his hands up. "Not even warm, Mr. President. We're still studying its function. No one is permitted to even touch it. The radiation readings are quite high so we're leaving it alone for right now."

"'Cause I'm thinking," the President continued, "if we could find a way to reverse that we could send an expeditionary force through to see what the hell's going on. Maybe some SEALS or something."

"Mr. President," Panny said, "it may be years before we understand the technology involved. It may be decades."

"That's unacceptable, Rolf. This country launched the Manhattan Project because it was necessary for our survival and the survival of civilization. This country put a man on the moon. Whatever resources you require, I want you working on it until you figure it out. Knowing it can be done, *has* been done, is half the battle."

"As you wish, Mr. President," the general said. "We're working with SETI and the Stanford physics department."

"Do you have a team trained to deal with extraterrestrials?"

Panny nodded.

"We've been working on it since the seventies," Brubaker said.

"What do these goddamn bugs want?" the President asked semi-rhetorically.

For a moment, no one stirred.

"Mr. President," Brubaker said. "I can only surmise they seek to displace man as the head of the food chain on this planet."

"But why go about it in such a haphazard manner?" the President said.

"Mr. President," Yee said in a thin, but tensile voice, "these creatures are alien. They are, by definition, unknowable. We can't think of them as sentient beings possessing any semblance of morality. We must regard them as an implacable, unknowable enemy, like the plague or an infestation of ... of spiders."

Burke nodded.

"Mr. President," Brubaker said. "The Russkies are launching mass cyber-attacks on our security system. So are the Chinese and the Iranians. They're terrified we'll crack this technology."

"Advanced Networks is on it," Yee said.

"Sir," Murray Compton said from the far end of the table. It was the first he'd spoken since they'd sat down. "You might want to address the issue of copy cats when you speak to the nation tonight."

The President arched his eyebrows. "Copy cats?"

"Yes sir. Loons issue a fatwa on Facebook, Twitter, Google—they're against the corporations or something. They go to the mall or the courthouse, douse themselves with gas and set themselves on fire. Six so far. Unfortunately, people believe the internet statements are part of a conspiracy and that these self-immolators are part of the invasion."

Burke rested his chin in his hands. "Why can't the invasion be the conspiracy they don't believe?"

"Murphy's law," Yee muttered *sotto voce*. Everybody laughed.

"Murray, get in touch with Sylvia—have her write something about the copy cats." The President looked around the table. "What else?"

All he saw were grim faces.

"All right, let's meet here again tomorrow and see where we're at."

The directors stirred, stuffing their laptops into their bags, pausing to shake hands with Burke on the way out. Yee was last in line.

"Margaret," the President said, "hang with me a minute."

CHAPTER
SEVENTY-NINE
MAGAZINE

Yee sat at the President's right, folded her hands on her lap and waited placidly like a tiny Buddha.

"Have we gotten everything out of Otto White that we can?"

"Mr. President, White was tasked with finding the source and means of these atrocities. He has fulfilled his mission. Legally, I don't see how you can continue to use him in the field after he shot a federal agent."

Burke rubbed his hands. "I don't want to lose someone with his skills right now. There's so much about these invaders we don't understand. We need people who can think fresh, see things in new ways."

"Otto White regards the invaders as satanic. He believes they are literally representatives of the devil."

"I don't see how that alters the equation. Murray says the same thing about you, Margaret."

Yee essayed a chilly smile. "Otto White has emotional issues. Shooting Hornbuckle—that's bound to have repercussions. I just don't think he's reliable."

Burke shook his head. "What a shame. Thank you for your candid assessment."

The President pushed his chair back, but Yee remained where she was. "Is there something else, Margaret?"

"Mr. President, there is disturbing evidence that Hornbuckle had a hidden agenda."

"What evidence?"

"Videotape taken four weeks ago of Hornbuckle searching White's home."

"Did White know this?"

"Yes, sir. He set the link up for real time streaming. I believe that someone close to you has initiated a rogue operation to learn the source of the immolations to sell to the highest bidder."

"That's a very serious accusation. Can you back it up?"

"Not at the moment. At least whatever it is can't be used as a weapon. Not by us, at least."

"Not yet," the President said. "Don't tell me whom you suspect. I don't want to know. Bring me some proof and I'll act on it."

"Yes, sir."

She remained seated, her mouth a grim line. "There is one other thing, Mr. President." She removed her laptop from her shoulder bag and opened it so that both could see the screen.

"This is an X-ray taken of Dr. Lewis Berman this morning at St. Mary's in Denver."

The President stared at the image on the screen. "Oh my God."

The X-ray showed six tiny black spaceships stacked vertically like ammo in a magazine.

CHAPTER EIGHTY
CLUSTERFUCK

Friday afternoon.

John Bullis arrived at the hospital at two-thirty Friday afternoon. He showed his ID and leather portfolio to the cop and the Fed and was admitted to Otto's room. Bullis was of medium height and weight with Geraldo-esque brown hair, glasses and a bushy mustache. He wore a light tan cotton sports jacket over khakis, a white shirt open at the neck.

Otto rose from his seat where he'd been watching the news. "Pleased to meet you," Bullis said, shaking Otto's hand.

Bullis turned and started to shut the door.

The cop said, "Door has to stay open, Mr. Bullis."

Bullis framed himself between door and edge. "No, it doesn't. Lawyer/client privilege." He slipped a surgical mask over his chin and shut the door.

Otto shut the blinds and turned off the lights. It was dark in the room but still visible. Wordlessly they went into the bathroom. Otto turned on the tiny night light by the sink. He turned on the fan, which made a loud mechanical noise.

"You are the fuckin' bomb, dude!" Bullis said quietly, removing several objects from his briefcase. "I can't believe I know you!"

"I can't believe it either. Let's move"

"Bullis" stripped off his wig, glasses and mustache and handed them to Otto. Kleiser took off his clothes. Otto slapped on the aftershave Kleiser was wearing. Otto's white cotton turtleneck concealed Kleiser's tats. They exited the bathroom. Kleiser sat on the bed and Otto sat in the chair. He turned the television to Cajun Pawnbrokers and turned the sound up. Kleiser turned on his laptop and angled it so that Otto could see.

Otto leaned forward and spoke softly. "Dr. Haas usually stops in between four and five. You won't be able to fool him. What about Bullis?"

Kleiser smiled. "A computer glitch has rerouted Mr. Bullis' flight to Kansas City. I doubt if he'll make it here until very late in the evening."

"Do you know how you're gonna get out of here?"

"No sweat, Holmes. I've done my homework. Do what you gotta."

"Thanks, Randy."

"Are you kidding? You the man with the plan!"

They huddled for fifteen minutes going over the plan. Otto put on the white cotton surgical mask that covered the mouth, nose and chin, checked himself in the mirror. They checked each other. Otto opened the door and stepped halfway out.

"I'll be in touch," he enunciated carefully and painfully. "You want the door open?"

"Leave it open," said the fed. Otto walked down the hall to the elevators.

Kleiser opened his laptop and went to work. Fifteen minutes later the fire alarm sounded and the ceiling-mounted sprinkler system turned on. Utter chaos. Two minutes after that, the hospital suffered power failure and was momentarily plunged into darkness.

"Stay where you are!" the fed warned.

"I'm not going anywhere," Kleiser responded seated placidly in his chair with his laptop open. The fed withdrew muttering into his headset. Kleiser put on a pair of swimming goggles and pulled the tab on the smoke grenade Otto had told him how to make.

Within seconds the room was opaque. Kleiser stood clutching his laptop with his back to the wall just inside the door and when the fed rushed in to save him, slipped out without being noticed.

The generators kicked in when Kleiser was halfway down the staircase. He exited the building into the parking lot along with dozens of employees and visitors, patients being wheeled out on gurneys. He left the hospital grounds as the first fire trucks arrived.

CHAPTER
EIGHTY-ONE
SAFE HOUSE

O tto had a window of opportunity to return home and grab what he needed before federal agents descended on his mountain. He'd had plenty of time to think out the plan. The battered old Subaru wagon was in the Sav*A*Lot parking lot where Kleiser had left it, the key on top of the left front tire.

Two hours and twenty minutes later Otto drove the exhausted Subaru off his mountain road into the bushes and unlocked the gate to his place. Working his way around the tank trap he came to a pile of two-by-sixes covered with a desert camo tarp. He placed the boards side by side until they completely covered the tank trap leaving him drenched through his shirt and his jaw aching.

He didn't waste time showering. He went straight to the monster truck, stripping it of its camouflage. He unlocked his gun safe and took what he needed. The truck consisted of an old Dodge Power Wagon mounted above twenty-six inch wheels powered by a twin-turbo small-block Chevy V8 through two differentials to all wheels.

It looked like tens of thousands of monster trucks all over Colorado.

There was no question in Otto's mind that Hornbuckle had planted a bug. It took him four minutes to find it. Rather than chip away at the epoxy he used a cordless drill to render it inoperable.

Truck loaded with gear he set off down the mountain. Two-and-a-half hours later, he pulled into the strip mall on Colfax housing Casa Bonita. Kleiser emerged from between two vehicles bearing a backpack, climbed up into the truck using the running board and handles.

"Wow," he said. "Great view from up here."

"I need this for later, but right now we've got to drive cross country in something less conspicuous. Any ideas?"

"I boosted that Subaru from Rocky's Autos. There's an old Ford we can use."

"Where?

"At the safe house." Kleiser gestured toward the restaurant. "You want to get something to eat?"

"I'm still on semi-solids. We need to hit a grocery. I have a list."

An hour later Kleiser emerged from King Soopers with a shopping cart filled with supplies that they loaded into the truck. Otto drove northwest according to Kleiser's directions toward Hygiene. In Hygiene, they entered a neighborhood of twisting roads and cul-de-sacs until they came to the address Kleiser had dictated, a rambling two-acre property at the end of Brigham Court. A FOR SALE sign in the front yard named a Denver realtor.

The battered mailbox said "Johnson" in hardware store paste-on letters.

They drove onto the property through the open gate, past the shabby ranch house to an old gray barn. It was dusk and Otto switched on the monster truck's lights. Leaving the truck idling they climbed down and Kleiser opened the barn's twin wood doors with a horrendous squeak. The interior was dark and dusty, with old farm implements visible in corners and on the wall. Otto drove the truck inside and parked it next to a battered Ford Taurus SHO covered in dust. Kleiser opened the driver's door, slid in and released the hood. He got back out, found a trickle charger on a shelf and hooked it up.

"Should be good to go in the morning."

Otto looked at the plates. They were five years out of date.

"No prob, dude. I got plates in the house."

"Whose car is this?" Otto said.

"My friend, Rich. He owns this place ..."

"Who's Rich?"

"An entrepreneurial type. He invented the computer rat."

"The rat?"

"Yeah, it's like a mouse only it sits on the ground and you operate it with your foot. You don't get that carpal tunnel syndrome. I don't know how you can avoid the rat, man. He's been pushing that thing 24/7 for months."

They carried their groceries into the house through the back door into the kitchen.

Otto went through the darkened house, through the living room where dozens of tiny lights winked at him to the front porch and sat in the rocker. It was the type of shabby genteel neighborhood that fifty years ago represented the American dream. The lots were a little bigger out here and less fussed over, with the occasional vehicle visible on blocks; the type of neighborhood where most men had a project car and the women had vegetable gardens.

He heard Kleiser putting the groceries away in the kitchen followed by the thin sound of a classic rock station playing "Black Water."

Kleiser came out to the porch. "Me and Rich are tight—he lets me use this as a home base. Come on in, I'll show you around."

No wonder they could never find him, Otto thought. He followed Kleiser into the dark interior, which smelled of dust, stale cat urine and electronics. Tiny lights glowed at him from every corner: red, blue, green, yellow. Kleiser turned on a table lamp. The living room was crammed with servers, routers, hard drives and monitors. It was warm inside. Kleiser went around opening windows.

"Must be a hell of a friend to risk numerous felonies by letting you stay here," Otto said.

"He's a good friend. I help him out from time to time."

"What kind of help?"

"Technical shit."

"I'll bet," Otto said, sitting on the long, low cloth sofa. He picked up a stack of magazines from the dusty side table. The Nov. 12, 2011 issue of *Barron's* was addressed to Richard Johnson, 14 Brigham Court, Hygiene.

Kleiser went into the kitchen and returned with two Fat Tires. "I got frozen pizza. What do you want, pepperoni or pepperoni?"

"I'll just have soup. Got a straw?"

Kleiser went back to the kitchen and returned with a straw, which Otto put in his beer.

"Do your neighbors know you're here?"

"We wave to each other."

"Can you get into national security from here?"

"Probably. What do you need?"

Otto told him.

"Just let me pop this pizza in the oven and we'll get started."

CHAPTER
EIGHTY-TWO
CLANDESTINE

K agemusha sat on the veranda of his coastal Virginia farm with a Tom Collins in hand, a Tom Clancy on his Nook and feet up on the ottoman, staring out at the blue waters of Chesapeake Bay while Doris fussed in the kitchen. As a young man, Kagemusha had been a field agent in East Berlin tasked with bringing out a Russian scientist, Nikolai Gohnkorov, who had been working on a weapon that caused people to burst into flame at a distance. Gohnkorov had allegedly successfully tested the device on dissidents at Makarov Station above the Arctic Circle.

Kagemusha's Control had been legendary spymaster George Brodsky, CIA Director under Bush Sr. Brodsky was among the original Cold Warriors including Dulles, McNamara and Kirkpatrick. Their guiding principle was that the Soviet Union was the U.S.' natural enemy, our greatest enemy, and was to be curtailed, discouraged and resisted on every front.

Operation Wicker Man, as the agency dubbed it, began in the mid-fifties concurrent with secret government programs to develop telepathy, teleportation, and discover alien intelligence.

"Black Ops" they used to call them. They'd recruited Control right off the Harvard Quad in his senior year. He'd been active in ROTC—back when Harvard had ROTC—majored in poli sci and minored in Russian.

He'd done two tours of duty in Beirut before being reassigned to Germany, where he received extensive training in spy craft, hand-to-hand combat, improvised explosive devices, spy ware and other tools of the trade. He began a remarkable string of successful missions that soon brought him to Brodsky's attention. Brodsky flew into Ramstein to personally bring Control up to speed on the Gohnkorov defection.

"The transfer will take place near Neustadt. We will launch a diversion at 0458, a quarter mile north. The diversion will cut power to the fence. You'll have a twenty-minute window to get your man across. He'll come alone. He'll wear a ghillie suit. Here are the particulars." Brodsky handed him a thick white manila envelope with TOP SECRET stamped in red.

"You're a young man with a great deal of promise, Brubaker," Brodsky told him. "I've got my eye on you."

"Yes, sir. Thank you, sir."

Three nights later Brubaker found himself freezing his ass off in the tree line in a windbreak on a ridge overlooking a wheat field and beyond that the ten-meter no-man's-land bordering the fence. Rain limited visibility to the tree line opposite, a quarter klick away. They'd been waiting for just such a night as this. The hurricane fence was eight feet high topped with concertina wire. The fence was electrified. Plowed earth planted with landmines extended ten meters past the fence. A guard tower was just visible a half klick to the north.

Brubaker wore a dark green down-filled parka with the hood up, heavy snowmobile gloves, Schnelling hiking shoes and ski pants and carried an Oakes Night Vision unit, a monocular that weighed four pounds. He also carried a radio, but there would be no broadcasts lest he reveal his position. The puncture point was miles from civilization or highways, a fertile valley devoted to hops, wheat and soy production.

He tried walking in place to keep warm and wished he'd brought some of the instant heat packets he'd been offered. His breath hung in front of his face like a word balloon. He checked his watch. Seconds to go.

At exactly 0458 there was a flash to the north followed by a dull whump. A column of flame lit up the sky, toasting the bottoms of the cumulous clouds a marshmallow orange. Brubaker trained his mono on the guard tower. The guy in the tower was trying to phone somebody. He looked frantic. His back was to Brubaker, who retrained his monocular on the field directly before him. Two flashlight blinks—space—followed by a third. Gohnkorov was in position. Now it was Brubaker's move.

They'd scanned the ground for mines from the trees and from the skies. Brubaker had memorized the route so that he could run it in his sleep. He ran it now, head down, heart pounding, right up to the fence, bolt cutter in hand. He fumbled trying to get the bolt cutter into the first groove, but after that it was like slicing salami. The fire to the north burned and burned demanding the attention of the local militia. The lookout had already leaped.

And here came Gohnkorov, breaking from the trees a half klick beyond the fence, wearing his ghillie suit like a great shambling pile of moss, running for the fence.

Then the unthinkable. Rising from the straw and mud like a giant mole, an East German op in his own mud-encrusted ghillie bringing up a bizarre apparatus, whipping off a protective tarp and FWOOSH! The flamethrower launched a gout of flame fifty meters, completely enveloping Gohnkorov whose ghillie suit went up like a month-old Christmas tree. He never stood a chance. The screaming would stay with Brubaker forever.

And then, as he watched transfixed, he could have sworn the E. German soldier looked right at him. The barrel rotated his way and Brubaker ran, ran through the rain praying he would make the tree line in time.

As Brubaker collapsed behind the ridge, Ghonkorov exploded.

CHAPTER
EIGHTY-THREE
QUINN

They reassigned Brubaker to the Sudan for six long years but then a new administration came into power and summoned him back to the capital to serve his new president with his expertise and experience. The East Germans simply had better intelligence that time. Brubaker waited years to become Director and once it happened he wasted no time in initiating a SHC program of their own. At first the infrared seemed to hold some possibility but the technical problems were overwhelming. The source of power simply didn't exist.

One more reason why it was vital to reverse-engineer the alien technology. Whatever powered the immolations and the central unit very likely represented a vast new source of energy. Whoever figured it out would pull so far ahead of the rest of the world it wouldn't even be close.

Brubaker never learned what caused Gohnkorov to blow up like a Roman candle, but he had his suspicions. For the past week, he had been searching for a link between the Russian scientist and

Pawnee Grove without success. Two different worlds. A different time. Perhaps there was a transfer station in Siberia.

A free White was a wrecking ball. Whatever he knew must not be permitted to pass into hands other than Brubaker's. Regretfully, it was far past the point they could have brought White in. He was officially rogue, a killer on the loose. Brubaker needed to take him out fast.

For that he had just the man.

But first there was the problem of finding White. Here is where Brubaker's long game came into play. He had been an original, behind-the-scenes investor in Brainiac, the gaming company whose CEO Bryan Ayres was among the early SHCs. Brainiac had developed the Ocelot secretly in conjunction with the Pentagon. While it was true the Ocelots were untraceable, Brainiac had designed a back door signal that activated a tiny transmitter inside the phone. There were only fifteen Ocelots in use. Twelve since Hornbuckle's murder.

White still had his. Of that, Brubaker had no doubt. It was time to activate the transmitter. He would do that from his study as soon as he contacted Quinn. Quinn was the agent of last resort. The U.S. wasn't supposed to have any Quinns, but they all had them. Quinn would find White, force him to talk and then kill him.

And then what? Would the knowledge put Brubaker in position to stage a coup? God knew the present pack of clowns in the White House and Congress had not the slightest clue how to save the republic from smashing into the iceberg. Reynolds had been clueless and Burke was no better. They had so distorted the meaning and intention of the Constitution as to render it irrelevant. The United States was the greatest, kindest nation that had ever existed. True patriots would not stand idly by as feckless heads of state and legislators played party politics and lined their pockets.

Kagemusha contained hundreds of patriots ready to act. Many were in the military, but there were also patriots planted throughout the civil service, the intelligence community, the Congress, and yes, the White House itself. There were even patriots in Hollywood. Thomas Jefferson's words about the necessity to water the tree of liberty with the blood of tyrants were never more true.

Mastery of SHC was essential to controlling the opposition.

Brubaker removed his Ocelot and placed the call. Now it was his turn to listen to the pings and crackles of the Ethernet. Invented by the Defense Department, you're welcome.

The phone rang twice.

"What's up, chief," came the low voice.

"Are you stateside?"

"I'm in Florida."

"Good enough. The subject's traveling with a transmitter—I'll send you the code directly. It will start transmitting the next time he makes a call. His name is Otto White."

"Aardvark?" Quinn chuckled. "How did that fool ever survive Firebrand?"

"He's lucky. And don't you forget it. I want you to find him, find out what he knows about the SHCs then kill him."

"Is he alone?"

"I don't know. I leave that to your discretion. Drop everything. Get it done."

"You know the numbers, Boss," Quinn said. "I'm on it."

Brubaker hung up.

"Honey," Doris called from the dining room. "Supper's ready."

CHAPTER
EIGHTY-FOUR
THE PLAN

F riday evening.

Kleiser sat at the terminal for forty-five minutes tapping keys and eating pizza. Otto was after the Russian report on Dmitri Yakovitch, CEO of Odessa Oil and international playboy. Kleiser kept up a running commentary on what he was doing, using worm programs to sneak in the back door and bypass passwords using Trojan updates designed to resemble the standard security measures sent out five to six times daily.

Otto only half-listened. Occasionally Kleiser would say, "ho shit," or "bite my schwanz," usually in response to a security warning. He would then describe his retreat and flanking attempts. At last, he exclaimed, "bingo." Kleiser slid out of his seat and gestured for Otto to take his place.

TOP SECRET/NSA SAFEHOUSE ODESSA/AUG7/20**/
INFORMANT UDO FLESKO SUBJECT DMITRI
YAKOVITCH

AGENT 2691 REPORTING

Yakovitch had invested in a lavish club called Scruples in the resort city of Anapa. The night before he died, he partied at his club, which had flown in the Korean hip-hopper Sis Boom Ba for a rumored half mil. Yakovitch was there until four in the morning snorting cocaine and drinking vodka. At one point, he required service from two Ukrainian prostitutes. His bodyguard Udo Flesko drove him home in the pre-dawn hours. Yakovitch was alone in his bathroom when he burst into flames.

Terrified at what might happen to him at Russian hands, Flesko was now in an American safe house in Odessa, the only reason the Russians had agreed to share their information. The police attributed the conflagration to Yakovitch's "gangster rivals" and had instituted a nation-wide crackdown on criminal gangs.

Yeah right, Otto thought. The Russian government *was* a criminal gang.

Something else was bugging him, a memory floating around in the short-term slurry tank waiting to be retrieved. Something about the way Yakovitch went out. Could a drug overdose trigger the combustion? These aliens had no experience of cocaine, marijuana, heroin. Did they become addicted too? Now he would have to go back through all the victim files searching for drug use. He wished he could call Gus.

The memory popped. Fonzelle Armstrong, rapper and hip-hop mogul. Los Negativos were one of his acts. Fonzelle admitted he'd used, but claimed to be clean since '10.

So what? Yakovitch had never been to the Grove but Armstrong had. Was Armstrong a delivery system for Sis Boom Ba and she in turn for Yakovitch? Was that how they spread? Armstrong's international empire made for an effective base of operations. But Sis was a woman. At least everyone believed she was a woman. Upwards of sixty thousand people attended her concerts in sports arenas in Spain, racetracks in France, parks in Australia. Not exactly the target rich environment the aliens sought.

Otto would have to find a way to get that information to Yee without revealing himself. By now every agency in the country had his name and face. He was afraid to turn on the television for fear of seeing himself.

Finally he checked *Drudge*. Nothing. If *Drudge* didn't have it, it didn't exist. The feds were keeping the lid on, which meant the hunt for him was widespread, intense, and sub rosa. The new administration had enough unforced errors on its plate.

Otto mentally reviewed the last few days. Who could connect him to Kleiser?

No one. They'd been careful. And Kleiser was good about covering his tracks.

How long could their luck hold? Some snoop was bound to ferret this out. Wikileaks. *The National Enquirer.*

Kleiser pushed himself away from the flat monitor in a wheeled mesh chair. He chugged a Red Bull. Two dead soldiers lay in the wastebasket. Otto wondered why Kleiser didn't self-combust from all the caffeine. Witherspoon had loved that shit.

"How would you find out if any of these victims drank a specific soft drink?" he said.

Kleiser put his hands behind his head and stretched. It was seven-thirty. "Oh mannnn, I don't know. Go through their trash?"

The FBI had gone through the trash. They spent the next seventy-five minutes hacking into the CJIS to go over the manifests. The room was uncomfortably warm from all the machines despite the open windows. Otto pored over the evidence lists. They found empty cans of Mt. Dew, Red Bull, Coke Zero and V8 in six victims' trash. Forget the Coke Zero and V8. Four of the victims favored Mt. Dew or Red Bull.

What did it mean? The alien mind craved caffeine? Causation was not causality.

By now it was eleven-thirty and even Kleiser showed signs of fatigue.

"What else?"

Otto looked at his watch. "It can wait. We've been at it for six hours."

"What's next?"

"We hit the road. We need to bust a guy out of a mental hospital in Virginia."

"What guy?"

"Lester Durant, the Below the Beltline Sniper."

"Seriously?"

Otto stood and stretched. "Ever since he got creased by a bullet Durant can see the aliens. Everyone of those people he took out had a connection to the Grove."

Every ace needed a wing man.

CHAPTER
EIGHTY-FIVE
On the Road

Saturday.

They left before dawn in the old Ford, tires inflated, gas tank full, back seat and trunk crammed with supplies and equipment. Using a McNally Atlas of the U.S., they drove blue highways. They could have used GPS, but that would only provide a homing signal. It was radio silence from here on out.

Besides. Kansas City was pretty much a straight shot.

Kleiser drove, slamming Red Bulls and periodically stabbing at the AM/FM/8 Track player in the center of the dash. Otto dozed in the shotgun seat, occasionally looking out at the flat, featureless landscape punctuated here and there by graying farm buildings and lonely windbreaks.

He dozed off.

Thumping bass and monotone braggadocio ripped him from sleep as Kleiser cranked the volume on a rap station out of KC. Otto's hand shot out like a piston and banged the whole control panel until the sound went off.

"Hey!" Kleiser exclaimed.

"No rap! Shit makes me violent!"

"That's my music, dude!" Kleiser said defensively, wondering whether he should put it on again. Otto sat like a coiled cobra glaring at the dash through slitted eyes. Kleiser refrained from turning on the radio.

"It's not music," Otto said. "Music is composed of rhythm, harmony, and melody. There's no harmony. There's no melody. It's just some ghetto crawler with bogus street cred braying about the size of his penis and his guns and that includes Marshall 'The Beav' Mathers!"

Sighing, Kleiser pulled out an iPod, fixed buds in his ears and bopped to whatever cacophony he wished. Otto went back to sleep. They were both awake by the time they reached the outskirts of KC at three p.m. They made a pit stop at a Bosselman's, stocked up on Slim Jims, corn dogs and pudding and hit the road. They were driving straight through. At five they switched places. Kleiser, who'd been driving for twelve hours, crawled into the back seat, heaved the duffels and boxes around until he created a cat-like space for himself, curled up and went to sleep.

The plan was to set up shop somewhere near the hospital and arrange for Durant's release into their custody that involved impersonating federal officers. Otto was making it up as he went along, trusting his unlikely partner more than he might have wished. Kleiser claimed to have contacts all over the country—fellow hackers and followers. He was much admired in the hacking community.

Kleiser started to snore, a low-level grinding noise. Otto turned the radio on low, switched to AM and found a news channel. From sea to shining sea the situation was FUBAR. Transportation had ground to a virtual halt as the TSA, Homeland Security, the Coast Guard, and all local municipal police departments went on the highest alert. Once, Otto spied a roadblock a quarter mile to the south on the interstate.

The No Fly order persisted. Long lines formed at all manner of public transportation as every traveler had to submit to a search and/or scan. Hysteria ramped up at every possible level. Parents kept their children home from school. Underlings refused to go to work for fear their bosses might go nova. Bomb squads rushed from office to hearth futilely trying to keep up with the avalanche of alarms.

Sen. Lamont Cranston, D, New Jersey, demanded that all regular immigration be halted and that all diplomats and citizens entering or reentering the country be subjected to the blood test. Sen. Marie de los Santos, R, Texas, introduced a bill requiring all members of Congress to take the test. Someone else proposed the test for welfare recipients. CDC didn't have enough enzymes for the tests. The whole world lacked the necessary ingredients. Pharmaceutical companies in Germany and the Sudan operated around the clock trying to keep up with the demand.

Otto switched to FM and quietly searched until he found a blues station out of KC. His plan had been to drive straight through, swapping off with Kleiser. But Kleiser claimed to have an ally in Mexico, MO with all the gadgets, bells and whistles. At one-thirty in the morning, Otto pulled off the blue highway into the entrance to a cornfield and shook Kleiser awake.

"Wha—?"

"We're about ten miles from Mexico. Call your friend."

"Yeah, right," Kleiser mumbled, opening the door and staggering to the three meter corn. He unzipped his pants and relieved himself. He came back to the car and pulled out his cell phone, poked at it.

"No service."

Otto reached into his pocket and pulled out the Ocelot. "Try this."

CHAPTER EIGHTY-SIX
PORTER'S A LITTLE WEIRD

Sunday morning.

Kleiser folded the phone and handed it back to Otto. "He's up."

They got back in the car and headed toward Mexico, a town of 12,000 twenty miles northeast of Columbia.

"I should warn you, Porter's a little weird."

"Of course he is."

"He had a snowboard accident up at Keystone a couple years ago and bashed a hole in his skull. They had to insert a metal plate. He's been a little funny ever since."

"Randall, I would be shocked if your pal was normal."

"Actually, he was a little weird before that. I think he's got a touch of Asperger's. He also hoards shit. He's still got all his old monitors and hard drives stacked in the kitchen. Collects all sorts of shit. If he weren't so paranoid, he'd be a big hit on *Hoarders: Buried Alive*."

Kleiser's friend Porter lived in a sagging wood frame farmhouse with a collapsed barn in back and a '72 Chevelle listing in the gravel driveway. The rear end was plastered with bumper stickers: "Coexist," "Occupy Kansas City," "We Are the 99%," and "No Nukes." The light burned in the living room window.

Porter opened the door before they got out of the car. He was six four and couldn't have weighed more than 160. His Emperors of Wyoming T-shirt hung on his bony frame like a flag of surrender. He had a mop of black hair with a purple streak, pierced ears, nose and lip. You could lead him around with a strong magnet.

Kleiser went up the creaky wood steps and they embraced, slapping each other on the back.

"Dog! When's the last time you took a shower?" Kleiser said.

"I don't know. What day is it? Hey, man! Welcome! *Mi casa es su casa.* Whassup? Whoozis? Your brother?"

Otto stepped up, wrinkling his nose. Porter smelled like graphite. "Otto White. Thanks for putting us up."

"No problemo," Porter said leading them into the house. His movements were quick and jerky revealing a patch the size of a half dollar on the back of his head hidden by lanky locks. Otto spotted the ubiquitous Red Bull on a computer desk, but the scarecrow might have been tweaking too. Dream catchers hung on the walls and in a window.

The grimy living room was filled with servers, hard drives, keyboards and monitors just like Kleiser's. It smelled of ozone, cigarette smoke and body odor. Ashtrays overflowed. Two monitors were lit: a chat room and scrolling numbers.

An ancient dog of unknown provenance crawled out from its doggie bed, tail sweeping. Otto stooped to pet.

"That's Opie."

Porter slid into a folding chair facing the monitor. "Dig it— I'm almost into Whole Foods' database. Ahmina publish all the board members' names and addresses. That'll teach that motherfucker to donate to Rethuglicans. You want something to eat? You want eggs? I got six dozen in the fridge. They were on sale for a dollar a dozen."

"Dude," Kleiser said. "I need to use your equipment to set up a prison break."

"Cool!" Porter enthused. "I coulda used that in January when the fucking pigs locked me up for holding a half fucking gram! I was in there for thirty-six hours before my PD got me out."

The scarecrow opened a drawer beneath the computer, withdrew a smeared hand mirror with a pile of white powder on it. "Either of you guys want a bump?"

"What is it?" Kleiser said.

"The finest crystal you can get."

"No, thanks."

Porter used a balisong to wrangle a line, which he snorted through a cut soda straw. "So what's the plan?" he said wiping his nose.

"We're going to fake an FBI pick-up to bust this prisoner loose."

"Radical!" Porter said. "What do you want me to do?"

"Let me sit there," Kleiser said.

Porter slid out. Kleiser slid in. The first order of business was to break into Tuscadero State Hospital's computers to study the security system and the transfer procedures. They would have to present the hospital with legitimate transfer orders and authentic ID. Otto could no longer use his current IDs because of the APBs. However, the sheer audacity of their action, carried out fifteen hundred miles from where everyone believed him to be, increased their chances of success, as did his knowledge of the bureaucratic mindset.

Otto was dog tired. Porter showed him to a sofa in the "media" room which featured a huge flat screen TV, speaker towers, and shelf after shelf of CDs and DVDs, long boxes covering the floor labeled "Marvel," "Dark Horse," etc. The sofa had an old Indian blanket buried under tons of graphic novels, books and rubble.

"Make yourself at home," Porter said leaving.

Otto carefully transferred the books to the floor, slipped the Ruger out of the small of his back, slid it between the sofa cushions and fell into a mercifully dreamless sleep.

The light woke him. His first impulse was to reach for Steve. He remembered and sadness filled him. He glanced at his watch. Seven-thirty. Sounds of a printer from the other room. Opie came into the room and began licking his face. Dogs were like that.

Otto sat up, rubbed his eyes, padded into the bathroom, took a shit, shave and a shower.

Kleiser stood next to the printer in the living room, Porter sprawled on a sofa. The room stank from Porter's intense body odor, exacerbated by the meth. At least Kleiser had resisted temptation. He looked up as Otto approached.

"What do you think?" He handed Otto a sheet of white foolscap affixed with the Bureau seal and heading.

"Very nice. But we're going to need a transfer order signed by a judge."

Kleiser turned, sifted through some papers and handed Otto what appeared to be an official FBI Request for Transfer.

"Holy shit! How did you get this?"

"You want the long version or the short version?"

"Never mind. Outstanding work, Randall! I'm putting you in for a No-Prize."

Porter lurched up off the sofa, popping a fresh can of Red Bull. "A Marvel No-Prize? I got one of those. Did you dig when they turned Spider-Man into a gay Puerto Rican?"

Otto and Kleiser stared blankly.

Porter looked around like a man discovering his surroundings for the first time. "I got that shit somewhere. Lemme dig it out."

"Not necessary," Kleiser said.

Porter got down on his knees and pulled two long cardboard boxes labeled "Spider-Man" from under the card table holding one of the servers. Otto envisioned a long fruitless meth-fueled search.

"I'll take your word for it," Otto said.

"No, wait. I know where it is."

Porter got up and headed into the kitchen. Otto looked at Kleiser and mouthed the word "great."

There was a pop and a thud followed by the snarl of an old dog defending its master.

CHAPTER
EIGHTY-SEVEN
: DEATH BY COMPUTER

Two more pops and an animal squeal.

Kleiser looked up quizzically while Otto moved. He'd left the Ruger in the bedroom! Stupid! No time to get it before whoever had snuffed Porter entered the room. Otto picked up a monitor and held it like a Crusader's shield in front of his chest. Kleiser suddenly noticed the electricity in the air and sat up with his mouth open in a state of uncomprehending anxiety.

The killer entered the room in a crouch, black cargo pants stuffed into black boots, heavy black turtleneck sweater and a black balaclava covering the narrow, deep-set killer's eyes. The figure wore a utility belt that would have drowned Batman and cradled a Glock with a fat black suppressor in both gloved hands, swinging the muzzle from one to the other.

The muzzle came back to Otto as the sinister intruder gave Kleiser the psychic brush-off.

"Have a seat," the intruder growled at Otto. Otto backed up and sat down on the deep cloth sofa. Not exactly conducive to fast movement. The figure edged toward one corner leaning against the computer desk, hostages at ten and two. He nodded toward Kleiser.

"Who's this?"

Kleiser shot Otto a fearful glance.

"Randall Kleiser."

The figure grinned beneath his stocking mask. "As a dog returneth to his vomit, so a fool returneth to his folly."

"If you're federal why are you wearing a mask?" Kleiser said.

"I'm not federal," the intruder growled.

"Take the mask off, Quinn. You're not fooling anyone."

Benson pulled off the mask revealing the bony skull and Mr. Sardonicus smile. Dark circles under his eyes belonged to an older man. "I tagged you for a screw-up back in Cairo," Benson said. "Kleiser—go sit on the couch."

Kleiser shifted to the sofa.

"Either you boys carrying? White? Nothing? No knives or shit? First sign of fast action and I put one through your knee. What happened to your face?"

"'With a donkey's jawbone I have made donkeys of them. With a donkey's jawbone I have killed a thousand men.' Only I fucked up. I used my own jawbone."

"You remembered. Stand up and turn around."

Otto did as he was told. He felt the hard muzzle of the Glock against the inside of his thigh as Benson patted him down one handed, stood and shoved Otto forward so he stumbled onto the sofa. Kleiser watched fearfully.

"Your turn," Benson said. Kleiser stood while Benson patted him down, shoved him back into the sofa.

"Who's Control?" Otto said.

"I don't answer questions. I ask them. I need everything you've got on the SHCs—how they start, everything you know or suspect about the perpetrators. Whose place is this?"

"Porter's," Kleiser said. "You shot him."

"You're awfully mouthy for a nerd turd."

"Fuck you."

Benson's left leg shot up and out, booted heel smashing into Kleiser's face knocking out a tooth and jamming his head hard against the wall with a bone-jarring thump.

"How can he get knowledge whose talk is of bullocks?" Benson said.

Kleiser leaned forward groaning, hands to his face dripping blood on the threadbare carpet.

"Aardvark. Who's behind the flame-outs?"

"Tiny aliens that look like spiders."

As casually as flicking lint Benson whip-kicked Otto in the side of his head with his right instep so fast the only thing that kept Otto up was Kleiser sitting next to him. Otto's head rang and he saw stars. It reminded him of Libya. His new jaw flamed with pain.

"Keep it up, I'm gonna get out the power tools." Benson reached into one of the pockets attached to his belt and removed two thick plastic wiring harnesses.

Otto knew that once those were on he'd be helpless. He judged kicking Benson in the groin, but the seasoned op remained just out of range.

Benson tossed the wire harnesses to Kleiser. "White, show him your back. Douchebag, put those on tight."

Porter appeared in the entrance to the kitchen backlit by the morning light, holding something over his head. As he stepped into the living room, Otto saw the blood streaming down his face. Mouth open in a wordless scream Porter lurched forward bringing the ancient sixty-pound monitor down on Benson's head screen first. At the last instant, Benson sensed something and started to turn but he was too late.

The massive diode screen shattered and the old monitor sank down onto Benson's bony skull to the ears. Benson swayed upright, pistol pointed at the floor and collapsed.

CHAPTER
EIGHTY-EIGHT
'ON THE ROAD AGAIN

Benson's bullet had struck Porter in the steel plate in his skull, and while he'd dropped like a stone he'd recovered a few minutes later to find his dog dead beside him and some freak with a gun in the living room. Filled with righteous rage he seized the first weapon at hand and brained the fucker.

Porter sprawled on the sofa with the mother of all headaches while Otto fixed a washcloth filled with ice. Kleiser washed himself off in the bathroom and emerged with a flesh-colored bandage the size of a package of Chiclets plastered across his nose. When they pried the monitor off Benson, they discovered that a shard of glass had pierced the carotid and the rounded side of the monitor had filled with blood. Otto went through his pockets finding his Ocelot, car keys and an ankle gun. The key ring included a BMW ignition key.

Porter stared at his hands. "Wow, man. Wow. I killed a pig."

"You killed a fuckin' pig with your bare hands!" Kleiser and Porter exchanged a high five.

"Well, technically, I used that old monitor. I got tons of that shit. I keep meaning to recycle, but loading all that shit in my car and carting it to the recycling joint is a drag, man, and plus you gotta pay them by the pound to take this shit. Prob'ly cost me five hundred bucks to get rid of this shit. I could sell some of my comic collection—I have a complete run of *Spider-Man* but I don't want to have to do that. I already sold all my *Youngbloods*."

Otto went out through the kitchen into the backyard, a jumble of discarded lawn furniture, tools, old bikes, old charcoal grills and bricks. He set his Ocelot down on the brick patio, picked up a cinderblock and gave it the Benson treatment.

Kleiser followed him out, raised his eyebrows.

"That's how he found us. Fuckers have been tracking me through my track-proof phone. Benson drove here. Let's find it. You go east, I'll go west."

It was a new BMW 540i with Florida plates. Otto drove it back to Porter's and stashed it in the backyard, which was pretty much invisible to neighbors. He went over the car with a magnifying glass. Kleiser rigged a signal locator out of Porter's pile of junk and they swept the vehicle for bugs.

The found a sawed-off Winchester twelve gauge in the trunk along with a cordless drill, enough electronics to bug a college dorm and clothes. Kleiser hacked the Florida Dept. of Transportation and discovered that Benson's plate didn't exist. How cool was that? He traced the VIN and found the BMW belonged to a Naples-based firm, Husted Securities. Further research revealed several military contractors on the payroll including Brainiac and a development grant from the Dept. of Defense.

"We're taking the Beamer," Otto announced. "Benson's off the grid—they don't know where he is or how long this is going to take."

"What about the dude's phone?" Kleiser said.

Otto pulled the Ocelot from Benson's pocket and tossed it to Kleiser. "Get a list of incoming and outgoing before we give it the heave-ho."

When Otto went back into the house Porter had conked out on the sofa making a noise like a wood chipper. Otto surveyed the damage. Dead dog, dead spook. They didn't have time to do a professional cleanup.

Five minutes later Kleiser came in. "Got 'em. What are we going to do about Porter?"

"We can't take him with us. Leave that fuckin' shit with his gun—let the cops straighten it out. Obviously Porter here is no killer—and when they finally figure out who Benson is there will be a lid on this tighter than a politician's college transcripts. They can't charge Porter—that would expose the agency. They'll hold him for a little while, figure out he's harmless and let him go. Maybe they'll even hire him. Is he a good hacker?"

"The best. Next to me. It's that Asperger thing."

"When I get an opportunity, I'll tell the right people."

Kleiser pulled out the Ocelot. "Why not let them know now?"

Otto held his hand out. Kleiser tossed the phone. Otto went out through the kitchen, laid the phone on the bricks. Kleiser followed him out and stared.

"We need some time to get in place," Otto said. "Did you get those numbers?"

Kleiser handed him a sheet of yellow legal paper.

"Okay. I need for you to send this to someone and then we're outta here." Otto picked up a brick and smashed the phone.

CHAPTER EIGHTY-NINE
CONTROL

Sunday evening.

Brubaker sat in his study, Macallan at hand, going through the latest intel on domestic terrorist activity. An unwelcome distraction, but it was his job. He tried not to think about how close he had finally come to his goal: the secret of spontaneous human combustion. Benson had never failed him. Benson was the most lethal and versatile op Brubaker had ever known.

Benson had estimated it would take him twelve hours to set up and get in place from the time he received the coordinates. By all rights, he should have results by now. Half expecting a phone call, Brubaker reluctantly turned his attention to a recently hatched group of Puerto Rican Separatists called *Quemarlo*.

Somewhere across the bay, a foghorn made the loneliest sound in the world. Brubaker looked outside, down the broad sweeping lawn to his two hundred feet of shoreline, still visible in the dying light. He'd bought the place eighteen years ago and had spent the happiest moments of his life there with Doris, the kids, the dogs. The 118-year-old Georgian residence had cost 4.3 million at the time.

Everything was about to change. The current President was a fop and a weak tit. Kagemusha included two cabinet secretaries, head of the Joint Chiefs, and several powerful members of Congress. The Speaker of the House was prepared to step in and declare martial law.

With the power of spontaneous combustion, a power that had fascinated him since childhood, he would restore the United States to its rightful preeminent position in the world. He would restore its moral fiber and return to the principles of Christianity, which the Founders had intended. At some point he would come forward and be hailed as the savior of America. Monuments would be built to him, songs written, movies made. Now that Gabe Winner was dead, Bradley Cooper could play him.

One of his two pedigreed vizslas started barking. A splash of headlights played across the evergreens at the turn around. Who could be visiting at this hour of the night? It was nine-thirty! Were things so bad the President couldn't take a chance on regular communications he had to send a car?

He heard the faint chime of the front door, Doris talking to someone. A minute later, she appeared in the door to his study. "Luther, Margaret Yee is here."

"Tell her to come in. And thank you, dear."

What could the National Security Director possibly want with him?

The grim-faced Director appeared in the door clad in a navy blue wool suit and carrying her omnipresent bag.

"Come in, Margaret. Would you like a drink?"

She looked at the Scotch on his desk. "I'll have what you're having."

Brubaker went to the wet bar concealed behind a sliding Oriental panel and poured Yee three fingers of Macallan.

"Ice?"

"Neat is fine."

Brubaker handed Yee the drink. She sat in an overstuffed Queen Ann, her feet barely touching the Persian rug.

"Margaret, you look like the grim reaper."

"Luther, I have Ray Benson's phone records. Earlier today we arrested Congressmen Peake and Wayans as well as Secretary of Energy Fulton and Joint Chiefs Chair General Macauley. Peake and Wayans are singing like a gospel choir. Benson spoke before he died. He said you ordered the hit on White."

Brubaker stared into his glass. "I see. And why haven't you arrested me?"

"The President felt, in light of your outstanding service to your country, that you might wish to avoid the ugliness of the trial and media frenzy."

Brubaker opened the top drawer of his desk and withdrew a 1911 Colt .45. He set it on the desk top. "Is this what you had in mind?"

"I'm so sorry, Luther, but you left us little choice. The warrant has been issued, federal marshals will be here in the morning."

She rose. "Thank you for the drink. I'll show myself out."

A minute later Brubaker heard murmured greetings between his wife and Yee and then the front door shut.

So this is how it was supposed to end? With Brubaker doing the "honorable" thing while the country slid further into chaos and penury? Brubaker had always believed that suicide was the coward's way out. A trial would provide him with the platform he needed to make his case to the American public.

But the public wouldn't buy it. The public was stupid. The public was a mass of security-seeking, ill-informed sheep whom politicians and the media played like a game of Space Invaders.

Brubaker had a dock that currently hosted his twenty-eight foot Boston Whaler.

In some ways, Brubaker had also been preparing for this moment his entire life. The safe house owned by a shadow of a ghost in Arlington. The fake passports and IDs, mounds of cash and South African Krugerrands. The Kagemusha network.

Doris appeared in the door, a crease of worry running up her forehead, her long blond hair fixed in an elegant bubble. "What was that all about?"

"Doris, I'm going away for awhile."

CHAPTER NINETY

TABITHA

Sunday evening.

Tuscadero was in Annandale not far from George Mason University. Kleiser's Black Widow sycophant lived in Alexandria and from the moment she opened her sixth floor apartment door, it was plain she was head-over-heels in love with the hacker whom she had only known previously in chat rooms. Tabitha Truskewitz was 200 lbs. of Goth with neon orange hair and tats on her fat biceps. Her lips were orange. Her fingernails were black. Her apartment was a shrine to Black Flag, Rage Against the Machine, pre-sellout Green Day, Che, Mao, and OWS.

Tabitha was a Queen Nerd Geek. There were posters of the Dragons of Pern, *John Carter*, *Chronicles of the Imaginarium Geographica*, *Hellboy*, *Lord of the Rings*, and *Witchblade*. Tabitha's Facebook handle was Ferociouscosplay.

Tabitha was a Gamer.

Tabitha was a Cosplayer.

Tabitha was a Hacker.

The tiny apartment hummed with monitors, hard drives and servers. A brand new HP full color printer occupied a corner of the living room, manual open on top. An old-fashioned fat cathode-ray television was tuned to CNN. Images of whole neighborhoods burning, police in riot gear, solemn politicians interspersed with insurance and network advertisements lent an air of absurdity.

"It's so good to finally meet you!" she gushed, hardly giving Otto a second glance. "You've been a hero of mine like forever!"

"Yeah thanks, Tab. Did you get the stuff?"

"Totally! As soon as I got your message I went out to Best Buy and picked up the printer. I hope I got the right paper. I hit an Office Max and bought about four kinds. Would you like something to drink? Beer? Whiskey? You want to do a bowl?"

"Got any Red Bull?" Kleiser said.

"No, but I have Mt. Dew."

Otto raised his hand. "Me too."

Tabitha left them in the living room as she went into the tiny kitchen. Otto looked at Kleiser, raised his eyebrows.

"She's cool," Kleiser said.

"Does she know she's gonna have to bail?"

Kleiser made a placating gesture. "Don't worry about it."

The next step was to inform Hospital Administrator Nicholas Beausoleil, M.D., by e-mail and phone that the FBI wished to collect Inmate #009327, Master Marine Sergeant Lester Durant, for interrogation at FBI HQ.

Otto would wait until tomorrow to make the call. Dr. Beausoleil was home for the weekend. While Kleiser prepped the message—including a fake callback number that he would intercept—Otto went shopping. At a nearby Men's Wearhouse he purchased plain suits, blue and gray, plain white shirts, ties with a vaguely patriotic theme, and Oxford tie-ups, one pair brown, one black. It was easy shopping for Kleiser, who was almost exactly the same size. The clothes had to entirely cover Kleiser's ink, as federal agents were not permitted to have tats.

Otto purchased two tiny ceramic American flags at the checkout counter.

By the time he returned to the apartment, Tabitha had transformed herself. She covered her orange hair with a drab gray wig of long, straggly hair. She'd changed the protest shirt for an XXL Redskins sweatshirt and sweatpants, and looked like any of the millions of denizens of Walmart.

"What do you think?" she asked Otto as he entered with his packages. She turned around sullenly as if looking for something.

"Brilliant," Otto said.

"Tabitha's going to rent the car," Kleiser said.

"Tabitha, you realize that you're about to become a federal fugitive?"

She'd removed her mascara and lip-gloss so that she looked like plain pudding, which made her vehemence all the more startling. "I've been at war with the fucking Feds since I popped out of my mother's womb."

"All-righty then," Otto said. "You got a place to go?"

"Commune in Vermont. I've been going up there every summer for the past ten years helping them with the sorghum harvest. They said I could come up any time."

"You realize you're going to have to take off as soon as you deliver the vehicle? The longer head-start you have the better off you'll be."

"She has to make us up first," Kleiser said, eyes on the screen.

Tabitha looked at Kleiser with cow eyes. "You'll meet me there?"

Kleiser stared at the monitor. "I said I would."

Otto felt a cold ball of disgust settle in his gut and immediately despised himself for it. He held up one of the suits. "Try this on."

"In a minute. Just lay it on the sofa."

Otto had seen enough of the screen to know that Kleiser was hacking into the FBI system, implanting a fake electronic trail. He sat at another monitor and gleaned what he could of Tuscadero, including a slide show and staff listings. Tuscadero was a high-security hospital for the study, treatment and containment of the criminally insane. John Hinckley had spent time there, as had the two Beltway snipers.

Otto stretched out on the sofa and fell asleep. He woke to the sound of the printer as Kleiser ran the transfer papers on FBI letterhead. Tabitha had gone out and returned with Chinese. Rubbing the sleep from his eyes Otto checked his watch. It was eleven-thirty at night.

He sat at the card table in the kitchenette and helped himself to the mu shu pork. They'd left him a fortune cookie. "YOU ARE OPEN HEARTED AND HAVE MANY FRIENDS."

"Yeah," he muttered. "Bingo."

It seemed crazy; the two of them marching into a high-risk facility and waltzing away with Durant, but Otto had spent time in a similar facility and had participated in prisoner pick-ups when he was an MP. He was also familiar with the bureaucratic mindset and planned to use the collapse of civilization to his benefit.

As did the President.

They would strike Monday morning during the time of greatest confusion.

Kleiser was still at it a half hour later when Tabitha called from the bedroom.

"Randy, are you coming in here?"

With a look of misery, Kleiser pushed himself away from the monitor and headed for the bedroom.

CHAPTER NINETY-ONE
TUSCADERO

onday morning.

Dressed as a drudge, Tabitha rented a black Yukon Denali from a Budget in Alexandria. She returned to the apartment by ten a.m. At ten-fifteen, Kleiser phoned hospital administrator Beausoleil posing as an FBI agent while simultaneously e-mailing a copy of the transfer order via a slave unit in the FBI's own computer system.

"I'll inform staff," Beausoleil said with a touch of relief. No muss, no fuss. Tuscadero was bursting at the seams with soothsayers, doomsayers, Napoleon, John F. Kennedy, Osama and Jesus Christ himself.

The makeover: a skull-snapping crew-cut black wig for Otto that transformed him instantly into a career government bureaucrat. The lifts in his heels raised him two inches. Tabitha expertly applied black make-up to his eyebrows. In his suit and horn-rimmed glasses, he looked like Bill Cullen. Kleiser received a slightly longer wig—but by no means radical—along with a fake mustache and cheek inserts that gave him a jowly look.

Tabitha wanted to photograph them, but Otto didn't think that was a good idea. "You'll be able to enjoy your work on surveillance cameras," he said.

They transferred their supplies from the BMW to the SUV in Tabitha's basement parking garage. Kleiser replaced the rental's plates with the fake federal units he'd prepared in Colorado. By eleven they were ready to go.

Otto turned his back on the icky-poo farewell. He'd memorized their route off the internet and took the wheel. The Yukon came with GPS, Blue Tooth, and Sirius XM. They pulled out of the dim garage into the bright glaring light of Virginia and headed toward Annandale.

They rode in silence for awhile, Kleiser burning with shame. Otto didn't know what to say. Kleiser had taken advantage of a lonely girl. On the other hand they were trying to save the world. Was that a fair justification? No. It reeked of the fanatic's "the end justifies the means."

Who was Otto to judge? He was no playboy but he'd had his share of girlfriends and not always treated them well. If things went according to plan, Tabitha could claim she'd loved a historical figure. They would never meet again.

Otto turned on a local news station. You knew things were bad when they stopped reporting the weekend box office takes. There had been no new combustions over the weekend, but tension was ratcheting due to other signs of the apocalypse: war in the Middle East, the collapsing economy, the imminent threat of terrorist attacks.

Traffic moved at a crawl due to numerous checkpoints. The District and surrounding environs had been adding CCTVs daily since President Reynolds' first national emergency address. They arrived at Tuscadero State, where Otto showed his and Kleiser's phony FBI badges obtained from the Bud K Company.

The guard waved them through.

Tuscadero was a Gothic monstrosity made of red brick. The Hippocratic Oath was inscribed on a bronze plaque on the left side of the massive concrete arched door. A plaque from the National Registry of Historic Buildings balanced it out.

Otto parked next to the red curb in the circular driveway entrance. He and Kleiser entered the building through the double-glass doors (retrofitted) into the seedy lobby where a stout black female receptionist sat behind a marble counter, metal detector set up at one end and a dozen folding card chairs half occupied with desultory family or lawyers.

The receptionist listened to something on ear buds connected to a freestanding iPod player and amplifier. Her nameplate said Clifton. As Otto and Kleiser approached, she removed the ear buds.

Otto showed her his badge. "Weeks, FBI. We're here to pick up Lester Durant." He showed her a copy of the transfer order.

"Just a minute," she said, picking up a phone. A moment later, she hung up. "The Director will be right down."

Otto and Kleiser sat on the metal chairs looking like two accountants. Shortly, elevator doors behind the marble counter opened and a harried-looking man in a gray suit, comb over and glasses came out from behind the barrier holding a clipboard. Otto and Kleiser stood. Beausoleil came over and shook their hands.

"Gentlemen. May I see your ID?"

Otto and Kleiser complied. Beausoleil gave them a cursory glance. On top of the clipboard was their transfer order. The director flipped that up revealing pages of notes.

"Is this strictly necessary right now? Mr. Durant is showing some progress."

"I'm afraid it is, sir," Otto said. "It's a matter of national security. If you have any questions I have the director on speed dial."

The director sighed, shuffled through his papers and put a release form on top. "Please sign here and here."

Otto did so.

"Mr. Durant will be down shortly. Have a good day."

The director took the clipboard and returned to the elevator. Behind the elevator was a yellow electronically controlled steel door with a square window crisscrossed with mesh wire. Otto and Kleiser sat, hands folded on laps, eyes straight ahead, perfectly still. Doctors, specialists, service people, visitors came and went. No one gave them a second glance. Otto took out a spiral pad and sketched.

Fifteen minutes later the yellow door buzzed open releasing two hefty orderlies and Durant in green hospital scrubs with leg and wrist shackles. The sepia-colored sniper looked like a child between his two enormous minders. He couldn't have been taller than five six. Same height as T.E. Lawrence, Otto thought. Durant glanced sharply at the receptionist who was bopping to an unheard beat.

The orderlies marched Durant out from behind the counter. The receptionist had her ear buds in and didn't even look up. Otto and Kleiser stood to meet them.

"Thank you, gentlemen. You can take the shackles off."

One of the orderlies, a black man with a shaved skull and a diamond earring, looked at him. "You sure? This guy's s'posed to know kung fu and shit."

"We're sure."

Durant stood meekly while the orderlies unlocked his restraints. "Sir, if you'll come with us," Otto said.

Durant followed them through the front door out into the bright sunshine. He looked at the ground, squinted and mumbled something.

Kleiser unlocked the van and got in.

"What did you say?" Otto said.

Durant looked up at him with burning eyes. "Can't you hear it? The devil's music! They hate the devil's music. It drives them mad."

CHAPTER
NINETY-TWO
THE DEVIL'S MUSIC

They exchanged the rental for the black Beamer. The plan was to avoid the interstate, stick to blue highways and drive straight through to Colorado in twenty-five hours. Sirens wailed in the distance as they drove away from Tuscadero. They rode in silence, a subdued Durant in the shotgun seat, Otto behind him.

Ambulances and police cars passed them three times in two different directions. Otto waited until they were cruising through the endless suburbs past strip malls and big malls and cineplexes with IMAX. Past pet hospitals, usurers, tire stores, Dollar Stores, automobile parts stores and karate studios.

"Lester," Otto said leaning forward. "I'm Otto White. This is Randall Kleiser. We know the spiders are real. We've seen them."

Durant slowly turned in his seat. "You've seen them?"

Otto took out his sketchpad and handed it to Durant. It was a drawing of one of the creatures from memory. Durant slowly nodded his head. "Yes. That's them. But there are always three of them."

"How big are they when you see them, Lester?"

Durant squinted, held his thumb and forefinger up so that they almost touched.

"How is it you can even see them over any sort of distance? You were a sniper, weren't you?"

"Yes but it's not a matter of magnification. The people they're in, they don't look healthy. Most people have a healthy aura. Kinda pink. Their aura is kind of gray, and this dead black space at the base of the skull. It's been that way ever since I got creamed by that IED in Kandahar."

"You're referring to your skull injury?"

Durant put a hand to a puckered pink furrow that creased the side of his crown. "Yo. All of a sudden I could see them. I only saw a couple in Afghanistan. Then I started seeing them around Washington. Like little tiny black holes walking around inside peoples' heads. And those people they were in? They were already dead."

"Why did you shoot them then?" Otto said.

"They're evil," Durant answered matter-of-factly. "Are you a religious man?"

"I believe in God and that his son Jesus is mankind's savior."

Durant nodded. "Me too. See, my pappy was a Baptist preacher. We believe in the holy Trinity. Father, Son and Holy Ghost. I know that's Catholic stuff, but we got some strange Baptist brews where I come from. So if you believe in a Holy Trinity, why not an Unholy Trinity?"

"Three spiders?" Otto said.

"Exactly. What are you going to do with me, anyway?"

"We're hoping you'll join us in taking the fight to the enemy."

Durant was a silent for a minute staring at his lap. "Seriously?"

"Yeah."

"Okay," Durant said.

"Okay?"

"Okay."

Otto clapped him on the shoulder. "Good man! What did you mean when you said the devil's music drives them mad?"

"What's the devil's music, dude?" Kleiser said, eyes on the road.

"Like I said, I was raised in a Southern Baptist church. I sang in the choir. I can play a little piano. My pappy, the Reverend Ezekiel Durant, God rest his soul, loved him some music. Jazz, soul, the Beatles, Beethoven, he loved it all. But there was one form of music he would not tolerate. Rap. Sir, he hated him some rap. 'Music,' he said, 'is made up of three elements: harmony, melody, and rhythm.'"

"You see?!" Otto crowed.

"Now rap ain't got no harmony nor melody. Oh sure, you may have some gal singers crooning a riff in the background, and what little melody there is has been taken from some other, better song. Which leaves you with some caricature of a nigga braggin' on his hos, his guns, and his rides."

"But now you have white rappers. You've got female and Puerto Rican rappers," Kleiser said. "It's a major part of the music industry."

"That ain't what the suburban white boys are buying," Durant said. "They want the gangsta rap, Death Row, all that ugly shit signifyin' a life without Christ."

"So rap's the devil's music," Otto said.

"Well that's my feeling. But that's not what drives them crazy. It's Sis Boom Ba."

Otto looked like a guppy. "Sis Boom Ba?"

"Yeah. That first guy I shot? I'd been scoping him out at that park for several weeks. He'd go down to the Ninth Ward, pick up some thirteen-year-old street hustler and bring them there. One day that little girl turned on the radio, found Sis doing "Boom-Ba Style" and those three tiny black holes got all agitated—like they were going to boil over. Racing around all in a jumble like. I knew he was going to blow. That's when I shot him. He blew anyway. I am very sorry about that little girl. I was trying to save her life."

Otto looked out the window. Sis Boom Ba?

Otto consulted his records. Durant's first victim had been Mortimer Kovsky, a lobbyist for Marville Chemicals. There was no direct connection to Pawnee Grove, but Kovsky had moved in high-powered circles and would have had ample opportunity to pick up a parasite.

Otto had sensed something like this out there. There had been clues all along.

Fonzelle Armstrong.
Dmitri Yakovitch.
Causation was not causality.
Could rap the Korean hip-hopper be their death ray?

CHAPTER

NINETY-THREE

BLASTER

Tuesday evening.

They rolled into Brigham Court at six-thirty. Kleiser emptied the mailbox while Otto checked the barn. They went inside. Durant stopped just inside the door mesmerized by all the equipment. He'd driven the last 800 miles. Kleiser showed him to the sofa in the den and let him drop.

Otto had slept through most of the day and was ready to go. "I need to phone Stella. Got something I can use?"

Kleiser held up a finger, went back to the master bedroom and returned a minute later with a plastic bin filled with about a dozen cell phones. "Take your pick."

Problem: Stella was undoubtedly under surveillance due to Otto's escape. Could they tap her cell phone? He couldn't take the chance. But there was someone he could phone. He fingered a Verizon unit.

"Give me fifteen minutes," Kleiser said, plucking the phone from Otto's hand. Otto went into the living room and switched on the flat screen to watch the parade of chaos and destruction. No new burn-outs. Maybe the aliens got the message. Maybe they were pulling out.

But if they were pulling out wouldn't they incinerate their installations? Would they just let the bodies fall? Kleiser came back out and handed him the phone. Otto hit the mute.

"It's going to bounce off the Frog Aegis System and a 470 gyro through Gasconne System outta French Guiana. Tony Stark couldn't trace this call."

"Thanks, Randall."

Otto got up and went out on the porch. It was still daylight outside, warm and pleasant with a hint of sage on the breeze as he sat on the creaky old glider and put his feet up on the banister. It could use a coat of paint if the owner really expected to sell the place, but maybe he didn't. Maybe it was just a front for Kleiser. Business and politics made strange bedfellows.

He dialed the Fort Collins number from memory. It bounced around the ether for a few minutes and rang six times before Crystal answered. "Hello?" she slurred.

"Crystal, it's Stella's friend Otto White. You remember me."

"Oh sure. How are you Otto?"

"Great! Say, Stella told me about your friend, the one who makes miniature amplifiers and speakers. I have a friend who's opening up a car stereo shop and he'd be interested in talking to him."

"Tom? Would you like me to give you his phone number?"

"And the address of his shop if you can."

"Just a minute."

Otto heard the Mamas and the Papas in the background. And emptiness. He imagined she was alone in the big house on the ridge drinking and listening to the old songs.

Crystal returned and gave him Blaine's phone number and the address of his shop in Loveland. He thanked her, hung up and phoned Blaine.

"Tom Blaine."

"Tom, this is Otto White. I'm Stella's friend. She may have mentioned me."

"Oh sure," Blaine, the natural salesman, said confidently.

"She told me a little bit about your product. What do you call it?"

"The Blaine Blaster."

"That's it. Do you have units for sale?"

"Not really. We're still scraping up seed money, but it is an amazing product."

"I wonder, if I came by, if you'd show it to me."

Pause. It was seven p.m.

"Sure. Come on by. I'm not going anywhere." Blaine gave him the address in Loveland. Otto promised to be there in forty-five minutes. Using the Beamer's GPS, he was there in fifty. Blaine's shop was actually the garage of his toney west side condo on a dead-end street. The garage door was open and Blaine stood at a workbench in his well-lit garage as Otto pulled up next to an old Porsche.

Blaine came forward hand outstretched. "Hi, how are ya? Any friend of Stella's is a friend of mine."

Otto looked at a row of about a dozen small blue boxes, one flat surface of which appeared to be a speaker. They were made of a soft plastic that was pleasing to the touch.

Otto picked one up. "They are small. Can I try one?"

Blaine put his hand on Otto's arm. "Not here. The neighbors complain. Come on in. Something to drink?"

Blaine's finished basement featured the usual entertainment wall with a flat screen TV. He mixed them both a tumbler of Buffalo Trace on the rocks.

Taking the unit from Otto, Blaine pointed to an input slot. "You download your songs or whatever just like you would for an iPod. The back's a touch screen—see how it lights up when I flip up the cover?"

He poked at it and showed it to Otto. The screen showed a play list including Rick Derringer's "Rock And Roll, Hoochie Koo."

Otto pointed, "Let's hear Rick."

Blaine opened a drawer in the marble-topped credenza and removed two shooters' sets of muffs designed to protect ears from loud sounds. Otto and Blaine put on the ear protectors. Blaine walked up to the tiny box, which rested on the credenza and pushed a button.

The sound was a physical blast that shoved you back—like that wall of fire that blew Otto into the desert. Even through the ear protectors, Otto could feel his ear drums distort. He nodded and signaled that he'd had enough. Blaine pushed a button and the ruckus mercifully died.

"Wow," Otto said, hardly able to hear himself. Even from the basement, it must have upset the neighbors. "How much for a couple of these?"

Blaine smiled and waved his hands. "Oh no. These are my prototypes."

"But you have so many. And I know some people who might be interested."

"Seriously?"

"Oh yes. Just because the world is going to hell in a knapsack doesn't mean there aren't smart investors out there looking for the next big thing. Could I borrow a couple?"

CHAPTER NINETY-FOUR
HYGIENE BASE CAMP

Otto returned to the safe house at ten-thirty. Durant was in the shower. Kleiser had transferred the guns, gear and grits into Otto's monster truck in the garage. He came back in through the kitchen scratching at a bite.

"We'll be ready to go as soon as Durant shapes up."

"You're not going."

Kleiser's face collapsed. "What?"

"Randall, you've already risked your life a dozen times. I can't ask you to participate in a mission from which we are unlikely to return."

"You asked Durant!"

"Lester's military. If he stayed here, he likely would have spent the rest of his life in prison. You can get away, start over. You're smart enough. You could reinvent yourself a million ways. Where we're going is almost certain death. More than likely we'll just blow ourselves up."

"That's my choice, dude."

"No, it isn't. This is a military mission and I'm in charge. Besides. Somebody has to stay here to tell the story."

Otto saw the nickel drop. Kleiser's face went dreamy. The book deal, the cover of *Rolling Stone, Scientific American, Wired.*

"I will give you John Bullis' contact information. You'll be charged with hacking and impersonating a federal officer for starters. But so many people will want a piece of you I don't see how they can railroad you. Tell them about the spiders. Tell them whatever you like. Speak the truth and stay out of trouble."

Kleiser laughed. "Yeah, right."

Otto laughed too. What else could you do?

"Hey, listen," he said. "Did you download 'Boom-Ba Style?'"

Kleiser held up a flash drive. "Rightchere."

Otto tossed him the Blaster. "Load 'em in there. But whatever you do, don't play anything!"

Kleiser looked at it. "Fuck izzis?"

"It's our secret weapon against the spiders."

Kleiser turned it over in his hands.

"Seriously. You'll be all right. Stella Darling will help you. What are they gonna do? You'll be the last man to see us alive, the only one who knows what happened. Expect congressional hearings. You'll find out who your friends are soon enough. Remember—we serve only the people of the United States, but our actions are on behalf of mankind as well. Remind them of Jimmy Doolittle's 1941 raid on Tokyo. Remind them we face an inhuman, implacable enemy. Actually you should turn yourself in."

"At FBI HQ!" Kleiser said.

"Now you're cookin'. Tell 'em I sent you."

Durant emerged from the spare bedroom in military fatigues. He reminded Otto of Audie Murphy in his lethal innocence. Otto wondered if Durant were a virgin, like T.E. Lawrence. No time to fix that now.

"What do I shoot?" he said.

Otto pointed to the sofa, on which lay an ArmaLite AR-50 and a Steyr AUG in 5.56 mm. He picked up the ArmaLite like an old friend, cradled it like a baby. "Are you my spotter?"

"I'll be your spotter."

"Now where are we going exactly?"

"Spiderland, I hope. They've got some kind of teleportation device set up in the mountains. We're going to try and reverse it."

"What if we can't breathe the air?"

"That'll be a problem. But they breathe our air."

Durant nodded. He was a good soldier. All he'd ever needed was direction. "Sir," he said. "How shall I address you?"

"Just call me Otto. Stick that hardware in the truck why don'tcha. Get squared away. We leave in ten minutes."

"Sir, I'll do a little recon."

"Call me Otto."

Durant grinned, his entire face breaking out in sunshine. "And you call me Lester, Otto."

Durant slipped out the back door with the rifles.

"Boy's a ninja, ain't he?" Kleiser said.

"He is."

"I want to thank you, man, for being my friend."

A bolus of shame crouched in Otto's gut. The hacker was dead serious. What had Otto done except involve him in a conspiracy against the government? "Don't say that, man. Don't thank me."

"Well you're my friend, aren't you?"

"I am."

"I didn't know what I was doing before, striking out blindly, any big organization. Public, private, it didn't matter. I was mad at everyone. Now for the first time I feel as I'm part of something that matters."

"Well that's kind of you to say so."

"Saving the fucking world, man! It doesn't get any bigger than that!"

Durant slipped back in the kitchen door shooting off sparks. "There are four SWAT teams at the end of the street. They're evacuating all the houses up to here."

"Well," Otto said. "I guess you're coming with us after all, Randall."

CHAPTER
NINETY-FIVE
INTO THE TREES

Early Wednesday morning.

The monster truck erupted from the barn in a screaming cacophony, churning up a dust storm as it doughnutted the yard and bolted west. A meandering stream formed the back line of the property and beyond that a series of fields chopped up with barbed wire for cattle, horses, and llamas. Otto switched on the running lights. Five quartz-halogen spots lit the landscape like a space launch from eight feet above the ground.

They were almost to the stream. Otto had a split second to judge whether the truck could bridge the steep but narrow divide, climb the slope on the other side and make it into the fields. No time to slow down. They hit the sagging barbed wire on their side of the property line and plunged down into the gully with a spine-popping jar, the three of them crammed together on the one bench seat, seatbelts fastened. The truck bungeed up and down on meter-long shocks.

They clambered up the opposite side like the Space Mountain ride in Orlando, rolled over a taut new barbed wire fence and bounded into the fields. In his rearview Otto could see flashing red and blue lights filling the yard, forming a line where they pulled up short, unable to take the plunge.

How had the feds found them?

The Cyber Unit may have found a link between Kleiser and Johnson.

Hornbuckle might have planted a second transmitter in the truck. Otto doubted it. If they'd been able to trace the truck they would have had agents in place long before they did. Not that it mattered. Now it was fox and hounds.

Minutes later, they heard the *whup-whup-whup* of a chopper.

"Shit!" Kleiser shouted from the shotgun seat.

"Chill," Otto said. "They're not going to fire on us. Randall, twist around and hand me those night vision binocs behind the seat. No wait—hand 'em to Lester—Lester get 'em going and slip them over my head."

The boys got busy. Otto switched off all the lights. It was a bright starry night in Colorado with good visibility. An edge of macaroni showed in the east. Durant turned on the night vision, put it on his own head, adjusted the level and placed it on Otto's.

"So bright out I don't really need it," Otto said as the vehicle rolled with surprising smoothness across the prairie. They could see clusters of cattle regarding them with curiosity. A line of Douglas fir marked the property line, and another barbed wire fence.

Otto hated to ruin those fences. He hoped the ranchers' insurance would cover it.

"God forgive me," he muttered and laughed.

Worried about the fences!

"What?" Kleiser demanded.

"Nothing. I'm going to drop you in Lyons. Any luck, they won't have time to close the roads. Pretty sure they didn't expect us to do this. Lester, turn on that police radio in front of you."

Lester complied. There was a frenzy of low-level chatter about an SUV headed west in Boulder County, discussion of how best to head them off. They couldn't do jack while Otto drove cross-country. He followed plat lines until he burst from the trees onto

Highway 66 about six miles east of Lyons. Traffic was non-existent until they passed the water pumping station and a CHP cruiser caught big drift as it turned west in pursuit. The cruiser was on their tail within seconds, better able to take the curves than the top-heavy truck.

"Fuck!" Kleiser said.

"Relax, boys. I hate to do this to an officer of the law, but ..." He reached under the dash and pulled a toggle. A ten-gallon tank welded to the backside of the frame dumped diesel oil all over the highway including the cruiser's windshield that immediately turned opaque. Kleiser stared in amazement through the big side mirror as the cruiser went into a clockwise skid and skated elegantly off the highway and into the ditch.

Kleiser giggled. "Man I wish Porter coulda seen that."

Otto drove through Lyons at a high rate of speed stopping only to drop Kleiser at Oskar's Brewery. He had to get off the highway ahead of the tsunami of police vehicles that were certain to ascend. Having driven these mountains for much of his life, he knew of a fire road near Glen Haven that would take him around to the northwest side of Pawnee Grove and the back of Mt. Pythagoras. They couldn't drive all the way to the top, but it might get them to the tree line.

Morning sun touched the top of Long's Peak.

Durant slid over to the shotgun seat. "Do you ever wonder if God has a purpose for you?" he asked staring ahead.

"Not anymore."

"I used to ask that question all the time. Now I know He does."

"But you were raised in the church."

"I still had doubts. I always had doubts. Even my preacher pappy had doubts. Faith doesn't always mean blind obedience. You know when I knew? When I saw that Senator come visit us and he had those spiders in his head. That's when I knew."

An electric current traveled down Otto's spine. "Which senator?"

"Colorado. Dearing or something."

"Senator Sam Darling."

"Yeah."

CHAPTER NINETY-SIX

MAX

Heavy clouds scudded in from the west. It looked like rain high up. They rolled through a nearly deserted Estes Park and up to Glen Haven, pausing for several deer and a long-horned Rocky Mt. sheep. Artsy hippie village Glen Haven was still asleep as they drove past the purple-painted coffeehouse and the Peoples' Bookstore.

Otto found the ancient fire trail that would eventually take them to the top of the mountain. As he used a bolt cutter to cut through the rusted chain, the helicopter reappeared sporadically through the trees.

They had to know where Otto was heading, but they had limited resources unless they wanted to announce to the world that Pawnee Grove was the epicenter of an alien invasion. They'd avoided a military display by treating the deaths as a police matter and never mentioning what lay beneath the mountain.

However, Otto doubted even the FBI and CIA had knowledge of his chosen route, which had been closed since the Wilderness Preservation Act in '88. They were under heavy tree cover now and the winds were picking up. Shortly it would be dangerous for the helicopter to remain aloft. Otto smelled the rain through the open window. He glanced at Durant.

The sniper had a white-knuckle grip on the grab handle and leaned his head out the window with a ferocious grin, which reminded Otto of Steve.

Branches whipping against the sides of the truck caused constant screeching. The huge wheels and tires clambered over barrel-sized rocks and the body jounced from side to side with an oddly musical squeak.

The first fat drops of cold water struck the windshield and then the heavens opened up. Otto could see well enough to keep the truck centered in the trough as they climbed and climbed, catching glimpses of the valley here and there, sun still gleaming off Lake Estes. Seconds later the clouds rolled in and blotted out the light.

They traversed a thirty-two percent grade, the enormous knobby tires slipping and catching on the rock-studded ground. Otto kept it in low gear. They rolled up the windows to avoid being soaked. That would happen soon enough. An abandoned prospector's shack looked like it was melting into the land.

Forty-five minutes later the road ended in a sheer granite wall, now a waterfall. They were just below the tree line at about 3,200 meters. From there it was another 900 meters to the summit. But they weren't going to the summit. They were going to just below the summit.

Otto had packed carbineer, pitons, and strap on metal climbing platforms, but if they could work their way around to the NW facing chimney they would have an easier go of it. They eased into nylon wet suits and stepped out into pouring rain. Each slipped into a fifteen kilo backpack. Each carried one of the sniper rifles. Otto carried two smoke grenades. They could have used the AKs in the cave, but Otto wanted Durant to be comfortable with his equipment.

They began to climb and were immediately enveloped in the dense gray cloud. Otto could barely see five meters. They had entered a Grey World. With gloves and crampons, they worked their way up rising switchbacks that worked counter-clockwise around the mountain. They paused on a ledge above the tree line and for an instant the clouds broke, offering a staggering vision of the Mummy Range to the north.

The weather was with them. It would keep the choppers off their back, as well as a potential ranger drop. Thunder rumbled across the vast range and lightning strobed in the distance. Each was acutely aware of the danger from lightning strikes. The preponderance of metal they carried didn't help.

Otto took the lead. They came to the boulder field. Boulders the size of Humvees, slick as cue balls. What cataclysmic event had polished them, then tossed them 4,000 meters above sea level? Some of the boulders were so perfect it made Otto think maybe the red bowling balls were nature's work.

He shook his head. The altitude was affecting his thinking. He turned around. Durant gave him the thumb's up. Otto approached two massive boulders just touching each other three meters up leaving a narrow passageway. It was better than trying to clamber over the slick surface. Otto removed his backpack and got down on hands and knees, his Harbor Freight kneepads absorbing the hard ground. Pulling the backpack by its strap, rifle attached, he crawled forward thinking this would be the perfect place for an ambush, if an enemy somehow knew he was going to be here, 4,000 meters up at five-thirty in the morning during a thunderstorm.

He crawled toward the misty light from beneath the boulders. The rain abated. Otto paused on hands and knees and breathed deeply, breath as thick as a contrail.

The sound was as unexpected as deep crimson. A startling snort, so close he could almost feel the warm breath. Otto slowly turned his head. And there was Max, curled up in an alcove, regarding Otto calmly through untamed yellow eyes.

Ever so slowly, Otto backed up and crouched, holding one hand out toward the breach to stop Durant. Five meters separated Otto from the big cat.

"Hello, Max," Otto said softly.

The cougar licked its chops.

From beneath the boulders metal clicked on rock. Max glanced once and was gone; springing effortlessly over Otto's head and disappearing in the gray. Seconds later Durant appeared dragging his pack. He got up, stretched, and looked at Otto still in his crouch staring into the mist.

"Did I miss something?"

Otto got to his feet. "It's all good."

CHAPTER
NINETY-SEVEN
:DIVERSION

Wednesday morning.

They reached the chimney and climbed above the clouds into brilliant sunshine. As they looked down, they saw an endless lumpy field of gray wool as far as the eye could see punctuated by mountaintops: Archimedes and Isosceles, Long's Peak and Flat Top. Soundlessly they obtained the jutting shelf of granite, from which Otto had launched his assault on Goldfarb.

Despite the sunshine, it was cold and they could see their breath. Dropping backpack and rifle, Otto inched out as far as he dared to on the ledge, Durant anchoring his legs and belt. He peered around the corner and caught a glimpse of a blue pop-tent tethered to the granite with nylon straps. A sentry crouched at the lip of the ledge cradling a thermos of coffee, wearing fatigues, an H&K machine pistol around his neck. There would be at least one other.

Durant pulled Otto back.

"At least two military. How do we get 'em out of there without hurting them?"

Durant shrugged. "Diversion?"

"What diversion?"

They discussed possible scenarios. The problem was there seemed to be no way for one of them to crawl around to the other side of the ledge. There may be other entrances to the cave, but they didn't have time to search for them.

"I got two smoke grenades," Otto said.

Otto's view of the money deck was so limited he could see only about twenty per cent of the shelf. If he leaned out far enough to heave a grenade back under the overhang, they would see him. But if they could get the grenade back there without being seen, the sentries would conclude that the smoke originated under the overhang.

Otto guessed there were two. It was the tactical thing to do. More than two were unnecessary in so remote a location, and one man alone had to take time to sleep. Of course, if they were being supplied inside the mountain they could change sentries on the hour but Otto didn't believe that.

The cave was too sensitive for the Army or the CIA to invade and occupy so quickly. They had no idea with what they were dealing with. So long as the burnings stopped, the heat was off and they would proceed with the utmost caution.

Of course, Otto had no idea whether the burnings had stopped. There could be hundreds—thousands infected.

By hanging from his hands, Otto could "walk" out to where he could see most of the ledge but he would be visible as well. He and Durant crouched in silence, each seeking a way out of their dilemma. The lumpy sea of cloud began to rise. Soon it was mere meters below. Then it began to engulf them. It was the opportunity they needed.

The dense fog cut visibility to a few meters. With a rope around his waist tied around the rock, Otto swung himself out over the mountain, caught the merest glimpse of one of the sentries with his back to him, triggered the grenade with his teeth and rolled it back toward the cave entrance. It rolled virtually soundlessly due to its plastic soft drink bottle construction.

A shout from under the ledge. "Hey Vic!"

Otto swung himself out onto the ledge, landing with a grunt.

"Fuck!" the sentry exploded stepping out from behind the pop tent three meters away. He immediately brought his H&K to bear and ratcheted one into the chamber.

"It's you," he said.

"Who?" Otto said. "Me?"

"Get on your knees and turn around. Bob! I got him! I got White!"

Otto knelt facing the sentry and put his hands behind his head.

"I said turn around!"

There was the slightest thump as the cougar landed next to the sentry and crouched calmly regarding the man. The sentry gasped soundlessly and stepped off the edge of the ledge. Max coiled his loins and was gone.

"Don't move!" the second sentry called.

Durant came up behind and choked him out.

CHAPTER NINETY-EIGHT
BOOM-BA STYLE

Otto looked over the edge. The sentry lay five meters below. Otto watched until the sentry began to move. He and Durant wasted no time entering the door into the armory and barring it behind them. The inner door—the one into the cave—appeared untouched. Durant moved from crate to crate, picking up guns, sniffing them.

"Let's go," Otto said. They moved through the inner door into the cave. As soon as they shut the door and let their eyes adjust to the light, Otto could see their footprints outlined in phosphorescence from the last time he'd been through. There were no extra footprints. No one had entered the cave from above since Otto and Alvarez. They followed Otto's previous tracks.

"Sorry about your dog," Durant said softly.

Otto tried not to look at the paw prints. "Thanks."

They proceeded in silence, awed by nature's magnificence. Durant's head moved like a swivel turret. The spot where Casey had died appeared untouched, the evil black stain, the lumps of metal and shards of fabric. There was no sign of his leg. Something had carried it off to eat.

When they arrived at the upper end of the spiral leading to the teleportation device, Otto drew his pistol. Durant followed suit. Back to the wall, Otto edged towards the chamber, light growing stronger. When he came into full view he froze and let his eyes sweep the vast underground gallery.

The chamber was deserted. The eerie lighting burned, still connected by cable to something beneath the wooden platform. With military at both the top and the bottom, the authorities believed the teleportation device too hot to handle for the time being. Otto could only imagine the bureaucratic infighting that had accompanied that decision with the hard-liners, Brubaker and MacCauley, pushing for an immediate investigation and reverse engineering while the one-worlders dithered. The President was sitting on the discovery like a penguin.

Otto edged further into the chamber. Witherspoon's headless body still lay where they'd left it. It writhed, the pale flesh rippled, the limbs twitched obscenely. A shroud of intense loathing and horror settled over Otto as he approached the corpse behind his Ruger.

"Hey!" he spat.

White cave spiders the size of saucers skittered out from beneath the corpse, out the ends of the corpse's sleeves and pants, some carrying gibbets the size of peas.

How ironic.

How appropriate.

"Jesus wept," Durant said.

They spoke in whispers due only in part to the magnificence of their surroundings.

"Just cave things. Bring your gear onto the platform."

They set their gear on the wooden platform beneath the looming seat. The two interconnecting rings that defined the sphere were four meters in diameter. There was plenty of room for both men and their gear.

Otto carefully eased himself into the black plastic seat. It was pleasantly warm causing him to both relax and shiver—an alien craft broadcasting conflicting signals, a funhouse mirror of normality with that flash of black chitinous wing at vision's edge.

He settled into the seat, feeling it conform to his body. He took the loose wire that dangled from the control panel and held it in his hand. He confronted the black triangular control panel before him. It was smooth and featureless. He laid his right palm against it and felt a snap of electricity as it suddenly lit up, a triangular screen filled with a swirl of green and blue, red parabolic lines running from top to bottom and a scroll of alien runes across the top. An electric sizzle swarmed up the hoops to the North Pole, which glowed blue.

Otto used a strip of Gorilla Tape to attach the bare wire to his forehead. He pressed the screen again and the scroll changed to numbers. Mathematics was immutable, or so Otto had believed. The laws of physics didn't change. The *Skorzh* must have been intent on becoming conversant with human thinking and mathematics. A series of symbols formed a pentangle. One was clearly Earth with the continents barely visible and the moon. It was numbered 624. One was red and had three silver moons. There were three other symbols surrounding a black triangle with three red dots. It was numbered 666.

"Lester we're in business. Haul your shit over here by the seat."

Durant crouched by the lake where he was filling canteens with water. What the hell. The transportation would probably kill them. The three Daleks surrounding the platform began to hum and their stones glowed red. Otto pulled out his spiral pad, wrote something in pen, got up and set it on the edge of the platform held down with a rock.

Durant stacked the water bottles beneath the chair. Otto resumed his position. He took out the Blaster and hooked it over a breast pocket. He looked at the menu. "Boom-Ba Style." Good to go.

The humming grew louder. The red stones pulsed. The hoops began to glow.

Otto strapped himself in. "Keep your hands on my shoulders."

Durant did so. "Our Father in heaven," he began, "hallowed be your name."

Otto joined in. "Your kingdom come, Your will be done, on Earth as it is in Heaven."

There was a scuffle and a shout down the slope. Lon Barnett burst into view running flat out with four special forces in combat fatigues carrying machine pistols.

"OTTO HALT!" Barnett shouted.

Otto pushed the symbol with the three red dots. A clap of thunder and light filled the chamber. Even with sound suppressors, the Special Forces brought their hands to their ears. The small group was stunned and blinded.

As their sight returned, they saw that the platform was empty.

Barnett walked up and found the note beneath the rock. He held it up.

"Lester and I have gone to fight the Spiders. God bless America. Yours, Otto H. White."

CHAPTER
NINETY-NINE
AFTERMATH

In the weeks that followed Otto's disappearance, incidents of spontaneous human combustions waned and finally disappeared altogether, like the last fireworks on the 4th of July or the tail end of a meteor shower. But there was no return to normal. There was no normal anymore.

Randall Kleiser turned himself in at the Denver FBI HQ. John Bullis was his lawyer. In return for consideration, Kleiser told national security about Sis Boom Ba. Much easier to simply blast "Boom-Ba Style" than individual administer blood tests. The problem was some or all of the hosts might very well be innocent and would go down with their parasites. The test was administered under the strictest secrecy.

In one sense, Durant had been mistaken. Hosts were not dead but often retained their original personalities for years, such as Sen. Darling. The Agency drafted Kleiser under a special wartime executive action exempting him from prosecution. Surprisingly, he fit right in and within days was instrumental in erecting a firewall against Chinese and Russian cyber-attacks.

The "Freedom and Prosperity" bill granted President Burke unlimited powers. Elections were "temporarily suspended" while the world roiled in fear and the heads of the great nations met without the UN causing further outrage and rioting.

Burke lifted the No Fly order a week after Otto's disappearance, about which the world knew nothing. Officially, it was a man-made terrorist wave. The government knew how it was done, but would never divulge the details lest it loose demons of flame upon the land. Two months following the President's immolation, Burke lifted martial law but most major cities and municipalities still had curfews in effect.

On an overcast Sunday afternoon in September Margaret Yee and Stella Darling met at the Chowder Shack on Oyster Bay on the Chesapeake. They sat on the deck despite a strong offshore breeze; Yee bundled in a trench coat and broad-brimmed hat, Stella in a CSU hoodie. Yee thought Stella looked liked she'd aged five years. She'd lost her father, her boyfriend, and Otto who obviously still meant something to her. In fact, Yee was cognizant of their renewed relationship.

Yee believed she owed the younger woman a debt, that was one reason she'd invited her to lunch. The other had to do with national security. They sat in a banquette at the back of the restaurant looking out at the wind-chopped bay, seagulls soaring and shrieking.

Yee squeezed the other woman's hand. "Thank you for coming, dear."

"I had to come. They won't tell me what happened to Otto. Not a word about alien invaders. What's going on, Margaret?"

"First of all I want to tell you how very sorry I am for your loss. No one has sacrificed more in this secret war."

"No one except Dad, Otto and Gabe, and all the other victims."

Yee remembered what made Stella such a formidable trial lawyer. "Of course. That's not what I meant. Know that you have the President's gratitude."

"For what? I didn't do anything."

"Well, he thinks you did and I'm inclined to concur. Would it be all right if he phoned you?"

"Of course."

"He says that when things die down he'd like to give you the Presidential Freedom Award."

"Whoop de do. Can I get a drink?"

Margaret flagged down the teen-age waitress. She ordered a Bloody Mary. Stella had a vodka and tonic.

The waitress subserviently took their order and withdrew.

"Do you want to look at the menu, dear?" Yee said, opening the heavy clapboard tome done in faux eighteenth century font with a gold fob.

"No, I'd like to hear what happened to Otto."

"He and your friend Durant are now on the Spider home planet wreaking havoc, it is devoutly to be hoped."

Stella stared and made a little smile.

"How'd they do it?"

"You know when we were casting about for someone to lead this project I placed luck at the very top of the criteria. Most of my associates snickered. Is it good luck, or bad luck? He did say that if he got through he would try to send us some kind of sign."

"When did he say that? I thought he and the feds weren't talking."

"We talked right up until the end."

"How'd they do it?"

"He must have figured out the control board. At least we haven't been sucked into a black hole. I find that highly encouraging. Needless to say, this is all unrepeatable. You're not recording me, are you?"

"Of course not."

"There is concern that the boys might open up some kind of space/time continuum and we could be sucked into a black hole. We pay people to think up these scenarios. We're like the apes in 2001 coming across the slab."

Stella felt her heart ache. It would always be there next to her memories of Otto. Even in another dimension, she refused to believe he was dead. Otto was lucky. It was possible he would return.

Yee picked up the parchment menu and opened it. "They say their crab cakes are to die for."

CHAPTER
ONE HUNDRED
SPIDER DAY

Spider Day.

The air was different. A slight hallucinogenic tint to everything and a sharpness—an unnamable mint. Otto felt as if his skull was expanding and contracting like a puffer fish. He looked at Durant. If the Marine felt anything he didn't show it. He was a calmly coiled snake ready to launch.

The view was breathtaking. They were atop a mountain from which they could see endless peaks undulating to the horizon capped with blue snow. The air was frigid. Their boots sank an inch deep in the blue snow even on the sturdy platform, made of a brown material that was neither wood nor plastic. Purple cirrus clouds lay like God's cursive across the caramel sky.

Otto looked around. They had materialized inside three towers; three cylindrical cairns made of blue stone fused together, each with a golf ball-sized red sphere on top. The cherry on the sundae. Otto looked up at three soaring peaks that dwarfed the one they were on. He had no doubt what he would find at the summits. The sun itself was red. He screwed in his earplugs. Durant did likewise.

Their breath streamed away in purple streaks. The wind wailed like lost souls. Thirty meters across the caldera of the extinct volcano lay a low installation made of blue bricks with a sloping purple roof, the color of the clouds, a sort of ziggurat. Framing the ornate oval door were two enormous black tusks.

The oval door slid open. Twelve spiders spread in front, all twitching, all armed with multiple bladed weapons including spears, swords, and harpoons. Nothing that resembled a gun. They had tumbled from the building in a semi-panic. They looked like a frenetic audio signal, jagged on the top and bottom, constantly shifting up down up down. They looked nervous, if such things could look nervous. They had never been invaded. Never in their wildest imaginations did it occur to them that their prey would boomerang using their own system.

They appeared to be about two meters tall.

For an instant, the wind stopped and all was still beneath a pale and distant ruby-colored sun. In one motion the dozen warriors hoisted their barbs, emitted a sound that scraped like a knife on glass, nails on a blackboard, a wolf pup's dying screams, every atavistic auditory horror that had haunted mankind's dreams since the dawn of time.

Otto and Durant held fire until they were at ten meters. Otto turned on the speakers. Sis Boom Ba's eerie adenoidal voice rolled across the tiny valley like a tidal wave.

May I please have your atencio! My plan is reprehencio!

 Lester leveled his ArmaLite .308 and methodically fired, working from left to right, hitting each spider in the center of its body mass. It was as if they had all been sucked into a blender. Those warriors that didn't die immediately from the gunfire went berserk, their limbs thrashing spasmodically. Otto could hear neither the gunfire nor the chitin cracking as they gyrated themselves to death.

The firefight lasted five seconds. The spiders hadn't managed to release a single barb. Otto turned off the blaster. He and Durant looked at each other in utter astonishment.

Durant thrust his fist in the air. "BOO-YAH!" He and Otto slammed into each other, embraced and exchanged high-fives.

In three seconds, the smile was gone and Lester had defaulted to semi-catatonic. He looked to Otto. Otto did a three-sixty. They were alone on top of the mountain. But there could be more spiders in the building. He motioned Durant forward. They approached the still open door in a pincer movement. Durant indicated he wanted to roll inside like a grenade and come up shooting. Otto didn't think that was a good idea.

Detaching one of the miniscule speakers from his shoulder, he placed it in the open doorway and turned it on. He gave it thirty seconds, shut it off and motioned Durant into the building. Durant rolled and came up. Otto followed. The large domed chamber appeared devoid of spiders. Thousands of nodules, each with a dime-sized hole in the middle, studded the walls except for the back wall, which was vertical and carved from the rock face. A rectangular screen with rounded corners, approximately two meters diagonally was tuned to CNN.

A camera was mounted on a tripod on a platform facing several chairs designed for the spider physique. A quarter section of the wall was lined with hairy-looking nests at the base. Sleeping pads. An incandescent globe hovered over the center of the big room. On closer inspection, it hung from an almost invisible spider-web like strand.

Every occupant had rushed out of the building. Evidently, the spiders were not used to strategy. Otto and Durant formed up in front of the screen. It was silent but the news scroll across the bottom was up to speed.

Otto looked at Durant, who mirrored his surprise. "Martial law?"

Durant gestured at the camera with the muzzle of his ArmaLite. "If they can receive broadcasts through that thing ..."

"Fuck an A, bob," Otto said.

Who knew how long they had before others arrived to investigate the silence? Who knew if the spiders would even investigate? The presence of the CNN feed only served to highlight the yawning gap between their cultures and made Otto wonder if it would ever be able to even understand this enemy.

Or whether that was even desirable. He had no wish to get inside their heads.

"It's going to take me a while to prepare an address," Otto said. Durant nodded and began to explore the room on his own.

Otto dreaded public speaking. Always had. But it was important that they let the people back home know they had arrived safely with encouraging results. He sat on the edge of the platform and pulled his pen and pad from his pocket. He focused totally on the message he wished to send, unaware of the passage of time.

He looked up. Durant was seated nearby looking at him.

"What?" Otto said.

"Reconnoitered. Lotta shit here we don't understand, but I think I can get those cameras working and the controls appear similar to those on the teleportation device."

"Okay. Give me a few minutes. See if you can get up top of this thing and take a look around."

Durant saluted and booted.

Stella collapsed on the sofa in front of her wall-mounted flat screen TV and turned it on. Talking heads debated the feasibility of the new international One World initiative. Was it better for a central authority to deal with worldwide perfidy, or should such decisions be left to hopelessly archaic and jingoistic "nations?"

The screen flickered. A snowstorm. Abruptly, in neon colors, Otto faced the screen in front of an indistinct brown/black background. A snap of electricity hit Stella like a bucket of ice water to the face.

"People of Earth—greetings from Spiderland. This is Otto White, along with Master Sergeant Lester Durant, on the spider home planet. For those of you who don't know who the spiders are, ask the President. Earth has been invaded by an alien species. It was they who caused spontaneous human combustions. Sgt. Durant and I succeeded in reversing their teleportation device and here we are. There's good news and bad news. The good news is that the spiders seem completely unprepared to deal with our weapons. We took this station with zero casualties and twelve spider deaths.

"The bad news is this is an alien culture and our resources are limited. It's only a matter of time before the natives tumble to our presence and send someone to investigate. We have no idea where we are in relation to the planet. We have no idea where the planet is in relation to the Earth. We ..."

Otto tilted back, eyes wide. "Oh shit! Stella I love you! Gotta go!"

The screen went blank.

ABOUT THE AUTHOR

Born in Wisconsin, Mike Baron is best known for his comics work on *Nexus, Badger, Punisher, Flash, Deadman, Star Wars, and Robotech*. A perennial fan favorite, he is the winner of the prestigious Inkpot Award and the Eisner Award. He has written for every major comics publisher.

He broke into comics with *Nexus*, co-created with artist Steve Rude. *Nexus* currently appears monthly in Dark Horse Presents. Baron also created *Badger*, one of the longest-lived and most intriguing of independent superheroes. The Badger is a multiple personality, only one of whom dons a costume to fight crime. *Badger* returns this winter from a resurgent First Comics.

In addition to the novel *Whack Job*, he has written *Skorpio, Helmet Head*, and *Biker*. Baron lives in Colorado with his wife, Ann and a bunch of mutts.

bloodyredbaron.net